"Her sexy cowboys are to die for!"
—*New York Times* bestselling author Maya Banks

"Lorelei James knows how to write one hot, sexy cowboy." —*New York Times* bestselling author Jaci Burton

"The down-and-dirty, rough-and-tumble Blacktop Cowboys kept me up long past my bedtime. Scorchingly hot, wickedly naughty."
—Lacey Alexander, author of *Give in to Me*

"Hang on to your cowboy hats because this book is scorching hot!" —Romance Junkies

"Lorelei James knows how to write fun, sexy, and hot stories." —Joyfully Reviewed

"Sexy and highly erotic." —TwoLips Reviews

"Incredibly hot." —The Romance Studio

"[A] wild, sexy ride." —*Romantic Times*

Also by Lorelei James

The Blacktop Cowboys Novels

Saddled and Spurred
Wrangled and Tangled
One Night Rodeo
Turn and Burn

CORRALLED

A BLACKTOP COWBOYS® NOVEL

LORELEI JAMES

A SIGNET BOOK

SIGNET
Published by the Penguin Group
Penguin Group (USA), 375 Hudson Street,
New York, New York 10014, USA

USA | Canada | UK | Ireland | Australia | New Zealand | India | South Africa | China

Penguin Books Ltd., Registered Offices: 80 Strand, London WC2R 0RL, England
For more information about the Penguin Group visit penguin.com.

Published by Signet, an imprint of New American Library, a division of Penguin Group (USA). Previously published in a Signet Eclipse trade paperback edition.

First Signet Printing, October 2013

ISBN 978-0-451-46639-6

Printed in the United States of America
10 9 8 7 6 5 4 3 2 1

To all the cowboys and cowgirls who follow the black roads and back roads in pursuit of that gold buckle, and along the way provide hours of entertainment for rodeo fans such as me

Chapter One

"Screwing two guys doesn't make you a slut."

Lainie Capshaw darted a quick glance at the crowd in Bucky's Tavern. Luckily none of her coworkers—her male coworkers—lurked about. "Maybe you could've said that a little louder, Tanna. I don't think they heard you on the dance floor."

"*Puh-lease*. The men in this joint are too busy gawking at the cocktail waitress with the watermelon-size tits to be eavesdropping on us." Tanna sucked down a healthy swig of beer. "Twenty bucks says ol' monster jugs pops a strap in the next ten minutes."

"No dice. If I take that bet, you'll sneak up behind her and slice the damn strap just so you can win."

"You're no fun." Tanna sighed dramatically. "I'm bored."

Lainie rolled her eyes. A bored Tanna was a dangerous Tanna.

"So let's talk about Lainie's lewd love life."

"Let's not."

Tanna wagged her finger. "Ah, ah, ah. Suck it up, chickie. You walk the walk, you gotta talk the talk. Besides, who cares if you're boning two guys? Cowboys are notorious for having a different buckle bunny every night, in every podunk rodeo town on the circuit. It pisses me off there's still a double standard for women."

"True. But . . ."

"But what?" Tanna looked at her quizzically. "You aren't feeling guilty, are you?"

She shrugged. "Maybe. Wouldn't you?"

"Hell, no."

Bull. Lainie called Tanna's bluff. "So if the buff babe in the yellow shirt sauntered over and said, 'I wanna screw your brains out against my truck right now,' you'd follow him out into the parking lot without question?"

"Or hesitation. Well, besides checking my purse for condoms."

"Even when you're already making time with that studly bulldogger from Austin?" Lainie challenged.

Tanna planted her elbows on the table. "I'd do it in a heartbeat, Lainie. What would *you* do if both your men showed up here tonight?"

Wet myself. "Umm . . . I'd probably run."

"Like a contest to see who wanted you more? Whoever catches you first wins?"

Good Lord. Talk about an overactive sense of drama. "No. More like running from my problem."

"Doesn't sound like a problem to me. Two sexy men angling to thrill you between the sheets." Tanna smiled brazenly. "Or against the bathroom stall, in Kyle's case."

Whoo-ee. Just thinking about the hot tryst with Kyle still fried Lainie's circuits. Never in her life had she warranted an I-need-you-right-fucking-now bout of raunchy monkey sex. So yeah, it'd earned her bragging rights.

Even been-there-done-that Tanna had been impressed by Lainie's balls-to-the-wall behavior.

Tanna's cell phone vibrated on the tabletop. She squinted at the number and snapped, "'Bout time, you dumb bastard," before she flounced out the side door, chewing the caller's ass.

Lainie hunched over the table to discourage any cowboys from asking her to dance. Probably an unnecessary precaution, since tantalizing Tanna usually garnered that type of male attention, not her.

Which was why it was so twisted that Lainie had captured the interest of not one, but two men. Two very hot, very alpha men on two different circuits.

Lainie liked working the rodeo circuits, even though the pay was crap. As a med tech for Lariat Sports Medicine, she split her time between the two largest rodeo organizations: the Cowboy Rodeo Association, known as the CRA, and the Extreme Bull Showcase, known as EBS.

The CRA was comprised of rough stock events: bareback, saddle bronc, and bull riding; as well as timed events: calf roping, team roping, steer wrestling—also known as bulldoggin'—and barrel racing. The EBS had just one event—bull riding.

The CRA bull riders didn't compete in the EBS and vice versa. Which was how Lainie ended up with a hot cowboy hookup on both the CRA and the EBS.

Fraternizing with cowboys could be career suicide for a woman in the male-dominated sport, especially when her job was to examine those glorious bodies. Lainie prided herself on avoiding the sexual temptation for damn near two years.

Until she'd met Hank Lawson.

She'd encountered the intense CRA bullfighter after he'd pulled his Achilles tendon during a CRA event and grudgingly limped into medical services. After she'd fixed him up, he asked her out on a date. Lainie refused—tempting as it'd been. Not only was Hank a hundred percent real Wyoming cowboy who handled bulls with ease and panache, but at six-three, with inky black hair and ruggedly masculine features, he embodied tall, dark, and handsome.

She kept refusing until Hank invited her to dance at a sponsors' dinner. A simple dance—what could it hurt?

If she appreciated Hank's moves in the arena, his moves on the dance floor were equally fine. Whenever hard-bodied Hank studied her with those eyes the color of new denim, she experienced a rush of adrenaline that must have been equal to spending eight seconds astride a two-thousand-pound bull.

Two weeks later, Hank asked her to two-step at another rodeo event. Too much wine and too much Hank went straight to her head. One slow dance led them directly to Hank's motel room for a little mattress dancing.

Revisiting that romp with Hank caused Lainie's thighs to clench with want. Intense concentration and instinctual reaction were the hallmarks of good bullfighters, and Hank had both in spades. No surprise his single-mindedness carried over into the bedroom.

The man took his own sweet time making love; it was as maddening as it was arousing. Leisurely undressing her. Running his work-roughened fingers over every inch of her bare skin. Kissing everywhere his hands roamed. Wringing at least two explosive orgasms from her before he rode her hard and fast, or slow and sweet.

As phenomenal as the sex was, Hank rarely deviated from missionary position. Even if Lainie started out on top showing off her excellent riding skills, she'd end up underneath Hank at the big finish. She'd shoved aside her niggling doubts about Hank's lack of sexual spontaneity because he made her come so many times she saw stars.

So why had she hooked up with bull rider Kyle Gilchrist from the EBS circuit? True, Kyle and Hank were opposites. Physically, Kyle was wiry rather than overly muscular. His green eyes sparkled with mischief, not intensity. With Kyle's blond locks and golden facial hair, he resembled a Viking.

After taking a year off due to knee surgery, Kyle returned to the EBS with a vengeance. He'd started dropping by the sports medicine room to chat, in the guise of having his previous knee injury reexamined. Very polite. Very much interested in showing her in explicit detail how a modern-day Viking would utterly ravish her.

Her resistance lasted two months. The square-jawed, sloe-eyed sweet talker had literally charmed the pants right off her in a bathroom stall at Denny's outside Chula Vista. That first weekend she'd had sex with Kyle six times—not once in missionary position.

It'd been freeing. Fun. Hot as sin . . . until the weekend ended. Away from the temptation of Kyle's consuming kisses, she questioned whether she'd become as loose and easy as the buckle bunnies trailing after the circuit cowboys.

But mostly Lainie wondered whether she could juggle both men at the same time.

She and Hank hadn't discussed exclusivity. For all she knew, Hank could be sleeping with half the barrel racers on the CRA circuit. Kyle hadn't demanded promises either. Given Kyle's charm and good looks, she doubted he spent his nights alone watching Country Music Television.

So it wasn't the "cheating" factor that bothered her. It was the fact that she really liked both men and she didn't know who she'd pick if she had to choose.

Luckily, Lainie was in the catbird seat for a while. In the big world of professional rodeo, the EBS and CRA circuits rarely intersected geographically. Chances were slim she'd run into Hank if she was with Kyle or vice versa.

Feeling a little cocky, she sipped her beer.

Lainie's smugness lasted all of thirty seconds before two rough-skinned hands covered her eyes and a deep, sexy male voice murmured, "Guess who."

∞

Kyle Gilchrist could not believe his luck. Mel was here. Right here. Her wild curls tickling his cheek. Her powdery scent teasing his nose. The sight of her lithe little body hardened his cock.

And to think he'd dreaded spending the eve of his CRA debut in some dive bar in Lamar, Colorado.

Cool fingers circled his wrists. "Kyle?"

He removed his hands and spun the barstool, forcing Mel to face him. "Hey, sugar. Surprise."

"Oh, my God. It is you. What are you doing here? This isn't your circuit."

"Came in to have a beer and coerce a pretty woman into dancin' with me. And look who I found first thing—the prettiest lady I know." Kyle's palms slid down her bare arms to grasp her fingers. "Come on." Allowing her no chance to argue, he tugged her to the dance floor, right into the thick of the crowd.

"Kyle, this isn't a good idea. What if—"

"It's the best idea I've had in weeks. Come on. Admit it. You missed me."

"Maybe." She smiled against his throat.

He wasn't much of a dancer, so he employed every seductive tactic he'd stockpiled over the years to draw her attention away from his two left feet. Brushing his thumb at the base of her neck. Gradually easing his thigh between hers. Swaying to the beat of the music while their bodies moved to a rhythm uniquely theirs.

The final chord of the tune rang out. He spun them until her back was to the main part of the bar.

She tried to push him away. "Kyle. Let go."

"Not until you give me a kiss."

"But I can't. Not here where everyone can see—"

Kyle settled his mouth over hers, treating her to the lazy kisses that always distracted her.

A soft protest exited her mouth, which he swallowed in another kiss. She thought too much. Worried too much. The best way to turn off her overactive brain was to turn her on in a whole 'nother way.

As luck would have it, that was one thing Kyle was very good at.

∞

Hank Lawson paced in the shadow of the sleazy honky-tonk. "No, sir. I understand. Yes." He grinned at the phone. "I'm committed to the next three weeks. Uh-huh. Well, sir—all right, Bryson—it's a good opportunity for me to work with some of the rankest bulls in the CRA. No. I'll cut it short if I have to. Absolutely, I'll be there. Tulsa. Looking forward to it." He clicked the phone off and pumped his fist into the air.

"Yes!" Hank couldn't wait to tell . . . He stopped. Wait a second. He couldn't tell anyone. Dammit. That sucked. Biggest news of his career and he had to keep a lid on it.

Bullfighting. In the EBS. It was a callback from his pretryout test last month at a second-tier event.

As much as Hank loved bullfighting in the CRA, for a bullfighter, the EBS was the big time. More money. TV coverage. More sponsorships. Fans. And he wasn't supposed to tell anyone? Screw that. Hank scrolled through his contact list and hit Dial.

"Hank?" she answered breathlessly. "What's up?"

"News, but promise me it'll stay under your hat."

"Fine. Spill it fast because I'm short on time."

The noise in the background sounded like she was at a rodeo. "I scored another audition with the EBS."

She squealed. "Seriously? That's awesome! When?"

"A couple of weeks. Once I'm done with Cowboy Christmas."

"They couldn't get you in sooner?"

"Bryson asked if I'd be available for the Huntington Beach event next week, but I can't. I've already committed to—"

"God, Hank, why can't you let Gilly navigate the CRA trail on his own? It ain't like he's a rookie."

He scowled. Would she ever get over her beef with his buddy? Probably not. The girl held a grudge like nobody's business. "I'm not goin' on the road as a favor to Gilly. Truth is, I'm doin' this for me."

"For the money?"

"Partially. But the more bulls I can get on the next three weeks, the better my chances in the EBS."

"Unless you get stomped by one and blow your goddamn big chance," she retorted.

"Thanks for the confidence, sis," he groused.

"I have the utmost confidence in you, bro. It's the bulls I don't trust. That said, I really *am* excited for you."

"I know you are. Remember, you can't tell anyone."

"Not even Abe?"

"I'll tell him."

"You'd better. But I'm afraid he won't be as thrilled. Come to think of it, if you do get picked, it'll be more work for me at the ranch. Maybe I oughta be rooting for the bulls."

Hank laughed softly.

"Glad I amuse you. Shit. I'm up. Later."

He said, "Up for what?" to the dial tone. He glanced

at the time. Damn. He'd been outside for thirty minutes. Not only hadn't he said hello to Lainie yet—and wouldn't she be surprised to see him—but he'd left Gilly hanging. Too bad he hadn't introduced them before he'd taken the call. He headed back inside.

The flashing lights from the stage show inside the honky-tonk screwed with his eyes. Hank blinked a couple times, scanning the tables. The band wailed a decent cover of Billy Currington's latest love song.

He stopped at the bar and ordered three Coors Lights. Hank felt like a fish swimming upstream, juggling three bottles of beer as the people rushed off the dance floor after the tune ended. He'd made it to the table he'd spotted Lainie and her friend sitting at earlier, but there was no sign of her now.

Huh. Hank looked around the bar. No sign of Gilly either.

His gaze wandered to the dance floor. One couple hadn't left yet, oblivious to the fact the music had stopped. They were twined together, mouths fused, body pressed to body.

Hank squinted. Hey. Wait a minute. Was that . . . ?

Holy fucking shit. That *was* Lainie—his Lainie—in a clinch with some happy-handed cowboy.

Fury filled him. He'd fucking lay the bastard out cold. *Come on, asshole—show me your face so I can figure out where I'm gonna put the first bruise.*

Then the loser in the cowboy hat kissing Hank's goddamn woman lifted his head.

Not just any cowboy had his hands and mouth on Lainie; *Gilly* had his hands and mouth on Lainie.

Hank's stomach dropped. And so did the bottles of beer.

Lainie and Gilly looked at him at the same time the raucous crowd broke into applause at his clumsiness.

The cocktail waitress snapped, "Maybe you oughta think about drinkin' one at a time, buddy."

But he couldn't tear his eyes off them. Tempting to punch his buddy in the kisser for kissing her. Equally tempting to pull Lainie outside and ask her what the hell was going on.

The couple stopped right in front of him.

Hank calmly said, "Lainie, sweetheart, I was gonna introduce you to my good buddy Gilly, but I see you two have already met."

Chapter Two

No way. This isn't happening. Any second, my alarm will blare and I'll wake up. Wake up and laugh hysterically.

"Hank, you know Mel?" Kyle asked.

Wake up, wake up, wake up.

"Intimately. Except I know her as Lainie. Right, darlin'?"

Any second now, the buzzing would jar her straight out of a dead sleep. And boy, wouldn't she welcome that intrusion for a change.

Kyle frowned. "Why is that name familiar?"

"Because that's her name, dumb ass," Hank snapped. "Lainie Capshaw. She's a med tech with Lariat Sports. Is that ringing a bell?"

Comprehension dawned. Kyle's head whipped toward her, his jaw nearly hanging to his championship belt buckle. "Your name isn't Mel?"

Shit. Busted. She was so freakin' busted.

Kyle faced Hank. "You're with her too?"

"Too?" Hank repeated. He didn't spare Lainie a glance. He shoved Kyle. "You'd better be fuckin' kiddin', Gilly."

"Don't fuckin' push me, Lawson." Kyle pushed Hank back.

Broken glass crunched beneath their booted feet.

"Back off," Hank snarled.

"You back off first."

"Not a fuckin' chance."

Kyle sneered, "Bring it, asshole."

A crowd gathered, anticipating a fight.

Should she jump between them and put a stop to this?

"Who's up for a wet T-shirt contest?"

All eyes zoomed to Tanna, standing on a table at the front of the bar. She'd stripped to an itty-bitty see-through white tank top, which showed the outline of her nipples in full detail, as well as the deep vee of her impressive cleavage.

Lainie's gaze briefly connected with Tanna's and her friend mouthed, *Go!* before she poured a bottle of beer on her chest.

Male whoops of appreciation echoed and Lainie ran as if the hounds of hell were chasing her. As she cut out the side door, her brain ran rampant with questions. What were the odds that both her men would show up here tonight? Or worse, that they'd know each other?

Stop thinking and run!

Boot steps slapped the pavement behind her. A hand landed on her shoulder, jerking her to a stop.

"Mel, please. Wait. Don't run off. It won't solve a damn thing."

Breathing hard, she didn't protest when Kyle whirled her around. No hint of amusement danced in his green eyes. His hands slid down to her arms and curled around her biceps, keeping her in place.

She braced herself for his recriminations. Angry words and accusations about her loose moral character would make it easier to walk away. Easier than admitting the truth: She wasn't sorry for her hanky-panky with Hank or for getting her kicks with Kyle. She was just sorry she'd gotten caught.

"What's goin' on? I'm confused as hell," Kyle said.

"That makes two of us."

"No. That makes three of us," Hank said as he sidled up beside Kyle.

Lainie tried to squirm out of Kyle's gentle hold, but his fingers tightened.

"Let her go," Hank said sharply.

Kyle's eyes searched hers. "Is that what you want?"

She nodded and he immediately released her.

"Step away from her, Gilly," Hank warned.

Kyle shoved him. "You first."

Hank shoved him back. "Keep it up and I'll hand you your ass."

"Try it," Kyle taunted.

"Stop it. Both of you." She wrapped her arms around herself and stepped sideways so she could see both men.

They were pissed. Rightly so.

The brutal silence caused her to blurt, "I'd say I never meant this to happen, but I doubt you'll believe me."

"Try us," Kyle said.

"Obviously I had no idea you guys were friends." She paused and her gaze flicked between them. "How good of friends?"

"Why does it matter?" Hank asked brusquely.

"It just does."

"Me 'n' Hank have been friends since junior high," Kyle said.

Lainie bit back a groan. It figured. "For the record, I've never, ever done anything like this in my entire life.

So it's no surprise . . ." A headache built behind her eyes, making the sockets ache and her temples pound.

Do not cry. You will not pull those goddamn crocodile tears like your mother would. Buck up and face the music.

Wrong. Run!

"I have to go. Right now."

"Now, wait just a damn minute. We're all adults here—"

She focused on Hank. "Did you or did you not get into a shoving match with Kyle when you saw us together?"

He scowled. "It caught me off guard, okay?"

"Me too," Kyle said. "You must know neither one of us is the type of man to back down."

Lainie threw her hands up. "Which is precisely my point."

"We aren't gonna come to blows over you," Hank scoffed.

"You're right. You won't. Because *I'm* backing down. *I'm* breaking it off with both of you."

⚮

"Lainie. Come back here so we can talk about this," Hank shouted.

Her wild curls bounced against her rigid back with every hurried boot step. She never stopped. She never looked back.

When she climbed in her truck, Hank started after her.

A strong grip on his forearm and a curt, "Let her go," stopped him.

Hank shifted to glare at Gilly. "What the fuck? Maybe you don't want her, but I sure as hell do. I ain't letting her go when she's like this."

Gilly got right in his face—a feat in itself, since the man was six inches shorter. "Don't think for a second I don't want Mel as badly as you do. But goin' after her when she has this stubborn mind-set is a fool's errand,

and you damn well know it. I won't have you fucking up my chance with her because you're too damn dense to let her be."

"Stop calling her Mel," Hank snapped. "Her name is Lainie."

"Stop bein' such a dickhead," Kyle shot back. "And for chrissake, if you're gonna be such a picky bastard about names, how about if you get mine right? I ain't been Gilly since I left Muddy Gap, Hank. The name is Kyle."

"Fine, *Kyle*."

The back door to the bar burst open, releasing a blast of steel guitar. Hank glanced in that direction, away from the dust plume as Lainie's truck barreled off. A woman's drunken whoop echoed, followed by a man's laughter, and the door banged shut again.

Hank scowled. This was how his evening played out? Standing in the parking lot of a honky-tonk? At ten o'clock at night? Completely sober, completely pissed, completely confused on how he and his buddy ended up fucking the same woman?

Kyle sighed. "Look. I need a damn beer, but the thought of heading back into the bar turns my stomach."

"Yeah. Me too. There's a package store around the corner."

Five minutes later, laden with a six-pack, Hank climbed into his truck next to Kyle. He set the brown bag on the center seat, tempted to crack a bottle—to hell with the open-container law. He needed a damn drink now.

The lights of Lamar zoomed past the truck windows. Hank had half a mind to whip a U-turn and drive out to the rodeo grounds. At least if they were getting drunk with a group of rowdy cowboys, they wouldn't be commiserating about having the hots for the same sexy-assed sports med tech.

"You thinking about her?" Kyle asked.

"Yeah. Are you?"

"Always."

Great. Hank knew Lainie starred in plenty of sexual fantasies of cowboys on the CRA circuit. He'd never expected she'd been part of his friend's sexual reality.

"How long have you been seein' her, Hank?"

"Roughly six months." As much as Hank didn't want to ask, he did. "How about you?"

"Two months."

Hank couldn't stop the smug feeling over having been with Lainie longer than Kyle.

Yeah? If you're in with her so damn good, then why'd she go looking for another man to knock boots with?

Damn.

"What'd she treat you for?" Kyle asked.

"Pulled my Achilles."

It'd pissed him off too, pulling a muscle during a performance. Instead of the usual gruff med tech, Lainie stepped up. Hank had scoffed at the little slip of a woman. How was she supposed to fix him if she could barely assist him onto the exam table? But as Hank half listened to her questions, he watched her. Her hair color was odd—somewhere between dark brown and rich red, a shade that reminded him of his quarter horse's glossy coat. Hank kept that observation to himself; few women found humor or flattery within workhorse comparisons.

Lainie had stretched him out on the padded exam table and dug her fingers into his sore calf. The strength and skill of her hands surprised him almost as much as the color of her eyes—the hue of burnished copper.

And so began his obsession with Lainie Capshaw.

At an event the next week, Hank popped into the medical aid station, only to discover that Lainie worked every other week with the EBS circuit. In the interim, he'd stumbled across information about Lainie's heritage that'd shocked him. The curly-haired cutie with the sparkling eyes and magical hands was the daughter of world-famous bull rider Jason Capshaw. An icon, a legend, a man who'd died way too young, way too publicly, gored by a bull in an arena filled with thousands of adoring fans. A man who'd left behind a young widow and a five-year-old daughter. A little girl christened Melanie—who'd been nicknamed Lainie by her adoring father.

When she'd checked out Hank's sprained pinkie the following week, Hank asked her about her famous father. Lainie's sunny disposition vanished as fast as a Wyoming rainstorm. Yes, she was Jason Capshaw's daughter. No, she didn't want to talk about him. So Hank seized the opportunity to steer the conversation in the direction he'd wanted all along: He'd asked her out.

Lainie's response? A vehement no. She absolutely did not date rodeo cowboys. Ever. Period. End of discussion.

Normally, he'd move on. Yet, something about her called to him. Hank didn't push, but he let her know he wasn't giving up on her either.

His luck turned the night of a sponsors' dinner. The wine had relaxed her and he swooped her onto the dance floor during a sexy, suggestive Dierks Bentley tune.

Lust exploded between them the instant he hauled her into his arms. Hank'd had his share of sexual conquests in his years as a bullfighter and a cowboy. But nothing in his experience was as potent as slow dancing with Lainie Capshaw fully clothed.

They'd managed to keep their relationship platonic for another twenty minutes. Sex between them rocked his world. He'd believed Lainie felt the same. So Hank hadn't demanded exclusivity, fearing it'd spook her, given her "no dating cowboys" rule. Now he wished he had.

"Hank? Buddy, you okay?" Kyle asked, breaking him out of his reverie. "You're awful damn quiet."

Hank sighed. "I don't know. Guess I'm more shocked than anything. Aren't you?"

Kyle shrugged as Hank parked at the far back of the motel lot. He hopped out and lowered the tailgate with a loud clank while Hank snagged the six-pack.

They sat on the tailgate, gazing at the sky. The stars were bright, despite the light pollution from the town. He passed Kyle a bottle. A *pop-hiss* sounded, followed by a metallic *ping* as he flicked the cap into the truck bed behind them.

Kyle spoke first. "You asked me if I was shocked. I'm not. She ain't the type to play games, but I suspected she was seein' someone else. I figured it'd be a guy who lived in her area."

"Lainie don't exactly seem like the 'what happens on the road, stays on the road' type, with a different fella in every town."

"Exactly. I figured her deal with the other guy couldn't be that serious if she was with me every so often." Kyle sent him a sidelong glance. "Am I right?"

"She and I never made promises to each other. It's been pretty casual." Hank knew it wouldn't help the situation if he admitted he'd wanted those promises from Lainie and had been prepared to offer them in return. Tonight, in fact.

"You been with other women since you and Lainie hooked up?"

Hank shook his head. "You?"

"Nope."

"That's a fuckin' surprise."

"Why?"

"'Cause I know you."

Kyle's back straightened. "No, you don't. I ain't the horndog I used to be."

Hank snorted. "Right."

"Did you ask me about screwing other women so you could run and tell her that she was just another meaningless tumble for me, while she was special to you?"

Heat rose up Hank's neck. Kyle had nailed his response and he knew it, which was what made this situation doubly hard.

Thick silence descended.

"Hell, Hank, maybe Mel—Lainie—has the right idea. Maybe we all oughta walk away from this."

He practically snarled, "I don't wanna walk away from her."

"Me neither." Kyle drained his beer and rattled the paper sack, reaching for another.

Hank finished his Bud and grabbed a second. "I'm open to suggestions as to what to do."

"Beats me. Ain't shit like this usually settled with fists?"

"You saw how she reacted when we got into a shoving match. Made it worse. That ain't gonna work." He sent Kyle a tight-lipped smile. "One of us could be a gentleman and bow out."

∞

"Go for it," Kyle said, flashing his teeth at Hank in a nonsmile.

Hank laughed. "Not a chance."

"I ain't bowing out; you ain't bowing out. Then we're back to square one."

"Appears that way."

Another bout of quiet stretched between them. Normally Kyle would fill the void with chatter, jokes, and bullshit, but tonight he was unnerved. For the first time in a long time he'd found a woman who invoked real feelings in him. Lainie wasn't his usual she's-hot-and-she-fucks-like-a dream type of woman, who he'd happily bang until he got sick of her. No, from the moment Kyle met her, he'd known she was different.

Immediately after rejoining the EBS, Kyle learned from the other fifty-nine guys on the tour that Mel did not fraternize with cowboys. Ever. Given her tragic family history, he understood her need to detach herself, especially from bull riders. Given the fact she was the only woman on the sports medicine team, he understood her need to keep a professional distance and reputation.

Everything changed the night Kyle landed hard enough on his riding arm that he feared he'd cracked his elbow, which sent him straight to the sports med room. Lainie had slapped a sling on him, never losing her good humor during the drive to the closest hospital for X-rays.

When he admitted to the attending doctor at the ER that he thought he might've cracked his tailbone too, Lainie's professional edge sharpened—as did her words. She asked if Kyle had neglected to tell her the full extent of his injuries in the sports med room because of her gender—or because she wasn't a doctor.

Kyle confessed he had a problem sticking his ass in the air for a woman. She'd snapped back that if it bothered him, she'd scratch her crotch, refuse to shower, and walk around with a ball-swaying swagger so he'd think of her as a guy.

From that point on, he'd become smitten with the oh-so-feminine yet ballsy woman called by a man's name. Kyle knew the attraction wasn't one-sided, no matter how many times she'd denied it. No matter how many times she'd told him she didn't mess around with bull riders. Period. But he'd worn her down with a mixture of charm and luck.

They'd ended up fucking in a restaurant bathroom ten minutes into their first date. Sexually, they meshed. Kyle proved her fears of locker room stories were unfounded, as evidenced by the fact that no one on the EBS tour caught wind of their raunchy rendezvous.

Now that he'd found a woman worth fighting for, Kyle wasn't giving her up without a fight.

Even to the point that you'll lose a good friend?

Maybe.

"Think it'll be hard with us both bein' on this circuit?" Hank asked.

"Probably. It ain't like I'm planning to get the shit kicked out of me just so she'll put her hands on me."

"Oh, I don't know. I've had her hands on me. It might actually be worth getting stomped."

Kyle punched Hank in the arm. "It's a damn cryin' shame we can't just share her until she makes up her mind which one of us she likes better."

Hank's beer bottle stopped halfway to his mouth. "You know, that ain't a half-bad idea."

"I was kiddin'."

"I'm not."

"Seriously? Like I'd get her Friday night and you'd get her Saturday night? Hank. Buddy. You know that'd never work. Especially when we'd be in the same town, knowing exactly what's goin' on behind closed motel room doors. Maybe in the motel room right next door."

"True. But what if . . . ?"

Now he'd piqued Kyle's curiosity. "What if . . . ?"

"What if we were both with her? At the same time. Think she'd go for that?" Hank asked.

Kyle froze. Maybe it was irony or fate or some such shit, but he and Lainie had once discussed that very thing. "One time we were watching porn in a hotel room and she admitted girl-on-girl action didn't appeal to her. But two guys taking care of her sexual needs? She said to sign her up."

Hank faced him and grinned. "Well, there you go. I knew this was a good idea. Problem solved. We'll pitch it to her first thing tomorrow."

"Now, hold on." Kyle took a drink of beer. "I ain't sure she wasn't just all talk."

"You trying to convince me? Or yourself?"

"Both, maybe. Hell, I don't know. This just seems really fucking weird."

"Was Lainie drunk during this conversation about being with two men?"

"No."

"That tells me she'd be open to it."

"That don't mean that I'm on board."

"For a threesome? Why the hell not? I'm totally on board." Hank snickered. "You ain't afraid Lainie will be comparing our dick sizes or something?"

"Fuck off, Lawson. That ain't what concerns me. What if part of her deal is she wants us to be together, kissing and touching and shit like them women in porn threesomes are?"

That visual immediately caught Hank's attention. His body went rigid before he shuddered. "No fuckin' way am I sucking your dick, Gilly."

They both went quiet.

Hank drained his beer and handed them each a fresh one. "But I'm gonna point out that Lainie knows us both well enough that she wouldn't expect us to be doin' each other when we're doin' her. And because she's had sex with both of us, if anyone can talk her into a three-way relationship, it'd be us."

"That's true."

"Best-case scenario: She agrees to be with both of us when she's working the CRA tour."

"What about when we are together? Will it always be the three of us? Or will I get to spend time alone with her?"

"I don't know the damn logistics," Hank grumbled. "We can sit here and plan the whole goddamn thing out how we want it, but we both know she'll have ideas of her own. Knowing Lainie, she'll probably bring up things we ain't even considered."

"You ain't whistlin' 'Dixie' there." Kyle listened to footsteps fading on the blacktop. An engine started. A Buick slowed as it drove past them. The occupant probably wondered why two cowboys were tailgating at the Broken Spur Motel at midnight.

"So we need to talk to her," Hank said. "But we have to present a united front. She either takes both of us or neither of us." Hank turned and Kyle felt his quizzical gaze. "Right?"

Rather than respond, *Fuck no. You're on your own, pal*, Kyle muttered, "Right."

"Good. You 'n' me will talk specifics on our way to her motel tomorrow morning."

"Where's she staying?"

"Cow Palace Inn." Hank jumped off the tailgate and gathered the empty beer bottles, dropping them into the crumpled paper sack with a muffled *chink*. "Well, roomie, I'm whipped and goin' to bed. You comin'?"

"Nah. I'll be along in a while. Think I'll sit out here and strategize covering my bulls tomorrow night."

"I looked at the roster from the stock contractor. He's brought some seriously rank bulls."

"All the better."

"Thought you might say that. Got your room key?"

Kyle nodded and aimed his face at the stars, hoping Hank would get the hint that they were finished talking.

Hank lumbered off without a word.

Somehow Kyle managed to put the bizarre conversation and situation out of his mind and focus on the reason he was here: to ride bulls.

Chapter Three

When the knock came on Lainie's door at eight a.m., she'd expected to tell housekeeping to go away, not Hank. And Kyle.

Dammit. She should've left the safety chain on. "Hey! What do you think you're doing?"

"Coming in, because Lainie, darlin', we need to talk." This from Hank as he brushed past her.

"There's nothing left to say."

"Wrong," Kyle said as he walked past her too and stood next to Hank.

She crossed her arms over her chest. The shrunken camisole and ratty boy shorts she wore as pajamas left little to the imagination.

Kinda late for modesty now, since they've both sampled the goods you're trying to hide.

"Can we please talk about this? What happened last night and what's been going on the last few months?" Kyle asked.

"Why? So I can hear you call me nasty names because I've been sleeping with both of you? No, thanks."

Kyle and Hank traded a look. Then they faced her again. Hank looked at her hard enough that she shivered. "That's the kind of guys you think we are, Lainie? Really?"

No. But with both of you here together like this? Being flip is my best defense against all this testosterone.

"What Hank is trying to say, sugar, is that we'd never do that to you."

"You two exchanged pretty harsh words last night." Lainie's eyes narrowed on the shadow below Kyle's jawbone. "Did you smack each other around after I left?"

"If you remember, I ride bulls for a living. I tend to get beat up by them on occasion," Kyle said wryly.

Lainie stomped over and peered at the dark mark. "Has anyone looked at this?" She reached up. Before her fingers connected with his stubbled jaw, Kyle snatched her hand and kissed her fingertips.

She didn't dare look at Hank. Would anger burn in his eyes with Kyle touching her so blatantly? Right in front of him?

"Just listen to us," Hank half pleaded. "If after we've had our say you don't like what you've heard, then you can kick us to the curb."

To be honest, she was interested in why they'd provided a unified front. "Fine. I'm listening."

After Hank noticed Kyle hadn't released her hand, he grabbed her other hand, throwing Kyle a pointed you're-touching-her look—which Kyle completely ignored.

Kyle's eyes searched her face. "We never talked about an exclusive relationship, Mel—er, I mean, Lainie. Damn, I gotta get used to calling you that." He sent her a soft smile. "You're an attractive woman. I didn't imagine you were sitting at home or in a hotel on the road, pining for me when we weren't together."

She opened her mouth to speak but Kyle shook his head.

"But I woulda been hard-pressed to guess you were whilin' away the hours with my buddy Hank," Kyle added.

"Same goes for me," Hank said. "Although I am sure I mentioned my friend Gilly a time or two."

"You did. But I didn't relate 'Gilly' with Kyle. No one else on the EBS circuit calls him that."

"Point taken." Hank kissed her knuckles.

Her belly fluttered at the sensation of his warm lips lingering on her skin.

"Why do you go by Mel on the EBS circuit anyway?" he asked.

"It was Dusty's idea of a joke. Bryson Westfield prefers male med techs, but Dusty was shorthanded when he assigned me to the EBS. So he listed me as Mel instead of Lainie so Bryson wouldn't bitch."

"Anyone who mistakes you for a man is obviously blind."

"Amen," Kyle said.

Flustered, she let silence fill the uncomfortable void.

"Look, Lainie, we don't want to say anything that'll make you run out again, but the bottom line is, we both still wanna be with you."

Her entire body froze. "You do?"

"Uh-huh. We understand part of the reason you were upset, besides the surprise factor of Hank and me bein' good buddies, is that you didn't want to choose between us."

"I don't. I won't. So it'll be easier if I—"

Kyle put his finger over her lips. "Do you want to walk away from this? From both of us?"

She didn't need time to consider her answer. She shook her head.

The guys breathed a collective sigh of relief.

"Good. Very good." Hank smiled. "'Cause neither of us wants that either."

"So what do you propose we do?"

"Share you," Kyle said.

"Share me?" Her gazed flicked between them. "I am not a hammer to be passed back and forth when you want to nail me!"

"That's not what we meant."

"Then what do you mean? How can you share me? You can't saw me in half. And I know it'd drive a wedge in your friendship if I was switching off weeks between you guys, even with Kyle in the EBS and you in the CRA. Both of you are too . . . alpha and headstrong to take a backseat to the other for very long."

"True. Which is why this sharing situation would work," Hank said.

"I don't see how."

Hank looked at Kyle with a hint of exasperation. "You have a better way to explain this?"

"Maybe I oughta point out that I fell in the standings from number fifty-eight to number seventy-nine and the EBS kicked my ass off the tour four weeks ago. Yeah, I know it's standard procedure, and there are lots of younger bull riders eager to take those top sixty spots. I've been off my game and I need to get it back. Nothin' changed when I hit the secondary circuits, so tonight I'm starting in the CRA," Kyle said. "That'll give me a chance to compete a whole bunch during Cowboy Christmas."

Lainie knew the annual ritual known as Cowboy Christmas was a three-week period when professional cowboys drove thousands of miles all across the country in sleep-deprived pursuit of prize money awarded in a string of rodeos leading up to—and directly following—the Fourth of July. "Why?"

"There's potential for me to earn cash and rack up points. I won't make it to American Finals Rodeo, but it'll allow me to ride lots of bulls, figure out why my buck-off rate is so high, and position me for the new season next year."

"Then we'll all be on the same circuit," she said inanely.

"Ain't that great? See why this'll work?"

"No!" Lainie stepped back. Way back. "How can you think that'll be better? That's worse. What do you think people will say if they see me with both of you? We'll be at sponsors' events together. I can't be with one of you one week and then the other the next week."

The guys swapped an indecipherable look.

Kyle crowded her first. "We ain't talking about you switching off. We're talking about you bein' with *both* of us at the *same* time."

Lainie let that sink in.

"The night in Chula Vista? You admitted interest in a threesome with two guys. You swore if given the chance, you'd grab it with both hands." Kyle grinned. "Well, darlin', Hank and I are here and ready to be grabbed."

She gaped at him. She remembered that night clearly, stretched out on the bed at the cheap motel, trash-talking while watching porn. Kyle confessed being at the mercy of two women did it for him; Lainie retorted that it'd be hot with two men catering to her. She never imagined that comment would come back to bite her in the ass.

But doesn't having these two sexy, virile men offering a dream sexual experience sound thrilling?

Yes. But Lainie wasn't the type of woman to just go with the flow.

Yet, somehow you found the guts to screw two different men at every opportunity and keep it a secret.

What would it be like to be with both men at the same time?

Delicious. Wanton. A chance few women were afforded.

Did she have the cojones to grab the opportunity with both greedy hands?

"Tell you what. We sprang this idea on you first thing this morning and we wanna give you time to think on it. But we also want to give you a little taste of what we have in store for you." Kyle curled his palm around the back of her neck, bringing her mouth to his. He let the kiss remain unhurried, a soft brush of lips on lips. Then he released her. She had about a split second before Hank invaded her space.

Hank's lips were firmer, his kiss more intrusive as he swept his tongue into her mouth.

She loved the full-out way Hank kissed. No holding back. Eating at her mouth like a starving man. His hand rested on her throat, allowing the jagged edge of his thumb to rub her jawline.

After a minute or five of scrambling her brain, Hank eased back to peer into her eyes.

The lust she saw wasn't a surprise. But his next action was—passing her back to Kyle.

Kyle threaded his fingers into her hair, angling her head to take her mouth in a no-holds-barred kiss. A tongue-thrusting swamping of her senses that made her weak-kneed and weak-willed.

For a second, she forgot the divine decadence of Kyle's kiss, unnerved by the knowledge that if Kyle's hands were in her hair, whose hands were on her chest?

Hank murmured, "Relax, Lainie. Let us touch you." He peeled the tiny elastic straps of her camisole down her biceps and past the tops of her breasts.

With the straps nestled in the bend of her elbows, her arms were immobilized. Not that she intended to push Kyle away when his lips followed the arc of her neck.

Lainie's eyes closed, her head fell back, and she momentarily lost her balance.

A big, warm hand steadied her. "Easy."

The wet flick of a tongue on the very tip of her right nipple made her breath catch. She moaned when a hot mouth enclosed the peak and suckled.

Another mouth toyed with the left nipple, using teeth and firm-lipped bites. Then hot, wet suction. How incredibly bizarre, feeling two different mouths on her breasts at the same time. How incredibly arousing.

She knew Kyle had commandeered the left side, even without the rasp of his goatee on her skin. He didn't tease. Hank, on the other hand, took foreplay seriously and worshipped her breast with single-minded concentration.

With both men seeing to her pleasure? No wonder her pulse was racing.

As she fought for breath, Hank's lips landed gently on hers, drawing out the intimacy with lazy kisses he knew she craved.

She felt Kyle retreat, leaving her in Hank's capable hands. Hank straightened her clothes, smoothed her hair. He rested his forehead against hers. "Think about this today before you make any rash decisions, okay?"

Lainie inhaled slowly. Exhaled. Worked to get her crazed hormones under control. "Okay."

"Good enough." He stepped back.

But he didn't depart fast enough; she noticed the bulge in his jeans. Whoa. Hank was turned on by what'd just happened.

Kyle sidled in front of her with that engaging devil-may-care grin and a serious hard-on. "You are one smokin'-hot woman. Thanks for not bootin' our sorry asses out." Kyle's kiss was flirty, fun, and Lainie was grateful.

"We'll see you tonight. Hopefully not in an official capacity." He winked and followed Hank out of the room.

∞

An hour later, when three solid raps sounded on her door, Lainie remembered to check the peephole first.

Tanna. Fully dressed in her barrel-racing cowgirl regalia.

Lainie unlatched the chains and Tanna burst in.

"You have to tell me what happened with Hank and Kyle right freakin' now. It's been driving me crazy." Tanna whirled to balance on the tips of her ropers so she could loom over Lainie. "No holding anything back."

"You mean . . . last night?"

"Yes, I mean last night. You freaked out when you realized they were there together. And damn, girl, what was up with the cowardly way you snuck out the back door?"

"I warned you I'd run."

Tanna's left eyebrow winged up. "So Kyle followed you first, then Hank. Then what?"

"How many people saw them chasing me down last night?"

"Two, three maybe. But mostly the guys were mesmerized by my unique brand of entertainment. Jiggling my boobs as a distraction entitles me to all sorts of juicy details."

Lainie hip-checked her. "I owe you, but you loved having them drool over what they'd never have."

"That is true. But it don't matter. Spill the deets."

"Kyle and Hank grew up together."

Tanna frowned. "You didn't pick up on the fact that they're both from the same hometown? Don't, like, four people live in Wyoming?"

"Gee, thanks for the vote of confidence, Tan."

"Sorry. Go on."

"Kyle's bio said he's from Rawlins. Hank's says he's from Muddy Gap. Without having a map in front of me, and knowing nothing about Wyoming, I had no clue the towns are thirty miles apart. They went to the same school, where Hank called Kyle 'Gilly'—an abbreviated form of Gilchrist. So yes, I'd heard Hank mention Gilly offhandedly, but the truth is, whenever he and I were alone together, because we saw each other only twice a month, we didn't do a whole lot of talking."

"And can I just point out how jealous I am of that fact?"

"Anyway, I made it halfway to my truck when Kyle stopped me. Then Hank showed up and saw Kyle holding my upper arms and warned Kyle to get his hands off. Kyle let me go and shoved Hank. Hank shoved Kyle back. . . ."

Lainie sat on the edge of the bed and shot Tanna a dark look. "This is not where you insert, 'That is so romantic.' It was horrible. These guys are really good friends. There's no way I can choose one over the other. So I broke up with both of them and left."

"That's it?"

"I thought so until this morning. They showed up here. Together. To talk about me leaving last night. And Kyle told me he was kicked off the EBS tour and he's competing in the CRA."

"Oh, no."

"Oh, *yes*. So I'll be seeing both of them all the time. But that's not all they wanted to discuss with me." Lainie gnawed on her cheek. She trusted Tanna, but Kyle and Hank's suggestion of sharing her sounded . . . outlandish.

"Come on. You cannot be seriously thinking about not telling me, Lainie."

"Fine, but you have to promise on your championship AFR belt buckle and your grandma's secret noodle recipe that you will not tell another person. Ever."

Tanna held up her hand in a scout's-honor pose. "I swear by all that I hold holy, Granny's noodles and my beloved gold buckle, that I will take this secret to my grave."

Lainie blurted, "Hank and Kyle wanna share me. Like, at-the-same-time type of sharing me."

"Holy freakin' shit." Tanna's big gray eyes went comically wide. "They're offering you a threesome? With them?"

"Yes! Can you believe it?"

"Well? What did you say?"

How could she confess to losing the power of coherent thought once they'd started kissing her in tandem?

She couldn't. Not yet anyway. But clearly they expected a lot from her. A lot of naughty sexual things she'd imagined, but never mustered the guts to try—or, more accurately, had never been offered the chance to try.

"Please tell me you said yes, Lainie."

Her gaze flew to Tanna's. "You're not appalled?"

"Hell, no. I'm jealous."

"So you're telling me you'd do it?"

"If they'd asked me? Girl, I'da jumped 'em both so fast I might've knocked teeth out." Tanna grinned cheekily. "Look, obviously they both think you're hot in the sack. Since you've been nekkid with them, multiple times, they each know exactly how to push your buttons. Having two gorgeous guys willing to satisfy your every sexual craving? *Sign. Me. Up.* And since we're being completely honest, for the record, it wouldn't be the first time for me."

Lainie stared at Tanna, half-amazed, half . . . not surprised at all. "You've been in a threesome?"

"Yep. Appalled?" she teased.

"No. Just . . . intrigued as to how it came about, I guess."

"Happened on the spur of the moment. Got a little

crazy one night with my boyfriend and his best buddy. We ended up spending the entire weekend in bed. It was awesome." She gave Lainie a pointed look. "No, it's not my current boy toy or anyone that you know. We broke up a couple of months afterward, but I don't regret a damn thing."

Regret wasn't Lainie's main concern.

"Did you give them an answer?" Tanna asked.

"No. But they didn't demand one either. They told me to think about it and we'd talk after the rodeo tonight."

"See? That right there is exactly why you should do this. Hank and Kyle will try their damendest to outdo each other in making you scream. They'll see what turns you flaming hot—by watching the other guy. The bonus? They already know what you like in bed, so they'll try to kick up the kink a notch or ten. So the person who benefits the most in this situation is . . . you."

Leave it to Tanna to cut to the chase. Lainie was curious about the logistics of two men and one woman in the throes of passion. How it'd feel to have two hard cocks demanding entrance into her body. Two sets of hands squeezing and stroking. Two mouths. Two tongues. Two cocks. Yeah. She was kind of stuck on that mental image.

"Here's my advice. Try it. If you don't like it you can still walk away, break up with them or whatever. But you'll be kicking yourself years down the road when you're a blue-haired little old lady if you don't seize the chance now."

Lainie flopped back on the bed and sighed. "You're right. For once in my life, I'm cutting loose. What happens, happens. No fear, no regrets, no holding back. I'm a woman in her sexual prime; hear me roar. Balls to the wall, right?"

"Right." Tanna flopped on her back right next to Lainie on the bed. They stared up at the stained ceiling tiles. "On a purely selfish note, I hate knowin' that you're getting laid all the damn time and I'm not."

"Tanna, you could get laid every night of the week by a different cowboy if you wanted. I've watched them ask you. Watched you turn every one of them down in the last two months." Lainie paused, knowing this was a touchy subject. "Are you really that crazy about Steve?"

"Yes. No. Hell, who knows? I was. It sucks because I can feel him pulling away and I can't do a damn thing about it. Sounds stupid, but the more he pulls away the harder I want to hold on to him."

"That's never good, T, and it's not like you at all."

"Ugh. I know." Tanna sighed. "Listen to me, whining about my pathetic love life. We oughta be celebrating yours, loading you up on lube at the local A & P."

"Think that'd raise eyebrows in Lamar?" Lainie mused.

"If they look at you funny, just tell them it's for rodeo medical services."

"Got all my bases covered, huh?"

"I'm a practical girl." Tanna rolled off the bed and onto her feet. "Look, I'll see you later. I've gotta put Jezebel through her paces before showtime."

Lainie kept her eyes closed. She hadn't slept worth beans last night and a catnap might be in order.

Hair tickled her nose. She looked up into Tanna's face, which hung directly above hers. "What?"

"I'd better not see you at the bar tonight. You'd better not chicken out, Lainie Jay. Although I will expect a fully detailed report tomorrow."

"Deal."

Tanna smooched her forehead. "Get some rest, chickie, 'cause with those two guys? You're definitely gonna need it."

Chapter Four

For the bigger rodeos, the Lariat Sports Medicine team showcased the giant semi with the gigantic logo emblazoned across the side. Most people expected the enormous cargo area was filled with medical supplies and equipment. While that belief was partially true, the real purpose of the tricked-out truck was advertising.

Yes, the sports medicine team fixed broken cowboys, but inexplicably, tying the Lariat brand name of clothing with the sponsorship of pro rodeo was the sole reason for the Lariat Sports Medicine team's existence.

As much as Lainie liked her job with Lariat, she was strictly part-time, which meant she freelanced as an EMT in Colorado Springs on her flex days. With her fluctuating schedule, the last half of the week she was on the road headed to the next Lariat event. So, basically, she'd had no life for the last two years beyond the folks she'd met in the world of rodeo.

Hooking up with Hank had eased her loneliness.

Sometimes she wondered why she'd tried so damn hard to keep her relationship with him hidden.

The door to the designated medical room opened and her boss, Dr. Dusty Bowman, sauntered in.

Right. Now she remembered why things with her and Hank were kept hush-hush. Doc Bowman didn't like bullfighters. Normally it wouldn't matter what her boss thought about her love life, but Doc was more than just her boss. He'd stood behind the chutes watching in horror as his best friend, bull rider Jason Capshaw, was gored by a bull and the bullfighters did nothing to stop it.

At the time, Dusty had been a bull rider as well as Jason's traveling partner. After her father's very tragic and very public death, Dusty dropped out of pro rodeo and returned to college, earning a medical degree specializing in sports medicine.

Doc Dusty blamed Jason Capshaw's death on improperly trained bullfighters and lack of safety gear for the riders. He took it upon himself to design a vest that offered protection from a bull's deadly horns. He'd sold his patented design to a small company, which also made protective clothing for policemen and loggers. Eventually Lariat Clothiers bought out the company. Then they approached Doc Dusty about spearheading a sports medicine program geared toward rodeo. With his background as a bull rider and rodeo safety promoter, Dr. Bowman became the "face" of Lariat Sports Medicine.

Dusty hired her, albeit part-time, with her lowly LPN and EMT degrees, when he could've hired any one of the hundreds of applicants—all with master's degrees. She wondered if he'd ever feel he'd repaid the debt he owed her because he was supposed to have been on the bull that killed Jason Capshaw.

But none of the grief or guilt was evident in Doc's eyes when he saw her. He grinned from beneath the brim of his ever-present cowboy hat. "Lainie! Good to see you."

"What brings the face of Lariat Sports Medicine to the trenches?"

"A business deal—what else? Plus, I've never worked this rodeo, and you know me—always lookin' for something new."

How true that was. The man was constantly on the go.

"Also, I wanted to talk to you."

Lainie's focus zoomed to him.

He shut the door and leaned against it, offering her a rueful smile. "That oughta buy us a little time."

"Doc, you're scaring me."

"You jump to the worst conclusion first. Just like your daddy."

"Am I in trouble?"

"No. Far from it. You have a great rapport with the contestants in both the EBS and the CRA."

"But?" she prompted.

"But I know you hire out as an EMT the days you aren't working for me. You look exhausted. I'm worried the travel schedule is wearing you down."

"Funny, I don't feel exhausted. And this must've come on real sudden, because I looked just fine to you the day before yesterday at the Lariat offices."

He glanced away. Guiltily. Which meant one thing.

Lainie pushed away from the wall. "Did my mother put you up to this, Dusty?"

He still wouldn't make eye contact with her.

"That meddling bitch."

"Now, that ain't no way to talk about your mama. You can't blame her for being concerned about you."

"So she goes to you, my boss, behind my back? Instead of talking to me first?"

"This is why she brought it to my attention, because we both knew you'd react like this."

"Act like what? Resentful that I'm a twenty-six-year-old professional woman and my *mommy* is still checking up on me?"

"Lainie—"

"Are you my boss right now or my family friend?"

Doc hesitated. "I hate that you draw these invisible lines in the sand and I'm forced to stand on one side or the other."

"Choose."

"Fine, I'm your friend."

"Then, *friend*, here's the side I'm standing on. I hate that you're still letting my mother lead you around by the nose. I hate that the last time I talked to her I told her to butt out of my life. She couldn't accept that and she took it upon herself to call you to rectify it."

"What was I supposed to do? She was crying. *Crying.* About you. It broke my damn heart."

God, Lainie was mad enough to spit nails. Doc Dusty was one of the most focused, headstrong men she'd ever known. She'd watched Doc stare down the head of a major television network when they demanded to televise his examination of life-threatening rodeo injuries. So his being reduced to an errand boy for Sharlene Capshaw Green burned Lainie's ass.

"And worst of all she was blaming *me* for *you* not staying in touch with her," Doc added.

"How is that your fault?" Lainie demanded.

"Sharlene said I'm keeping you too busy working both circuits and you have no life outside of this job. Which, she felt entitled to point out, is only a part-time position."

Dammit.

"After I talked to Sharlene I checked your personnel file. You haven't taken any time off since you started working for me."

"So?"

"So you're overdue for a vacation. Long overdue."

"When was the last time *you* took a vacation?"

His eyes narrowed. "This ain't about me. This is about me and your mama being worried about you."

"Why doesn't she worry about her other kids and leave me the hell alone?" Lainie fumed. Paced. Cursing her mother's need to control everything, which had always been a major sticking point between them.

A year following her husband's tragic death, Sharlene Capshaw was wooed by Marcus Green—an ambulance-chasing attorney—to sue the venue where Jason Capshaw had been killed. Sharlene refused. Yet a romance between the grieving, beautiful young widow and the greedy, hotshot lawyer blossomed. By Lainie's seventh birthday, her mother had remarried.

They moved out of Oklahoma to Marcus's house in California. Which would've been fine, except Sharlene decided Lainie acted too rural for Sharlene's new station in life. She enrolled Lainie in a private school and cut Lainie off from anyone who'd mattered in her old life. Her grandmother, Elsa Capshaw, wasn't allowed contact, under the guise of Lainie needing to acclimate to her new surroundings.

By age nine, Lainie refused to travel with her mother and stepfather, demanding instead to spend her summer vacations at her grandma Elsa's house in Oklahoma.

During those hot summers she fell in love with the world of rodeo her mother had left behind. The month Lainie graduated from high school, she moved back to Oklahoma for good. Partially because her grandmother needed a caretaker; partially because Lainie's career goals weren't lofty enough for her mother.

It hadn't mattered that Lainie had earned a CNA certificate and become an EMT while a senior in high school. Or that after moving to Oklahoma she'd earned a degree as an LPN, as well as becoming a licensed massage therapist. Sharlene constantly harangued Lainie to go back to college for an RN or PA degree, with an eye toward medical school.

Medical school didn't interest her. She couldn't fathom the extra burden of attending classes and finishing homework at the end of a brutal workweek.

So Sharlene had been beyond infuriated when Lainie accepted Dusty's job offer to work in the world of rodeo. Things had spiraled to the point where she and her mother rarely spoke at all these days.

"Lainie? You went awful quiet. You all right?"

"No. I'm not all right, Doc. Don't do this."

"Too late. After tomorrow night's performance, you'll officially be on vacation for three weeks." He raised his hand, stopping her automatic protest. "This is nonnegotiable."

Seething, Lainie itched to smack something. She inhaled two deep, long breaths and exhaled with deliberate care. "Okay. Say I agree to take this blasted vacation and don't just quit outright. What happens when I come back? Will you knuckle under to Queen Sharlene every time she feels I'm being mistreated?"

Doc scowled. "No."

"Because as a fully grown adult woman, I tend to get a little pissy about stuff like that."

"I imagine so. Look, I'm not knuckling under to her. In fact, I'd planned to approach you about this and another issue *before* Sharlene called me. It seemed a good idea to get what I want—forcing you to take the break you need—while allowing Sharlene to believe I abided by her wishes and keeping her happy."

Warning bells rang in her head. "Whoa. Back up. Approach me about what other issue?"

"About you going to work for Lariat full-time."

"You're joking."

"Nope. But before you get all hyped up about it, I'll tell you this: It wouldn't be under the same structure we are right now. We've been in negotiations for months about serious changeups. By the time you get back, hopefully we'll have all the details ironed out."

Trying to contain her excitement, Lainie casually asked, "Can you give me any ideas on the full-time job?"

"Off the top of my head? It'd be administrative duties. There'd be no traveling," he warned. "You wouldn't work either circuit, which I know is your favorite part of the job."

"Would I be in Colorado Springs?"

"Of course."

Lainie scowled at him.

"I know you don't like living there, but suck it up."

"Fine. Who's working the circuits as an official Lariat rep while I'm gone?"

"No one."

"So I'm not the only one forced to take a vacation?"

Doc smiled sheepishly. "No. It's pretty much everyone across the board. This time of year, with Cowboy Christmas, it's notoriously slow as far as big official events."

"I find it hard to believe no one gets injured during that time."

"Actually, there are more injuries, being as the contestants are racing from event to event. But treatment is sporadic. Very few of the smaller venues can afford to do more than park an ambulance beneath the stands, get a local doctor to volunteer, and hope like hell there aren't life-threatening injuries."

Two knocks sounded; then Doc's assistant, Randy, poked his head in. "Parnell is lookin' for you, Doc."

"Tell him I'll be right there." Doc rubbed his forehead again. "Never fails. I'm damn surprised we had a conversation this long without bein' interrupted. At any rate, we'll talk more later, okay?"

"Okay."

Then Doc was gone.

The closer to performance time, the busier Lainie was. She taped wrists, thumbs, ankles, and ribs—with the Lariat-stamped medical supplies. She fielded phone calls. Dealt with the little crap the sponsors required, making sure the logo was visible everywhere in the assigned room, down to the positioning of the water bottles in the coolers. She was low woman on the totem pole—in fact, she was the *only* woman on the totem pole. Which meant she did a lot of fetch-and-carry.

She loved the bustle, the action, and the sense of family on the CRA circuits—maybe because the family aspect was sadly lacking in her life, but she felt she belonged here.

No matter how many times she heard the announcements over the PA system of the night's rodeo sponsors, the names of the rodeo queens in attendance, the entertainment, the call for veterans to stand, when the local singer began "The Star Spangled Banner" she still got goose bumps from being part of something so wholly American.

If things were boring in the medical room—which they all hoped for—Lainie and the other Lariat employees took turns watching the action in the arena. Normally she preferred barrel racing and team roping to the rough stock events, but tonight she had the overwhelming urge to attend the bull riding section.

It was no coincidence the rodeo promoters kept the most popular event for last. In some of the bigger venues, the bull riding was interspersed between other events. The crowd went wild at the announcement of the first rider. Lainie hustled through the barricades separating the chutes and gates from the arena, flashing her Lariat pass at the guards policing the area.

The buzzer echoed and a smattering of applause followed. The guy was bucked off with no score. Lainie climbed up the metal rungs and rested her arms on the top of the fence.

Oh, looky there. One very hot bullfighter was bouncing from foot to foot. His nylon performance shorts brushed the backs of his muscular calves. Hank's loose-fitting sponsorship shirt covered the tight vest. Not as thick as the vest required for bull riders, but it offered some protection against horns and hooves.

Three bullfighters worked the chutes. Because they dealt with all the bulls rather than just one, bullfighters were injured more frequently than bull riders. Why any man would willingly go head-to-head with a bull confounded her.

She zeroed in on the guy on the bull behind the gate. He wore a black cowboy hat, not a protective face-mask helmet. She shook her head at the poor choice. Before too long she hoped helmets were required safety equipment for all bull riders on all circuits, the same way vests were required.

The rider nodded his head and the gate jerked open. The bull leaped out; strings of snot flew from his nose; his hindquarters left the ground as he attempted to fling the rider into the air. The bull succeeded and bucked the rider off at 4.8 seconds.

Again Lainie was reminded of where the spectator's focus was: on the bull and rider. Not on the bullfighters who distracted the snorting beast so the rider could scramble away unscathed.

Dammit. Even she hadn't watched Hank during the

bull ride—and she had a vested interest in making sure he kept his big, hot body safe. She squinted at the scoreboard across the arena floor to see what rider was up next. No one she recognized. The announcer blathered on and she focused on the far chute. Namely on Hank, ten feet off to the side of the chute, still bouncing in anticipation. Lainie could hang stark naked from the ceiling and Hank wouldn't notice her; his concentration was absolute.

The gate opened and Hank stayed out of the way—until the rider hit the dirt. Then he ran straight at the bull and danced to the right, weaving and bobbing, forcing the animal to charge him rather than the guy who was still struggling to get up.

Then the bull abruptly switched direction and trotted back through the livestock gate. But Hank was already down by the next chute, waiting for the next rider. It was fascinating to see Hank working. She knew other bullfighters deferred to him, which was a big deal, because Hank wasn't that old. For the first time she wondered if Hank had aspirations of moving up. Since the EBS dealt only with bulls and not other rodeo events, getting a job as a bullfighter with that organization would be a huge boost.

It bothered her, not knowing Hank's future plans.

That's because it's just sex between you two, remember?

Except now, it'd be sex between the three of them.

Lainie wasn't exactly sure how to proceed. Did she just saunter up to them tonight and say, "Ride me hard, boys"?

The way things looked right now, this would be a one-time-only threesome. As Hank and Kyle traveled from rodeo to rodeo during Cowboy Christmas, she'd be holed up in her apartment. Maybe she'd head up into the mountains, see if her buddy Mara could snag time off and hop a flight to Vegas. Or visit the beach.

"Now up, a name we haven't seen on the CRA circuit, but that might be familiar to those of you who follow the EBS."

A few boos echoed. Her attention snapped back to the chutes.

"Kyle Gilchrist comes to us from Rawlins, Wyoming. Let's make Kyle feel welcome in his CRA debut."

She peered at the figure behind the bars but couldn't discern whether he wore a safety helmet or a cowboy hat. Whenever he'd come into the sports medicine room he'd already stripped out of his chaps and riding gear. She'd never watched Kyle ride, but many people in the rodeo world compared Kyle's fluid, graceful riding style to her late father's technique.

Lainie's breath stalled when the chute opened and the bull jumped so high all four hooves were off the ground at the same time. Landing hard, the speckled body spun to the left. Spun to the right. Twice. Jerked its rear around. Kyle held on. His body flowed with the angry bull's every twist and turn, his free arm up in the air, his feet spurring.

The momentum of the crowd grew. The clapping and whistling nearly drowned out the buzz of the timer.

Kyle pulled the release from the hand wrap and bailed off the bull, landing right square on his ass. He clambered to his feet, immediately making a beeline for the fence surrounding the stands, when the bull gave chase.

But the bull didn't get far before Hank slapped it on the rear flank. The ornery beast spun toward the new potential conquest. Hank raced to the livestock gate and the bull trotted in without looking back.

"You ready for this, Lamar? We've got a new high score. How about an . . . eighty-nine-point-five debut for the cowboy from Wyoming?"

Thunderous applause echoed from the stands and

Lainie clapped along, laughing as Hank and Kyle did a jumping chest bump on the arena floor, much to the delight of the crowd. Then Kyle picked up his flank strap and tipped his hat to the fans.

Only four riders remained and chances were good none would knock Kyle off the leaderboard. Lainie returned to the medical room and busied herself stacking towels. When she heard the shuffle of boots and the muffled clank of spurs, she turned and saw Kyle wearing a sexy grin a mile wide.

She couldn't help but smile back and give him a once-over. It ought to be illegal to look that damn good in a pair of dusty chaps.

"Nice ride," she said.

His eyebrows rose. "You watched it?"

"Yeah. Been pretty boring in here tonight."

"I can't say I'm unhappy about that."

Her gaze dropped to where he was cupping his right elbow. "What happened?"

"Nothin'—just jerked my riding arm a little hard on my dismount."

"Where?"

He pointed to the outside of his forearm.

"Think it might be fractured?" Most bull riders had broken so many bones they knew the difference between a sprain, a bruised muscle, a fracture, and a break.

"No. I'm fine. That's not why I—"

"Sit. Let me look at it."

"Lainie—"

"Now."

Kyle grumbled. But he sat.

Lainie rolled his shirt cuff up as far as it would go. She poked the skin surrounding the bone. Just slightly swollen. She let her fingers trace the bend in his elbow and move up his beefy biceps. When Kyle sucked in a breath, she finally looked at him. The desire she saw made her mouth dry.

"Every damn time you touch me, Lainie. Whether it's in a professional capacity or when we're alone—"

"Kyle—"

"There's no one here but us. Let me speak my piece while I've got the chance."

She nodded.

"I like bein' with you. A lot. It probably seems weird, what Hank and me have proposed, but neither one of us wants to walk away from you."

"I get that. But I won't pit you guys against each other."

Kyle reached out to touch her face, but let his hand fall back to his leg at the last second. "We both know that."

"Are you here speaking on Hank's behalf?"

"Yes. We figured it'd be easier if we didn't come blazing in here together. So I am here to ask if you've made a decision."

"You want my answer right now?"

"The rodeo is almost over. People are gonna be heading out, and me 'n' Hank wanna know which direction we'll be goin'."

Lainie searched his eyes. No smugness. Just curiosity. And an underlying hint of cautiousness. Kyle wasn't looking at her like a sure thing, a done deal. Would her answer be any different if Hank had asked?

No. It'd be exactly the same: a resounding yes.

She rolled his sleeve down and snapped the buttons before she met his gaze again. "I'll see you both at my room in an hour."

Chapter Five

Kyle and Hank sat in Hank's truck in front of Lainie's hotel. The allotted hour was nearly up. They'd rushed back to their room, showered, changed, and counted up the condoms between the two of them. Nine. Enough for one night.

"Should we've brought her flowers or something?" Kyle asked.

"Hell if I know," Hank said.

Kyle blew out an unsteady breath. Might as well get this confession over. "I ain't ever been in this position before."

Hank's head whipped around. "Meaning what? Getting ready to have a threesome?"

Kyle felt the tops of his ears burning. "Yeah. Maybe that makes me lame or something—"

"I've never done this either," Hank blurted out, which was unlike him.

They stared at each other. Then they both laughed. Hard.

Tension broken, Hank drawled, "Three threesome virgins—imagine that."

"So do we let Lainie know we're greenhorns?" Kyle asked.

"I guess we'll see."

"I'm thinking we keep that info to ourselves unless she asks. But we gotta act like we know what we're doin'."

"How do you propose we do that, Kyle?"

He shrugged. "Just like this morning. Take charge. If we don't let her overthink every move, chances are we won't either. We'll just go with it."

"True. But I keep thinkin' we'll get to her room and she'll have changed her mind," Hank said.

"We'd hafta actually get out of the damn truck to figure out if that's true or not," Kyle pointed out.

Hank straightened his hat and grabbed the door handle. "Let's do this thing."

Inside the hotel at Lainie's door, they looked at each other. Hank nodded and Kyle knocked.

Locks disengaged and the door swung open. Lainie stepped back and jammed her hands in the pockets of her jeans. "Um. Hi. Come in."

Man. She was nervous. That made three of them.

For some odd reason, it calmed Kyle. There were no rules. No right or wrong way to approach this. For all he knew maybe they'd sit around and watch TV tonight.

But then, looking at her lush lips and breasts, Kyle threw caution to the wind. He vaguely heard the door slam when he cupped Lainie's face in his hands and kissed her.

He didn't devour her mouth; he kept the kiss soft and easy, laced with heat and intent. She leaned into him without taking her hands out of her back pockets. Kyle broke his lips free in tiny biting increments. "Mmm.

That's what I'm talking about." He sidestepped her, curious as to how Hank would react.

Hank didn't play it cool. He swooped in, picked her up, and gently tossed her on the closest bed.

Lainie's shriek of surprise was muffled as Hank kissed her thoroughly, leaving her arms trapped behind her.

Kyle knew Hank had taken the right tack. Tipping Lainie off balance from the start, making the situation light and fun. No pressure. No discussion. No time for nerves—from any of them.

"See what we have here, Kyle?"

He leaned over and peered at Lainie. "Yes, I do. But you've got way too many clothes on, hot stuff."

"You get her boots off while I make sure those hands of hers stay right where they are," Hank said.

Thump. Thump. Boots hit the floor. "Now what?"

"You work on her bottom half and I'll work on her top half. Up you go, sweetheart."

Once Lainie was standing again, she spoke. "Guys, I'm not sure—"

Hank briefly pressed his mouth to hers. "We are. Trust us."

Kyle was impressed by Hank's take-charge stance; Lainie complied immediately. But that didn't mean he'd allow Hank to call all the shots. Kyle said, "Drop your hands by your sides." He worked the button and zipper on her jeans. The instant he caught a glimpse of her pink bikini panties, his cock went from semihard to fully erect. He dropped to his knees and placed a kiss on the alluring section of skin above the waistband.

A soft gasp escaped from her parted lips.

"Help me yank these off," Kyle said to her. She seemed strangely shy after her jeans hit the ground and she stood in front of him in her panties. He looked at Hank. "Your turn."

Six loud pops from the pearl-snap buttons and the floral Western shirt hung open, revealing a pink bra. And all that pearly skin. He peeled the shirt down her toned arms. Hank's breathing had changed, but Kyle wasn't about to check out the crotch of Hank's jeans to see if Hank was sporting wood.

Kyle hooked his fingers beneath the elastic band of her panties. And slowly—very, very slowly—he tugged the lace down her legs, letting the coarse tips of his fingers scrape against her soft skin. "Your turn," he said hoarsely to Hank.

Hank stood behind Lainie. He unhooked the bra and allowed the shoulder straps to ease down her limbs with the same painstaking precision Kyle used removing her underwear. But Hank mixed it up too, dragging his mouth across the slope of her shoulder as he rid Lainie of her last scrap of clothing.

Kyle knew what he wanted to do next: bury his face in her pussy.

But Lainie demanded, "Take off your shirts, both of you."

"Why?"

"Because if I'm gonna be the filling in a Hank-and-Kyle sandwich, I want to feel every inch of those hot, hard chests against my front and my back."

That was when Kyle knew Lainie was truly in. Her bossy surrender was typical; she never did anything half-assed. He wanted to fuck her like a madman, but he kept his motions unhurried as Hank nibbled and licked down the side of Lainie's neck.

As soon as he'd doffed his shirt, he fell in front of her. He pressed his mouth into the sweet-smelling mound. At her soft moan, he looked up.

Hank squeezed and cupped her tits, pulling at the nipples until the tips were long and hard. He expected

Lainie would let her head fall back, giving herself over to the moment. But she watched Kyle with those mesmerizing copper-colored eyes.

Keeping their gazes connected, Kyle licked from the top of her slit down to the hot, wet heart of her. Once. Twice. Three times.

She trembled.

Three more agonizingly slow passes of his greedy tongue.

Then Hank said, "Switch."

Hellfire and damnation. He'd just gotten his mouth close to paradise. Forcing him to move seemed like a cruel power play on Hank's part. But Kyle also understood Hank's reasoning: proving to Lainie her pleasure was a team effort. Either man could call a halt or switch it up at will. And Hank could be damn sure Kyle would also exercise that option.

Kyle rose to his feet, following the curve of her upper body until he reached her succulent mouth. By the time he stepped behind her, she was rubbing her legs together.

She cried out and Kyle knew that bastard Hank had gone straight for her clit.

Fine. If Hank got her off first, Kyle would be first in line to fuck her. And he wouldn't tone down his aggressive side. If Lainie expected sweet lovin', Hank could give her that. Kyle would be the one to give Lainie fire.

"Hank. I'm so close; don't stop."

Kyle alternated between watching Lainie's blissful expression to watching Hank's head moving between her thighs. Seeing Hank in that position wasn't as weird as Kyle had imagined. In fact, it was sort of hot.

As Lainie started to come, Kyle pinched her nipples and used his teeth against her throat. She moaned one of the sexiest sounds he'd ever heard.

Once Kyle was sure Lainie was stable, he said, "Get on the bed, sugar." He toed off his boots and stripped down. Holding a condom, Kyle looked at Hank and said, "Switch."

Hank's mouth opened. Then closed. His jaw tightened. He nodded and leaned against the wall, arms crossed over his chest.

Fair was fair.

Lainie reclined on the bed on her elbows. Her lips parted. Her eyes looked dark and sated. Color dotted her cheekbones. Those crazy curls surrounded her face, giving her the appearance of a tousled angel.

Kyle ripped open the condom and put it on.

She shot a worried look at Hank, then at Kyle. "How does this work? I mean, am I supposed to—"

"Relax; we'll ease into it. We ain't gonna jump on you with the double-rider special first thing."

A slow smile curled her lips. "Appreciated, although I am looking forward to it."

Kyle circled his hands around her ankles. "Lookit this body. Shame you ever have to wear clothes, sugar."

Her gaze dropped to his erection. "You're not so shabby yourself."

Hank didn't utter a sound, but they were both completely aware he was in the room.

"Get up on your hands and knees facing the end of the bed."

She smirked. "You do like to do it from behind."

"Is that a complaint?"

"God, no. You know I love it this way."

"Mmm. There's something mighty appealing about watching my dick pounding your pussy as your ass is shaking."

"Don't forget how much you like to wrap your hands in my hair while you're watching my badonkadonk shake."

"Sure shocked me to figure out you liked that tiny bite of pain." Kyle leveled a soft slap on her ass as he positioned himself behind her on the bed. He loved the upthrust angle of her ass. The curve of her spine. The dimples above those sexy rounded butt cheeks. He bent forward and tongued the indentations, tickling the fine hairs with his goatee and breathing across the damp spots.

She moaned.

He kneed her stance wider and layered his chest to her back, basking in the power of this position. Normally he didn't get off on power-play stuff, but with Lainie, his dominant side pushed front and center. Kyle followed the line of her spine with his tongue from tip to bottom.

"Kyle. Stop teasing me."

"I've only just started to tease you." He took himself in hand, swirling the head of his cock through the cream gathered at the mouth of her sex.

Lainie pushed her hips back, trying to impale herself.

That action earned her another swat on the ass. "Naughty girl. Behave. You don't get to be in charge. At all. I'm tempted not to fuck you."

Hank snorted softly at Kyle's half-assed bluff.

"No. Please. I'll . . . behave."

"Since you asked so nice." He squeezed her hips in his hands, holding her steady as he plowed into her pussy in one stroke.

She arched hard. "Yes. God. Just like that."

He grinned as his shaft eased out. When just the tip of his cock rested against the opening, he slammed back in.

And stopped.

Her strong interior muscles attempted to draw him deeper into her cunt. But Kyle didn't budge.

Movement out of the corner of his eye caught his attention. Hank strode toward the end of the bed as he loosened his belt. The rasp of his zipper sounded loud in the room, as did the rustle of his jeans and boxers hitting the floor.

Kyle kept still, but not as still as Lainie.

Hank centered himself in front of Lainie. His free hand threaded through her curls and he tilted her head up. "How about you wrap those pretty lips around my dick?"

Lainie's pussy clenched around Kyle's cock.

"That's it," Hank murmured. "Open wide, baby, and suck me in."

It was sexy as shit having Lainie at their mercy. Kyle saw the appeal of threesomes—lust, flesh, urgency, power. He waited until Hank pulled out of her mouth and he mimicked the movement, easing from her gripping channel. When Hank snapped his hips and buried his cock between Lainie's lips, Kyle plunged to the hilt in her cunt.

Meeting Hank's eyes as they enjoyed the same woman didn't freak Kyle out. Hank either, apparently. Hank grinned. "I need it faster. You?"

"Yeah."

Hank placed both hands on Lainie's face and pumped his hips in a quicker rhythm. "This hot fuckin' mouth of yours makes me crazy. Send me over, Lainie. Send me over and swallow every drop."

Lainie's answering head bob caused Hank to snarl.

Kyle knew he should reach around and stroke her clit, but his selfish side took over. He pounded into her harder and faster, greedy for the quickest path to blowing the seed from his balls. He closed his eyes when he heard Hank's hoarse shout and the sounds of Lainie swallowing.

Four hard thrusts later, Kyle clenched his ass cheeks as pulses of heat shot out the end of his dick. He grunted as he came with each thrust, keeping a tight grip on Lainie's butt cheeks so he didn't fall off the damn bed. Oh, yeah. Fuck, yeah. That was what he needed. Just like that. He slowed his thrusts to short and shallow, feeling too damn good to withdraw.

She moaned, "Yes, Hank. Faster."

Whoa. Hank? Had Lainie already mixed up their names? Kyle opened his eyes and saw Hank standing at the side of the bed, his left hand braced in the middle of Lainie's back, his right arm moving below her as he stroked her clit. Hank murmured in Lainie's ear as he brought her off. Again.

That's two he's given her, pal, and none from you.

Dammit. Lost in an orgasmic haze, Kyle hadn't even noticed Hank had moved. Nor that Hank's fingers were mere inches away from Kyle's cock.

You would know if you'd been an attentive lover.

Rhythmic spasms of Lainie's cunt clamped down on his softening cock as she climaxed. Fuck. That was almost enough to get him hard again.

She sighed contentedly, nuzzling the side of Hank's face as he murmured in her ear.

Probably sweet nothings. Silver-tongued motherfucker.

There it was. Kyle realized he'd have to step up his game if he wanted to keep up with Hank.

He withdrew and retreated to the bathroom. As soon as Kyle returned, Hank took his turn cleaning up.

Which left Kyle alone with Lainie. She'd already slipped on an old T-shirt and chosen the bed farthest from the door. The first night they'd spent together, he'd expected Lainie to be cuddly as a kitten after sex, but she definitely wanted her own space.

Kyle crawled next to her, not caring whether it pissed Hank off. First come, first served. Hank would get his chance, but not tonight.

Hank sprawled in his lumpy hotel bed—alone—listening to the whir of the air conditioner and Kyle's snores.

Kyle, that opportunistic bastard, had gotten into Lainie's bed while Hank had gone to take a leak.

You'da done the same thing, hoss.

True.

It just proved he'd made another tactical error. This situation with Lainie wasn't as simple as Hank first believed. He'd rather cockily imagined he had a leg up on his buddy because he'd been with Lainie longer. Apparently Hank had also deluded himself that their rockin'-hot sex would weigh in his favor too.

Now Hank knew why Lainie had strayed with Kyle: Kyle ratcheted sex to a level Hank hadn't.

Didn't that feel like a kick in the balls.

Hank flashed back to the times he and Lainie had been naked together. He'd eked sighs and moans of sexual satisfaction from her every damn time. Several times. As soon as the hotel room door closed, they'd always been crazed to get their hands on each other. But Hank realized that somehow he always slowed it down.

Why?

A mistaken belief that all women needed extended foreplay? Because he feared he'd be too quick on the trigger if he didn't pace himself? No, the truth was, Hank had never gotten sexually inventive with her. He'd considered her too sweet to be interested in doing the darker, kinkier things he'd imagined.

So he'd played it safe. And in playing it safe, Hank damn near lost her. He could *still* lose her. Kyle had brought his A game to the bedroom and Hank had rested on his belief that he had it in the bag.

Christ. He was a twenty-eight-year-old man with

plenty of sexual conquests under his belt. He'd had no complaints. Still, he was worried. How could he take this to the next sexual level? He'd never been a book guy, so reading up on the thousand ways to please a woman in the sack wasn't happening. He'd watched a fair amount of porn. Too bad he couldn't remember specifics, now that he needed knowledge of acrobatic or unusual sexual acts.

Or . . . did he? Was that what Lainie wanted? A different sexual scenario every time? With props, crops, cuffs, and toys? That wasn't what happened with her and Kyle. So what had Kyle given Lainie that put such a wanton look on her face and a whimper of anticipation in her voice?

Demanding her obedience? Showing her who was in control? Maybe. Fuck. It shouldn't be this hard to figure out where he'd made his sexual misstep. But then again, Hank hadn't imagined he'd be lying by himself in a double bed in a hotel room while Kyle was five feet away sleeping with his woman.

Your woman? Get your head in the game or Gilly will steal this prize right from underneath your nose.

Hank turned on his side and watched Lainie sleeping. Her arm curled under her head. Her cheek nestled into the pillow.

Damn. He wished it were him in bed next to her. It did little to curb his feelings of envy to know that it *would* be him next time. Something sweet and protective flowed through him at the humming sigh Lainie made in her sleep.

He rolled over and stared at the opposite wall for a long time before he finally fell asleep.

Chapter Six

Lainie woke to the smell of coffee. She blinked at Hank sitting on the bed across from her, completely dressed. She sat up.

"Mornin'," he said with a smile.

She smiled back. "Morning. You're up early."

Hank shrugged. "Habit. I'm always up early at home. I brought you coffee. Didn't know if you used sugar or cream so I got some of both."

"Thank you." Lainie yawned and took the to-go cup. She scraped her tangled hair back. "Lord. Talk about extreme bedhead. I must look a mess."

"I think you look beautiful."

"How much sugar did you put in your coffee to turn your tongue so sweet?" she murmured.

"None. I reckon you just bring out the sweet side in me."

Lainie rolled her eyes, but her belly swooped.

"Didja bring me a cup, sweetheart?" Kyle grumbled sarcastically from beneath the covers.

"Yep. I also bought a couple toothbrushes out of the

vending machine. Yours is still in the package on the sink."

Still muttering, a naked Kyle scooted off the end of the bed, snatched a coffee, and shuffled to the bathroom.

For some reason, Lainie was nervous about being alone with Hank. Maybe it was his unexpected sweetness. Maybe it was the contemplative look that darkened his eyes to a deep midnight blue. "What?"

"This." Hank leaned over and closed his mouth over hers. He tasted like coffee and mint.

She pulled back. "Sorry, I haven't brushed my teeth."

"I don't care." He dove back in for another kiss, keeping it lazy and gentle. "Mmm. I like kissing you first thing in the mornin'."

The bathroom door opened. Lainie almost jumped back guiltily, but then she remembered what they'd done last night, all three of them. "Umm. I'll just hop in the shower."

Hank drawled, "Need help scrubbing anything in particular?"

"No. Thanks. I'll be fine." She locked the bathroom door and stripped off the oversize, completely unsexy T-shirt she'd slipped on after last night's fun and games.

Whoo, yeah. Last night redefined wickedly naughty.

When Kyle started fucking her from behind, she'd expected Hank to sit back quietly and watch the scene unfold with those brooding eyes. Then after Kyle finished with her, she expected Hank would swoop in, lay her on her back, and fuck her face-to-face, as he always did.

So Hank's dropping his pants and commanding her to suck his cock had blown her expectations all to hell.

The forceful way he'd inserted himself into the situation was sexier than his command that she get him off. He'd never acted so aggressive. Never demanded she swallow, since he'd never let himself come in her mouth.

And his grip on her hair had been just shy of painful. Seeing that side of Hank was a real eye-opener—and a serious turn-on.

Between the dual sensations of Hank's cock tunneling in and out of her mouth as Kyle rhythmically fucked her, Lainie had spiraled into a place where she existed as a conduit for their pleasure. A different kind of pleasure, laced with feminine power.

The buzzing rush became dreamlike when Hank fingered her to another orgasm. She hadn't remembered much after that, beyond collapsing onto the bed.

After showering, Lainie brushed her teeth and smoothed on lotion. Leaving her hair wrapped turban-style and a second bath towel tucked around her torso, she exited the bathroom in a cloud of steam. When she glanced up after digging through her suitcase, she noticed both Kyle and Hank were staring at her. Namely, staring at her ass. "What?"

"Darlin', it's a damn good thing that suitcase ain't any lower on the floor. Or you'd be givin' us a real good show," Hank said.

"Not that we'd mind," Kyle added with a grin.

Her cell phone rang. Flustered, she answered without checking the caller ID. "Hello?"

"Melanie?"

Ugh. "Hi, Mom."

"How are you?"

Pissed off that you called Dusty. Pissed off that you insist on calling me Melanie. Just pissed off at you all around.

Not a good way to start the conversation, let alone the day. "I'm okay. How are you?"

"Oh, we're fine."

If Lainie didn't cut to the chase her mother would drone on about the fabulous weather or the twins' latest exploits, or her stupid dog. "So, to what do I owe the honor of this call?"

"I can't call my own daughter to chat? To see how she's doing?"

"I'm sure Dusty told you exactly how I was *doing* when you called him."

Dramatic pause.

Lainie paced, waiting for Queen Sharlene to deign to speak.

"You're upset."

"Damn right I'm upset."

"I don't see why. I'm the one who put myself on the line with Dusty, getting him to see reason about you needing a vacation. You should know he refused to talk to me at first."

"Pity it didn't stick."

Sharlene laughed. "I can be very persuasive. I know you think you've got Dusty wrapped around your little finger, Melanie, but the truth is, he's manipulating you like always."

Lainie froze even as anger raced through her veins like liquid fire. "Since you brought it up, Mother, let me be perfectly clear: You were out of line calling Dusty. He had a right to refuse to talk to you and I have a right to be pissed."

"That man is slaving you, for slave wages. This part-time obsession is holding you back from starting a real career or having a real life."

"It's my life, Mom. This *obsession* is making me happy."

"Are you sure? Because it's not making me happy, Melanie Jay. You haven't been home in nearly two years!"

"The road runs both ways from Colorado Springs to Belmont. You could've come to see me."

"So I could spend my time in a hotel while you flit off

to another rodeo? No, thank you. But since Dusty is giving you a three-week vacation, you have no excuse not to come to California. There are some things we need to talk about. Now that our schedules—"

"Look, I'm sick of pretending we haven't seen each other just because our schedules don't mesh. So don't waste your breath. We have nothing to talk about, and I will not spend a single minute of my vacation time in Belmont."

Silence.

"This is the thanks I get for going out of my way to help you?"

"You went out of your way to try to fuck up my personal relationship with Dusty, as well as my business relationship with him. So don't wait for my gushing thanks. Jesus. Do you have any idea how goddamn mortifying it is that my *mommy* called and cried to my boss about my supposed unfair treatment?"

"Don't you use that foul language with me, Melanie."

"Don't you talk down to me, Mom. I am not a child."

"Then stop acting like one," Sharlene snapped back.

Lainie exhaled in a rush, unaware she'd been holding her breath. "You're right. This is completely unproductive. I am not in the wrong. You are. Think about that for the next three weeks while I'm on vacation and you don't hear from me."

"You're serious. You're really not coming home?"

"No. And don't call me until you're ready to apologize."

"Why are you punishing me? That's not—"

"Good-bye." Lainie hung up. She clutched the phone, half expecting it'd ring again. But it didn't. Maybe she'd finally gotten her point across to her clueless mother.

Not fair—she means well. She acts out of love, even when she has a piss-poor way of showing it.

"Lainie. You okay?" Kyle asked.

Crap. She'd totally forgotten Kyle and Hank were here. "No, I'm not okay. I'm never okay when I'm forced to deal with my mother. It pisses me off that she doesn't think she did a thing wrong." Lainie closed her eyes. "I'm just sorry you guys had to hear it."

"Did she really call Doc and demand he give you vacation time?"

"Yes. But Dusty pulled one over on her, since he'd already planned on forcing me to take time off before she called."

"Does she do this often?"

"Often enough, but never on this level. Since Dusty and my dad were best friends, she thinks nothing of playing Dusty. Then she accuses *me* of being manipulative, ungrateful, and having unresolved Daddy issues. Oh, and I'm wasting my life with the rodeo because of those issues. Then she usually starts in on how I should be furthering my education. God. It never ends." She exhaled again. "Sorry about the drama. Probably not anything you guys wanna deal with."

"If it affects you, Lainie, it affects us," Hank said.

It was so kind she felt the urge to bawl.

Hank's big arms enclosed her from behind, urging her to lean into him. "Do you want to talk about it? Or forget about it?"

"Forget about it."

"We can help you with that," Hank murmured. "Of course, first you'll have to lose the towel."

"I'm not in the mood for sex."

"Not everything is about sex. I reckon you could use some food."

"We definitely want you to keep up your strength," Kyle said.

"I could eat."

"Good. How about you get dressed and we take you out for breakfast? Then we can talk about how *we'd* like you to spend your vacation."

∞

The Adobe Inn boasted greasy fare that typified diner food. Lainie tried not to eat at places like this too often, so when she did, she went whole-hog.

Still, having breakfast with Kyle and Hank was almost more bizarre than having a threesome with them.

From behind the menu, Kyle said, "What're you guys havin'?"

"Three eggs, bacon, sausage, biscuits, and gravy," Hank answered.

"Sounds good. Lainie?"

"Looks like Hank and I are on the same page, because that's what I'd decided on."

Kyle folded his menu. "Little slip of a thing like you? Where you gonna put all that food?"

"Hey, I'm hungry."

"I like to see a woman with an appetite," Hank said. "I'da been disappointed if you'd chosen dry wheat toast and a cup of herbal tea."

She snorted. "That's what I eat when I'm sick. But I'll confess I don't eat like this every day."

"Me neither." Kyle sipped his coffee and looked at Hank curiously. "I'll bet Celia rolls outta bed at the crack of nothin' and whips up something like this for you when you're home, huh?"

Lainie's hand tightened around her coffee cup. Who was Celia, and why was she cooking Hank breakfast on a regular basis?

"She can't cook worth a shit, Kyle. Nice shot, putting me on the defensive first thing." Hank faced Lainie in the booth. "Now's as good a time as any to exchange family history. I don't have to ask about yours, since it's rodeo legend, but the Celia that Kyle was referring to is my baby sister."

"Baby." Kyle sneered. "She's what? Twenty-one?"

Hank ignored Kyle's interruption. "I have one older brother, Abe. Me 'n' him run the family ranch outside of Muddy Gap. We raised Celia after our folks died ten years back."

Weird to think that in all the times she and Hank, or she and Kyle, had been together, they hadn't talked about family. Lainie placed her hand over Hank's on the table. "I'm sorry. Both your parents died at one time?"

"Yeah. Dad was elk huntin' and Ma went along because they did everything together. Some freaky malfunction happened with their hotel heater and they died of carbon monoxide poisoning. Anyway, Celia was only eleven, so she was stuck growin' up with me and Abe. Which means she's pretty much a tomboy clear through."

"That girl would rather be with her horses than with people," Kyle said.

"Probably why she has an eye for good horseflesh. Celia ain't interested in datin', thank God."

"Only because you and Abe chased off all the guys in the county that dared look at her."

"Lookin' is one thing. Touchin' is another."

The waitress returned to take their order. As Lainie was thinking about all she didn't know about Hank, she realized Kyle was as much a mystery. "What about you, Kyle? You from a Wyoming ranching family?"

Kyle shook his head. "Just me 'n' my mom. My mom worked a lot, so I rode the bus home with Hank or our buddy Eli. I practically lived at the Lawson place." Kyle gave Hank a conspiratorial smile. "Your mom was the greatest. She loved bein' surrounded by rambunctious boys. And you finished chores three times as fast with me 'n' Eli helping."

Lainie had no problem imagining Kyle and Hank as rough-and-tumble teenage boys. "So what'd you do after chores were done?"

"Raised hell," they said in unison, and laughed.

"Raced horses, raced four-wheelers, taunted bulls, fished, worked some more, target shot, the usual stuff ranch kids do for fun."

"I had ranch envy," Kyle admitted. "We lived in a two-bedroom apartment in low-income housing in the crappy section of Rawlins, close to where she cocktail wait-ressed. Whenever I was out at Hank's place or Bran's place I felt like I could breathe."

Another punch of guilt surfaced at hearing Hank and Kyle talk about their growing-up years. These guys had a connection stronger than any bond they'd started to form with her.

"Hey." Kyle leaned across the table and peered into her eyes. "You got an awful serious look all of a sudden. What's wrong?"

"I can't do this."

"Can't do what, sweetheart?" Hank asked.

"Can't come between you two."

"I'm hopin' you come between us often."

Lainie glanced at Kyle after his smart-ass response. "This isn't funny. I'm serious."

"So are we, Lainie. We're big boys. We've talked about it."

"You have?"

Hank nodded. "Actually, that's why we think the sharing option works. Because we'll both give this time with you our best shot. So if you do choose one of us over the other—which we all know might not even happen—it really is because the best man wins."

"Wins? I'm not the prize you think I am."

"Sugar, obviously that ain't true, because Hank and I are both here."

Their reassurances didn't bolster her confidence.

"We know you had fun with us last night," Hank said.

"That's an understatement," she muttered in her coffee.

"We also know you've been pushed into taking a vacation. Since you're not sure about your travel plans, here's what we propose." Kyle looked at Hank and Lainie saw him nod. "We want you to spend those weeks with both of us during Cowboy Christmas."

Her gaze whipped between blue eyes and green. "You're serious."

"Completely. You said you don't get to see much of the areas you're working in. Here's a chance for you to learn the life of a rodeo cowboy. Think how much better it'll be for your career as a med tech to know firsthand the stresses our bodies are subjected to as we're getting from place to place."

"But—"

"When was the last time you went to a rodeo and just had fun?" Kyle demanded. "Watching all the events, not just stuck in the medical aid room?"

Lainie racked her brain but she couldn't come up with a reasonable answer.

"Doesn't it sound like a blast to attend rodeos—big and small—across three different circuits?"

"Trust us, there's nothin' like a small-town rodeo in the summertime. It's why the rodeo lifestyle is addictive. Hearing the roar and the groans of the crowds. Knowing people paid their hard-earned cash to see us entertain them."

The food arrived and they tucked in, eating in silence except for requests to pass the salt and the occasional scrape of forks across plates.

Hank and Kyle made short work of their breakfasts, while Lainie dawdled.

Finally, Hank spoke. "You getting ready to turn us down?"

"No. It's just . . ." She drained her cold coffee and blotted her lips. "Say I agree to do this. Where would we all sleep? Even cheap hotels get expensive. Right now, Lariat pays for my rooms when I'm on the road."

"My brother has a fifth wheel he won in a poker game a few years back. We'd planned on heading to the ranch tonight after this event and hitching it up."

Kyle added, "It's cheap to stay at the rodeo grounds, if not completely free."

She raised her eyebrows. "All three of us living together in a camper?"

"Trust me—it's good-sized, even for me and Abe, and we're both big guys."

"Think of how fun it'd be with you cooking for us all the time," Kyle said.

Silence.

Laughing, Kyle sagged back against the booth seat. "If looks could kill, I'd be dead. Lainie, sugar, I was kiddin'."

"Kyle, you're an asshole," Hank snapped.

But Kyle provided levity about the prickly situation and Lainie appreciated it.

"Darlin', we ain't asking you to come along because we want a maid and a cook. Truthfully, inviting you is not only about the smokin'-hot sex, at least, not on my part. Is it on yours, Kyle?"

"Nope. I'm in complete agreement with Hank on this. We want to get to know you better."

And still she didn't speak.

"Would it be so bad spending time with us? In and out of bed? Getting to know us? Letting us get to know you?"

Lainie picked at her biscuit as all sorts of objections swirled in her head.

The biggest problem is you're dying to do this and you're working hard at playing it cool.

After the waitress refilled their coffee, Kyle said, "Are you worried about people finding out that you're traveling with both of us and we're staying in close quarters?"

"Maybe a little."

"It probably won't convince you, but there's lots of 'don't ask, don't tell' musical horse trailers goin' on across all the circuits."

Lainie knew the truth of that statement after listening to Tanna's tales of life on the blacktop.

"We'll be switching from circuit to circuit, following the money. I know you haven't worked as a med tech on the CRA often on the Upper Mountains and Plains, Badlands, or Montana circuits, which is where we'll be concentrating our efforts."

"What are you really afraid of?" Hank asked softly.

"Maybe she's worried that 'Lainie Capshaw, Daughter of Legendary Bull Riding Great Jason Capshaw, Shacking up on the Road with Two CRA Cowboys!' will be a headline in *Bull Riders*, *American Horseman*, and *Western Woman* magazines?"

Hank scowled at Kyle but Lainie laughed. "Maybe. I don't know. I've never considered doing anything this impulsive."

"Which is why you should do this with *us*, Lainie," Kyle urged. "Take a chance. It'll be an adventure."

"What'll be an adventure?" Tanna asked.

All three surprised gazes flicked to the hot-bodied woman standing at the end of the table.

"Hey, Tanna, fancy meeting you here." A total lie. Lainie had texted her, not knowing whether she'd need an escape plan.

"A girl has to eat."

"Tanna Barker, this is Kyle Gilchrist, a transplant to the CRA from the EBS."

"Nice to meet you, Tanna," Kyle said.

"Likewise. Great ride last night."

"Thanks. I got a good bull. I'm hoping my luck holds tonight."

"Amen. Be nice to take home part of that purse, wouldn't it?"

Hank immediately stood and thrust out his hand. "Hank Lawson, Tanna. We've met a time or two. Would you like to join us?"

"If it's no trouble."

Kyle also stood, gesturing to the inside of the booth. "No trouble at all. Any friend of Lainie's is a friend of ours."

Small talk about the night's previous rodeo dominated the conversation, but eventually they ran out of things to say.

Hank and Kyle exchanged a look. "Hate to be rude and take off, but we've gotta check out of our hotel by noon. Then I'm obligated to attend sponsor events this afternoon."

"I understand. By all means, go," Lainie said.

"You rode with us. You need us to give you a ride?"

Sure, you can ride me, cowboys, but I ain't talking about in your truck.

It felt so good to be bad.

Tanna waved them off. "I'll get her where she needs to go."

"Thanks." Hank snagged the bill and squinted at Lainie, his eyes dark with purpose. "We *will* see you later."

Not a question. "Be careful tonight. Both of you."

"Always, sugar," Kyle drawled. The men sauntered away after nods of their hatted heads.

"Oh, my freakin' God. Greedy, much?" Tanna demanded.

"What?"

"I might actually hate you."

Lainie frowned. "Why?"

"Can I be blunt?"

"When have you ever not been blunt?" Lainie asked.

Tanna folded her arms on the table and leaned in. "You're fucking not one hot man, but two. Individually, I was a little jealous. But now? After seeing the way those buff guys gazed upon you with utter adoration? And I know you're doin' both of them at the same time? I'm green with envy."

"Yeah? Well, color *me* confused, Tanna. I don't know what the hell I'm doing."

"What you're doin', right this freakin' second, is telling me if it's all that, bein' between those cowboy beefcakes?"

Lainie tried not to grin like a lunatic, but it was pointless. "Absolutely. And this oughta stick in your craw: They've asked me to go on the road with them during Cowboy Christmas."

"You're considering it?"

"No, I'm doing it."

Tanna's gaze turned shrewd. "Weren't you keeping quiet about banging Hank because it might damage your professional reputation? Ditto for Kyle on the other circuit? Now you're jumping aboard the traveling sin wagon, letting your freak flag fly for all to see?"

"Yes, but it's different now, because I won't be on any of the circuits after my vacation. This has to stay between us, but Doc is switching me to a full-time office position at Lariat. I'll have a normal Monday-through-Friday, nine-to-five job, and it's about damn time."

"So no more working on the CRA or EBS circuit?"

"Nope. No more traveling." At Tanna's dour look, Lainie said, "Hey, we'll still see each other."

"When?" Tanna demanded. "I live in Texas. I get to Colorado Springs once a year as I pass through for the Denver Stock Show. Over the next couple months we'll lose touch. So maybe I just oughta say 'good-bye and have a nice life' to you right now."

Stung, Lainie reared back. "Fine, if you really feel that way—"

"Dammit, Lainie, I'm sorry." Tanna snatched her hands and squeezed. "I'm happy for you about the job, because you deserve it. But I'm a selfish bitch and I'm sad for me. You're my best pal. We've had some great times and I'll miss you something fierce."

"I know. Me too." Lainie's thoughts tumbled a mile a minute. "Give it to me straight, Tanna. Will anyone notice I'm shacked up with both Hank and Kyle?"

"Yes. And no."

"That's helpful," Lainie grumbled.

"Yes, some people will notice. The 'Jesus cowboys' will advise you of the error of your adulterous ways. The newly married women will give you the wink-wink-nudge-nudge, and act smug, like they're not on the road to keep a close eye on their hubbies. The women with kids won't notice you unless you're on fire.

"The youngsters, rookies, whatever, will ask you the most inappropriate questions and get indignant when you don't answer. A few older women will high-five you for getting it on with two hotties. The buckle bunnies will offer to do you in front of your men—and then demand you watch while your men do them. So it'll run the gamut from 'you slut!' to 'you go, girl!' to 'hey, baby, how about let's you and me have a private party?'"

Lainie was positively goggle-eyed. "That much speculation?"

"No. Jesus. Lighten up. I was kiddin'. No one will notice this time of the year."

"Would you do it if you were me?"

"Lainie, we've had this conversation and my answer hasn't changed. Yes. Hell, yes." Tanna smirked. "And, sugar, if you don't do it? Well, I'm sitting in fourth right now in my circuit, so I can afford to take the next three weeks off. If you chicken out, I may offer myself up to them in your place."

"Smarty. After last night, I think they're awful determined to keep me." Lainie smirked back.

"I really hate you."

"Any chance we'll cross paths on one of these circuits?"

Tanna's long, glossy braid fell over her shoulder as she shook her head. "I'll be in Texas. Lots of rodeos within two hundred miles. I need a dose of my mama's cookin'. I need to be home for a while to regroup."

Lainie wondered what that'd be like, the overwhelming need to reconnect with roots. Her mother and stepfather's house in California wasn't homey, but more of a showplace. Grandma Elsa's cozy house had seemed like home, but it was gone now too.

"Come on. I'll drop you at your hotel."

∞

Lainie packed her suitcase and loaded up. She'd called Doc and double-checked that he'd be at the rodeo grounds before she headed there. She drove past the horse trailers and campers, paying particular attention to the fifth wheels. Hank's pickup was a Cummins 350-horsepower diesel quad cab with an extended bed, so maybe his camper wasn't the claustrophobia-inducing box she feared.

She walked through the tamped-down weeds, dust kicking up with every bootstep. Kids and dogs ran everywhere. Tack of all shapes and sizes hung on horse trailers. Men and women stood in groups shooting the breeze. Lawn chairs were scattered between campers in semicircles. It resembled a minitown. Why hadn't she noticed that before?

Because you're not usually among people in their element; you're stuck inside, missing out on real life.

Activity was minimal inside the arena this time of day. The livestock entrance gate was open at the back of the building. She ducked in, skirting the loading ramps. The familiar odors of manure, dirt, and hot air hit her, but didn't offer the comfort they usually did.

The concession stands were empty. Cleaning crews mopped the cement floors and cleaned the bathrooms, nattering back and forth in Spanish. For them this was just another day getting ready for the crowds. For Lainie it felt like a new beginning.

She rapped twice on the door of the medical room. Doc motioned her in as he finished a conversation on the phone.

"No, that's not what we agreed to. Fine. Send it to corporate. Mark it 'Attention Jackie.' She'll straighten it out." He hung up and sighed. "Remember the good ol' days, when running a sports medicine team meant I could actually practice medicine?"

"Umm, no. During my tenure the motto's been: 'We're building a family brand as strong as cowboys who depend on us.' "

"Smart aleck." But he said it with a soft smile. "Did you ask for this meeting because you intend on chewing my butt?"

"Maybe."

His gaze pierced her. "You talked to your mother."

Not a question. "Yes. I won't bore you with the details, except to say I won't be flying to Cali for my vacation."

Lainie smiled tightly. "However, you are right. I need time off. I'll take it and come back in three weeks ready to take on whatever you throw my way."

"Okay," he said slowly, drawing it out to about four syllables. "What's the catch?"

"No catch. I just want to know who's on staff tonight."

"Marty. Shorty. Me. You. Why?"

"If you've got it covered, I'd like to leave right now."

"You're really on board with this vacation, Lainie?"

She shrugged. "I understand why you did it. I don't agree with Sharlene's railroading you into it. However, I wouldn't have done it on my own. So I'll admit I'm looking forward to time off."

"Lie down. I need to check you for a head injury."

"Funny, Doc. I'm fine."

He measured her with his gaze. "You know, you do look better than I've seen you in months. I won't ask what brought it on. I'm just happy that something did."

Thank God Doc hadn't demanded specifics.

"Have a great vacation, and I won't be calling you unless it's an absolute emergency." His phone rang again and she sneaked out.

As she debated on calling Hank or Kyle or texting them, she heard, "Lainie?"

She wheeled around. Lo and behold, Hank was there. "Hey, I was looking for you. I didn't think you'd be here," she said.

"Sponsors wanted to meet. I just go where they tell me." He jerked his chin toward the medical room. "Everything all right?"

"Everything is fine. I had to tell Doc I wouldn't be around for tonight's performance."

Hank's face fell. "What? Lainie, I thought we'd—"

She briefly put her finger to her lips and towed him down the secluded hallway. "I'm not backing out. I need to take care of a few things before I'm gone that long. I thought if I had a head start, I'd be ready to be picked up at my place in Colorado Springs tonight."

"That'll work. We're driving straight through to Muddy Gap. I have a few things to help Abe with on the ranch before I'm gone for that long too."

"See? This will save us time."

Hank crowded her against the wall. "I want to kiss you. Right now. Makes me a selfish bastard, because I don't care if Doc sees or if the cleaning crew sees. I don't give a flying fuck if the whole blasted arena is watching, Lainie. This is about you and me. About what we bring to each other when we're alone."

His mouth descended and she was lost.

Velvety soft lips brushing hers. Crushing hers. His tongue stroked and teased. Coaxing. Devouring. He repositioned his head, taking the kiss down to the depths of her soul.

Ignoring the undertone of possession, Lainie wallowed in the intensity of his kiss. Of his power. Confidence. Lust.

Yet Hank didn't touch her. He kept one forearm braced above her head. His palm lay flat by her shoulder. But she felt as if they were both naked as he drew her into a cozy world where nothing existed but him. And her.

And Kyle, her conscience prodded.

Damn.

When she broke the kiss and looked in Hank's eyes—that bottomless blue, deep and dark enough to fall into—she wondered if she could handle this competitive side of him. Or Kyle.

Was Hank pulling out all the stops because he wanted her more than any other woman? Or did he just want to be the victor over Kyle?

Did Kyle feel the same way? Was she truly a prize in their eyes? Or just a game to be won?

He traced the line of her jawbone. "So serious."

"That was a serious kiss."

"A reminder I'm not taking anything that happens between us now, or what happened between us in the past, for granted. Or as a given because you were with me first."

"Are we supposed to tell Kyle everything that happens between us?"

"It was just a kiss, darlin'."

No, it wasn't, and he damn well knew it. She fiddled with the collar of his snap-front shirt. "So what happens now?"

"Wanna sneak behind the concession stand and have a quickie?"

Yes! "No." She lightly cuffed him on the chin. "Maybe another time."

"I'll hold you to that. While you're getting your stuff ready for three weeks on the road, toss in any sex toys you might wanna have fun with." He grinned. "Soon as the rodeo is over tonight we'll be on the road. I'll call you when we're close." Hank gifted her with another soft kiss. Then another. "Drive safe, Lainie."

He'd reached the end of the corridor when she called out, "Promise me you'll stay out of the paths of the bulls tonight? Both of you."

"We'll try, but no guarantees."

Chapter Seven

As Kyle adjusted his chin strap, he heard the announcer droning, but it was just background noise. Sweat trickled down his spine. His shirt stuck to his back like a second skin. Heat from the helmet dampened his hair. His face burned. His heart thundered. The bull jumped beneath him in the chute, ready to play the man-versus-beast game. Eager to hurl Kyle on his ass and stomp him into nothing but blood and bones.

"Bring it, fucker," he snarled at the slobbering animal before he slipped in his mouthpiece. He set his feet. He tested his hand wrap one last time and vigorously nodded at the gatekeeper as his free hand flew up.

Immediately out of the chute, shock vibrated up his tailbone and rattled his spine. The bull's rear legs kicked up and twisted left at the last second. Kyle shifted slightly to keep his balance. He spurred and the bull spun right, jumping sideways, damn near jerking Kyle's arm out of the socket. He held on, readjusting his position as every bone and joint in his body screamed for him to get the fuck off.

The roar of the crowd barely permeated his concentration as the words *hold on* kept repeating in his head. Time had no meaning when he rode. None. He was in a whole 'nother dimension.

Failing to dislodge him, the bull switched directions and started to spin. Faster and faster. Kyle bore down on his mouthpiece, keeping his back straight and his feet moving.

The buzzer sounded and Kyle snapped out of his riding stupor. His free hand automatically tugged on the rope to release his riding hand. As soon as the wrap gave, the bull jumped, bouncing Kyle high into the air like a piece of popcorn.

The spectators gasped. While he was airborne Kyle knew he'd land hard. He twisted and hit on his left side, avoiding his knee, taking the brunt of the impact on his hip, rib cage, and shoulder.

Fuck, that hurt.

Dust kicked up and he heard, "Hey-hey-hey-hey-hey-hey!" the bullfighter's attention grabber. Shoes entered his vision as the bullfighter directed the bull's attention away from stomping Kyle's stunned ass. He scrambled to his feet and raced to the fence.

Only then did he notice the crowd was still whistling and clapping. Kyle ripped off his protective helmet, shoved his mouthpiece in his vest pocket, and squinted at the scoreboard.

No score yet. The bull loped through the livestock arena gate. Kyle hopped down from the fence and raced across the dirt to snag his flank strap.

Hank met him with an enormous grin. "Nice ride. Figure that'll put you in the money. You're buying the first tank of gas."

Kyle grinned and draped his rope over his shoulder. "Fair enough. Thanks for savin' my ass."

"All in a day's work, buddy." Hank clapped him on the back.

The announcer said, "How about if y'all put your hands together for a score of . . . eighty-eight! Ladies and gentlemen, we have a new leader."

More whoops and hollers.

Waving to the crowd, Kyle exited into the contestants' area. Two more riders remained. Both guys had covered their bulls the night before. If either of them rode, he could be knocked out of first place. He'd still finish in the money, but the extra points for first would let him start that slow climb in the CRA standings.

He took congrats from the other guys milling about. The difference between the CRA and the EBS was that as soon as the contestants in the CRA knew they weren't in the money, they loaded up and lit out. In the EBS, all the riders stuck around until the end of the event. After the mandatory postevent autograph session, some guys—usually the Jesus cowboys, guys who liked a little preachin' about hellfire and damnation with their bull riding—headed for their hotel for a prayer group or something wholesome. Single riders scoped out the buckle bunny offerings. Married guys traveling with the missus were whisked away from temptation.

Winners of the timed events, and the bareback and saddle bronc winners, bullshitted with their impatient traveling partners. Life on the road was expensive. Sometimes two or three guys shared the expenses and the driving time, especially those hauling horses for the timed events.

Kyle looked for Lainie's friend Tanna. She must've lost out on a top-three finish, since she wasn't cooling her boot heels with the other barrel racers waiting to pick up a check. He brought his attention back to the arena as the gate opened.

The bull shot out and made a hard right, leaped, and turned right again, sending the rider sailing. But ejecting the guy wasn't enough; the bull snorted and headed straight for him as he sprawled in the dirt. No matter how many times he'd seen it happen, Kyle still held his breath.

Before the beast reached the rider, Hank jumped between them. The bull's horn hooked Hank's vest and the massive head tossed Hank aside like a pesky crow. The bull focused his fury, nostrils dripping snot as its head came down and aimed horns at Hank.

Hank rolled out of the way, but not before the bull's hoof clipped him on the thigh. The other bullfighter ran alongside the bull, attempting to lead it away from Hank. By then the pickup man galloped alongside the bull and roped him, cutting a sharp right with his horse. They dragged the ornery animal through the livestock gate.

"Folks. Let's give a big round of applause to our fearless bullfighters tonight, Hank Lawson, Kipper Pitch, and Bebo Smith."

Lackluster clapping. Fans would stand all day for a great ride, but the bullfighters saving life and limb never brought the same thunderous response.

Did that bother Hank? They'd never talked about it. Kyle watched Hank limp off to the side and a member of the sports medicine team yakked at him through the fence slats. Hank shook his head and waved off his concern. Would Hank have waved Lainie off so quickly? Or would he play it up, hoping she'd give him a little extra TLC?

Maybe you shouldn't be so fast to dismiss exaggerating an injury to garner Lainie's undivided attention.

Never. He'd never do that, and neither would Hank. All might be fair in love and war, but playing on a woman's natural sympathies was cheating and cowardly.

The last rider burst out of the chute. The bull wasn't anything special. It kicked and jumped. Spun a little. The rider stayed on the full eight seconds, but Kyle knew it hadn't been an eighty-nine-point ride, which was what the guy needed to overtake the leaderboard. The score came back seventy-seven. Kyle breathed a sigh of relief. He'd won his first CRA event.

Hot damn. Serious celebrating would wait. He glanced at the arena scoreboard clock. Nine thirty. It'd be eleven by the time they finished here and left Lamar for the three-hour trip to Colorado Springs to pick up Lainie. Then they'd drive straight through to Muddy Gap.

They could take it easy and stay the night in Colorado Springs, but Kyle understood Hank's push. The sooner Lainie got used to the hours spent traveling from event to event, the better. Plus, he suspected the man missed home.

Or Hank wanted to show off his ranch to Lainie. And for that, Kyle didn't blame him a bit. The Lawson Ranch was a breathtaking piece of heaven on earth. But it'd give Hank another advantage. After seeing the gorgeous Lawson Ranch, no way would Kyle drag Lainie to where he hung his hat when he wasn't on the road—a shitty trailer he rented dirt cheap.

"Gilchrist? They're waiting for you in the winners' tent."

Kyle went to collect his buckle and his check.

∞

An hour later Kyle tracked Hank to a bench outside the main arena entrance. Hank sat next to a woman—no more than eighteen in Kyle's estimation—who jabbered like a parrot on acid. Teased hair, pouty red lips, skintight clothes—she looked like every other bunny trolling for a new notch on her rhinestone belt.

Hank's blank face became animated when he caught sight of Kyle. He pushed off the bench, wincing as he bumped his thigh into the woman's knee. "Hey, partner, you ready to hit the road right now?"

"Yep."

The woman leaped to her booted feet, crowding Kyle's personal space with her toothpaste-commercial smile, stinky-ass perfume, and—holy shit—stripper tits. "Hi. I'm Gia. I was just telling Frank here that I love the rodeo lifestyle. It's so exciting!"

Kyle bit back a grin. *Frank?* Yeah, she was the type of woman in for the long haul . . . *not.* No wonder Hank wore the spooked-rabbit look. "I got all my stuff loaded, *Frank*, so I'm set."

Hank scowled.

"Gosh, are you a bullfighter too?" the woman said in a breathy, baby voice.

"Nah. I'm on the cleanup crew."

Her nose wrinkled. "Oh." She whirled back around to Hank. "Like I said, I don't have a thing going on, and I'd love to keep you company on the road. I'm very"—her red-tipped fingers inched up Hank's shirt—"inventive with ways to make the time fly by."

Hank twisted sideways to escape the wandering claws. "Ah, I'm sure you are. But I'll pass. Have a good evening." He ran out. The man with the injured thigh literally raced outside.

Entertained by Hank's discomfort, Kyle followed Hank to the truck. He'd barely shut the door and Hank was burning rubber out of the parking lot.

"Jesus Christ. Save me from women like that."

"Now, *Frank*, don't you think you're bein' a little hard on her?"

"Fuck off."

Kyle laughed.

"And thanks for nothin'. What was the bullshit 'I'm on the cleanup crew' comment?"

"You see how fast she dismissed me? Works every time."

Hank sent him a sidelong look. "She wasn't your type?"

"Meaning . . . easy?"

"If it weren't for Lainie, would you've boasted about bein' a bull rider and banged her brains out?"

The judgment should've bugged him, but Hank was dead-on. Kyle used to take pride in his horndog reputation. "Yeah, I would've done her. She don't give a shit who you are beyond that you're wearing Wranglers, a hat, and boots. She'd brag to her friends how she bagged a bull rider. I wouldn't remember her name even while I was fucking her. Sorta sad. But that's the way I was. I ain't that guy so much anymore."

The blinker clicked as Hank steered onto the ramp to Highway 50, heading west out of Lamar. It wasn't until he'd set the cruise that he spoke again. "Why the change?"

He deflected. "Everything in my life went to shit after my injury. After I healed enough to get around, Ma was pissed that I turned down her boyfriend's offer to sell used cars in Cheyenne."

"Selling used cars don't interest you at all?"

"No. Hell, no." Kyle squirmed in his seat. "Bein' laid up, I had nothin' to do but think. I realized riding bulls is what I know. What I do best. But it ain't something I can do for the long haul. So I figure if I save money like a miser and focus on my riding, not chasing every hot piece of ass that crosses my path, maybe I'll earn enough to buy myself a chunk of dirt someplace."

"What was this event purse?"

"Twenty-two hundred."

"Not bad for sixteen seconds' work," Hank said, grinning at their old joke.

"I ain't complaining. But I've been on the famine end of riding. Bein' bucked off a dozen times in a row sucks."

A semi roared past, the amber and red lights bright against the dark road and dark sky, and Kyle blinked, surprised to feel sleepy.

"If you wanna crash, go ahead. I'm wired."

"Thanks." Kyle closed his eyes.

Seemed he'd just fallen asleep when the truck lurched and jolted him awake. An orange sodium glow flooded the window. "Where are we?"

"A truck stop outside Colorado Springs. I thought we'd fill up and call Lainie before we burst in on her."

Kyle stretched. "Man. I was out that long?"

"Yeah. And you talk in your sleep too. 'Oh, no, please don't spank me, master, I'll be good,'" Hank mimicked in a falsetto.

"Fuck off."

"Your turn to pay at the pump." Hank bailed out of the truck.

While Kyle filled the big diesel gas tank, he watched Hank talking on the phone, trying to cover a yawn. The man was wiped out. No way could he drive to Muddy Gap.

Kyle loaded up on caffeine-laced soda and returned to the truck after paying. "Was Lainie up?"

"Says she was sleeping but I don't buy it. We're not too far from her place." Hank yawned again. "Damn. I'm gonna need to crash. You okay to drive after we pick her up?"

"No problem. You sure you wanna keep goin'?"

"Yeah." Hank muttered directions to himself, squinting at the street signs.

Lainie lived in an apartment complex, which surprised Kyle. But the truth was, he didn't know much about Lainie beyond the physical, and that was something he aimed to change.

She waited under the security light of her building. A duffel bag and a backpack were at her feet, an enormous pillow tucked under her arm. She'd secured her riotous curls in a ponytail and jammed her hands in the front pockets of her jeans. She looked very young, although he and Lainie were the same age. Were they taking advantage of her? Would any of them walk away from this situation unscathed?

Probably not.

Both he and Hank got out to help her load up. Kyle asked, "Either of these bags need to go in the cab? Or can they both go in the truck bed?"

"The backpack can go in the cab if there's room."

"That pillow is looking mighty tempting," Hank said.

"Here. Have it. I'm wide-awake now. Am I driving?"

"Kyle's driving. I'm beat."

Lainie's eyes narrowed, then scanned him head to toe. "What happened tonight?"

Crickets chirped in the sudden silence.

"Hank?"

"Ah, darlin', it wasn't nothin'."

"Don't make me get out my rubber gloves and check you myself first thing. Tell me."

"Just a little misunderstanding between me and the bull. I went left; he was supposed to go right, but he didn't. Caught me on the quad. I'm sore. But mostly I'm tired. No worries, okay?"

"Fine. I'll let it go for now, but I want to take a look at it in the morning."

Hank muttered, grabbed the pillow, and limped off to climb into the back cab of the truck.

While Kyle had the chance, he pecked Lainie on the mouth. "Nice to see you out here waiting for us."

"Were you afraid I'd chicken out?"

"Nothin' is a sure thing."

Lainie returned his smooch. "Lucky for you, I am." She situated herself in the passenger side. "Need me to navigate?"

"Nope. I reckon this truck can almost drive itself to Muddy Gap. We'll head north on I-25 to Cheyenne and then west on I-80 to Rawlins. You ever been in that area?"

"Doc keeps me to the Southwest and Midwest areas for the CRA, which is why I always run into Hank."

"Lucky Hank," he muttered. Kyle wouldn't admit it to them, but it bugged him that Lainie and Hank had known each other longer.

"No sniping," she warned.

Might be a long couple of weeks.

Settled in, with the truck on cruise, he asked, "So even when you live in Colorado Springs you've never worked the 'Daddy of 'Em All' in Cheyenne?"

Lainie's body went stiff. She shook her head and aimed her gaze out the window.

Way to stick your boot in your mouth.

Kyle felt like a total fucking heel. Of course Lainie hadn't worked Cheyenne Frontier Days. Frontier Park was where her father had been killed. He grabbed her hand from the console. "Sugar, I'm sorry. Sometimes I don't think before I open my big trap."

"Actually, it's probably stupid I've never been there. My mother suggested I steer clear of the place, since she claims I already have enough issues with the hero worship of my dead father. But the morbidity keeps me away, not her."

"Have you talked to her since this morning?"

"No. And I feel guilty, but not guilty enough to call her, know what I mean?"

"Yeah. My mom gets on my nerves too. We butted heads big-time when I stayed with her after my surgery."

"Sharlene and I get along for a while and then *kaboom*! We don't talk for months. My grandma Elsa reminded me I might not like what my mother does, but at the end of the day, she's still my only mother." She sighed. "I miss Grandma putting things in perspective for me."

"When did she pass on?"

"A little over two years ago."

"I'm sorry. You're lucky. I never knew my grandparents." Heck. Kyle never knew his father. That was one thing his mother never shared—the name of the sperm donor who impregnated her. "What was your grandma like?"

"Elsa was an amazing woman who lived a hard life. Her parents married her off at eighteen to a family friend who was fifteen years older than her, right after he was discharged from the military. They had nothing in common and she didn't get pregnant until she was thirty-eight. My dad was her miracle baby. Arthur, my grandfather, died when my dad was six, so Grandma raised her son on her own. She cleaned houses, took in sewing and ironing. She grew most of their food and hunted and fished for their meat."

"She does sound amazing."

"My dad's death nearly killed her," Lainie said softly. "And then my mom moved me away. When I was nine I ran away and my mom finally agreed to let me spend summers with her. After I graduated from high school, I packed up and moved to Oklahoma. Gram needed a caretaker and I was all she had. Times with her were the best of my life. She was . . . real—know what I mean?"

Kyle squeezed her hand. "I like seeing this sweet, sentimental side of you, Lainie. I'm just sorry I didn't take the time to notice it before."

The conversation died. Had Lainie taken that the wrong way?

"Kyle, can I be honest?"

"Sure."

"I liked that you saw me as sexy, not sweet. I really liked that you were so hot to have me you couldn't wait." He felt her curious stare. "Do you remember that first time?"

"Remember? Hell, how could I forget?" After two months of flirting, Lainie agreed to meet him for a late-night breakfast.

She'd sauntered in wearing a pair of short shorts and a tank top. Kyle had taken one look at her copper eyes and freckled skin and lost his cool. Without a word, he'd dragged her into the women's bathroom and locked the door. He'd been absolutely fucking crazed to feel her soft curves, heated skin, and wet pussy clinging to him as he fucked her. He took her against the wall.

Then Kyle rushed her to his motel room and nailed her in the shower; he bent her over the vanity and they fucked in front of the mirror. There hadn't been a whole lot of talking. To some extent all their sexual encounters played out that way—urgent.

And hot. Holy freakin' hell, did the woman turn him inside out and upside down with pure animal lust.

"Can I tell you something that sounds ironic?"

He nodded, hating that his stomach tumbled.

"That night I'd planned to tell you I was already seeing someone. But then you looked at me like that . . ."

"Like what?" he asked hoarsely.

"Like I embodied your every secret sexual fantasy." A giggle escaped her. "It was thrilling stuff, Kyle. No way could I resist you."

"Ditto, sugar."

Her nervous energy amused him. Lainie messed with her cell phone. Stared out the window. Checked on Hank. They didn't speak again until they'd passed through the Denver metro area.

"Was your grandma proud you chose sports medicine?"

"I didn't go to work for Lariat until after she died. She was just glad I took advantage of getting a higher education. I'd already earned my EMT certificate and certified nursing assistant diploma my senior year in high school. I graduated with an LPN degree after I moved to Oklahoma. At some point, massage therapy interested me, so I went to school for that."

Kyle smirked at her. "The masseuse thing explains those magic hands."

She batted him on the biceps. "I probably don't have the medical degrees needed to work for Lariat, but Doc offered me the part-time position and I jumped at it—much to my mother's eternal dismay."

"Working part-time is enough to pay your bills?"

Lainie sighed. "No. I work third shift as an EMT when I'm not on the road with Lariat. I'm hoping once I get the—" She stopped. "Sorry. I'm boring you, huh?"

"Never. I could listen to you talk all night."

"I guarantee it's better than listening to me sing," she said glibly.

The discussion changed to general topics. Music. Movies. TV shows. When they hit Fort Collins, he exited off the interstate and cut through town. The residential sections disappeared and they zipped through rural countryside again.

"Are we filling up with gas way out here?"

"Slight change in plans. We're taking the scenic route on Highway 287 instead of goin' through Cheyenne.

We'll hook up with I-80 in Laramie and head to Rawlins."

Lainie went motionless. "You didn't have to do that, Kyle. Avoid a whole city because of my paranoia."

"It's no big deal. It *is* a shortcut, okay? Driving through Cheyenne, right past Frontier Park, ain't something you need to deal with right now."

She lifted her cool fingers to his face to trace the outline of his mustache and goatee. "Thank you. I'm really glad to be seeing this sweet and sentimental side of you too."

Kyle angled his head and kissed her palm. "Anytime."

Not long after that, Lainie yawned and slumped against the door. Neither of his snoring passengers woke when he topped off the tank in Laramie.

Five miles from the turnoff to the Lawson ranch, Hank stirred.

He sat up and draped his forearms over the middle of the front seat. "Man. Talk about sawing logs." He jerked his chin toward Lainie. "How long's she been out?"

"Since outside of Fort Collins."

"How're you holding up?"

Kyle yawned. "Don't mind telling ya, I'm hitting a bed for a few hours before we load the camper and all that shit."

Lainie stretched. Yawned. "Where are we?"

"We're just about home, darlin'."

Home. Kyle snorted. Hank's home.

It's not like you can offer that to Lainie. You don't have anything to offer her. Hank does.

Fuck. That thought jarred him wide-awake.

She smoothed her hair and cracked her neck side to side. "Well, boys, as long as we have a few minutes, let's get our stories straight."

"What stories?" Hank asked.

"Why I'm traveling with both of you. I doubt Hank wants his family to know he's sharing me with you, Kyle. So the question is, when I'm asked, which one of you guys am I 'officially' with?"

Kyle and Hank answered, "Me," simultaneously.

Chapter Eight

Hank was groggy. But not that goddamn groggy. No fucking way was Kyle getting the upper hand on Hank's home turf.

"We're staying at my fucking house, driving my goddamn truck, so it makes sense that Abe and Celia believe Lainie is with me."

"Which is exactly why it makes more sense for them to think Lainie is with me," Kyle said calmly.

Which just pissed Hank off more. "That don't make a lick of sense, Kyle."

"Guys. Please."

"Maybe we oughta have Lainie choose." Kyle sent Hank a smug look.

That'd sounded confident. Had something happened between them while he'd conked out? Hank looked at Lainie. "Well?"

She shook her head. "I won't choose. Try again."

"You said it yourself, Hank. I have a reputation—a *former* reputation, I might add—as a player, so Abe and

Celia would think nothin' of me shacking up on the road with a sexpot like Lainie." Kyle waggled his eyebrows at her.

"Should I be offended by that statement, Kyle?"

"Sugar, you oughta be flattered. Unlike some people, I've never brought a woman home to meet the family."

Hank bit back a sarcastic remark at Kyle's cheap shot. "Your reputation precedes you, Kyle, but that's exactly why *my* family would be skeptical. They ain't gonna believe I'll travel with you and *your* woman of the month, driving *my* truck, living in *my* camper for three weeks. But they'd have no problem believing you'd tag along with me and *my* woman."

After fifteen seconds, Kyle muttered, "Shit. You're right."

Hank fought the urge to gloat. And lost.

Lainie didn't say anything, although he sensed her questions as her gaze winged between him and Kyle.

The sun was starting to peep over the horizon when the turnoff to the ranch came into view. Kyle cranked a hard left on the gravel road leading to the house.

"So that's how we're playing it?" Kyle asked testily. "Lainie's with you?"

"Yep. Lainie? You all right with that?"

"I guess." She studied Kyle quizzically, rather than meeting Hank's gaze.

Which bugged the crap out of him—not that he'd say anything.

The road snaked three-quarters of a mile around trees and up a hill until the house, barns, and outbuildings appeared. The house wasn't fancy, just a one-story ranch that'd been added onto over the years. Abe's truck was parked in his usual spot. Celia's pickup was absent. Where the devil could that girl be at five thirty in the morning? Dollars to doughnuts she wasn't up doing chores.

The lights were on in the kitchen. Abe started chores every morning at six, just like clockwork.

Kyle parked beside Abe's rig and shut off the engine. He turned around, resentment in his eyes. "I'm agreeing to this on one condition."

"What's that?"

"If Lainie's in your bed alone with you for one night, turnabout is fair play."

The thought of Kyle and Lainie alone together made him gnash his teeth, but it also strengthened Hank's determination that his time alone with Lainie tonight would be memorable. Maybe even unforgettable. He said, "Fine."

By the time they'd unloaded the luggage, Abe leaned on the front rail with a mug of coffee, watching them.

"Hey, bro," Hank greeted. "Is there coffee left or did you drink it all?"

"Drank it. But I started a fresh pot when I heard you drive up," Abe said. "Got quite the merry little band with you, Hank."

Hank tugged Lainie beside him. "Abe, this is Lainie Capshaw. Lainie, this is my brother, Abe."

Abe switched his coffee mug to his left hand and thrust out his right. "Good to meetcha, Lainie."

"Likewise, Abe. Thanks for having me as an extra houseguest."

He smiled. "No trouble at all. How long are y'all stayin'?"

"Just tonight. We're heading to Gillette early tomorrow."

Kyle dropped his bag and dust puffed out from where it hit the ground. "Hey, Abe."

"Gilly."

Hank smirked at Abe's use of Kyle's old nickname.

"Well? Don't keep me in suspense. How'd you do in your CRA debut?"

"First place."

"Outstanding. Was the purse worth more or the points?"

"Definitely the points. Although the money wasn't bad. Ain't gonna make me rich, but luckily I've hooked a rich travel partner to share expenses with for the next couple weeks." Kyle nudged Hank when he snorted.

"You guys taking the camper?" Abe said to Hank.

"You're not using it for huntin', are you?"

"Have at it. I'll get Bran and a couple of guys to help us load it."

"I'll call him," Hank offered. Part of the reason he wanted to see his friends was to show Lainie off.

She's not really yours.

But she will be.

"Where am I crashing?" Kyle asked Abe.

"Probably be quietest down in the basement. Back bedroom."

"Cool. I'll be bright-eyed and bushy-tailed after a little shut-eye." Kyle shouldered his duffel and lumbered into the house, the screen door slamming behind him.

No doubt Kyle was sore about the Lainie situation.

Hank focused on Abe. "Where is Miz Celia?"

"Who the hell knows? She's been coming home at the butt crack of dawn for the last two weekends. Then she sleeps all damn day. She won't tell me nothin' about where she's been or what she's been doin'. Maybe you can coax something out of her. I sure can't." Abe drained his coffee and grimaced. "Sorry for rambling, Lainie, when it appears you're ready to fall asleep on your feet."

"It's okay. If there's anything I can do while you guys are checking cattle or whatever, I'd be—"

Hank smothered her babbling with a decisive kiss. When he eased back, she blinked up at him. "What was that for?"

"For thinking you're gonna be a maid, housecleaner, and cook. What part of 'guest' is confusing to you?"

"The offer to help out is deeply ingrained in me. A

little kiss ain't gonna stop it, sorry to say." She yawned. "As much as I'd love to chew the fat, if you don't need me I will hit the hay."

"I'll be waiting in the machine shed whenever you two get done." Luckily Lainie missed Abe's lewd wink.

Lainie didn't gawk at the surroundings of his home. He steered her half-stumbling form down the hallway. Damn woman. He'd bet she hadn't slept a wink waiting for them to pick her up. He opened the door to his room, praying he hadn't left it a pigsty.

She sighed dreamily. "That's the biggest bed I've ever seen. Is it real? Or am I asleep, dreaming about an enormous marshmallow?"

"It's real." Hank managed to catch her before she face-planted on the carpet. "Whoa, there. Lemme help you." He guided her to the edge of the mattress. "Let's get your boots off."

"I can do it." She frowned. "Probably." Another frown. "Maybe."

While she debated, Hank lifted her foot and yanked off her right boot. Then her left. She fell back onto his puffy goose-down comforter with another blissful sigh. "Night, sexy bullfighter."

He laughed. "You need my help getting undressed?"

"Why can't I just sleep like this?"

"Because I've fantasized about getting you nekkid between my sheets since the first time we met and I ain't about to let the opportunity pass me by." He stroked her hair. "It's not like I haven't seen you in the buff."

"True. But I'm too tired to move."

"I know, baby. Lift your arms." Hank removed her shirt. Sweet Jesus. She wore the sheerest black bra he'd ever seen outside a lingerie catalog. The way the mounded flesh popped over the fabric hardened his cock. The tease of her peaked nipple poked into the material and begged for his hungry mouth. Somehow he tore his gaze away and tugged off her jeans.

Fuck. It figured she wore matching sheer black panties that hugged her sweet, feminine cleft. He peeled back the covers and gave her a gentle nudge until she scooted in.

When her skin slid over the cool cotton sheets, she moaned. Loudly.

He half hoped Abe heard that.

No, hopefully Kyle heard that.

Hank smoothed the springy curls from her face, reluctant to leave her. She looked so small and vulnerable . . . and perfectly at home in his big bed.

"You're staring at me, Hank."

"Does that bother you?"

"Depends on if you're planning on doing more than looking."

"Not right now. I ain't gonna take advantage of when you can't be a full participant in what I've got planned."

"But tonight, when it's just us, will you take advantage of me?"

He squinted at her, unable to tell if her words were exhausted babble. "Is that what you want?"

No answer.

"Lainie?"

"I want you to do all the things you've fantasized about doing to me when I'm in your bed."

Had to be the tiredness talking. "No reason to hash this out now. We'll talk later."

"No." Her eyes flew open. "Maybe it is lack of sleep giving me the courage to bring it up."

"Bring what up?"

"You've held back with me, Hank. From the start six months ago, when we first starting sneaking around."

Hank wasn't sure if his tongue or his guts were tied in a bigger knot.

"Show me that side of yourself you've hidden from me."

He swallowed hard. "And if it scares you?"

"It won't. I'm tougher than you give me credit for. If I'm all in for everything a threesome entails, then you should be all in with me."

"Hmm." Hank let the back of his knuckles float up and down her jawline. "I'm not sure you're completely coherent."

"Try me."

"If I spend the rest of the day getting primed to show you my kinky side, and I crawl into bed with a bottle of lube and a rope, will you freak out?"

"That won't happen—"

"Good. Because, darlin', you asked for it." He smooched her forehead. "Sleep. If you think you're exhausted now, it ain't nothin' compared to how you'll be when I get through with you tonight."

"Bring it, cowboy." Lainie rolled over, leaving him staring at her back.

∞

Hank filled an insulated mug with coffee before he wandered outside. The hazy sky weakened the light, a signal that they were in for a barn burner of a day. He tracked Abe to the new steel shed, which housed piles of odds and ends and busted machine parts beyond repair.

Abe had torn a motor out of an antique exhaust fan and was cursing at it under his breath.

"You oughta take that to Bob to fix. Quit pissing with it, Abe. Jesus, it's been, like, four months."

"I'm not trying to get it to work, dumb ass. I'm trying to figure out if those guys building the wind turbines are using this old technology. If I can reverse-engineer it, I'm planning to build a turbine down by the west end of the creek. Take advantage of the fact that the wind blows so goddamn hard here and harness it into energy."

That was ambitious. Although Abe hadn't gone to college, he was the smartest man Hank knew. "Why's this the first I've heard of it?"

Abe shrugged. "Been doin' more thinking about it than talking." He stared pointedly at Hank's leg. "You were limping after you got out of the truck. You okay to work?"

Hank waggled his mug. "A little caffeine therapy and I'll be fine. What're we doin'?"

"What do you think?"

He groaned. "Fixin' fence. Damn. I hoped you'd finished that up while I was gone."

Abe gave him a droll stare. "You ain't been gone that long."

The sound of tires crunching on gravel echoed through the open door.

"Guess who decided to grace us with her presence?" Abe said with an edge.

"I'll talk to her." Hank hustled out and caught Celia just as she'd started up the steps.

Why the hell did she look like she'd been rolling in the dirt? The back of her jeans were dusty, from the frayed white strings dragging on the ground by her boot heels to the dark smudges covering her back pockets.

"I assume you ain't goin' to church dressed like you've been mud wrestling?"

Celia spun around, as much guilt on her face as mud splatters. "Oh. Hey, Hank. I thought you probably got in late and you'd already be sleeping."

"Obviously." Celia's resemblance to their mother increased damn near every day and spooked him a little. He let his eyes sweep over her, from scuffed boots to mussed hair. Yep, the front side of her clothing was as filthy as the backside. "Where you been?"

"Did Abe send you out here to grill me?" she demanded.

"No. I can see you've been up to no good with my own eyes."

"See? You're just like him! You automatically assume I've been doin' something bad."

"If it wasn't bad, then why don't you answer my question?" He sipped his coffee, waiting for the wildcat to hiss and scratch.

"Because I don't answer to you. Or to Abe. I'm not a child, Hank, and I— "

"Spare me the rant and the reminder of your age. You're right, Cele, you don't have to answer to me. But what you *do* have to do, as long as you're living here, is pull your weight. Which it don't sound like you've been doin'. I count on you. So does Abe. And when we can't even talk to you about it without you flying off the handle? Something's goin' on. Tell me."

She glared, then focused on kicking the crap out of a clump of red dirt that had fallen off her boot.

"I don't give a good goddamn if you were out all night partyin' in some damn mud hole. Suck it up and check the cattle. Right now." Hank held up his hand at her automatic rebuttal. "Before you ask, me 'n' Abe will be fixin' fence before it gets too hot, so by all means, complain and I'll send you with him instead."

"You suck."

"Yep. Also, be warned—Kyle is sleeping in the guest bedroom downstairs, so you'll be sharing a bathroom with him."

"What? Why can't he stay in the guest bedroom upstairs? He's *your* friend, Hank, not mine."

"Because I already have someone staying with me."

Celia's bloodshot eyes narrowed. "Who?"

"My girlfriend, Lainie."

"Yeah, right. Since when do you have a girlfriend?"

"You answer my question about where you were last night and I'll answer yours."

Another mulish look.

Hank grinned at her. She was so damn easy to tease. "I'll introduce you to her later. Now git before I change my mind and find something worse for you to do than mope as you ride around in the truck."

"You really do suck." She flounced past him and roared off.

"Nicely done," Abe said behind him.

"Thanks. Think she's got a boyfriend she's hiding from us?"

"Maybe. She's at that age."

"She's *past* the age, bro. Most of her friends are already married. Hell, she's only two years younger than you were when you got hitched."

"Don't remind me," Abe said.

"Fine. Where we workin'?"

"Section over by the bluffs. It's a two-man job, so I've been saving it special for when you got back."

"You suck," Hank shot back, and Abe laughed.

∞

When they returned hours later, Lainie was sitting in a patch of sunshine on the front porch. Alone. Had she and Kyle already fucked like bunnies while he'd been out sweating like a pig? Jealousy surged through him.

You've no right to it. Lainie has all the control in this situation, so buck up and deal with it or you'll just piss her off.

Besides, she was his tonight. All night. Any way he wanted her. By the time Hank reached the steps his smile for her was genuine. "All rested up?"

"Mmm-hmm. I've been out admiring the scenery and the solitude. Gorgeous place you guys have."

"Thanks. We like it."

Her gaze lingered on his upper thigh. "How's the leg?"

Sore as hell. "Fine. Is Kyle up?"

"I haven't seen him."

Good. "You hungry?"

"Starved."

"I'll hop in the shower and then rustle up something to eat."

"If you point me toward the kitchen, I can fix lunch."

Abe ambled up. "Tell you what. Hank tells me you're a med tech."

Lainie nodded.

"How's about you check his leg, because he's been favoring it all damn morning, and I'll figure out what to feed us."

Abe. What a fucking traitor.

"I knew you were lying." She drilled him in the chest with her index finger. "Get your butt in the shower. And after that I'm looking at that leg."

"Lainie—"

"Move it or I will drop your pants right here in front of God and everybody."

"Promise?"

Lainie made a threatening noise and pointed to the house.

"I'm goin', I'm goin'."

He cuffed Abe in the back of the head as he walked past him.

A shower helped loosen some of the kinks, but his thigh boasted a bruise the size of a hoof. He wrapped a towel around his waist and crossed the hallway to his bedroom.

Lainie was perched on the end of the bed waiting for him. "Oh, good. No clothes will make it much easier for me to examine you. Towel off. Now."

Cursing, Hank stood in front of her and released the towel. For some stupid reason heat rose up his neck.

He heard her sharply inhaled breath. "Damn, Hank, talk about a serious contusion." Her fingers trailed over the swelling. "The whole muscle is sore?"

"Yeah." One muscle in particular wasn't sore at all, but it was leaping for her attention.

"You should ice it down. Sit on the bed and I'll be right back with an ice pack."

Hank started to argue, but she'd already sailed out the door.

∞

Lainie cut through the living room to the arched doorway she assumed led to the kitchen.

Abe stood at a center island, chopping lettuce. The knife stopped midchop. "Something I can get you?"

"A plastic bag and a towel. Hank needs to ice down his injury if he expects to work tomorrow."

"No problem." He rooted in a drawer, passing her a gallon-sized Ziploc and a frayed hand towel. "Ice is over there."

She scooped several handfuls into a makeshift ice pack. When she looked up, Abe was staring at her. His eyes were a steely gray, not a deep blue, but had the same intensity as Hank's.

She stared back at him with equal curiosity. Definitely a family resemblance, which would be more pronounced if Abe shaved off his goatee. The brothers were roughly the same height, but Abe appeared rangy and compact, whereas Hank was bulkier and broader. Both men were total cowboy hunks in every sense of the word. She'd rubbed elbows with the best of the best in her line of work, so that was really saying something.

"Anything else?" Abe prompted.

"Umm. No. I'm just gonna get this to him." Yikes. Abe and Hank both had that don't-waste-my-time attitude down pat.

Lainie hesitated outside Hank's door. Icing his injury wasn't the only way she intended to soothe him. When he'd shuffled into his room in pain, his cock fully erect—both proud and begging—something inside her fragmented. The woman, not the med tech, had the urge to pacify her man.

Time to take the bull by the horn.

Lainie opened the door and locked it behind her.

Hank scowled at the ice bag in her hand. "You're overreacting."

"Quit being such a pain and let me do this for you." She moved between his legs and gently kneed them apart. "Close your eyes. Then you won't tense the muscle until after I put the ice on it."

He grunted.

As soon as Lainie was sure his eyes were closed, she placed the ice pack on his thigh and pressed her lips to his. When Hank's hand lifted to her face, she replaced it by his side.

Kissing him let that sweet heat build until she abruptly ripped free from the kiss and dropped to her knees. She had his cock in her mouth before he'd figured out her intention.

"Sweet Jesus, Lainie. That's . . . Ah, damn. You don't have to . . . Fuck. That's good."

She hummed and sucked, briefly releasing him with a soft pop. "This is a new therapy I'm trying."

Hank laughed quietly, although it resembled a strangled groan.

She wrapped her fingers around the base, pleased that the gruff cowboy kept the pubic hair trimmed. She lost herself in the warm smoothness of his shaft sliding back and forth over her tongue. With each sucking pass she brought him deeper until the cock head rubbed against her soft palate. Then she teased him by flicking her tongue over the sweet spot below the plump head. The clean taste of him flowed through her. Hank always came to her clean. Just once she'd like to taste him natural. No sweet-smelling soap. Nothing but the raw, salty, dark taste of Hank.

Lainie took her time, eking out every ounce of pleasure for him, every bit of power for herself.

Hank's moans escalated. His hips twisted off the bed. Lainie knew he struggled not to grab her hair, forcing her to satisfy him the fast way he preferred. His fist stayed clenched at his right side, while his left hand maintained a death grip on the bag of ice on his leg.

She looked up at him when the entire length of his cock was lodged deep. He peered at her from beneath heavy-lidded eyes. His nostrils flared. His full lips were parted, allowing his breath to escape in short, hot bursts.

"Lainie. Finish me. Please."

With a slight nod, she reached between his legs and stroked his balls. She rubbed the section of skin in front of his anus and his shaft seemed to lengthen across her tongue. Using her hand in tandem with her mouth, Lainie sent him soaring.

She swallowed each creamy spurt as he came. His unintelligible mutterings were as musical to her ears as the sweet nothings he murmured on occasion.

After Hank's softened dick slipped from her mouth, he flopped back on the bed.

Grinning, Lainie rolled to her toes and kissed his taut belly. "I'm going to help Abe make lunch, whether he wants me to or not. Leave that ice pack on for at least ten minutes."

She'd made it to the door when he rasped, "As far as therapy? Darlin', that's my very favorite ever."

Chapter Nine

In the kitchen, a long-legged blonde was stretched out on the barstool at the center island.

Abe scowled at his cutting board.

". . . not fair and you both know it," the woman said.

Lainie accidentally tripped over a dog sprawled on the rug. At the dog's yelp, both heads snapped in her direction.

"Sorry, I didn't mean to interrupt." She bent down to pet the black Labrador. "Sorry to you too." The dog licked her palm.

"Murray is very forgiving, unlike *some* people I know," the blonde huffed.

"I can't forgive you until I have an inkling of what you've done wrong." Abe gestured with the knife. "Lainie, this is our sister, Celia. Celia, this is Hank's girlfriend, Lainie Capshaw." His tone and posture said, *Be nice.*

Lainie braced herself for the inevitable *Are you related to Jason Capshaw?*

But Celia offered her hand. "Nice to meetcha. Whoa.

You're a lot . . . smaller than Hank's other girlfriends. He usually goes for the tall and lanky type."

"Celia Rose Lawson," Abe scolded. "What is wrong with you?"

"What? Just sayin'. She's petite. And stacked. It's a refreshing change." Celia smiled coyly. "Welcome to the testosterone ranch."

"Thanks. Anything I can help with, Abe?"

"Nah. This is for supper tonight. Got a few guys coming over to help us load the camper and I promised them food and beer. If you're hungry now, there's sandwiches in the fridge."

"Thanks, but I'll wait for Hank to wake up."

"Wore him out good, didja?" Celia snickered.

"Dammit, Celia, knock it the hell off," Abe growled.

Celia blew Abe a kiss before facing Lainie with determined eyes. "So, you and Hank, huh? He's been pretty mum about you. I had no idea he was seeing anyone."

"I knew."

Lainie looked at Abe. "He told you about me?"

"Not specifics. Just that he'd met someone on the tour."

"This is exactly what I meant by unfair, Abe. If I woulda brought a guy home and announced, 'He's staying with me in my room,' both you and Hank would've trussed him up and dragged him off Lawson land."

"Not the same thing, Celia."

Her gray eyes narrowed. "Why? Because you both have dicks? Or because you both *are* dicks?"

Abe's knife thwacked into the cutting board. "Goddammit, Celia, drop it. Can you at least try to act civil when we have guests in the house? This is pointless and you know it."

"We need another female opinion on whether it's a pointless discussion." Celia whirled around on the bar stool, giving Abe her back. "Lainie, help me out. Since Abe's whiny ex-wife left, there've been no female views here but mine, which, naturally, they think is totally wrong. Isn't it a double standard? They can have overnight houseguests of the opposite sex and I can't?"

"I really don't think I should—"

"Go ahead. I'm dyin' to hear your opinion," Abe encouraged.

Lainie examined Celia from bare toes to ponytail. "How old are you?"

"Twenty-one."

"Oh."

"Oh, what?" Celia demanded.

"You're an adult. It seems the 'do as I say, not as I do' rule is in effect for you. I don't see why you can't have an overnight male guest if you want."

Abe studied her coolly. "How long you sticking around, Lainie?"

"I'm hoping forever," Celia retorted. "Of course, this is all hypothetical, because few cowboys around here arouse my interest. Or if they do, they're my brother's buddies and treat me like a pigtailed third grader."

Abe leaned over and playfully yanked on her ponytail. "If the hairdo fits, baby sis . . ."

"So, you teaching Celia to rebel?" Hank said behind her, right before his arms circled her waist and his chin grazed the top of her head.

Lainie wasn't used to the demonstrative side of Hank in public, but it gave her a little thrill . . . which lasted until she saw the smiles his siblings beamed at them.

They're happy for him. They think this is real.

"At least someone has taken Celia's hell-raising education to task."

All heads turned to Kyle leaning in the doorway.

"You'd know all about that, Gilly," Celia said.

"Yes, ma'am."

"Why don't you share a few hell-raising pointers with me?"

"Because I don't have a death wish, girlie. Your brothers would kill me. And I need Hank to keep me alive in the ring, not let a bull trample me into a bag of meat."

"I am not a girl," Celia sniped.

Kyle purposely avoided meeting Lainie's eyes. He'd forgotten her father had become a bag of meat at the horns and hooves of a bull.

Lainie wanted to reassure Kyle that offhand comments like that didn't bother her. She'd gotten used to them in the last two years. But he wouldn't look at her at all now.

"I'm outta here," Celia announced, and hopped off the barstool. She whistled and the dog followed.

"Maybe you can work on her surly attitude while you're at it," Abe said to Lainie.

"I heard that," Celia shouted just before the door slammed.

"I'll talk to her," Lainie said, trying to free herself from Hank's embrace and Kyle's too obvious indifference.

"She's fine. Just hotheaded. It'll blow over." Hank kissed her crown. "Stay put, since I've got you right where I want you."

∞

Stay put, since I've got you right where I want you.

Kyle gritted his teeth. It ticked him off that Hank was acting so possessive with Lainie the first chance he got.

If you were standing in your mother's kitchen, wouldn't your arms be around Lainie? Wouldn't you bury your nose in the sweet scent of her hair?

Hell, yeah.

So it pissed him off that he couldn't fault Hank for his behavior, because Kyle would do the same damn thing.

Regardless, it'd be a long damn night if he had to watch the two of them playing grab-ass.

Kyle pushed off the doorjamb. "I'll see if wannabe wild child is out loading her pistols, gunning for me, since I'm the one who set her off."

"Thanks, man," Hank said as Kyle passed by him.

He paused on the porch steps. Well, looky there.

Celia had already bent the ear of the first non–family member of the male persuasion who'd crossed her warpath. She stood on the running board of Bran Turner's rig. And Bran was getting a huge chuckle out of whatever tale of woe Celia spun.

The instant Celia noticed Kyle, she scowled. She whistled for the grungy dog, which was never more than ten feet away from her, and sauntered off to the horse barn.

Bran's head whipped around as he shamelessly watched her walk away.

"Fuckin' perv," Kyle said.

"And proud of it." Bran craned his neck for one last look. "Jesus. That woman has the finest ass. Sometimes I wonder if she rides as good between the sheets as she does on a horse."

"Probably. Wouldn't be bad if you could keep a bit in her mouth. Or take a crop to her if she got too bossy."

"Who's the fuckin' perv now?"

Kyle grinned. "And proud of it."

"So, you ain't all busted up, which is a good sign. The bull ridin' biz went well?"

"Placed first in Lamar."

"Gotta feel good to put a little jingle in your pocket after the run of bad luck you've had the last couple months."

"That it does."

Bran adjusted his hat, attempting to keep the sun out of his eyes. "Rumor is you and Hank are hitting the road as traveling partners."

"Yep."

"How long's Hank planning on bein' gone this time?"

"About three weeks—give or take. Cowboy Christmas can stretch clear up until the Days of '76 Rodeo in Deadwood the end of July."

"Huh. Hank's never gone off like this before in the summer, during this . . . what'd you call it? Cowboy Christmas? I wonder what the big deal is now. Why this year?"

Kyle's ears burned. Hank had volunteered to drag him from rodeo to rodeo because he knew Kyle wouldn't go alone.

"Don't mind tellin' ya, since they bought that new parcel out by Green Bluffs, it's getting harder for Abe to handle the ranch when Hank ain't here."

"Does Hank know that?"

"Abe ain't exactly the type to run off at the mouth about his feelin's."

"No kiddin'. So what's Abe been doin' about it instead of talking?"

"Workin'. More workin'. Hell, what else can he do? What can *any* of us do?"

Growing up within a ranching community, Kyle knew the amount of time, money, and energy it took to run a ranch, even a small one. No days off. No sick days. Livelihood depended on the whims of the weather and the cattle market. His friends had either made the choice to stay on when tragedy struck—like Abe and Hank did after their parents died—or move on—like their friend Max Godfrey, who sold the family land to pursue his love of leatherwork. Or like Bran, raised by his grandparents and living on the ranch that'd been in his family for over a century. Kyle couldn't count how many times over the years, over many beers, he'd heard his buddies discussing the pressures of the legacy left to them, whether they found it to be daunting, confining, or stimulating.

Bran sighed. "So, Hank said anything to you?"

"Hank is a world-class bullfighter, but he's a rancher first. He cares more about this piece of Wyoming dirt than he does about hooking horns every weekend."

"Sorry I said anything. Don't say nothin' to him."

"No worries. Even on the road Hank ain't any chattier than Abe, believe it or not."

The porch door banged. They both looked in that direction.

"Who's she?" Bran asked, keeping his gaze focused on the couple headed toward them.

"Lainie. She's traveling with us."

"Ah. It makes perfect sense why Hank's ready to hit the road and ditch his brother. She's the woman he's been goin' on about the last few months?"

That green-eyed monster reared its ugly head when Kyle realized Hank had talked to Bran about Lainie. Did that mean Hank was more serious about Lainie than he'd let on?

Aren't you?

Hank kept his arm around Lainie's shoulders. "Bran. Glad you could help out today."

"No problem. Abe mentioned he was whipping up a batch of Wyoming jambalaya. Speaking as a bachelor, I'll do anything not to eat my own cooking." Bran thrust out his hand to Lainie. "Bran Turner. Friend and neighbor of the Lawsons."

"Interesting how you threw in the *bachelor* part of your bio right away," Hank said sarcastically. "This is Lainie Capshaw."

Bran cranked the Turner charm to high, kissing Lainie's knuckles. "I am so pleased to make your acquaintance, lovely Lainie. Are you by any chance related to—"

"Jason Capshaw?" she supplied.

He paused thoughtfully. "No. The Capshaws by Mule Creek Junction."

"Never heard that one, but I'm afraid I don't know them."

"Pity. If you think you might be kin to 'em, I'd be more'n happy to drive you over and introduce you while Hank is off chasin' his bulls."

"Quit trying to steal my girl, Bran." Hank dropped his hands low on Lainie's hips protectively.

The situation would've amused Kyle highly if he hadn't wanted his arms around Lainie. If he hadn't been dying to introduce Lainie as his girlfriend. He managed a tight smile. "We gonna do this camper thing or what?"

"We're waiting on Eli and Max."

"Really think it'll take six guys?"

"I can help," Lainie offered.

"Like hell," came from three different men.

"But—"

"I'm showing you the chauvinist side Celia referred to, Lainie, by saying no way. We've done this before and it'll go lickety-split if I'm not worried about those magic hands of yours getting crushed," Hank said.

Lainie didn't rail or argue like spitfire Celia would have. She shrugged. "Suit yourself."

"If we're waiting on Eli and Max to get here, I need to catch up on some other stuff before we take off tomorrow." Kyle wandered back inside, pausing when he heard Abe's angry voice in the kitchen.

"Fuck that, Janie. No way. Why? Because you lost that fuckin' right when you walked out on me." Angry footsteps stopped.

Holy shit. Abe was arguing with his ex-wife? Far as Kyle knew, Abe and Janie had severed all contact after the divorce. He hated to interrupt the phone call, but the access to the basement was through the kitchen. Before Kyle booked it downstairs, he saw Abe press his forehead to the sliding glass door in total defeat.

In the guest bedroom, he dumped the contents of his duffel on the floor. Sorted the clothing from the other junk he'd shoved inside the bag. It'd all fit in one load. He stripped to his boxers, gathered the dirty clothes, and trudged to the laundry room.

As he jammed the whole shebang in the washer and poured soap on top, he grinned, thinking his mother would be appalled. She hated how he did laundry. Which reminded him that he hadn't called her about his win in Lamar.

Not that she'd be thrilled. Maybe secretly thrilled, but she wasn't happy about his getting back into bull riding.

He sprawled on the bed before he dialed her at home.

She answered, "If it isn't my wayward son."

"Hey, Ma."

"Hey, yourself. You ain't calling me to bail you outta jail, are you?"

A real comedienne, his mother. "Nah. Can't a guy call his mom just because he misses her?"

"Lord have mercy, Kyle Dean Gilchrist. You must've lost your entry fee in Lamar if you're sweet-talking me. Hoping for a loan?"

"Nope. I got first."

"You did? Congrats! Tell me about it, but leave out the parts where you get the shit kicked outta you by a two-ton beast."

Kyle detailed the rides. He talked about the differences in the EBS and the CRA. He said nothing about Lainie or about her joining him and Hank on the road.

The click of a lighter. A sharp inhale. Damn cigarettes. He wished she'd quit, but nagging her did no good.

Like it did her no good with you and bull riding?

"So, where are you right now?"

"Hank's place. We're loading up Abe's camper."

"If you tell me you drove through Cheyenne to get to Muddy Gap and didn't stop to see me, so help me God—"

"We cut across from Fort Collins and came up through Laramie. You'da chewed my ass if I'd showed up on your doorstep at three a.m. anyway." Two soft raps sounded on his door. He held his hand over the mouthpiece and said, "Come in."

The door opened and Lainie was framed in the doorway, acting strangely hesitant. He motioned her in.

"Look, Ma, I'll call you from the road. We'll be in Gillette the next two days." Her threats burned his ear, but he still managed to grin. "No topless dancin' on the bar tonight for extra tips. Love you too." He snapped the phone shut and stared at Lainie.

"You give that warning to your mother often?"

"Every time we talk. It's a private joke."

"Must be nice."

"It is what it is." He smoothed his fingers over his mustache and goatee. "Something you need?"

Lainie shuffled closer. "Just checking to see if you're all right. You've been upset since we got here."

"I'm fine."

"You're not hiding an injury from me?"

"No." He'd completely forgotten he wore just his boxer briefs, until her gaze lingered on his crotch and slowly, very, very slowly, inched up his torso. "You really oughtn't be here, eating me up with those hungry eyes, sugar."

"I can't help it. You have such a yummy body. I want to rub my face in the hair on your chest. I want to feel your goatee teasing my nipples. I want you to kiss me. Do I ever want you to kiss me, Kyle."

"Jesus. Lainie. Have you been drinkin'?"

She laughed—a sultry sound that matched the heat darkening her eyes. "No."

"Hank won't be happy you snuck down here."

"The question is: Are *you* happy I'm down here?"

Kyle squirmed. "Of course. I just don't want Hank to get pissed off at me. Or think I lured you into the basement."

"It's not Hank's decision where I go. It's mine. I can tell him that if you like. After."

"After what?"

"After you kiss me." She paused by the edge of the bed. "Are you really all right?"

"I am now." Kyle jerked her on top of him. His mouth was on hers, catching her giggle. He rolled her beneath him, pinning her arms above her head. His dick had gone from zero to hard in about four seconds. His lips slipped across her jaw to her ear as he ground against her. "Tell me what you want."

"Get me off. And then I'll get you off. Just do it fast."

"Deal." Kyle twisted to his left hip, unsnapped her jeans, and yanked them and her underwear down past her knees. After popping the buttons on her blouse, he pressed on the front of her bra until the plastic clasp released. Kyle wiggled his boxers off and was right back on top of her. "Spread your legs wider."

"That's the farthest they'll go with my jeans on."

"Good enough." Kyle sucked in a breath when his cock connected with the damp heat of her mound. He rocked until his shaft was nestled into that sweet cleft.

"Kyle, what are you doing? We don't have a condom."

"I'm making you come, like you asked me to. And I don't need a damn condom to do it." He thrust up, then pulled back, dragging the entire length of his cock across her clitoris. "Gimme that mouth," he growled, kissing her urgently. His chest hair rasped over her nipples with his every upward movement.

"I like that."

"I know. That's why I freakin' love to do it." He felt goose bumps prickling across her arms. No matter how he touched her or what sexual position he suggested, she turned her pleasure over to him.

Or to Hank.

Dammit. He was not thinking about his buddy when he had Lainie in his bed.

When Lainie started to bump her hips up, he stilled, until she understood he was in charge. She sagged into the mattress and kissed him harder, squeaking those sexy, needy sounds into his mouth.

He shortened his strokes, keeping constant pressure on the slippery nub he could almost feel pulsing beneath his shaft.

Lainie's thighs trembled and she broke the kiss. "Kyle. Oh. Don't stop."

"Shh. Baby, I won't. Give it to me. Let me see you come."

Her beautiful neck bowed and she moaned as her orgasm hit. Biting her lip. Nipples stabbing into his chest. Her skin flushing a pale rose.

Watching her come proved to be his undoing. Kyle propelled his hips faster, letting the underside of his cock head graze across the hard bone of her mound.

Yes. Balls tight. Ass cheeks tight, stomach muscles tight. *Almost. Almost.* "Yes. Oh, sweet Jesus. Lainie."

He rammed one last time, resting his cock on her belly as spurt after spurt shot out on her warm, soft skin.

Everything went fuzzy for a second. Then Kyle pushed up on his palms and looked at her. She wore a catlike grin. "What?"

"You did follow through on your promise to make me come fast."

"Ditto." He licked at her lips, placed soft smooches on

the corners of her smile, and dipped his tongue into her mouth for a flirty kiss that left them both wanting more.

"Kyle. I have to—"

"I know. But I can't get enough. I love the way you taste." He nibbled on the baby-soft section of skin at the base of her throat. "The way you smell." Kyle brushed his nose over the sweat-dampened hair at her temple. "The way you feel under me. On me. Around me."

"The way I feel at this moment is sticky. Get off me so I can get cleaned up."

One last smooch to her chin and he flopped over on his back. His gaze sought the seed he'd left on her belly. Might make him a Neanderthal, but damn, did he love seeing his mark on her.

Then it was gone. Lainie swiped it away with a tissue. She was zipped and buttoned in no time flat.

She gave him a once-over and tossed him his briefs. "Where are the rest of your clothes?"

"In the washer. They're probably done by now."

"Want me to throw them in the dryer on my way upstairs?"

Lainie's thoughtfulness, even for the smallest things, always moved him. "If it's no trouble."

"No trouble. See you." She headed for the door.

"Lainie. Wait."

She whirled around.

"If Hank asks where you've been . . . will you tell him what just happened?"

Indecision warred in her eyes, but she nodded. "The reverse would be true too, Kyle. Anything you want to know about what happens between me and Hank, just ask. It's only fair."

The door closed behind her.

Chapter Ten

Turned out it wasn't Hank that Lainie should've been worried about.

She'd just tossed Kyle's clothes in the dryer when a voice spoke behind her. "Lucky Kyle. You'll do him *and* his laundry?"

Lainie threw in two fabric-softener sheets and started the machine before she turned around.

Holy crap—Celia was pissed. Arms folded over her chest. Slim body vibrating with anger. Mouth set in a grim line. Eyes hard and mean.

"It's not what you think," Lainie said evenly.

"Oh, it's *exactly* what I think. I heard you moaning Kyle's name. Same for Kyle gasping your name in praise."

Lainie's face heated. Not out of guilt. Celia's eavesdropping on a private moment irked her.

"What kind of woman is all lovey-dovey with my brother one second, and not an hour later she's fucking his friend?"

"I won't answer that, Celia."

"Why not?" she demanded.

Because it's none of your business. "Because it's complicated."

"Maybe when I talk to Hank it'll *uncomplicate* things for you."

Equally belligerent, Lainie pointed to the door. "Go ahead. If you bring it up with Hank, don't do it in front of his friends."

"Why not?"

"Because Hank doesn't deserve to be embarrassed. Especially not by his hotheaded sister, who doesn't have a freakin' clue about what's really going on."

Worry crept into Celia's steely eyes. "That's why I'm asking *you*, Lainie. What's goin' on?"

Lainie yanked the ponytail holder out of her hair. The damn thing was giving her a headache. Right. It was the elastic's fault her head pounded. Not this sneaking around and lying shit. "Look, Celia, no offense, but I don't know you or if you can keep a secret."

"Believe it or not, I'm good at keeping secrets." Celia snapped, "I'm good at recognizing a bullshit excuse too."

"The truth is, I'm with both of them."

"With both of them . . . As in sleeping with both of them?"

She nodded.

Celia's mouth nearly hit the laundry room floor. "Holy crap. For real? And Hank and Kyle are okay with it?"

"No." Lainie smiled ruefully. She summarized the situation and finished with, "For obvious reasons Hank didn't want to share the truth with you and Abe."

"God. It never even crossed my mind that a hinky thing could be goin' on between the three of you." A bewildered look darkened her eyes. "Kyle and Hank aren't . . . together? And you're just along as their beard?"

"No. God, no." Where in the hell had Celia picked up that term?

"Not that there's anything wrong with that," Celia rushed to say. "It's just, well, Hank is my brother. Some folks around here already think it's weird he ain't married at his age. Especially since he's not ugly or mean or a drunk—or all three."

Lainie seized her chance to get the lowdown on Hank. "Why isn't Hank married?"

Celia's face became contemplative for a second before she answered. "Partially because Abe's marriage went to hell. Obviously it was hardest on Abe, but it wasn't a picnic for me 'n' Hank because we lived here too. After that, Hank started traveling as a bullfighter, leaving more of the ranch responsibilities to Abe and me."

"You've known Kyle a long time. Why do you think he's not married?"

"Because he's a douche bag."

Lainie stiffened.

"Sorry. I shouldn't have said that. I used to get along great with Kyle. Until he . . ." Celia smiled slyly. "Can *you* keep a secret?"

Swapping secrets with Hank's sister? Bad idea. "On second thought, don't tell me. My buddy Tanna always says—"

"Tanna. As in Tanna Barker? The seventh-ranked barrel racer in the CRA? You know her?"

"Yeah. She's a really good friend of mine. Why?"

Celia squealed. "Oh, my God! She's totally my hero. I've memorized all her stats and watched her winning performance at the AFR on DVD a billion times. I even changed my saddle to one like she uses. What's she like? Serious? Dedicated? I'll be she spends all her off time training."

Countering the hero worship with, *No, she spends a good amount of her time trolling for studs not of the equine variety*, wouldn't be fair. Accurate, but unfair. "Tanna is the best. If you bought a saddle like hers, are you a barrel racer too?"

"Shh." Celia tossed a panicked look at the closed door. "This is a secret you absolutely cannot tell anyone, especially not Hank."

Before Lainie could stop her confession, Celia blurted, "Two years ago I bought Mickey to use as a cattle horse. But he was fast and agile, so when I started running him around barrels . . . Holy crap, me 'n' Eli were stunned. Mickey was made for barrel racing. We're talking a championship-grade horse. But Hank and Abe don't know anything about Mickey, let alone that I've been training him and competing."

"Who's Eli? A secret boyfriend?"

She snorted. "Not hardly. Eli Whirling Cloud is my brothers' buddy. He ain't happy about keeping this secret from Hank and Abe either."

"Why is this so hush-hush?"

"Because I broke my leg barrel racing when I was fourteen and we had to put the horse down. Abe and Hank freaked out and made me quit the rodeo team and promise I'd never compete again. I did quit competing, but I never stopped training. I love it too much. So when Eli agreed Mickey was ready to compete, I snuck off to a couple of rodeos within a day's drive and entered us under another name."

Lainie stared at Celia. Stunned. "Your brothers don't know anything about this?"

She shook her head. "You saw how they are. I'm still treated like a fourteen-year-old girl. What sucks is I'm acting like one too. Sneaking out at night. Lying about where I've been. Conning Eli into helping me maintain the lie. I'm exhausted from the secret traveling and late nights. Abe thinks I'm lazy. I can't even tell them my alter ego CeCe Murray is currently ranked seventeenth in the standings for this circuit."

"But seventeenth is great, Celia!"

"I know. I worked hard for it. I wish I could tell them, but they'll be seriously pissed."

"Don't you think they'd be proud of you?"

"Maybe. On the other hand, Abe feels Hank is pulled in two different directions with the ranch and the bull-fighting. It'll get harder for Hank if he's picked as an EBS bullfighter."

Hank had an audition for the EBS bullfighting team? The cream of the crop were chosen for the EBS. In addition to great money, there was more travel. Which would keep Hank away from the ranch. But how could he turn down such a great career opportunity? It appeared she wasn't the only one keeping a career change close to the vest. "When is that again?" Lainie asked casually.

"The final tryout is in Tulsa after Cowboy Christmas. Far as I know Hank hasn't told anyone besides me and Abe. And you."

But he didn't tell me; you did.

"So you won't tell Hank about . . . ?" Celia asked.

"My lips are sealed." She pushed away from the heat, scent, and comforting white noise of the dryer. "But you need to do the adult thing and tell your brothers the truth about what you've been up to."

"I will. Soon."

Lainie returned upstairs. Hank sat at the eating area of the kitchen. She plastered on a smile, hoping she didn't look like she'd been burdened with secrets she hadn't wanted. "How's the leg?"

His eyes narrowed suspiciously. "Fine. What were you doin' in the basement?"

That tipped Lainie over the edge. Rather than stammer about talking to Celia, or make an excuse about laundry, she met Hank's hard gaze dead-on. "Fucking around with Kyle. Why?"

"Need I remind you you're supposed to be with me, as my girlfriend, when we're here?"

She didn't say a word.

"Why did you go down there in the first place?"

"Because I care about him, Hank. This isn't easy on him. I went to see if he was all right."

"What happened when you were down there, Lainie? Did you blow him too?"

"And if I did?"

Hank growled.

She skirted the kitchen island and got right in his face. "This was your idea, remember? Yours and Kyle's. You both swore you'd have no problem sharing me. You'd have no issues with jealousy. So you don't get to make that caveman noise."

Hank jerked her against him. His mouth crashed down on hers. He pushed his tongue between her teeth, forcing her to take his brutal, commanding kiss.

Her body tingled from her lips to her toes. As she attempted to regain her balance, Hank's mouth brushed her ear. "Tonight I won't have to share you. Tonight you're all mine." He abruptly released her and ambled off without a backward glance.

∞

Supper was over. The camper was loaded. Sitting outside on a gorgeous summer night, drinking cold beer, bullshitting with his friends. It'd be a perfect night if Lainie were by his side.

The woman was flat-out ignoring him.

Hank supposed he deserved it, after his chest-thumping behavior in the kitchen.

"So you're all staying in the camper? For three weeks?"

He sipped his beer, looking across the picnic table at his brother's best friend, Max Godfrey. "Yeah. Why?"

"Seems a tight fit." Max dropped his voice. "What happens when you and Lainie wanna get busy? Do you tell Kyle to take a hike?"

"Max, leave it alone," Eli warned.

"I ain't worried. It'll work itself out." Hank glanced at Lainie talking to Bran and Kyle on the far side of the deck. Her hair fell in ringlets around her sweet face. Damn. He couldn't wait to thread that wild, coppery hair through his fingers as he kissed her. Fucked her. Over and over.

"See what I mean, Eli? The way Hank watches her all the damn time. Poor Kyle's gonna be taking lots of walks."

Eli grunted.

For once Hank was glad Eli was a man of few words.

Celia bounded toward their table. "I'm staying at Harper's. We're visiting her college friends for a couple days."

"Did you ask Abe?"

"No, but I told him about it." Celia and Eli exchanged an odd look.

What was that about?

He wouldn't be around the next couple weeks to run interference between Celia and Abe, and God knew they needed it. "Just be careful."

Celia hugged Hank from behind and kissed his cheek. "I will. You too."

"You coming with us tonight, Hank?" Max asked.

The group was cruising to Cactus Jack's, a favorite honky-tonk in Rawlins. Hank looked at Lainie. Thought of his plans for her after he locked his bedroom door. "No. We're goin' to bed early, since I'm driving tomorrow."

"Then that explains why Kyle's coming along." Max stood. "Let's get 'em rounded up. Eli, you the DD?"

"I reckon."

After everyone left, Lainie leaned on the wooden porch post opposite him. The air between them crackled with energy.

"Hank—"

He held up a hand. "My rules tonight."

Indecision clouded Lainie's eyes for a moment. Then she nodded and moved to him, letting her fingers scrape against the razor stubble dotting his jaw. "No pain, okay?"

"No intentional pain. I promise." He angled his head and kissed her palm.

Inside, Hank stopped in the entryway. "Strip in my bedroom and then come into the kitchen."

"Strip . . . as in down to nothing?"

"Yep."

Less than five minutes later she returned. Totally buck-ass nekkid. If the rosy flush on her body was an indication, Lainie wasn't used to walking around in the buff. Which was damn fine with him.

"Look at you. So pretty in just your skin." He reached for her, cupping his hands around her neck. Kissing her, teasing her with soft nibbles, little licks, and the smooth, wet glide of his lips.

She relaxed into him, gave herself to him.

Eventually he allowed his hands to slide down the front of her body to those lush, tempting tits. His thumbs rasped the pale rose nipples until the tips were rigid. Intoxicated by her breathy moan, he let his fingers skim the side of her torso, slipping over the curve of her spine. He whispered, "Hold your tits together for me."

It was sexy as hell seeing Lainie's hands mashing the mounds together, an offering to him.

As he stroked the crack of her ass, he flicked his tongue back and forth, dampening the tips of her breasts. Then he blew over the wetness, making the peaks tighter yet.

She let her head fall back. "Hank."

"Baby, can you do something for me?" he asked, rubbing his face into her soft, supple flesh.

"Anything."

Hank clasped her hand and dragged her past the massive dining room table to a buffet against the wall. He picked up the antique china tea set, placing it next to the candlesticks on the other end. He snagged a ladder-back chair. "Use this to climb up on the buffet."

She looked at him in shock. "What? No. I'll break it!"

"It's three-inch-thick solid walnut, darlin'. A sledgehammer wouldn't put a dent in it, so it's safe from your very fine ass. Get on up there. Now."

After she'd situated herself, Hank shucked off his clothes and rolled on a condom. He sat on the chair and scooted it between her knees.

Lainie's glistening sex was at his mouth level. All soft and pink and wet. When he ran his index finger through the slippery folds, Lainie's body jerked. The china tea set wobbled on the end of the buffet. "Hank. What are you doing? I don't want to break—"

"You won't. As long as you stay still while I'm tasting my fill of your sweet, sweet pussy."

"You can't be serious."

"I am. Call it a test." Hank had to know how far he could push her.

"A test? So you're not going to let me come?"

"Why wouldn't I let you come?"

"Because you know how much I thrash around whenever that wicked mouth of yours is sucking between my legs."

Hank grinned. "Oh, you'll come. Remaining still when you come? That'll be a challenge for you. Think you can do it?"

Her uncertainty disappeared and her stubborn chin notched higher. "Yes."

"There's my girl. Now lift." Lainie carefully placed her palms flat by her hips and pushed up. Hank's hands slid beneath her ass and he angled her lower half so it was barely resting on the edge of the buffet. Then he bent his head and licked her.

Her hips jerked and the china rattled.

He warned, "Steady," and lapped at her slit from bottom to top again.

Lainie gasped, but didn't make any sudden movements.

He licked the salty-sweet proof of her desire, tongue swirling through those petal-soft folds to the entrance of her sex. He suckled her pouty pussy lips. Flicked her clitoris with the tip of his tongue and plunged it deep into her channel, bathing his face in her essence.

Hank dragged openmouthed kisses up the inside of her thighs. "I was starving for a taste of you, Lainie. I could spend an entire day right here, with my face buried in you."

"I wouldn't survive. I-I can't hold out much longer."

Neither could he. His cock dug into his belly. His hands were cramping from the grip on her ass. Plus, he had a lot more in store for her tonight. He fastened his mouth to her clit, alternating hard sucks with butterfly flicks.

Her breathing changed from slow and steady to ragged bursts. Her legs trembled. He squeezed her ass in warning when the candlestick started to wobble.

"Hank. Please."

The continual strike of his tongue on that spot did the

trick. Lainie gasped, but otherwise held herself still as the orgasm rolled through her.

Hank swallowed the sticky sweetness, prolonging her climax by keeping his mouth sealed to her cunt. He looked up, her naked body motionless after the last pulse ebbed.

Lainie's eyes smoldered with an intensity that would've hardened his cock if it weren't already as rigid as a steel beam.

He couldn't fucking wait to plow into her. Sate the hard edge of his lust within her softness.

She kept staring at him. Her chest rose and fell with every jagged breath. "Let me down. Right now. Let me touch you. I'm dying to put my hands all over you—"

Hank stood and kicked the chair out of his way. He plucked her off the buffet so fast the candlesticks tipped over and clanked into the tea set. But he didn't give a damn if the things shattered; he couldn't see beyond the red haze of *want need want need* looping in his brain.

Her legs circled his hips and she was kissing his neck frantically. Hot, wet, hard love bites that sent chills skittering down his spine.

He debated laying her across the dining room table as he nailed her from behind, but he wanted those abundant curves wrapped around him. "Hold on." He sat on the dining room chair. "Hook your feet into the bottom rungs."

She kept her hands on his shoulders and her knees wide. He aimed his cock, sliding the head through her wet folds before thrusting up and seating himself completely.

Fuck, that was good. He suppressed the urge to ram into her until those gripping cunt muscles clamped down and sucked every ounce of seed from his balls. His body craved that rush. The completion of mating. Hank had to rein the impulse in sharply or it'd be over before it began.

Give her control.

He kissed the graceful sweep of her collarbone. "Fuck me, Lainie. Fast. Slow. Easy. Hard. Dirty. Sweet. I don't care. You're on top. You're in charge."

Her supple lips and moist breath tortured his ear. Tingles raced from his nape straight down to his sac. "I wonder . . . can you stay still while I'm riding you?"

Cheeky damn woman, turning the tables on him. "Whatever you want."

"Mmm." Her teeth nipped his earlobe. That sassy tongue soothed the sting. "Will you really let me fuck you my way? Or were those just the pretty words of a man desperate to get off?"

"I am desperate, but I believe in offering equal opportunities."

"Meaning, if I fuck you my way now, next go-around it's back to Hank's choice?"

He flashed her a wolflike grin. "Yep."

Lainie fisted a hand in his hair and jerked his head back to peer into his eyes. "Deal." She fused her lips to his, devouring his mouth in a fierce kiss.

Oh, sweet darlin', you just jumped headfirst into a devil's bargain.

She tormented him. Dragging out the withdrawal of his engorged cock. Letting the sweet spot below the cock head rub on the entrance to her pussy. Hank groaned every time. Wanting constant friction, wanting it faster. Being denied. She'd change the angle of entry and quickly plunge his shaft to the root. Bounce on his pole faster and faster . . . only to slow down and contract her interior muscles in a slick, intimate kiss when his cock was buried deep.

Lainie the temptress pleased herself by grinding her

clit against him. Forcing the smattering of hair on his chest to abrade her beaded nipples. Burning his ear with her throaty sighs and sexy female grunts.

It was fucking torture. His body was coated with sweat. Slippery thighs, slick chest, drenched back. Hell, even his feet were sweating. He licked his upper lip and tasted salt. And Lainie. God, he loved the taste of her on his lips. In his mouth. Pouring down his throat.

Her command, "Suck my nipples," nearly set him off.

As he tongued one tip, he murmured, "Lainie. Darlin'. You're killin' me."

"Mmm-hmm. And it's so darn fun."

He groaned. He needed to come so badly his teeth ached.

She licked the whorl of his ear and murmured, "What will get you there, cowboy?"

"Ride me faster."

"Help me. Show me."

Hank's hands slid around her rib cage to grab two handfuls of her ass. He lifted her up, never completely dislodging his cock, and pulled her body back down. One, two, three times in rapid succession. "Like that. Just like that."

The chair squeaked with her every bounce. The sound of skin slapping skin as her thighs connected with his reverberated in the air and through his body. His mind drifted into a hazy, urgent state, where nothing mattered but finding release.

"Hank? Oh, God, I'm there—"

He latched onto the section of skin below her ear and sucked.

Immediately Lainie's cunt spasmed around his cock, drawing him deep.

And it was over. Hank grunted, squeezing his eyes shut as his dick emptied. The last pulses were squeezed out by the contractions of her pussy and they rode out the last of her orgasm together.

Hank's head dropped back as if too heavy for his neck. He fought the buzzing inside his brain that urged him to sleep.

Whoa. She'd popped his top that time.

A smooch to his chin brought him out of his sexual trance. "You all right?" She petted his jaw.

"It was so fucking good I zoned out." Hank slid his hands up her damp back. Was anything sexier than the glow of satisfaction surrounding a well-fucked woman?

No. And he couldn't wait to put that look on her face again.

"What are you thinking about?"

"You. Me." Hank pumped his hips. "How I ain't nearly done with you tonight. The next go-round is my choice, remember?" He grabbed her wrists and held them behind her back. "How do you feel about ropes?"

"Ropes? As in, you want to tie me up? During sex?"

When she said it in that breathless, hushed tone, his cock twitched inside her.

Lainie's eyes enlarged. "The idea of tying me up makes you hard?"

"Completely." Hank pressed his lips to hers. "But that ain't really news, Lainie. Even when I've just had you, I can't see beyond the next time I can have you again."

She let her eyes drift shut and Hank sensed her surrender.

Instead of roaring his masculine satisfaction at her silent submission, he kissed her, keeping it soft and easy. Until she began to demand more. Fast dueling of tongues. The escalated breaths of endless openmouthed kisses. Their heads constantly adjusted to find the best angle to take the kiss deeper yet.

The tight clasp of his dick inside her cunt loosened.

Heated. The aroma of her renewed arousal drifted up from where their bodies were still joined.

Hank's lips nibbled. Teased. Slid over to her ear. "Lainie."

"I love your voice. Especially when you whisper in my ear as you fuck me."

"You like it when I whisper naughty nothings?" he murmured.

"Yes."

"I have a specific naughty in mind." He lightly sucked the air from her ear. "I want what no other man has had. I want to grind my cock into that hot little ass of yours."

Lainie's body stiffened.

"Me 'n' Kyle will both be taking our turns in your ass. You had to expect that, getting involved in a threesome." Hank nuzzled his lips up a fraction of an inch. "One of us has to have the privilege of being first, and I want it to be me."

Chapter Eleven

"Why you?" she asked breathlessly.

"You want prettied-up words, or the God's honest truth?"

"Find a way to give me both, Hank."

He smiled against her cheek, enchanted by her response. "Because I was with you first. Because I was a little vanilla in bed with you. I've seen the error of my gentlemanly ways"—he licked the shell of her ear—"and let's see if you can handle my rougher side."

She looked at him with clear desire. "I can."

He needed her to say the words. Out loud. "Tell me what it is you want me to do to you so there's no misunderstanding."

"Hank—"

"Say it," he demanded.

"I want to feel you in my ass. No time for me to think about it or change my mind. I just want you to do it."

Hank growled. "Bedroom. Now." He carefully lifted her, holding her up until her feet touched the ground.

She flounced off, that perfect ass shaking with her every step. He couldn't wait to watch his cock disappearing between those soft, round cheeks.

Needing a minute to compose himself, Hank wiped the top of the buffet with a dish towel. Righted the candlesticks and the tea set. Shoved the chair back where it belonged. Satisfied he'd left no sign of their sexcapades, he picked up his clothes. In the bathroom, he ditched the condom, washed his hands, and splashed cold water on his face.

Jesus. His skin was on fire. Hank peered at his reflection in the mirror. Eyes wild. Jaw set. Pulse jumping in his throat. Breath sawing in and out of his lungs. Cock slapping his belly. He'd be goddamn lucky if she didn't put a halt to this upon seeing him so reckless with need.

Lainie wants this just as much as you do or she would've said no.

He must've looked calmer than he felt when he entered the bedroom, because Lainie smiled at him from the edge of the mattress.

Her smile slipped when he slammed the door shut and locked it behind him.

Feeling far edgier than his ambling walk suggested, Hank snagged an unopened tube of K-Y and another condom from the top drawer in his dresser. He tossed the whole shooting match beside her and climbed on the bed.

"Umm. What about the ropes?"

"Another time."

She scrambled backward as he stalked her across the mattress. "Why?"

Hank got right in her face. "Because I'm impatient as hell. Because it'll be so much more satisfying that you're giving me this, rather than me tying you up and just taking it."

Her kiss-swollen lips formed an O of understanding.

"Get on your hands and knees, Lainie, before I lose my ever-lovin' mind."

His eyes feasted on her, noticing the strength in her shoulders. Her slim torso flaring into the beautiful curve of her hips. The deep dimples above her ass. The sleek line of her shapely thighs flowing into muscular calves and tiny feet.

"You look as gorgeous from the back as you do from the front."

She arched her neck and waggled her rear, reminding him of a mare in season.

Hank donned the condom and popped the top on the bottle of lube. "Widen your stance. Good. Angle your hips so I can reach you." Kissing between her shoulder blades, he traced the crack of her ass and swept one lubed finger over the snug little pucker.

She hissed in a breath.

"Breathe out, baby. Relax." On her next exhale he wiggled his finger inside to the webbing of his hand.

Christ, that was tight. He moved that finger in and out until she seemed to relax. Then he added more lube when he inserted the second finger.

"Shit. Hank. That hurts."

He placed a string of soft, wet kisses down her spine. "It'll get better."

"For you or for me?" she shot back.

A laugh rumbled out. "Oh. Definitely for me." He shoved both fingers in knuckle-deep. He put his lips on the back of her neck and breathed, letting the air drift across the dampness.

She shivered.

"If you wanna stop, Lainie, say so now. Because once I get goin', I ain't gonna hear anything beyond the pounding of my flesh as I fuck this virgin hole until my balls burst."

A pause. Then she said, "Don't stop."

Hank kissed her nape. "I'll make it good for you. And if I can't do that, I'll at least make it memorable."

She laughed delicately. "No vanilla?"

"Definitely not. Hard and fast and dirty." He plunged his fingers in and out, biting back his growl of pleasure at how firmly those untried muscles clamped down. After twisting the digits deep, then scissoring them wide, he decided Lainie was as loose and ready as he could make her.

He wouldn't last long once he'd buried his dick in that hot, snug passage. He thoroughly slicked up his shaft. Grabbing a pliant butt cheek in each hand, he positioned the head to her hole, watching the muscles tauten, trying to deny him entry.

"Lainie. Don't tense up. Push out. Breathe out. Lemme in. That's it, darlin'." He popped the plump cock head past the ring of muscle.

"Is it in?" she asked, panting.

"No." Hank lifted her hips higher so he could watch his cock pushing through her resistance, an inch at a time, until her sphincter was stretched around the base of his cock. "Now I'm in all the way."

"Fuck. That burns."

"It'll get better." Hank couldn't tear his eyes away as he pulled out. Completely out. He circled the spasming hole and rammed in.

Lainie started to raise herself up, but Hank centered his palm in the middle of her back and shoved her down until her chest rested against the mattress. "Steady. Relax, okay?"

She nodded and sucked in another breath at his slow withdrawal and harsh plunge.

His brain was stuck on a continual loop of pleasure. In: slick, tight, hot.

Out: Dragging across the sensitive tissues, he felt the squeeze of her muscles tightening.

"Hank?"

"Mmm?"

"Why did you slow down?"

Hank's balls were tight. His body was sweating, shaking. His brain focused on the basics: the primal need to come and the hot release dangling just out of his reach. "Because I don't want to hurt you."

"You're not. Give it to me the way you promised. Fast, dirty, and hard. I'm ready."

With a snarl, he jackhammered into her, lost in that primitive male need. His fingers clutched her ass as his cock reamed her. A line of fire zigzagged from the top of his head down through his spinal cord, zapping his balls into giving up the goods.

He held himself still as he came, locking his knees, his jaw, his ass as her rectum constricted around his spasming dick and he lost himself to the haze of release.

The clouds behind his eyes cleared. The fog in his brain lifted. He blinked. "Holy fuckin' shit. That was . . . Wow."

Lainie hadn't said a word. She hadn't moved at all.

Like she could with the goddamn death grip you've got on her with your dick embedded in her ass.

He glanced down. Damn. He'd probably left finger-shaped bruises. Would it bother her to see the marks on her skin? Would it bother Kyle?

He fought a snarl. He didn't want to fucking think about Kyle right now.

Maybe you oughta think about Lainie *right now, dumb ass.*

Hank stretched across her back and kissed her shoulder. "Baby, you all right?"

"You weren't kidding about rough, were you?"

He froze. "Did I hurt you?"

She angled her head to rub his cheek. "Yes. But it was inevitable. At the end it was a good kind of hurt."

"That's a relief. Hang on." He slipped out of her anal passage and retreated to the bathroom to clean up. When he returned quickly with a warm washcloth, he gently rolled her over. "Open your legs. This will help a little."

She smiled but didn't open her eyes. "You're sweet beneath that gruff bullfighter exterior."

He snorted and wiped her tender and swollen flesh. After he'd cleaned her, he kissed the baby-soft section of skin between her hip bones. His mouth meandered south and he ran his tongue along her slit.

"Hank. I—"

"Let me see to you. I'll be gentle, I promise."

Lainie sighed. "If you insist."

"I do." Hank took his time and savored her. Delving into the soft pink folds. Suckling. Licking. Lapping at the sweet cream pouring from her sex. Tickling her clit with the barest tip of his tongue. Not teasing her. Just enjoying her and the trust she'd bestowed on him tonight.

"I'm close. Don't stop."

He latched onto her clit with soft suction and tongued that nub until her hands squeezed his scalp.

"Yes. Yes!" She arched and came in throbbing wet pulses against his tongue.

He stayed right where she needed him until her body relaxed. What a beautiful sight: her skin flushed, her limbs trembling, her hair strewn across his pillow.

Lainie belonged in his bed. But not just for a night.

She pushed up on her elbows wearing a goofy grin. "That was fantastic. Thank you."

"My pleasure."

"But I'm done in. No more."

"I'm pretty done in myself. You want me to shut off the lights?"

"Yes." She yawned and hopped up to dig through her duffel bag. She yanked on an oversize T-shirt and crawled between the sheets. "Good night, Hank."

"Good night, Lainie."

Yep. He knew this woman was right where she belonged. And he had three weeks to convince her.

∞

The next morning, Kyle and Lainie flipped a coin for shotgun, since Hank was driving. She won. But Kyle's consolation prize was a lingering, soft-lipped kiss. Not a bad way to start his day.

"What time is check-in?" Lainie asked.

"Noon."

"This is a two-day event?"

"Yep. Rodeo starts at seven." Kyle rested his forearms on the bench seat and looked at Hank. "I don't imagine you're any more used to waiting around beforehand than I am."

"Depends. Sometimes I have a meet and greet with sponsors. Usually I roll in a couple of hours before showtime. Give myself time to limber up." He offered Lainie a sly grin. "Or get my injuries checked out ahead of time by my favorite med tech."

Kyle rolled his eyes.

"I'm always busy before the event starts," Lainie said. "I've either been on the road or in a plane. Then I'm helping wrap injuries or applying salve. Or listening to Doc argue with cowboys about why they shouldn't be competing."

"Do they listen?"

"Never."

Hank and Kyle laughed.

"You planning on stopping by the medical room to offer your services?" Hank asked.

"Maybe. I brought my official Lariat badge. Doc said at the smaller rodeos the event sponsors use local doctors as medical volunteers. Or they have an ambulance standing by."

"Most promoters put their money into the purse and the stock contractors. Everything else is volunteer. I'm imagining Lariat gets a big chunk of money from the CRA," Hank said.

"Almost as much dough as we get from the behemoth known as the EBS," she said sarcastically.

Kyle said, "Why does it sound like you're not a fan of the EBS?"

"It's not that." Lainie looked over her shoulder at him. "The EBS's demands increase every week. The money is excellent. But I predict in the next year Lariat will have to choose between providing services for the CRA or the EBS. The EBS is always adding new venues to the schedule, usually second tier. We're continually short staffed, which is partially why I'm bounced between both circuits."

"I hope they're paying you well, sugar."

Lainie blushed and faced forward.

Hank cast a questioning look at Kyle. After Lainie's conversation with her mother, he and Hank discussed whether Sharlene's concerns were valid or if Lainie refused to listen to reason simply because of the source of information. It didn't sit well with either of them that Doc might be taking advantage of her, especially since he was supposedly a family friend.

Seeing that Lainie was uncomfortable, Kyle changed the subject. "Hank, do you remember that prick Marshall Townsend?"

"The guy from outside of Rawlins?" Hank asked,

meeting Kyle's eyes in the rearview mirror. "Who wouldn't let us hunt on his place after we helped him with two days of haying?"

Kyle nodded. "He tried to corner me last night."

"What'd he want?"

"Who the hell knows? He was drunk as shit, babbling about some damn thing. Know who else I ran into? Harper Masterson."

"Harper? Was Celia with her?"

"No, which was weird, because didn't Celia leave early last night because she was goin' somewhere with Harper for the weekend?"

"Was there a live band? And dancing?" Lainie asked. "I like to dance. That band in Lamar the other night was good. What I heard of it, anyway."

Kyle sent Lainie a suspicious look at her abrupt subject change. Sounded like she was covering for Celia. But that didn't make sense. Lainie and Celia were the least likely types to become bosom buddies.

No one spoke for a while. The radio was off. Lainie stared out the window. Hank kept his eyes on the road. Kyle let his head fall back and his thoughts drift.

When he'd returned to Lawson's ranch house with Abe last night, the lights were off in Hank's bedroom. Somehow he'd tamped down his jealousy as he tramped downstairs.

As he lay in the dark of his bedroom, he cooked up several scenarios of how his night alone with Lainie would play out. Part of him hated thinking up new sexual tricks to use on Lainie that'd give him a leg up on Hank. But another part of him loved the chance to unlock his kinkier fantasies. Who knew if the opportunity would ever appear again?

Two hard bumps jarred him and his eyes flew open.

"Sorry. Potholes I didn't see until I was right up on 'em."

"Can't believe I almost dozed off." He stretched. Yawned.

"It's a damn boring drive."

"No, it's not. The landscape is stunning. You can see forever," Lainie murmured.

"Says the woman who grew up by the ocean."

She whapped Hank on the arm.

"What was that for?"

"Because your tone annoyed me."

Kyle grinned. Lainie was no shrinking violet. She'd definitely keep them on their toes the next few weeks. He was looking forward to it.

Hank navigated the inevitable road construction and pulled into the Campbell County Fairgrounds outside the CAM-PLEX. He offered to accompany Kyle to the contestant check-in area, but Kyle declined, as much as he hated leaving Hank and Lainie alone again.

The stillness of the arena during the day spooked him. It smelled the same—hot dirt, manure, animal flesh, and popcorn—but the air lacked the vigor of the raucous crowd and the nervous energy of the contestants behind the chutes.

The plump woman behind the window eyed him. "Lemme guess. Bareback rider."

"Nope. Bull rider."

She rattled off the entry fee. Kyle handed over the cash. The woman pushed a clipboard with the release-of-liability forms under the ticket window. "Sign here." That done, she stamped a receipt, initialed it, and passed it back. She pointed to another ticket booth. "You'll get your number over there. Good luck."

He mumbled thanks and moved over to the longer line.

The guy in front of him looked familiar, but Kyle couldn't place him. Luckily, the guy spoke first.

"I feel like we've met before, but I'll be damned if I can remember where." He stuck out a hand. "Breck Christianson."

Kyle shook his hand. "Kyle Gilchrist."

Breck snapped his fingers. "Now I know where I know you from. The EBS. You finished in the top ten in the world finals a couple years back."

"Seems a lot longer ago than that."

"Didn't you have some kind of injury?"

"Blew out my knee and was out for a year after surgery. The EBS let me start this season, but after my piss-poor showing they dropped me from the main tour."

Breck frowned. "Why didn't you stick with the EBS's secondary circuit?"

"Not enough venues. I need to get on as many bulls as I can to figure out what the hell I'm doin' wrong."

"I hear ya. Cowboy Christmas is my favorite time of year because of the number of stock I get to test out."

"So what is your poison?"

"Saddle bronc. If there ain't many contestants I sometimes dabble in bareback. Plus tie-down roping and bulldogging."

Kyle whistled. "Glutton for punishment?"

"It's the price of reaching for that all-around title." They shuffled forward in line. "How's the CRA compare to the EBS?"

It'd sound like pandering if he mentioned that the CRA people were nicer. "I've only done one CRA event, so it's too soon to tell."

"Where'd you compete?"

"Lamar."

"How'd you do?"

Kyle grinned. "First."

"Nice." After Breck picked up his contestant "back" number, he said, "Good meetin' you. See ya tonight."

Kyle rolled up the square piece of paper listing his contestant number and jammed it in his back pocket. He wandered around, familiarizing himself with the grounds. Just as he was about to call Hank, he saw a flash of wild curls duck beneath the bleachers. Only one person had hair like that. He tracked her to a tiny room with a medical symbol on the door.

Lainie was talking to a scrawny male kid who didn't look old enough to shave, let alone to run a medical station.

"I thought I'd offer," Lainie finished. She spun around and her fake smile slipped when her gaze landed on Kyle.

"Everything okay?" he asked outside the room.

"Fine. They have plenty of 'qualified medical professionals,' so I'm free to be a spectator tonight."

He recognized her disappointment. "That's not all bad. It'll really feel like you're on vacation. Did you guys get the camper set up?"

"Yeah. Let's head that way. I could use food."

They walked through the bustling campground to a fenced-in section outside the arena reserved for contestants and their families. Despite the steel horse trailers and campers, the area held the feel of an Old West town. Dust and tents and campfires. Whinnying horses, kids shouting, and barking dogs.

"This your first trip through a campground on the CRA tour?" Kyle asked.

"No. Sometimes Tanna and I hang out in her horse trailer. She usually takes off right after the event on the second night." Lainie avoided a pile of beer cans. "Talk about a shock. I figured the inside of her horse trailer would be covered in hay. She'd have a couple of plastic buckets to sit on, a dorm-size fridge, and a cot."

"Were you surprised?"

"Yes. My God. Her horse trailer is nicer than my apartment. Cleaner too."

"At Tanna's level of competition she can afford creature comforts." He shot her a grin. "And I do mean *creature* comforts, because I'll bet she pampers her horse way more than she pampers herself."

"True." She pointed. "We're this way."

"Where's Hank?"

"Called in for some last-minute sponsor event at a Western clothing store. They picked him up at the front gate an hour ago. Then he has to meet with the head honcho afterward."

At the campsite, Lainie hopped up on the metal stair and twisted a key in the lock. She tilted her body sideways and swung the door open.

Kyle followed her inside. The air conditioner worked well; the space was nice and cool.

She cracked open the fridge. "I didn't check to see what there is for food." She rummaged and muttered, "Meat for sandwiches, but I don't see bread. If I'd known that before we set up I would've insisted on a trip to the grocery store."

"Tell you what. I saw a store across the road. Make me a list of what'll get us through tonight and tomorrow and I'll head over there and pick it up."

"Really?" Her eyes lit up. "That'd be great. I planned on making the bed and taking care of general housekeeping stuff. I'll do that while you're gone and then I'll fix us lunch when you get back."

Kyle snagged her wrist. "Neither me or Hank expects you to cook and clean for us, Lainie."

"I know. But it makes sense for me to keep track of it, since you guys will be busy. I'm sure we can work out some kind of beneficial trade."

He bussed her cheek. "Count on it. And for the record? I'm better at fetching and carrying than I am at cooking."

"Good to know." Lainie jotted down a few items and passed him the paper with a breezy, "And anything else that strikes your fancy."

At the store, after he'd loaded what he could comfortably carry across the busy road, Kyle saw a bunch of sunflowers. He immediately thought of Lainie's sunshiny smile and added those to his basket before he checked out.

Holding the flowers behind his back, Kyle knocked on the camper door.

She peeked out the small window inset in the door before she opened it. "Why did you knock?"

He whipped the flowers out and said, "Surprise."

"Kyle!" Lainie plucked them from his hands. "They're beautiful. You are so sweet. Thank you." She peppered his face with kisses. "I might have to send you to the store all the time."

As they shelved the groceries, Kyle watched Lainie covertly, surprised at how much he enjoyed doing simple domestic things with her. Usually he had the overwhelming urge to run when women set up housekeeping. But she was fascinating. The sexy way she bit her lip when she was thinking. The continual—but completely pointless—way she smoothed back the loose tendrils of hair.

He wanted her with an all-consuming ache.

Lainie gulped the last of her water. As soon as the bottle cleared her lips, Kyle's mouth was on hers, taking the kiss he'd craved. Then he slowed the passion. Stroking her velvety wet tongue against his. Each pull into the soft depth of her mouth tightened his balls. Lengthened his cock.

Lust and comfort were a potent combination.

Kyle ended the kiss in playful increments. "Damn. I've been dying to do that all day."

"Don't let me stop you." She teased the hollow of his cheek with her lips. "You smell good. I could lick you up."

"Don't let me stop you," he murmured.

She froze. "Wait. Are we supposed to stop? Can I just jump on you? Or are we supposed to ask Hank? Or do we tell him after?"

Kyle cupped her jaw and tilted her head back. "Can't we just go with the jumping-on-me part and figure the rest out later?"

Lainie plastered her body to his and kissed him stupid.

He worked the buttons on her blouse until she shimmied out of it and ditched her bra. His cock pressed painfully against his zipper when he bent to tug her jeans free from her legs. "Thank God you wore sandals and not boots."

"Who cares about my footwear; hurry up."

Was Lainie impatient to fuck him because it was so good between them? Or in a hurry to get off and get it over with before Hank came back?

Does it really matter?

No. Not really. Sometimes a quick fuck was a quick fuck and nothing else.

Kyle pushed her against the ladder hanging from the bed platform. "Grab the top rung," he urged between kisses.

When Lainie grabbed the bars, the arch of her spine lifted her breasts exactly to his mouth level. He groaned and suckled the tips until she writhed, undulating her hips closer to his.

"Condom," she said, panting.

"Got one right here." Shit. No, he didn't. "Do. Not. Move." He dug through his duffel bag, found one, rolled it on, and was back between her thighs within thirty seconds. "Hold on." Palming her soft ass cheeks, he canted her hips, impaling her in one fast, deep thrust.

She moaned. "Yes. Like that."

Plunge and retreat. The creamy whiteness clinging to the latex was a fucking rush, proof that she wanted him as much as he wanted her.

Her breasts bounced with his every thrust, nipples hard and begging for his mouth. But he was beyond focusing attention on her beautiful tits. He needed to come so fucking bad it was like a fever.

"It's . . . right . . . there." She practically sobbed as she started to come.

The intimate internal kiss of her cunt muscles spasming around his dick drove him over the edge. His hips flexed of their own accord as his balls drained.

"Mmm."

Kyle lifted his head from where he'd buried it in Lainie's neck. "I'll have to buy you flowers more often."

Chapter Twelve

"Hank. Good to see you."

Hank returned Lyle Barclay's vigorous handshake. "Good to be here."

"Have a seat."

The Barclay Investment Group had been Hank's biggest sponsor for the past five years. The group kept their fingers in quite a few rodeo pies, including fronting the money for stock contractors, sponsoring rodeo PA systems and electronic scoreboards, as well as supplying big-screen TVs and live entertainment.

Hank usually met with a rep from Barclay informally under their signature white tent. But this time he was meeting the big boss. Out of the blue. Their annual discussion about sponsorship dollars normally took place at the corporate offices in Cheyenne. Not in a tent with kids hollering and rock music blaring from the Coors party tent.

"Am I in trouble or something?" Hank said lightly.

"No, son, not at all."

It amused Hank that Lyle always called him *son*, even when the man was barely ten years older.

"I'll admit I was surprised to see your name on the request sheets for various events over the next couple weeks."

Hank remained mum. Banker types loved to hear the sound of their own voices. Lyle would get to the point in his own sweet time. It wouldn't do Hank a lick of good to try to press the issue.

"Looks to me like you're wanting to fill the bullfighter spots across the upper Western circuits. A different one every night, with a few exceptions of two-day events. Plus, you requested afternoon and evening performances at a couple of unrelated events back-to-back." Lyle pushed his glasses back up his nose and set the sheaf of papers on the picnic table. "You develop itchy feet all of a sudden?"

"Not me so much as my buddy Kyle Gilchrist."

Lyle frowned. "The bull rider? Isn't he in the EBS?"

"Formerly." Hank gave him a brief rundown. "Since we've been buddies for years, I offered to travel with him. I've heard a lot about Cowboy Christmas, but never participated, so I figured now was as good a time as any to get the lowdown."

"So does Gilchrist plan on going back to the EBS?"

Hank shrugged. "This is only his second event in the CRA, so I don't think he knows. Why?"

"Just wondered if he planned to return the favor. Getting you an introduction into the EBS."

"Well, Lyle, with all due respect, I don't need Kyle Gilchrist to get me an introduction to the EBS. My reputation as a bullfighter speaks for itself."

"I take it you've been approached by the EBS staff?"

It never crossed Hank's mind to lie. "Yes. I talked to Bryson Westfield last weekend. He's interested in me."

Lyle's fingers did a rolling tap across the papers. "How interested?"

"Interested enough to offer me a second audition in Tulsa."

Silence.

"I appreciate your candor, Hank. I hope you'll appreciate mine. If it's only about the money, well, we can work on that part." Lyle leaned across the table. "The EBS has their own way of doing things."

"Some say the same about the CRA," Hank volleyed back.

"True. But the difference is they're trying to build an empire. We're trying to sustain a way of life. A life you lead on your family ranch when you're not facing off with a bull."

"Are you saying you don't want me to audition for them, Lyle?"

Lyle shook his head. "I encourage you to audition for them. I'm glad they see the talent in you we've always seen. But before you take their offer, will you give us a chance to counter?"

How bizarre. Hank never imagined his services were worth a price war. "You speaking for the CRA now?"

"No. I'm speaking as your sponsor. Bear in mind the EBS has their own set of official sponsors. Their bullfighters are only allowed to wear those names—on and off the dirt. So if you choose to go with them, I'll have no choice but to sever our sponsorship."

That sounded almost like a threat, which never sat well with Hank. "Lemme ask you something."

"Go ahead."

"If I'm worth more money, why hasn't it been offered to me before now?"

Lyle grinned a greasy banker's smile. "Because you never asked. Also, we assumed you were content working at the level you've stayed at the last five years."

"The level I've stayed at?" Hank repeated.

"Filling in where needed. Even though you're immensely qualified, you've never been selected for the AFR or the Circuit Finals. But only because bullfighting seems more like your hobby than your vocation."

Much as the truth stung, Lyle had a point. Hank's main responsibility was to the ranch. So why hadn't Abe protested when Hank told him he was flitting off for three weeks?

Good question. Hank never wanted to be a hobby rancher any more than he wanted to be a hobby bullfighter. But it appeared he was both. It smarted that it'd taken someone like Lyle Barclay to point it out.

Hank stood. "You've certainly given me plenty to think about. Right now, I have to get my head in the game for tonight."

"The stock contractor definitely brought rank stock. Be careful out there."

"I will. Thanks." Hank reseated his hat and ambled out of the tent, more confused than ever.

∞

Lainie was sated after the sexy interlude with Kyle.

Sated and completely unapologetic.

Lord. When Kyle had looked at her like that, green eyes hooded beneath sooty lashes, lips parted, everything feminine inside her purred. Roared, actually. She'd acted on that animal instinct without hesitation.

No awkwardness lingered after they'd slipped their clothes back on. They'd laughed and eaten lunch. Explored every nook and cranny of the camper.

The place was bigger than she'd thought. The narrow living and dining area was bookended with a bedroom at the back and another bed in the crawl-up sleeping compartment above the truck cab. The kitchen boasted an almost full-size refrigerator, a sink, and a two-burner cooktop. A minuscule bathroom contained a toilet, a sink, and a shower stall that seemed cramped even for someone her size. She had no idea how Hank fit in there.

Kyle had stretched out on the bench seat with his hat low over his eyes.

It'd been so long since Lainie had leisure time she had no idea what to do with herself.

"Why you so antsy, sugar?" Kyle said without moving.

"I'm always doing something. Sitting here feels like I'm wasting time."

"Welcome to life on the road."

She crossed her arms over her chest. "What do you do on the road?"

"I'm either driving or sleeping or at the grounds."

"That's it?"

"Yep."

"I won't survive three days, let alone three weeks," she muttered.

He pushed his hat up and looked at her. "Maybe you oughta rest up. Me 'n' Hank ain't gonna be too happy if you're too tired and cranky to be with us when we get done rodeoin' tonight."

That made her blush.

Kyle smirked and tugged his hat back down.

She unpacked her bag. She found two drawers beneath the bed frame that were already half full of hunting shit. She consolidated the stuff into one, which left her with a puny drawer. Damn good thing she hadn't overpacked. She kicked the drawer shut and attempted to hang her clothes in the shallow closet. But the door kept sticking and she had to slam it a couple of times to get it to shut.

When Lainie turned around, Kyle leaned in the doorway. He wasn't sporting his usual devil-may-care grin. The glint in his eyes sort of scared her. "What?"

"You done makin' enough noise to wake the dead?"

"It's not my fault the cabinet door is broken—"

"Enough," Kyle said with a sharp edge she'd never heard from him. "You're bored. I get it. I've got a cure." He advanced on her. "Strip to nothin' and lay on the bed."

Lainie's heart started beating faster.

"Not a request, Lainie. Get cracking." Kyle unhooked his belt. Toed off his boots. Kept staring at her as he unzipped his jeans.

"What are you doing?"

Off went his shirt. "I'm solving the boredom problem for you by giving you something to do with your mouth and hands." Off went his Wranglers.

He wasn't kidding. His cock bounced against his belly. He was already fully erect.

They'd just had sex an hour ago. Why was his unusually high-handed behavior turning her on?

"Last warning, woman. Or I'll get the cuffs out."

Kyle had brought handcuffs?

The camper door slammed. Two seconds later Hank stood in the doorway. His gaze moved over Lainie—still fully clothed—and then to Kyle, who was buck-ass naked. "What'd I miss?"

"Little Miz Lainie is bored."

Hank's eyebrows winged up. "Already? We've only been here five hours."

"I was fixing to focus her restless energy. Wanna help?"

"Damn fine idea." Hank's clothes flew off him.

Lainie's clothing should've gone up in flames from their fiery gazes, yet she remained locked in place.

"I warned you. My warnings ain't idle, sugar. Come here," Kyle said.

She backed up, but there was nowhere to go.

Kyle and Hank laughed.

"Hank, get her nekkid. I'm grabbing the cuffs."

Hank folded his arms over his bare chest. "I'll count. When I hit fifteen, whatever clothes you're wearing will be cut off. We clear?"

She nodded.

"One."

It was hard to undo buttons with shaking hands because Hank's deep voice enunciated every number. She swore the deep sound vibrated in her blood and pulsed between her legs.

"Eleven."

Lainie kicked off her jeans. "Done."

"Good. On the bed. Arms above your head."

The mattress had no give when she bounced butt first. Her breasts jiggled, which caught Hank's attention.

Then Kyle clicked a set of steel handcuffs around her wrists after he'd threaded the links through the headboard. She automatically tested them. Like the bed, there was no give.

If the look in Kyle's eye was any indication, there was no give in him either.

This darker edge inflamed her and she swallowed hard.

Kyle straddled her chest, tucking his knees under her armpits and his cock in the valley of her cleavage. His shaft rubbed the soft swells while his thumbs strummed her nipples.

"Where do you want me?" Hank asked.

"Your choice. I'm gonna fuck her tits and then her mouth."

His matter-of-fact tone dispatched another jolt of desire from head to toe and everywhere in between.

"Hand me a pillow."

Kyle yanked up both pillows and tossed them to Hank.

"Lift your hips," Hank commanded. "This pussy is mine."

Lainie obeyed, keeping her eyes on Kyle's face—not that he was looking at her.

"Hand me the lube," Kyle said to Hank.

The tube was passed. He squirted a line between her breasts. Then his hands were squeezing the fleshy globes together as his cock pushed in and out of the tight tunnel he'd created. "Ah, fuck. I like that."

Hank used his finger in a side-to-side motion on her clit as he worked his cock into her pussy.

More, *more*, *more*, echoed in her lust-addled brain. She tried to arch up to force Hank to sink into her completely, but his grip on her hips kept her locked down. He growled at her.

Kyle's eyes were riveted to her chest as he snapped his pelvis. Driving against her pliant flesh. Thumbs strumming over her nipples. Focused on the visual of his cock disappearing into the narrow channel he'd created, then watching as the head peeped out below the hollow of her throat.

The sexy look of need on his face was almost enough to get her off.

"This isn't working," Hank said. Kyle stilled as Hank scrambled to his knees. He adjusted the pillows under her ass and she let him angle her lower body, placing the backs of her thighs against his muscled chest. He withdrew and slammed back in.

Lainie gasped. Goose bumps dotted her legs, creating a tightening in her groin. *God, yes!* she thought, but didn't shout, because Hank would probably stop fucking her, just because he could.

Hank groaned. "That's better."

"She likes it too," Kyle murmured.

Her hands clenched into fists and she jerked against

the cuffs as the men fucked her. Showed her who retained control. Who was in charge of her pleasure.

Being bored had never been so good.

The humid, heady scent of sweat and sex, mixed with the sounds of harsh male breathing, turned the room into a sultry playground of carnal delights. Both men were lost to sexual greed. Skin—slapping, rubbing, sliding, gliding—against skin.

Abruptly, Kyle released her breasts and rose up on his knees. He brought one hand beneath her neck, using the other to guide his cock to her mouth. "Suck the head."

Her lips closed over the crown, beneath the rim, and she flicked her tongue back and forth over the sweet spot.

"That's it. Faster. I'm fucking close."

He stayed still, one hand braced on the wall, the other behind her neck, eyes avid as her mouth worked his cock. Kyle's musky, masculine scent overwhelmed her, as did her need to please him. To hear that grunt of satisfaction as he came. To know she'd brought him there.

Then it happened. He growled, "Open," and shoved deep.

She'd barely gotten control of her gag reflex when he started coming down her throat.

"Swallow," he demanded. "All of it."

She watched Kyle's face. He threw back his head, closed his eyes, letting his mouth go slack as his cock pulsed on her tongue. His grip loosened on her neck as he gave himself over. An incredible feeling of power rolled through her at seeing his lack of control.

When their eyes met, he grinned widely, tracing her lips still wrapped around the root of his cock. "You look so gorgeous with my dick buried in your mouth."

Hank snorted.

That was when Lainie realized Hank hadn't moved at all while Kyle had gotten off.

"You done?" Hank asked.

Kyle glanced over his shoulder at him. "Impatient much?"

"Fuck, yeah. I was bein' polite, not letting her come so she didn't sink her teeth into your dick."

"Thoughtful." Kyle caressed Lainie's face as he pulled out. Then he moved and lay alongside her.

"My turn." Hank curled his big palms over the tops of her thighs above her knees and hammered into her.

As much as Lainie loved the driving force of his thrusts, she needed direct contact with her clit. "Touch me."

"Eventually." Kyle toyed with her nipples. Dragging his rough knuckles up and down her damp skin until that skin quivered beneath his roving touch. Flirting with her bikini line, but his fingers never breached the curls covering her mound.

Lainie made a disgruntled noise.

Then Kyle's grinning face was inches from hers. "Still bored?"

Hank laughed.

Somehow she stopped herself from cursing at both of them.

A slippery finger skated across her clit. She gasped as it happened again, but on a slower pass. A more thorough pass.

Then it stopped.

Dammit. She moaned and thrashed, to no avail.

Hank grunted and stroked two more times, shoving deep on the last plunge. "Fuck."

Lainie felt his cock lengthen inside her. Even through the condom she felt the pulses of his cock head jerking against her swollen tissues. She bore down on him, hoping that extra stimulation would kick her into orgasm.

"Jesus, Lainie, keep doin' that."

She squeezed and released. Hank emitted a whimpering moan she'd never heard before, which made her forget about her own lack of orgasm and focus on giving him one that would utterly blow his mind.

He slowed. Stilled. Hank pulled out, dropped to his knees, and settled his mouth over her clit at the same time Kyle licked her nipple.

"You've been very obedient," Kyle murmured as he pressed her breasts together to tongue both her nipples at the same time. "We should reward that."

"Yes. God. Yes. Please."

Hank's lips nipped at the flesh surrounding her clit. A teasing scrape of his teeth. Then he suctioned his mouth over the throbbing heart of her and began a full-out assault with his clever tongue.

Lainie screamed as the orgasm flattened her. Throbbing pulses zapped her body as she thrashed against the hungry mouths devouring her most intimate spots. She wanted more, and yet the stimulus was too much. The handcuff chain rattled as she attempted to jerk free to push them away.

Then the twinges faded. And stopped. She floated into a fuzzy state where sleep beckoned.

Low male voices teased the edges of her subconscious, but movement to or away from the sound was impossible. Two clicks echoed and her arms were freed. She immediately curled up on her side.

"I think we plumb wore her out."

"I reckon you're right. Lainie? You okay?"

"Tired. Just wanna rest my eyes a bit."

Two sets of hands skated over her skin. She sighed. A blanket covered her. A pillow was tucked under her head.

More male chuckles, and then nothing.

∞

Hank made sandwiches. He ate light before an event, something he and Kyle had in common. They didn't speak of what'd gone down with Lainie. No reason to rehash it when they'd both been there.

After they finished the food, Kyle said, "What happened with Barclay?"

Hank rubbed the bridge of his nose. "Somehow he got wind of the meeting I had with the EBS. It don't take a genius-level IQ to see I'm thinking about jumping ship." He sipped his water. "So will it bother you if I do get selected for the EBS bullfighting team?"

"Nah. They'd be fools not to choose you. You're damn good."

That gave Hank pause.

"When you talked to Bryson Westfield with the EBS, did he ask if you'd competed in any of the ABA competitions?" Kyle asked.

"Actually, yes, he did."

"Not surprised. Bryson believes those kinds of competition separate the men from the boys. The wheat from the chaff. The cream rises to the top and all those lame-ass sayings that he'll bore you to fuckin' tears with if you let him ramble on." Kyle fussed with the brim of his hat. "Have you entered any of them bullfighting showcases?"

"Yeah, I just don't advertise it much."

"Because you lost?"

"No. I've done well. It's just not my thing."

Kyle frowned at him. "Why not?"

Hank struggled to explain. "Don't get me wrong. The guys I work with in the CRA are great. But I don't live close enough to anyone to work out the details of competing as a bullfighting team when I'm running a ranch during the week. So that leaves me in the freestyle form. Not my fave."

"Am I to take that as saying Hank Lawson's competitive streak has mellowed?"

Fuck no. Especially where Lainie was concerned.

"That's another reason why I don't like to compete in those showcases. For me, squaring off against a bull is business. I'm there to save bull riders. Period."

"Knowing the EBS, they'll offer to pay you very well to save riders."

"I wasn't hedging when I told Lyle Barclay I haven't decided."

"Does Lainie know about the potential gig with the EBS?"

Hank shook his head. He got the vibe that working the EBS circuit wasn't her first choice.

"Speaking of Lainie . . ."

Hank's head snapped up at Kyle's not-so-casual tone. "What about her?"

"Tomorrow night she's mine. You had her in your bed for a night. I get equal time, remember?"

"We're still in Gillette tomorrow night. What am I supposed to do on your 'special' night with her? Sleep in the bunk with my iPod cranked? Pretend you guys ain't even here? How about tonight? I could hang out with the guys for a few hours."

"No dice." Kyle showed his teeth. "You had her to yourself most of the day yesterday and all night. I'd only get her from nine o'clock on after the rodeo ends. Plus, after me banging her earlier and then us double-teaming her just now, I want her to be fully alert and rested, not sore."

Hank's smile dried up. "You fucked Lainie while I was at the sponsors' meeting today?"

"Is that a problem?" Kyle asked evenly.

Fuck, yeah. But he'd be goddamned if he'd give Kyle the satisfaction of seeing his jealousy. His eyes flicked to the flowers and then back to his smarmy friend. "Did you gift her with posies before or after you fucked her?"

"What do you think?"

Before.

Bastard had it all planned how he'd edge Hank out. Flowers, cozy domestic scenes, and the all-important time alone, where he'd probably do Kama Sutra–type sex shit to Lainie that Hank had never even heard of. Or some multiorgasmic tantric stuff.

Fuck that.

Kyle didn't know how far Hank would go in this battle to win Lainie's heart.

Hank smiled. "Sure. She's yours tomorrow night. Fair's fair, right?"

But the truth was, this was all-out war.

Chapter Thirteen

For Hank, the next day was a whirlwind of sponsor activity.

He barely had time to eat with Lainie, let alone fuck her. Which made him cranky, since tonight was Kyle's one-on-one time with her.

But she wasn't lounging in the camper wearing slinky lingerie, waiting for Kyle to take her to heights of sexual ecstasy. She was sitting in the stands watching the performance.

In the ready room, Hank began the ritual of dressing. He dressed the same way every time. First he slipped on the spandexlike athletic shorts, which were lightweight, yet contained panels that offered additional protection from hooves and horns. Next he donned the vest crafted out of the same material as the shorts. The piece wasn't as bulky as the vests required for bull riders. The formfitting, nonconfining vest allowed bullfighters to make the faster movements they needed.

He dropped to a crouch. Leaped into the air, drawing

his knees tight to his chest on the jump. Then he landed back in a crouch. Swinging his arms, letting his elbows lead the way as he loosened up his midsection. Side stretches. Elbow-to-knee crunches. Shadowboxing. Lifting his shoulders. Lowering his shoulders. Neck rolls.

Then he slipped on the long nylon basketball shorts emblazoned with the sponsor's logo. At most rodeos Hank wore the Barclay uniform, although sometimes he wore the one from the Big J Rodeo Stock Company.

Depending on the situation and previous injuries, he'd wrap whatever body part needed it. But tonight he felt good. No additional wrapping was required—even though Lainie would disagree about his needing extra protection over the contusion on his quad. Hank tugged on long athletic socks that ended below his knees. Tied his shoes. Strapped on his knee pads. Once he wore all his equipment, he repeated the stretching exercises.

Some bullfighters smeared greasepaint on their faces, which was their choice. But Hank figured that, as most guys in his profession were still trying to change the public's perception about the differences between rodeo clowns and bullfighters, donning greasepaint was a step backward.

Hank ambled out and noticed the other two bullfighters leaning against the concrete waiting for him. "Peck and Strand!"

Peck gave him a nod of acknowledgment.

"Hank Lawson, you look like dog shit," Strand drawled in his thick Texas accent.

"Must've happened when I started hanging out in the Lone Star State."

"Har, har. You see the docket tonight?"

"Didn't have much of a chance to study it. What've we got?"

"They ain't limiting the number of contestants. Thirty-seven entrants. Don't recognize half their names. So I'm hoping like hell it ain't a bunch of rookies."

"Are there enough bulls?"

"Appear to be," Peck said.

"Let's head up to the corrals. I wanna take a peek so it looks like I did my homework."

Chaos ruled behind the scenes. Usually the excitement behind the chutes was enough to make him grin, but tonight his enthusiasm was a bit lackluster.

"Only one thing puts a sour look like that on a man's face." Strand waggled his bushy black eyebrows. "Who is she?"

He muttered, "She's everything."

A tall, thin woman, decked out in a rhinestone shirt and skintight pants, brushed past them. She was surrounded by a group of cowboys, and every man hung on her every word. Hank stopped and stared after her. Something about her seemed familiar. Mighty familiar. But he couldn't place it.

Then she was gone.

Huh.

Hank wandered through the bullpens. While he waited for the bull riding to start, Hank watched the bulldogging. Normally he concentrated on limbering up. But tonight, Hank wanted to see the rodeo through a spectator's eyes.

Lainie's eyes?

Yes. Dammit. He hated that she was sitting alone. She spent way too much time by herself.

Music blared as the official rodeo sponsor truck rolled into the arena. Men jumped out of the truck bed, positioning the Coors barrels for barrel racing at the designated intervals.

Sixteen competitors was a big showing for the field of barrel racing. Sometimes he wondered how Celia would've fared if he and Abe hadn't insisted she quit after the disastrous fall that'd broken her leg and forced them to put her horse down. After losing their parents, he and Abe had gone ballistic; they couldn't fathom losing Celia too. So they'd done the only thing to keep her safe—forbidden her to compete.

And your job fighting bulls is so much safer?

Hank blinked. It'd been a long time since he'd thought of Celia's old argument. Did she resent them for making her quit the sport? Especially after Lainie agreed that they treated her like a child?

The barrel racers were milling about on their horses. Hank limbered up as he watched. He half heard the announcement of the last competitor, CeCe Murray from outside Rawlins, Wyoming. The home-state girl raced to the best time and finished in first place with a damned impressive ride.

As the barrels were pulled, Hank, Strand, and Peck waited across the arena from the chutes for their names to be called. National honors and winning bullfighting competitions were touted as each bullfighter made his way across the dirt. When the announcer boomed the standard, "Who's ready to see some bull ridin'?" that same lackluster crowd went wild.

Hank was oblivious to everything but the rider on the back of the bull. Not many of them lasted. One rider had gotten hung up in the rope and was taken for a ride before Hank freed the wrap.

Kyle was up next. He'd drawn White Lightning Kiss, a Charolais/Brahman cross with a reputation for trying to pulverize riders into meat. According to the stats, White Lightning Kiss had been ridden only two times on thirty-two outs. Both those rides had scored ninety-three points.

Come on, buddy. Stay on.

After a last-minute adjustment on the bull's back, Kyle nodded to the gatekeeper. Hank was right there. Close enough to the rider to offer immediate assistance if need be; far enough away from the bull to let the ride progress unimpeded. He didn't watch the ride as much as think what could go wrong with it.

Luckily, nothing did. Kyle hung on for the full eight seconds. After the buzzer sounded, Kyle released his rope. He sailed into the air and landed on his hands and knees before booking it to the fence.

The boot stamping and clapping signaled the spectators' opinion of Kyle's ride. The announcers filled the time waiting for the judge's decision. Finally the announcement came. "Ladies and gentlemen, how about a . . . ninety-one?"

Whistles, more clapping.

"Our leader from last night proved it ain't no fluke he's on the top of the board. Only eight riders to go. Let's see if the Wyoming cowboy can hang on to the top spot."

The rest of the rides went quickly as only one guy managed to cover his bull. Folks began to leave—which boggled Hank's mind. Didn't matter where the rodeo was held, few spectators stuck around for the award ceremony. Some people claimed handing out the money was less interesting than a rodeo participant getting handed his ass. But Hank believed that since most folks in attendance were ranchers, they just wanted to get on home. Since Kyle had finished big, Hank hung around for the presentations.

Bareback and saddle bronc winners were announced first. Kyle bumped fists with a guy named Breck. Then team roping, tie-down roping, and steer wrestling. Barrel racing and bull riding winners were named last, in rapid succession.

The strangest thing happened when CeCe Murray

walked up to claim her Black Hills Gold belt buckle and her check. Kyle went rigid, then grabbed the woman by the arm and hauled her up to the tips of her ropers.

Shit.

The Breck guy intervened long enough for Kyle to get his buckle. Afterward Kyle continued to berate the poor woman with the misfortune of standing next to him in the awards line.

Hank leaped the fence and raced across the arena to calm Kyle down. But when he arrived, he understood Kyle's behavior. He barked the first thing that popped into his head: "Jesus Christ, Celia. What the hell are *you* doin' here?"

Holy fucking shit . . . this tarted-up woman was his baby sister? His plain-Jane baby sister? Who wore cast-off men's flannel shirts, ripped jeans, and the same damn ugly pair of work boots every damn day? Who was this beauty with the perfectly made-up face? The artfully braided hair? The skintight shirt that shimmered with beads and metallic thread and showed off her cleavage? Not to mention the rainbow-colored rhinestone belt and painted-on jeans that highlighted the curve of her hips? She was an absolute fucking knockout.

And he'd knock out any man who looked at her. Lay him out cold. His eyes scanned the other winners, but the only guy paying attention to the outburst was Breck. His gaze was firmly glued on Celia's ass.

Hank stepped forward, between Breck and his sister's butt. "What the fuck you looking at?"

"Her." Breck's arms stayed crossed over his chest. "'Cause, hot damn, is she ever mighty fine. She yours?"

"Yes, she's mine; she's my fuckin' sister, asshole."

"Hank, knock it off," Kyle snapped. "Breck, thanks for sticking around, but we've got this under control."

Breck sidestepped Kyle, addressing Celia. "Damn fine

ridin' tonight, sugar pie. Any time you wanna get a beer or something, let me know."

"How about right now?" Celia asked through clenched teeth.

He laughed. "Oh, I like to flirt with danger, believe me, but I ain't getting in the middle of this. Later." Breck winked at Celia and ambled off.

"I really like your friends, Kyle," Celia cooed.

"You didn't answer Hank," Kyle reminded her sharply. "What in God's name are you doin' competing in barrel racing? Far as I know, *sugar pie*, you were banned for life from this activity."

"Not by any official organization, just my overprotective brothers. When I turned eighteen I made my own decision about what I wanted to do with *my* life and *my* time." Her defiant chin kicked up a notch. "I get that you're surprised—"

"I'm shocked down to the bone," Hank snapped. "So this has been goin' on for three years?"

"It's been goin' on for a hell of a lot longer than that. Did you see her ride? Jesus. She was amazing. No fuckin' way did she get that damn good in such a short amount of time." Kyle loomed over her. "You never quit, did you?"

"I didn't quit practicing. I quit *competing*. Big difference."

"No difference," Hank retorted. "Where'd you get the money to start hitting the rodeos? Because I know it ain't cheap."

"I earned it."

Hank laughed. "Doin' what?"

"What the hell does it matter to you? I pay my own traveling expenses. And my entry fees. I take care of boarding my horse. It's my money—"

"What horse you riding? It ain't one of ours."

There was that stubborn look again.

"Where'd you get a horse of that caliber, Celia?"

She grudgingly said, "I bought Mickey from Eli as a cow horse. But neither of us knew how much natural ability he had until I started putting him through his paces."

Hank gave Kyle a look that promised he'd deal with Eli.

A look Celia intercepted with a terse, "Leave Eli out of this. I mean it, Hank. You wanna piss me off worse—"

"Piss *you* off? You wanna talk about torqued off, little sis, just how long have you been sneaking around behind Abe's and my backs? Lying to us?"

Her mouth flattened. Her eyes glowed with pure anger.

"Answer him," Kyle demanded.

When Celia remained mum, Hank also got in her face. "Fine. I'm tired of arguing with you anyway. Get your shit packed and get on home. Abe will hafta deal with you until I get back."

"No."

Hank froze. "What did you say?"

"I believe she said no," Lainie said behind them.

Both he and Kyle turned around.

Fucking great. He tried to calm down, if only for Lainie's sake. "Lainie. Darlin'—"

"Don't you dare *Lainie, darlin'* me, Hank." Lainie glared at Kyle. "You either, Kyle." She moved beside Celia. "You okay?"

"Yes and no. Yes, because I won." She held up the gold buckle. "No, because . . . well, you heard."

"Ignore them. Celebrate the good. It was a great ride. I videotaped it with my cell phone, if you want me to send it to you. I'm definitely sending it to Tanna."

"You are?"

"Yes, but I'll warn you it's not the greatest quality—"

"Wait a second. How did *you* know to videotape CeCe. . . ?" A fresh burst of anger erupted and Hank loomed over Lainie. "You fucking *knew* she was competing in barrel racing?"

"Yep."

"How?"

Lainie stabbed him in the chest with her index finger. "It doesn't matter. What does matter is that you are being a complete and total dickhead to your only sister."

Hank's mouth opened. Closed.

"I'll say this once. Celia is not a baby. She is a twenty-one-year-old woman who you and Abe still treat like a girl. I watched you both do it, so don't tell me I don't understand where you're coming from. I do. Believe me, I do. If you want to drive her away, by all means, keep it up. Continue to make all of her life decisions for her, because she'll decide to leave, and that'll be the best decision she makes."

"Hank and Abe only want what's best for her, Lainie," Kyle said.

"No. They want to control her. But you're in the same 'she's a little girl' mind-set they are."

"Maybe if Celia started acting responsible, Abe and me would take her more seriously." Right after Hank said it, he knew it was the wrong damn thing to say.

Celia stomped up to him. "Responsible? Who does all the books for the ranch? Makes sure the bills get paid on time? Checks that our grazing permits and all that other federal, state, and tribal paperwork is filed in quadruplicate?"

Lord. He'd really stepped in it.

"I've always done anything you've asked, Hank. Both you and Abe. The one thing I wanted in my life? You guys denied me. For my own good. So yeah, maybe it was rebellious to keep up with my training. There were so many times I wanted to tell you, but I knew you'd react like this. And guess what? I wasn't wrong."

Lainie rubbed Celia's arm in a show of support that both inflamed Hank and endeared her to him.

Kyle said, "What's wrong is that you're putting yourself at risk. It is childish not to give a shit that Hank and Abe both worry about you. It's selfish as hell, Celia."

"You're one to talk, Kyle. Didn't you tell me your mama begged you *not* to get on the back of a bull again? After you were seriously injured? What did you do after a full year's recovery time? Said 'too bad, so sad, Mama, see you later; I got me some bulls to ride.' So don't you dare lecture me about selfishness and childishness."

Hank bet Kyle was sorry he'd opened his big trap too.

Yet the man kept going. "Dressing like that ain't helping." He gestured to her clothing. "Don't lie and say this whole thing is only about you wanting to race around a buncha barrels. It's about you getting noticed by every damn cowboy in the place."

Celia shoved him. "You arrogant fucker. I caught you looking at my ass earlier tonight when you didn't know it was me."

Kyle's mouth dropped open. "I did not."

"Yes, you did. So what if guys notice me? It's a nice goddamn change from the pats on the head I get from every man within thirty miles of Muddy Gap, Wyoming, who only see me as Hank and Abe Lawson's baby sister."

Silence. But the glaring contest between all four of them could've started the hay bales on fire.

Nothing would get resolved tonight. Hank knew a cooling-off period was definitely in order. "Look. Can we talk about this later? When I get back to the ranch? I'll call Abe and give him a heads-up—"

"See? This is what I mean! *I* can talk to Abe. I don't need you running interference—or interfering—in my life, Hank."

"Fine." He threw up his hands. "Do whatever you

want. I keep forgetting you're a big girl. Are you gonna be pissed off and snap at me to mind my own business if I tell you to drive safe and call me when you get home?"

"No. I'll call you." Celia muttered, "Asshole."

Lainie took Celia aside and they spoke so quietly Hank couldn't hear. Which just added another layer of frustration to the already frustrating situation.

Kyle leaned over. "When the fuck did they get so chummy?"

"Fuck if I know."

The women hugged and Celia walked off without a backward glance.

Lainie approached them, hands jammed in her pockets. She started to speak, but apparently thought better of it. Then she too wandered off without a word.

Kyle grunted, echoing Hank's sentiments exactly. They headed to the changing rooms.

Most guys had already cleared out. The showers were empty, but Hank preferred the noise. Maybe he could block out the idea that his sister had lied to him for years. How had he not known?

Because you're so involved in your own life that you fail to see what's going on around you.

Not entirely true. Celia must've done a damn good job of hiding it, because Abe hadn't known about her secret barrel racing either. He snorted. Secret barrel racing. Like it was some sort of crime. When he put it in that context it was almost funny.

Almost.

He half listened while Kyle and some other bull rider rehashed every second of Kyle's ride. He hefted the shoulder strap of his bag. Those stories could go on forever, and Hank was anxious to talk to Lainie.

He'd made it about twenty steps when Kyle called out, "Hank, wait up."

He stopped.

"Don't it just figure that it's my night to be alone with Lainie and this happens."

Sad thing was, Hank couldn't even feel happy about that.

"Think she's cooled off by now?"

"I don't know. She ever been mad at you about something?"

"Nope. It's only been half an hour."

They walked through the campground. It was eerily quiet. No groups sitting around drinking beer. No kids running about. No teenagers groping in the shadows.

The lights were on in the back of the camper. Hank looked at Kyle, who pantomimed, *After you.*

Lainie was in her pajamas, brushing her teeth. She didn't acknowledge them besides slamming the bathroom door shut.

Not a good sign.

Kyle dumped his equipment bag and flopped in the chair by the table. Hank stood there like a dumb ass, waiting for her to respond to them.

Screw that. He was a take-charge guy. And as far as he could tell, she liked it when he exerted control. He knocked. "Lainie?"

"What?"

"Can we talk to you?"

The door banged open. Lainie's gaze zoomed from Hank to Kyle and she snapped, "Nope," ducking under Hank's arm.

Hank's hand blocked the upper doorframe, kept her from slamming the bedroom door in his face. "Why're you so pissed off at us?"

"Because of what you said to Celia. I watched how all of you—you, Abe, Kyle, and your assorted buddies—treat her. I've been treated that way, so maybe I am overly sensitive on her behalf. I know what it's like to have people who claim to love you try to keep you from doing something you really want. But what bugs me is *you* don't want to change. You expect *her* to."

Hank stared at her, openmouthed with shock.

"I don't want to get in the middle of your family issues. As you know, I have plenty of my own."

"Then why *are* you getting involved in them?" Hank demanded.

There was the look that indicated he'd gone too far. Shit.

"Back off, Hank. Go to bed and let me do the same."

"Fine. Let's go to bed." They could work out their issues between the sheets. When he started to enter the bedroom, Lainie held up her hand.

"No way are you sleeping in here with me tonight."

Kyle snickered.

Lainie peeked around Hank's shoulder. "Don't know why you're laughing, Kyle, because you're not sleeping in here either."

"What? Where the hell are we supposed to sleep?"

"Not my problem."

Hank was so stunned by the turn of events that when Lainie put her hands on his chest and shoved him, he stumbled back.

Then she slammed the door in his face.

Unbelievable.

He lifted his hand to knock, when Kyle spoke. "Let her be."

"Now, why would I do that?"

"Because she asked you to." Kyle stood and stretched. "She'll probably cool down by morning."

"And if she's still pissed off?"

"I guess we'll deal with it then. Looks like you 'n' me are bunk mates."

"Fuckin' awesome."

"Sucks worse for me, Hank. I thought I'd be snuggled up to soft, sweet-smelling curves and instead I'm stuck with you."

"Ain't no snuggling between us, hoss. You touch me and I'm decking you."

"Same goes," Kyle shot back.

Hank flashed his teeth. "But at least you showered and don't smell like the ass end of a bull."

"Ditto, buddy."

They undressed, Kyle down to nothing but skin. Even as a teen, Kyle had slept naked as a jaybird. After the threesomes with Lainie, it seemed prissy for Hank to ask him to put on a goddamn pair of underwear.

In the upper bunk Hank was wide-awake.

Kyle sighed. "I can hear them damn gears spinning. Whatcha thinking about so hard?"

"The EBS. If my tryout goes good, how it'd leave Abe running the ranch, mostly by himself. Especially if Celia is off running barrels."

Kyle was quiet. Too quiet.

"What?"

"You're a damn good bullfighter, Hank. I ain't just sayin' that. But don't give up what you've got to chase something that maybe ain't worth it in the long run."

"You don't think bein' in the EBS is worth it?"

"Maybe. I know if I had what you already do, I wouldn't be chasin' this rodeo life so damn hard."

He'd always known Kyle wanted a place of his own in Wyoming, around their hometown and their buddies. The only way Kyle could ever scrounge up the kind of money required to put a down payment on a ranch was to keep riding bulls. So Hank already had the dream Kyle was working toward.

"Just . . . be careful. You can get sucked—or suckered—

into doin' things with the EBS you wouldn't do otherwise. It's easy to overlook some of the behind-the-scenes stuff when the big paychecks are rolling in."

"Would you go back? If you switched to the EBS second-tier events and hit the top sixty again?" Hank asked.

"I don't know. Ask me when I've been in the CRA for more than a couple events."

Silence.

"So what're we gonna do about Lainie?"

"I say we wake her up with an apology she'll never forget."

Chapter Fourteen

Lainie was up and dressed early the next morning. By the time she'd roused the sleeping men, she'd knocked back two cups of coffee.

Hank stumbled down from the upper bunk. He wore the bleary-eyed look of a man whose routine had been interrupted. Served him right.

"What're you doin' up so early?"

"Says the rancher," she replied dryly.

"Funny. Maybe me 'n' Kyle had plans for this morning." He waggled his eyebrows.

"Maybe you and Kyle should've gotten up sooner." She sipped her coffee. "The early cowboy gets to stick his worm in the cowgirl and all that."

Kyle laughed. "We'll remember that for next time, sugar. Hank, hand me my duffel, will ya?"

He tossed it up to Kyle without looking away from Lainie. "You still sore at us?"

"Nope." She addressed Hank. "But figure out a different way to deal with Celia. Adult-to-adult would be a good start."

"That I can do."

"You guys want breakfast?"

"Lainie. You don't have to cook for us," Kyle said.

"I'm already cooking for me. Might as well add a couple more eggs to the frying pan. Scrambled all right?"

"Sounds good."

"Count me in." Kyle hopped down wearing a pair of surfer shorts. She had half wondered if he'd arrive at the table naked. Hank also looked relieved that Kyle had covered up his dangly man bits.

Lainie cracked a half dozen eggs in the electric skillet. Hank set the table and poured Kyle a cup of coffee. Hard to believe they'd never done this domestic scene before. It seemed so routine.

When they finished eating, Kyle flipped open his cell phone and checked the time. "Bein's I'm on the day driving shift, let's hit the road and get to Sheridan so I can check in."

"What's after Sheridan tonight?"

"Billings has an early afternoon performance tomorrow and Red Lodge has a performance tomorrow night."

"So we're not actually camping anywhere for a couple of days?"

Hank shook his head.

"Hank, since you're driving tonight, you gonna crawl back up in the bunk and get some more shut-eye?" Kyle asked.

A look of challenge passed between them.

"What's going on with you two?"

"Ask Kyle," Hank said curtly.

Lainie's hands stayed curled around her mug. "Kyle?"

Kyle shrugged. "At the ranch Hank had you in his

bed all night. I want equal time. It'll be you and me alone in the back of the camper on the way to Billings tonight."

Part of her wanted to ask if she had a say in whose bed she ended up in. Another part wished they'd spend time together only as a threesome. Then she wouldn't have to worry whether each man was getting equal time. Or that she was picking one over the other.

"You okay with that, Lainie?" Kyle asked softly.

"Are we being completely honest here?"

Two nods of agreement.

"I'll remind you that even though I fucked Hank a couple of times and slept in his bed that night, I also messed around with Kyle during the day." She let her gaze move back and forth between them. "Does that mean in order to be fair I have to mess around with Hank at some point today?"

"*Have* to mess around?" Hank repeated.

"You know what I mean."

"No, I guess I don't," he said brusquely.

"Hank—"

"Have to," he grumbled. Then he snaked his arm around her waist and brought her onto his lap, one hand curving around her neck as he kissed her.

Boy, did he kiss her. Pressing the rough pad of his thumb against her carotid, gauging every increased beat of her pulse. He teased and nibbled, keeping her off balance with the sensual blitz of his mouth.

Have to mess around. Right. If Hank kept it up, there'd be no question how she'd spend the traveling time to Sheridan: on her back.

Lainie lost herself in the immediate punch of need Hank's drugging kisses delivered. Beneath the surface of passion was a sense of comfort. Hank could rev her up and soothe her, all within the same kiss.

On the periphery of her awareness, she heard Kyle get up, walk to the bathroom, and close the door.

Hank released her mouth reluctantly and buried his face in the curve of her throat. "Will you stay back here with me? Let me love on you a little bit this morning?"

She pushed out of his arms. "No offense, but I'm ready to be out of this camper for a spell."

"Understood." He pecked her on the mouth and set her on her feet.

Lainie expected him to cajole her, to attempt to change her mind. But he didn't.

Aren't you disappointed he didn't try harder?

"I'll scrub up that skillet before I get myself ready." He squirted dish soap in the pan and poured water in.

She turned and smacked into Kyle's bare chest. His hard, muscular bare chest. Damn. He smelled tempting. A mix of toothpaste, deodorant, and warm male skin. Without thought, she brushed her lips across the delineated line of his pectorals, letting his chest hair tickle her chin and cheek. She kept nuzzling until a chuckle rumbled beneath her roving lips. Lainie tipped her head back to look at him. "What?"

Kyle hooked a chunk of hair behind her ear. "You constantly surprise me."

"What surprises you?"

He traced the shell of her ear down to the bottom lobe. "You've embraced this threesome business wholeheartedly. No inhibitions. If you want to make out with Hank, you do it. And here you are, just a few minutes later, giving me the sweetest morning kisses. I'll admit, I didn't know how you'd react faced with Hank's and my sexual demands."

"Have I passed?"

"With an A plus." He grinned. "But if you're looking to earn extra credit, I'll let you blow me right now."

"Nice try, but I am not a suck-up."

Hank snorted behind her.

"Well, I've planned some good stuff for you and me later tonight anyway, so I can wait."

Although Lainie was intrigued by his taunt, and she sensed Hank's curiosity, she waved Kyle off. "Bring it, bull rider. For now, let's get this rig on the road."

∞

They topped off the tank and hit the RV dump station. Kyle took the wheel for the relatively short trek from Gillette to Sheridan. The drive was stunning—flat dusty hills, rolling prairie, crested buttes, and the Big Horn Mountains looming west of the interstate. Big, bold, beautiful Wyoming.

She also enjoyed the ease with which the three of them were together. No mindless chattering. No awkward silences. No blathering one-sided cell phone conversations. No fighting over the tunes on the radio. No annoying food consumption. Just peace.

Sheridan was a quaint town with a main-street shopping district that boasted everything from high-end Western clothing boutiques to a bait and tackle shop. Lainie wasn't much of a shopper on her best day. But she had the strangest compulsion to duck into one of those exclusive stores and buy an outrageously sexy outfit to wear to the rodeo.

Or to wear tonight for Kyle?

Right. She'd be lucky if she kept on whatever she wore for fifteen seconds.

As soon as they'd entered the contestants' area and found a temporary place to park, Hank's cell phone rang.

"You have an eagle eye, Arvin; I just pulled in. Uh-huh. Who? No, I don't. No problem. Thirty minutes? Sure. See you."

Kyle cranked his head toward him. "What's up?"

"I'm bein' summoned. Evidently the rodeo promoter is requesting me. Says he knows Abe—and me by association."

"What's his name?" Kyle asked.

"Renner Jackson. Ring a bell?"

"Vaguely."

"With me too. Guess I'll get the scoop on him firsthand and report back." He clapped his hat on. "Lainie, what'll you be doin' while Kyle is registering?"

"I hadn't really thought about it. Why?"

"Just checking. We wouldn't want you to get . . . bored."

Heat curled in her abdomen when she recalled how thoroughly they'd dealt with her boredom.

Kyle choked back a laugh.

"Grab your stuff and come to the sponsors' tent with me. We'll see if the promoter is also supplying the medical team. Maybe there's room for you to help out tonight."

Any objection to accompanying him died when Hank put it like that. Even Kyle didn't lodge a protest.

"Do I have to wear a dress or anything?"

"Why're you asking me? You've been to sponsors' events."

"At night, the banquet, formal type of events, not during the day. Doc handles all that promotional stuff while I'm prepping the medical room and pimping the Lariat name."

Hank frowned. "Don't worry about it. You look great."

Lainie rolled her eyes. "No makeup, my hair in a ponytail. Yeah, I look real great."

"You look awesome. No matter what you do or don't wear," Kyle offered.

"I think so too," Hank said.

Maybe fishing for compliments smacked of neediness, but Lainie was compelled to ask the question that'd been weighing on her mind for months. "Why did you guys hook up with me? You both could've had your pick of the litter of buckle bunnies. Or rodeo queens. I'm not in the same league as those women."

Kyle angled across the seat, trapping her face in his calloused hands and her eyes with his. "Don't ever let me hear you say shit like that. When I saw you for the first time? With those wild red curls, that devilish smile, and beautiful, kind eyes, my heart just sort of . . . stopped. Then you checked out my injury in that no-nonsense manner, but you had such a tenderness about you, Lainie, a tenderness that knocked me sideways."

Oh, God. Kyle really had thought about the answer, apparently before she'd mustered the guts to ask him the question.

"I ain't as eloquent as Shakespeare here, but that's awful damn close to what I was gonna say," Hank said.

Flustered, she smiled. "Such sweet-talkin' cowboys, laying it on thick when I'm already a sure thing. But I'll take it. Even though I'd like a minute or ten to freshen up before Hank drags me to the sponsors' tent."

"Whatever you want. I'll wait." Hank leaned back in his seat.

"Me too," Kyle said, with a hint of challenge.

As Lainie jumped out of the cab she heard them snap at each other, but she didn't stick around to see what it was about.

∞

Lainie wore her Lariat ID, so at least she didn't look like a freeloading girlfriend. She half expected Hank to abandon her once they were ensconced in the tent, but he was determined to introduce her to everyone. It'd seemed like a good idea at the time. Now she wondered if she was being unfair to Kyle by acting like Hank's girlfriend in public.

Not that it would've mattered if she and Hank were a couple. A number of scantily clad women were roaming around checking out male buckle and bulge size. Including Hank's. If Hank had worn his official bullfighter clothing, the predatory ladies would've glommed onto him even more than they were already trying to.

How would you react if you were his girlfriend?

Rage. She wouldn't put up with another woman's hands on her man. Ever. Not in private and certainly not in public.

Was that what Hank and Kyle had fought about? How Hank would explain who Lainie was at an official event? How could Hank expect that Kyle wouldn't be upset?

"Lainie." Hank placed his hand on the small of her back and brought her forward. "I'd like you to meet Arvin Zimmerman. Arvin is an old bullfighter, but mostly an old BS-er these days."

She shook his hand. "Mr. Zimmerman. Nice to meet you."

"Miz Lainie. The pleasure is all mine. Especially since Hank here usually flies solo." Arvin's gaze fell to her name tag. "How long have you worked for Doc Dusty?"

"A little over two years."

"He seems to have his share of employee turnover in that company."

Snarky thing to say right off the bat. Lainie smiled tightly. "I wouldn't know. It's been the same people in my office since I started."

"At any rate, welcome. Hank, I'll need to bend your ear at some point before you take off." *Alone* was implied.

"Not a problem," Hank said smoothly, and steered Lainie to the food table.

The food was standard: a meat and cheese tray, sliced fresh fruit, crackers, a veggie tray, and assorted chips and dips. She'd barely loaded her plate and found a place to sit when Hank was called away.

A bevy of buckle bunnies sat at the opposite end of the long table. They glanced at her dismissively and gossiped about some poor girl's sluttish behavior.

A camera-toting man took candid shots of the partygoers. Lainie ducked her head, swirling a carrot stick through the puddle of ranch dressing, wishing she were anywhere else. She heard, "Excuse me?" and looked up.

The photographer had aimed the lens close enough to see every pore on her face and snapped off a shot.

She lifted an eyebrow. "The painted ladies at the end of the table are far more photogenic than me."

"But the fact that you don't want your picture taken makes you a more fascinating subject."

"Why would you think I'm camera-shy?"

That surprised him. "Because you ducked when you saw me."

"No." Lainie leaned closer, as if to confide in him. "I ducked because of the guy coming in behind you. You blocked me from his view, so thanks."

He turned, allowing her time to tuck her name badge inside her shirt. "Which guy?"

"Oh. He's gone now," she lied.

The photographer was distracted by a pair of double Ds and wandered off.

Hank plopped down. "I'd planned to swoop in and rescue you from Larry the Lech, but you did just fine on your own, darlin'."

Lainie kept her eyes on the pudgy man as he waddled outside. "Who is he?"

"Larry works for *Pro Rodeo* magazine. He gets great arena action shots but he also considers himself an investigative reporter and tries to stir things up." Hank snatched a green olive from her plate. "Nice deflection, by the way."

"Hank Lawson?"

Both their gazes darted to the man standing at the end of the table. "Yes?"

"I'm Renner Jackson."

Hank stood and took his outstretched hand. "Renner. Good to meet you. What can I do for you?"

Lainie watched the men sizing each other up. Renner was a good-looking guy. Dark blond hair sun-lightened to gold, deeply tanned features. Silvery blue eyes. Around the same height, build, and age as Hank, but nowhere in Hank's league, in Lainie's opinion.

"I thought I'd have Martin give you a heads-up that I wanted to talk to you because I wasn't sure if you remembered me."

"I'll be honest; I recognized your name. But you don't look familiar."

Renner chuckled. "Probably because the last time we saw each other we were about seven or eight years old. I lived in Muddy Gap with my grandparents, Rona and Bill Harking, for a year when my dad was stationed overseas. Second grade? In Miz Tatanalli's class."

"Ah. Miz Tata's class. I forgot all about her, even when I recall certain parts of her vividly."

"Yeah. Me too."

Hank smiled. "Hey, now I remember. You were the kid that projectile vomited against the bus window."

"Highlight of my young life," Renner said dryly. "I left Wyoming right after that when my dad was stationed at Ellsworth Air Force Base in South Dakota."

"I gotta say, I'm surprised you remember me."

"What stuck in my head was that you and your brother, Abe, were nice to a transplanted city kid. Much as I appreciated it then, I appreciate it even more now, when I know how locals feel about outsiders." A quick grin. "Anyway, I got into the rodeo promotion/stock contracting business a few years back and recognized your name as available for bullfighting services. But I haven't run into you before now. Mostly I stick to the Midwest circuits and don't get out West much."

"I hear ya there."

"You've got a great reputation, so I was happy to see we'd booked you. Anyway, at some point I'd like to sit down and talk to you about a couple of things."

Hank's skepticism was evident. "What kind of things?"

Renner looked behind him. "Personal things. As you know, my grandmother sold the place right after my granddad died, which was strange because they only lived there a couple years."

No response except a cool stare from Hank, which sent an odd chill down Lainie's spine.

"My dad was a little sketchy on what really happened. It's always bugged me. Thought maybe once this rodeo season slows down, I could come by your place in Muddy Gap and pick your brain a bit."

"Sure. I don't see why not."

"Great. Thank you. I appreciate it."

Then Renner did a double take, appearing to have just noticed Lainie. He gave her a wily smile that might've made her weak-kneed if she hadn't spent the last two years steeling herself against those sly cowboy grins.

Yeah, and that had worked so well with Hank and Kyle.

"Shame on me for overlooking such a lovely woman." He offered his hand. "My sincere apologies. I'm Renner Jackson."

"Lainie."

"Lainie . . . ?" Renner repeated, politely inquiring her last name.

"Capshaw," she supplied. Hank rarely used her last name when introducing her in an effort to protect her from the morbid interest that came along with being the daughter of the infamous and beloved Jason Capshaw.

Almost on cue, Renner's blue eyes sparked with recognition. "Capshaw . . . As in bull rider Jason Capshaw?"

"Yes. He was my father."

Renner squeezed her hand. "I'm sorry. I'm sure with people asking you questions about him they forget you lost your father that day, not just one of the world's greatest bull riders."

Insightful and good-looking. That was refreshing. "Ah, thank you."

"I don't know if you're aware," Hank inserted, "but Lainie works for the Lariat Sports Medicine team."

"I thought you looked familiar. You worked Silver City Round-up last year?"

Lainie tried to recall. "Probably. Why? Did I screw up or something?"

Renner laughed. "No. I remember warning my stock handlers that I'd be watching they didn't fake injuries so the hot female med tech would treat them."

She blushed, but managed, "If you need an extra hand tonight in the medical room, I'll be around."

"Really? That'd be great." He pulled a business card out of his ID badge and wrote on the back of it before handing it over. "Give this to Beau."

"I will. Thank you."

"No, thank you." Renner faced Hank and handed him a business card too. "Good luck going up against my stock tonight. If you're interested in specifics, Pritchett, the chute boss, could fill you in on some of the nastier ones."

"I might meander over there and see what's what."

"Good enough. I appreciate your time and I'll be in touch about that other matter."

Renner ambled off and Hank stared after him with an odd look.

"What's wrong?"

"Nothin'. It's strange how things come full circle."

She frowned. "That's cryptic."

Hank refocused on her. "Not when you consider my mom and dad bought the Harkings' acreage from Rona after Bill died."

"So it's part of the Lawson ranch now?"

"It was. We had it a year and then our parents died. We couldn't make the payments so we sold it to a buyer out of Montana. It's changed hands a couple of times since then. People claim it's bad-luck land. So I ain't surprised he's curious about his grandpa dying there." He blinked and the shadows in his eyes vanished. "Anyway, far as I'm concerned, we're done here."

They exited out the back entrance and the sun scorched Lainie's eyes. She slipped on her shades. "If you're checking bulls, I'll wander around."

"You want to meet at the camper later?"

His tone was sexy enough to send a shiver of longing through her despite the heat. "I promised Kyle my free time today."

"But, Lainie—"

"I didn't make the rules, Hank, but I'm abiding by them. I'll see you later." She whirled around in the opposite direction.

On impulse, Lainie ordered an icy-cold draft of Moose Drool beer. She detoured to a secluded shady spot and took out her cell phone.

"How's the luckiest woman in the world?" Tanna asked in her Texas twang.

"Great. Can you hear me enjoying my tasty beer?"

"Drinkin' and whorin' in the afternoon? Dude. I could totally hate you."

Lainie laughed. "It's bizarre. I cannot remember the last time I sucked down a cold one in the middle of the day."

"That said . . . I'll bet you're getting used to sucking down lots of things during all times of the day and night, huh?"

She choked on her beer. "Jesus, Tanna, warn me next time."

"Now, where's the fun in that? How's it goin' with your men, sugar?"

"Okay."

"Just okay? How many times you been the filling in a hot and hard manwich?"

"Define filling." There. That should get the conversation going.

Pause. "Now, see, it's a good thing I know you so well, or I wouldn't recognize your sly way of asking me for advice. So what's the problem?"

"This is gonna sound so . . ." Slutty? Whorish? Nah. Lainie was just . . . impatient. And that was damned embarrassing to admit.

"Come on, girlfriend. I know those camper walls are rockin', so it ain't like you're gonna shock me with your kinky tales of ménage à trois."

"When we stopped at Hank's house in Muddy Gap it was easier to explain that I was just with him. I ended up spending the night in his bed. But Kyle demanded equal 'alone' time with me at the next opportunity. So tonight it's just me and Kyle."

"I don't see how that's a problem. Unless . . . you've gotten used to bein' with both of them at the same time and you prefer a threesome scene to one on one?"

"No, this goes back to your filling comment." Lainie took another drink of beer. "We've done variations on all of us being together, but not what I expected, where they're both . . ."

Silence. Then, "Ah. The old double-penetration threesome."

Lord. Her face heated. How could she do it if she couldn't even say it?

"That's what you want?" Tanna asked carefully.

"Yes. Wouldn't you? I mean, didn't you?"

"Uh-huh. But maybe they're leading up to it. It does take a bit of choreographing and some preparation, if you get my drift. And, sugar, it's only been four nights, right?"

Is that all? Then why was she so antsy? "Right."

"What happened last night with all three of you?"

Lainie drooped against the tree trunk. "I got pissed off about how Hank and Kyle treated Hank's sister, Celia—the barrel racer I sent you the video about? They spouted off nasty things to her. In front of me and some other people."

"And you always stick up for the underdog," Tanna muttered.

"Yes. Anyway, I locked myself in the back bedroom and made them share the upper bunk, so nothing happened. But Hank is pissy. Tonight after the rodeo, while he's driving to Billings, Kyle and I will be alone together in the camper."

Tanna sighed. "Look, Hank needs to get over it. Not your job to soothe his ruffled feathers, Lainie. He had his solo shot with you. It's only fair to give Kyle the same."

"You make it sound so easy."

"Sugar, this situation might be fun as all get out, but I never said it was gonna be easy."

"Great." She closed her eyes.

"As far as the threesome biz, tell them what you want."

"I should demand they give me double-rider special?"

A deep, throaty laugh. "Put it that way and I guarantee it'll happen before you can blink."

"Thanks, T. You're the best." Lainie shut her phone. When she opened her eyes, Kyle stood four feet away. Her stomach cartwheeled. Sometimes she forgot how sinfully hot he was, with that ripped body and chiseled face. Oh, have mercy—he was giving her the look that usually sent her clothes flying. "Um. Hi."

He smirked. "Interestin' conversation."

"How much did you hear?"

"Just the tail end, to be honest." He stepped close enough that his belt buckle brushed her belly. His position blocked her from view of the casual passersby and he used it to his advantage to outline her lips with the pad of his thumb. "You have the prettiest mouth."

"Kyle—"

"Let me touch you, Lainie."

He mesmerized her. The sexy tilt to his lips. The slight flare to his nostrils. His pupils expanded. Those impossibly thick black eyelashes lowered as he continued to trace the swell and seam of her lips. "Are you looking forward to bein' with me tonight?"

"God. Yes."

"You're not nervous, are you, sugar? We have been alone and nekkid together before. Plenty of times."

"True. But I have a feeling tonight won't be like any of the other times."

"And you'd be right." He replaced his wicked thumb with his enthusiastic mouth. Kissing her like he'd already stripped her bare and spread her out beneath his muscled body.

"Kyle. Please. Stop."

He muttered, "For now. I guarantee you won't be begging me to stop at all tonight."

The low timbre of his voice against her wet, trembling mouth sent a jolt straight to her core.

Kyle eased back. "We have a little time. Let's hit the carnival."

That shocked her—and made her do the happy dance inside—but surprise won out over joy. "Really?"

His smile vanished. "What? Hank's the only one who can be with you in public?"

"No. It's not that, it's just . . ."

"You embarrassed to be seen with me, Lainie Capshaw?"

Lainie fisted her hand in his shirt, hauling herself up to her toes so they were nose-to-nose. "Not even close, bub. I'm embarrassed to admit that in my sheltered dating life, I never went to a carnival with a guy. Never had a guy win me a stuffed animal or a goldfish. Not only that, the rides make me dizzy and sometimes I throw up, so you should know what *you're* getting into before you offer to take me."

Kyle trapped her face in his hands and laid a big wet kiss on her. "Let's see if I can't pop your carnival cherry and win you something big to remember me by."

Chapter Fifteen

What a great night. Kyle finished first in the bull riding and he finally had Lainie right where he wanted her: alone.

The camper swayed and she gasped, blindly reaching for the wall behind her.

"Might be a little bouncy. Luckily that plays into what I've got planned."

"Should I be nervous?"

He traced the edges of the blindfold. "I'm hoping you're excited."

Her lips curved into a purely feminine smile. "Of course I'm excited. That goes without saying."

Kyle began undoing the buttons on her blouse. He could've undressed her before he blindfolded her, but he wanted to keep her off balance. He kissed the corners of her smile, trailing more kisses down her stubborn chin and the column of her throat.

His sweet Lainie tasted even better than she smelled. When his lips met the front snap of her bra, he sank his teeth into the plastic clasp and twisted until it popped open.

"Oh. Man. That's a handy trick."

But Kyle didn't tongue her nipples. Or nuzzle the swells of her breasts; he kept moving southward. He unhooked the button on her jeans. Lowered the zipper. He let his breath fan the delicate area between her hip bones, watching the skin quiver in response. Then he shimmied the denim to the middle of her calves and left it. He jerked her shirt to her wrists, keeping the cuffs buttoned, knotting the material so her hands were incapacitated.

"What are you doing?"

"Hobbling you. You can't see. You can't touch. You can't thrash. You are completely at my mercy. And I've been looking forward to it all damn day." Swallowing her protest with a kiss, he spun them and sat her on the edge of the bed. "Lie flat." Kyle gave her a gentle nudge.

The camper hit a bump. He braced his hand on the wall as he stripped. "Can you wriggle yourself up until you're in the middle of the bed?"

"Will you be staring at me while I do it?"

"Seein' your tits bounce is the stuff fantasies are made of. So hell, yeah."

She grinned and put an extra wiggle in her movement. Sassy thing. "Be right back. Don't go nowhere."

"You're as funny as you are sexy, Kyle."

That stopped him. "Really? You think so?"

"I can't remember the last time I laughed so hard. I had a blast with you at the carnival today."

"Same goes. Although next time I'll just take you to a toy store and buy you a damn giraffe. It'd be cheaper."

"But not nearly as much fun." She emitted a sigh. "I especially loved when you swung the love hammer. Seeing your muscles straining as you hit it hard enough to ring the top bell? The whole time I just wanted to lick your biceps. Then lick the rest of you."

Kyle chuckled. "You did lick me in the haunted house, remember?" Lainie's playful mood had been infectious. All afternoon she'd teased him. Feeding him cotton candy. Sneaking kisses on the Ferris wheel. Offering to give him a hand job in the Tunnel of Love—which had been damn hard to turn down.

"I still think you cheated at the water-balloon game. No one shoots a water gun that well."

"Sugar, I've been shooting all types of guns since I was eight years old, so give it a rest. You lost." He lightly swatted her. "We're getting off track. Sit tight."

He filled a Styrofoam cup with icy water and returned with candles and matches.

"Did I hear you rattling around in the freezer?"

"Maybe." Kyle set his supplies inside the small dresser drawer next to the bottle of lube and the condoms. Then he straddled Lainie's hips and palmed her breasts.

She stilled.

"I ain't gonna fuck your tits. I figured out that ain't your favorite position."

"Is it yours?" she asked hesitantly.

"Not even close. I'd rather be buried balls-deep in your wet pussy. Or your hot mouth." He lazily stroked the edge of her areola, but avoided direct contact with her nipple. "Or your tight ass."

Lainie bit her lip and turned her head away.

But Kyle wouldn't let her. He slid his hand up her throat and he curled his fingers around her jaw, forcing her to face forward, even when she couldn't see him. "That thought excites you. My cock stretching your ass as I plunge my fingers into your cunt so all you feel is me fucking you everywhere."

Her chest lifted with each stuttered breath.

"Answer me."

"Yes. I want that."

"You'll get it, but on my time frame tonight, understand?"

She nodded.

"Good girl." He reached for the cream-colored taper candle. With shaking hands, he struck a match, releasing a whiff of sulfur.

"What's that?"

"Your cue to hold still." Kyle scooted back and trapped her hips between his knees. He grabbed the cup of ice and rattled it. When the candle built up a pool of wax, he tipped it sideways at the same time he tilted the cup of ice. A bead of hot wax and a drop of cold water landed on her belly simultaneously.

Lainie gasped and her stomach rippled.

He did it again. She gasped again.

Fourteen water and wax droplets landed on her trembling flesh. Each time her belly muscles constricted, so did his balls. He gritted his teeth against giving in to his urge to fuck her hard and fast this first time.

She held her muscles taut, her mouth parted slightly to allow harsh pants to escape. She cried out when water fell on her right nipple at the same time as wax splatted on her left nipple. "Oh, my God. Kyle."

"Does it hurt, sugar?"

"The anticipation is killing me."

"It's good for you. Anticipation is its own reward."

Kyle brushed his mouth over hers to quell her protest, tasting the seam of her lips with his tongue. She opened her mouth for a tongue-thrusting kiss, but he denied her. Not to be cruel, but to ratchet her need to the highest level.

"Let's try an experiment. You tell me if what I'm dripping on you is hot or cold."

Her answering smirk was the response he'd hoped for. Little Miz Lainie thought this'd be easy-peasy.

Wrong.

Kyle watched the wax splat on the creamy section of her flesh above her left hip bone.

Her breath caught.

"Tell me," he demanded.

A beat passed. "Um. Hot?"

"Yeah, but next time I'll penalize you for takin' so long to answer." Kyle pinched her nipple at the same time wax landed above her right hip bone.

"Hey! Not fair."

"Tough. All's fair. Tell me."

Kyle saw her nose wrinkling as she tried to reason her way through a response. He grinned. She had no clue.

Finally she guessed, "Cold?"

"Wrong." He placed the candle in the candleholder lodged inside the dresser drawer. He shuffled back on his knees and let his mouth linger above the missed hot spot. First he used his teeth to scrape away the hardened wax. Then he sucked on the pink dot with enough force to leave a love bruise.

Lainie shrieked and tried to twist free, but Kyle held her hips down until he was finished.

She slumped back on the bed, not relaxed in the slightest. Her body vibrated with tension.

He kissed the hickey. "How many people did you see in sports med tonight?"

"Ten." She frowned. "Why?"

"'Cause that's how many times we're gonna test your sensitivity to cold and hot." His cock slapped his belly as he reached for the cup and candle again.

His gaze took her in, spread out before him like the ultimate feast. The thrust of her pearled nipples atop the soft swells of her breasts. The arch of her neck that begged for the heated touch of his mouth. The sex-kittenish habit of biting her lower lip. Her made-for-sex body was dotted with dried white wax like he'd marked her as his with his come.

A primitive roar gathered in his chest and he had to clench his teeth to keep from letting it loose.

"Kyle?"

Then he was right in her face. But he couldn't tell her he wished to steal her away for himself. Screw his friendship with Hank. Screw being the civilized man waiting for his turn. Screw the whole stupid fucking sharing idea.

In his fit of jealousy or neediness or whatever fucked-up thoughts crowded reason from his brain, he accidentally splashed water on the center of Lainie's chest.

She smiled brassily. "Cold."

"Guess I'd better pay attention to what I'm doin'."

"What distracted you?"

"Your nekkid body. See, whenever I'm nekkid with you, my brain schemes on how I can stay nekkid with you all the damn time." He dribbled wax beneath her rib cage.

She hissed, "Hot."

"That you are, sugar." He sipped from the cup before he licked the sweep of her collarbone and simultaneously dripped wax on the swell of her abdomen.

"Kyle! That's cheating."

"You've got a fifty-fifty chance of guessing right," he offered.

"Cold."

"Wrong."

She inhaled a sharp breath. Wiggled a bit in suspense.

After Kyle set aside the candle and cup again, he scooted down until his feet touched the floor. He splayed his hands below the cute indent of her belly button, framing the dried wax chunk. Using his teeth and tongue, he pried the wax from her skin. He dragged his goatee over it enough times that he knew he'd have no trouble discerning the spot. He set his mouth on her and sucked without pause.

Lainie had no prayer of staying still. With Kyle this close to her pussy, her arousal wafted into his nose, making his mouth water for a complete taste of her.

"You're torturing me."

"Uh-huh. And just think—I ain't even half done yet."

She groaned.

He tracked openmouthed kisses straight up to her mouth. His biting nips on her lower lip pushed her to that edge of pain she craved. An edge she usually brought upon herself with the sexy way she dug her teeth in. Kyle soothed the sting with his hot breath, letting it drift across her kiss-swollen lips.

As he followed the angle of her jawbone up to her ear, she whispered, "Fuck me. With your tongue, your fingers, your cock, I don't care. I just need—"

"I know what you need, and I'm getting around to giving it to you." He blew in her ear, gloating when her whole body shuddered.

But Lainie wasn't about to give up. "I feel your cock when you slide up my body. It's hot and hard." Lainie turned her head and murmured, "Let me blow you. Bring that dick up here and let me suck you dry, Kyle."

Just to see how far she was willing to go, Kyle let their lips meet. She poured everything into the kiss. Soft female moans. Attempting to suck his tongue down her throat. Undulating her lower body against his. While he enjoyed the hell out of it, it didn't sway him one iota. He broke the kiss with a smile.

"Afraid the answer is no, sugar. But I'll tell you what I will do, since your methods of persuasion are commendable. I'll give you a freebie for the cold-and-hot game."

It was apparent Lainie wanted to snap at him in frustration, but somehow she refrained. Which also made him smile.

He grabbed the candle and tilted it so the wax dripped directly on her left nipple. Or it was supposed to, but the camper hit a bump, and his aim fell short. The wax missed its mark and slid down the slope of her breast. When she jerked up, Kyle placed his hand below her collarbone and pushed her back to the mattress. "Stay still," he warned. He reangled the taper, so the next splash of wax landed on the puckered tip.

"Oh, man."

"Does it hurt?" he murmured.

"Um. No. It just surprised me."

"Hot or cold?" he asked as he directed more wax over that circle of rose-colored flesh.

"Hot. Really hot."

Kyle shifted the candle and let wax stream down to her right nipple. He gave her credit; she didn't squirm. Drop after drop coated the areola. Soon as he was visually satisfied—and holy fuck, was that smokin' hot—he traded the candle for the cup and spilled water droplets on each breast. Slowly. One at a time.

Eventually, he asked, "Cold or hot?"

"Cold. Oh, God, is that cold."

"Very good." He pressed his mouth to the section of skin where her neck flowed into her shoulder. "You oughta see yourself, Lainie. All those spots of wax on your tits. The shine on your skin from the water. It looks like I marked you with my seed. Sprayed you until I had no more juice left in my balls because I spent it all, coating your sexy body over and over." He nuzzled her temple. "Does it turn you on that your body is my canvas?"

He watched the curvy form he'd reveled in marking flush with color. Yet she didn't utter a sound.

"You don't have a clue what you do to me. I want to take you in every way I've ever imagined. Bite you. Suck you. Mark you. Come on you. Come in you. You bring out my untamed side."

"Show me."

Kyle squeezed her breasts, watching as the wax cracked and peeled away. He brushed the tiny shards free until no trace remained. Then he set his mouth on her. He suckled her nipples so thoroughly Lainie actually came.

After he'd petted her and brought her back down to earth, his cock screamed, "My turn!" and took control of his brain.

His blood pounded a tribal rhythm. Perspiration beaded his forehead. His upper lip. His hairline. His body pulsed from his heels to the tips of his ears, as if he were about to get on the back of a bull.

He tucked his knees under her armpits and tapped her lips with the tip of his cock. "Open."

Lainie's tongue darted out and flicked the head. She sucked the knob and rimmed the tip with fiery flicks of her hot tongue. He'd gone beyond the need for foreplay, to that overpowering need for immediate release.

Bracing one hand on the wall above him, Kyle used the other hand to hold her jaw open. He fed his cock into her mouth until his sac rested on her chin. His fingers outlined her lips, stretched around the base of his shaft. He knew that if Lainie weren't wearing a blindfold her eyes would be locked on his. Bold, yet patient. Even though she was bound, with his dick in her throat, there was no doubt who had all the power. "Take me over the edge, Lainie."

Her hum of assent let loose the beast in him just as surely as pulling the gate in the arena released the bull.

He let the rim of his cock head rest against her bottom lip and slammed inside that wet haven, barely allowing her time to snatch a breath before he was fucking her mouth without restraint.

So good. So fucking good. Heat and wetness and suction.

Kyle lasted longer than eight seconds, but not by much. His cock swelled, bumping her soft palate. He stopped thrusting, keeping the tip on the back of her tongue. "Swallow. Now. All of it. Harder. More. That's it, baby. More."

Her throat muscles squeezed every pulse from his dick and made him groan. Long. Loudly. And without apology.

Another humming noise, a bit sharper than before, brought him out of his orgasmic stupor. He looked down. His cock was still lodged in Lainie's mouth. "Sorry," he said, easing out. His hands floated over her face. "You okay?"

"I'm pretty sure that one fell into the 'hot' realm."

What a card. Kyle grinned. "You'd be right."

She squirmed and sighed. But it was a different type of sigh.

"Something wrong?"

"Can you at least take my jeans off? They're cutting off my circulation."

"The hands stay bound." Kyle hopped off the bed, forgetting they were attached to a moving vehicle, and he smacked into the paneled wall before righting himself. He removed her jeans.

Lainie brought her heels up on the mattress, lifting her hips, wiggling her arms slightly. "Much better. Thank you." She turned her head, trying to figure out where he was.

"Gotta keep my captive happy so we can continue our game."

Her face fell. "We're still playing?"

"Yep."

"But I thought I'd won."

"Nope." Kyle sipped from the cup of ice water. He curled his hands around her knees and spread them wide. Then he placed his cold mouth right on the hot center of her and sucked. Ignoring her shrieks, he continued to run his cool tongue up and down the molten folds of her soft, juicy flesh. He raised his head long enough to ask, "Hot or cold?"

Her mouth opened. Closed. A cunning smile appeared. "I'd have to say . . . hot."

"Wrong." Kyle dropped to his knees. He licked the crease of her thigh, one side, then the other, tasting the salty sweetness of her skin. He used his fingers to keep her pussy open, settling in for a good, long torture-Lainie-until-she-begs session.

He wowed her with every erotic trick he'd ever learned about going down and going to town on a woman. Butterfly licks and gentle scrapes of his teeth across her clitoris, combined with slurping sucks and soft puffs of air. Burying his mouth, his tongue, his fingers, his face in the wet core.

"Oh, please. Don't stop. I'm . . . right . . . there." Lainie shrieked and bucked up hard.

Kyle kept his mouth fastened to the bit of flesh. She groaned and gasped as he sucked. Her thigh muscles were rigid, cradling his head as he stayed with her until the last pulse faded.

Then that throaty, sated sigh emerged and Lainie went boneless.

And Kyle went completely hard again.

"So was that the last test? Because I totally think I aced it."

He smiled against the curve of her hip. "That was the

last test. But we aren't done." He peppered kisses over her mound, straight down her slit, but he didn't stop and wiggle his tongue in her entrance. He kept going, letting the very tip of his tongue swirl around the bud of her anus.

Rather than jerking away, Lainie gasped.

Kyle did it again and again, painting that tight pucker with his saliva. "I want this part of you. To be crude, I want you facedown on the bed, bound, blindfolded, spread open, and at my mercy as I fuck your ass." He pushed to his feet and waited for her response. Breathing hard, ready to pounce on her the second she gave the all-clear.

"You don't intend to be gentle, do you?"

"There's that fine line between pleasure and pain. One can feed the other."

"Would you be as rough if this were my first time?"

"But you're not a virgin to anal sex. Although I'm betting it was a recent deflowering. Real recent."

Pause. "How did you know? Did Hank tell you all about it?"

He fought a flare of jealousy. "No. But I'm guessing he demanded you give it up to him the other night when you two were alone at the ranch. Am I right?"

She huffed out a breath. "Yes, but that still doesn't tell me how you knew he popped my anal cherry."

"Easy. Because if I'd been in Hank's position I would've demanded the same thing from you."

"Oh." Another pause. "I have to ask, is this roughness you've warned me about punishment because Hank got there before you?"

"Never. I ain't mad at you or at Hank, Lainie; it was your choice. I respect that. I told you how I wanted it for one reason: I don't think I can be gentle with this." Kyle crawled up her body and rubbed his goatee over her neck. Under her chin. Tickling her ear and the cup of her shoulder. "Say yes, sugar."

She whispered, "Yes."

His kiss turned brutal. Almost feral. Lainie didn't balk. In fact, she gave back as good as she got.

He pushed on her shoulder, but she couldn't roll without his help. Once she was on her belly, Kyle hiked her hips up. His damn cock jumped and twitched as if it had a mind of its own. He snagged a condom, the lube, and the candle. He watched half of Lainie's beautiful face pressed against the white sheet as he suited up and slicked up his impatient cock. "What are you thinking?"

"How strange it is, bound, knowing you're going to fuck me hard in a place that's not used to hard fucking. I'm still hazy and glowy from that orgasm, so I wonder if I'm dreaming. But my heart is racing. My blood is pounding in my temples, my ears, my throat, my chest, and even between my legs."

"Pounding in fear?" Kyle asked, squirting lubricant in a thick line down the seam between his first and second fingers.

"No, that's what so strange. My whole body is like one big, throbbing mass."

"Mmm." He leaned over and captured her earlobe between his teeth while he inserted a finger in her ass.

When Lainie reared up, his body absorbed the startled motion. He said, "Relax," and inserted another finger. Once both fingers were inside her, he fluttered the slick digits open and closed, trying to stretch muscles that didn't want to be stretched.

She was as ready as he could made her.

He applied gel to the pink pucker and added more lube to his cock. Aiming at the tiny entrance, he commanded, "Push out to me."

The second he felt that give, the slight relaxing, he

plowed forward. Once. Twice. Three times. Stopping on the fourth thrust to feel the sphincter clamp down on the thickest part of his shaft. While he remained lodged there, Kyle plucked up the candle and slipped it between her legs.

"What is that?"

"A makeshift dildo." He rubbed it up and down her slit lengthwise. "You want it in this wet cunt? So you know how it'll be to have both me 'n' Hank fucking you?"

"I'll wait for the real thing . . . oh, God," she said when he pulled out completely.

Gripping her hips, he set to fucking her hard. It was right there. Kyle gritted out, "Bear down on me."

She did and Kyle fucking lost it. His body vibrated with every hot expulsion of his seed. Over and over. The sheer blinding pleasure had him squeezing his eyes shut. His mouth hung open and he might've actually . . . howled.

Christ. Talk about a mindblower. His fingers dug into Lainie's flesh as the last vestiges of his orgasm threatened to topple him from the damn bed.

Seeing her waiting, Kyle yanked off her shirt, freeing her arms. Then he braced one hand by her head and slipped the other between her thighs. He fingered her clit while remaining embedded in her ass. "Help me get you off."

"Move your finger faster. Yes. Like that. No, don't slide it down. Keep it right there and, oh, sweet Jesus, yes, yes!"

Her cunt muscles clamped down as her clitoris pulsed. He felt every contraction. He hardly dared breathe as he listened to her come. The last thing he wanted was to fuck this up for her, after taking her ass so ruthlessly. The sexy gasps and the tightening of Lainie's anal muscles would be enough to get Kyle hard again—if he hadn't just come like a fiend.

She hissed when Kyle pulled out of her ass and dropped to the mattress.

He returned from the bathroom with a hot washcloth and gently rolled her over. She still wore the blindfold and she didn't say anything beyond making a contented purr as he wiped the front of her body. Three times he rewarmed the rag with hot water, enjoying taking care of her in a nonsexual way.

Somehow he removed the top sheet, with the flakes of dried wax, as she lay on the bed. He dragged the comforter over them and slid the blindfold free as he kissed her.

Released from captivity, Lainie's wild hair brushed his cheek and forehead. He chuckled and opened his eyes to find her already looking at him. "What?"

"I like that you don't treat me like a delicate flower. I like that you're kinky, bull rider. I like that you took the time to play with me today. Not just in the bedroom, but before, at the carnival. That was something new for me." She pressed her mouth to his. "So thank you for tonight."

"My pleasure." And it was. Kyle couldn't wipe the smug smile off his face that he'd given Lainie something that no man had.

But he still wondered if it was enough.

Chapter Sixteen

Hank scored a parking spot in the Metra Park in Billings. No place to hook up, but it was free. It'd be hours until the contestants' area opened at the roundup grounds.

It'd been hard as hell, getting comfortable in the truck cab. Around hour four, Hank cursed Kyle's name pretty severely. Especially since on the night Hank spent with Lainie, Kyle had his own damn bedroom with an actual bed, not the cramped cab of a pickup. Kicking him out of his own camper so they could fuck seemed unfair.

You're just worried Kyle is wowing her with sexual tricks that'll make your seduction scenes laughable.

Screw this.

He snatched his sleeping gear and trudged to the camper. Inside, he threw his bedding into the upper bunk and sat on the bench to remove his boots. Each movement took longer than the last, and Hank knew that if he didn't get in that bunk soon, he'd sleep where he fell.

A considerate friend would give them a heads-up that you're here, in case the sexual screams of ecstasy get out of hand.

Dread weighted his stomach like an anvil as he opened the bedroom door and poked his head in.

Naked Lainie was sprawled on her stomach, facing away from naked Kyle. Hank's gaze moved to the rumpled sheet on the floor, then to the candles poking up out of the nightstand next to the packs of rubbers and the bottle of lube.

Son of a bitch. Resentment arose. Thick. Sharp. Bitter.

First Kyle bought her flowers? He took her on carnival rides and won her a stupid stuffed giraffe? And then the smarmy bastard finished off his night of seduction with candles? Jesus. No fucking way could Hank compete. He just wasn't that smooth.

You'd better get smooth if you want a level playing field. If you want a serious shot at winning Lainie for good.

But how? He sucked at this kind of stuff. Which was why one-night stands worked best for him. Fuck and leave. He hadn't dreamed he'd have to come up with some romantic shit to keep Lainie interested.

Kyle grunted and rolled over, looking at Hank groggily. "What's up?"

"We're in Billings at Metra Park. I'm so damn tired I can't keep my eyes open. Wanted to let you know I'm crashing for a few hours in the upper bunk."

"Thanks. When Lainie starts stirring, I'll warn her to be quiet. I'm gonna catch another couple of hours of shut-eye myself."

Hank waited for Kyle to toss off something flip, like that he and Lainie hadn't done a whole lot of sleeping last night, but Kyle turned on his side and hunkered into his pillow.

Huh.

Hank lumbered up the ladder to the sleeping berth and closed the heavy vinyl curtains. Flopped on his back, staring at the backs of his eyelids didn't spur his creativity in the seduction department. Was he supposed to shower her with gifts? Another thought occurred to him. Kyle knew his way around a guitar. What if he started writing love songs? Serenading her by a campfire? Or in the moonlight? How could Hank compete with that? Would Lainie expect him to pen poetry?

For fuck's sake, snap out of it. You're so goddamn tired you're actually considering writing a tribute to her tits just to one-up your friend. Go to sleep.

He jerked the sleeping bag over his head and conked out.

∞

Hank was having the best dream about being pillowed between Lainie's lush breasts when he heard, "Hank?"

He peeled his eyes open.

Lainie was right there, lying next to him.

Her cool fingertips drifted across his cheek. "Morning."

"Morning. What time is it?"

"Almost eleven."

"Christ. I feel like I'm in a time warp. Did Kyle get checked in?"

"Yep. You slept like the dead. Didn't move even when we drove the camper to the fairgrounds."

"I was tired. It ain't so comfy sleeping in the truck cab, that's for damn sure."

"I don't imagine it is." She leaned over and pressed her lips to his. "Thank you for giving Kyle last night. I don't get why being alone with me is such a big bonus to either of you, but now Kyle feels he was treated fairly, so he's happy."

Hank said, "Did he make you happy?" even when he knew he shouldn't have asked.

Lainie blinked at him.

"Sorry. Never mind. You don't have to answer."

"You both make me happy. That's why you're sharing me, remember? I told you guys I wouldn't choose. I still won't."

Didn't she know he and Kyle were hoping that was exactly what she'd do? Pick one man over the other? His best option at this point was to deflect. "Isn't Kyle back yet?"

"He's waiting around to see if his new buddy Breck is hitting this event or if he swung over to one in North Dakota. I'm also supposed to tell you he called Red Lodge and confirmed he's competing there tonight." She frowned. "Why don't all places have the call-in option? It'd be easier than racing from town to town to make the entry cutoff times."

"The only places with the call-in option are when there are two events very close together and only hours apart in start times. Like Billings and Red Lodge. Most competitors hit both events. Neither venue wants to lose the entry fees or make the contestants choose. So they work together, but it's not the norm."

"Oh."

"Anyway, what about you? Did you scope out the medical-services situation while I was sawing logs?"

"I wasn't sure it'd be a good idea. I didn't want to get stuck here when we're racing to make the Red Lodge rodeo. Plus, since it's probably my turn to drive, I should rest up while you guys are in the arena." Lainie rubbed at the bristle on his face. "I haven't driven yet. I expect to pull my weight, Hank."

"Neither of us has a problem telling you what we want or need, do we?"

She shook her head and kept stroking his morning beard.

"Sorry. I'll shave."

"No. Don't. I like this rough side of you." She smiled. "Which is why it's so hard to ask you if I can have a hug."

A hug. Lainie wanted to hug him? Hank's gaze tried to catch hers, but she'd ducked her face from view. "Sure, darlin', hug away. Whenever you want. You don't even have to ask."

Lainie crawled right on top of him. Tucking her head under his chin and stretching her body the length of his. She expelled a soft, feminine sigh.

"Something goin' on?"

"Like what?"

"Like why you're bein' so damned cuddly all of a sudden."

"You don't like it?"

Hank clamped his hands on her ass when she attempted to squirm away. "Of course I like it. Just surprised me, that's all." He trailed his fingers up and down her spine. Soothing her, because something had spooked her.

Or someone. Maybe Kyle had taken things too far last night. Hank wouldn't push her for answers, even if it killed him, because he hated to be grilled when he wanted time to think things through.

They remained wrapped together for the longest time.

Lainie's voice was whisper soft when she finally spoke. "Know what's sad?"

"What?"

"I don't know what to do with myself on this trip. It's been so long since I've had free time that I honestly don't remember what I used to do when I didn't have to fill the hours with work."

"That's not sad, Lainie; that's life."

"What do you do when you have free time?"

"Sometimes after we get chores done, Abe, Celia, and I target shoot. Or we hang out and watch TV or movies. Head to the bar and play pool or darts with the guys. We do a lot of ranch-related stuff; seems like the work is never-ending."

"But I mean when you're by yourself. Do you read? Or whittle? Or craft things out of leather?"

Hank snorted. "Not hardly."

Lainie propped her chin on her hand and looked at him. "When I was taking care of my grandma, she told me a woman has to have interests of her own. Not just the ones that please her husband or her kids."

"Did she follow her own advice?"

She smiled. "Oh, Grandma was great at handing out advice, especially if you didn't ask for it. She was good at traditional things. She knitted. Embroidered. Sewed. Did crossword puzzles and word searches. Made her own soap. Grew her own vegetables. Planted flowers and fruit trees. She started out having to can and freeze foodstuff if she wanted to feed her family. But it became more. Something she enjoyed and took pride in."

"Didn't you want to learn to do any of that?"

"I did learn a lot of it. But it's not . . . portable. I can't drag ripe fruit, jelly jars, paraffin wax, and an enamel pot with me to whip up a batch of jam. I never really 'took' to sewing and embroidery, as she used to say. I loved working with her in the garden. But again, not something I can do either at my apartment complex or on the road. Been a long time since I did any word searches, but I sure loved them. I'd buy us identical books and we'd have races to see who finished first."

He stroked her back, letting her get it out.

"I feel . . . displaced. And not because I'm bored traveling. This feeling has been building for a while now, and

I was too busy to think about it before. But now that I've got time on my hands . . ."

"It's all you can think about."

"Exactly."

Hank almost wished they wouldn't have to hurry from Billings to Red Lodge for tonight's performance. After the Red Lodge rodeo ended they'd be back on the road, headed to Miles City, leaving them no time to play tourist. Lainie knew what she'd signed on for—rodeo cowboys hitting a whirlwind of events, and in between the arena performances were the lonely miles of blacktop.

But he wanted to give her one real vacation day, where they could hang out, relax, and not have to worry about busting balls to get to the next event.

So whisk her off someplace on your own. You're not doing this Cowboy Christmas for yourself; you're doing it for Kyle.

That wasn't entirely true. Hank needed to square off with as many bulls as possible to nail his EBS audition.

A brilliant idea pinged in his head. There was a place on this route—or close enough to it—where he could take Lainie for a day and night of R & R. A secluded cabin outside Great Falls. A cabin that boasted all the amenities of a fancy hotel, but without the people. His buddy Devin had given him an open invitation to use it whenever, so he'd have to call and make sure the cabin was available.

"You're acting serious, Hank. I didn't mean to bring you down."

He smooched her forehead. "You're not. I'm just trying to come up with a response that don't sound flip."

"And what have you come up with?"

"Not a damn thing."

She laughed softly.

"It'll be good for you to take the time to think, not just for the short term, but maybe with an eye to making some changes when you get back to Colorado."

"You are so smart." She wiggled up his chest for a better angle to kiss him. Sweetly. Lazily. Not without passion, but without urgency. As if the feel and the fit of his mouth moving on hers were satisfaction enough.

Except it wasn't enough for his cock, which rose to the occasion promptly. He knew Lainie couldn't help but notice the erection digging into her hip.

She broke the seal of their mouths and murmured, "Hank, if you want we can—"

"Ignore it. Just an automatic reaction to you, darlin'. Not everything has to do with sex. I like bein' with you. Holding you like this. Nothin' else needs to happen, okay?"

"Okay." She snuggled deeper into him.

Hank felt her contentment and could've stayed wrapped up in her softness and sweet need all day, but duty called. "Much as I hate to leave, I've gotta shave, clean up, and get to the grounds."

"Thanks for listening and not thinking I'm some kind of whiny drama queen."

"Never even crossed my mind."

∞

Lainie opted to hang out in the camper during the rodeo. That didn't sit right with Hank. Especially in light of their conversation about her restlessness.

Neither Hank nor Kyle was a spill-his-guts kind of guy, but they were smart enough to recognize something was up with Lainie.

They hung on the fence away from the contestant area, watching the tie-down roping. Kyle smacked the end of his bull rope into the wooden post. "What do you think is goin' on with her?"

"I figure it's a combination of not having the daily stability of her job and her worry about wanting to be with both of us."

"You got that feeling too, huh?" Kyle said. "I caught the tail end of her phone conversation with Tanna yesterday."

"What'd you hear?"

"Nothin' specific, just the impression she's ready, anxious even, to be double-teamed by us. Not the way we've been doin' it, if you get my drift."

"We talking no-holes-barred?" Hank asked casually.

"I reckon. I ain't exactly sure how that'll work."

"Me neither."

The announcer tried to rile up the crowd for the next event.

"This morning after you went to check in, Lainie crawled up in my bunk," Hank said, during a lull.

Kyle's head whipped toward him. "She did?"

"Nothin' happened, but I got the feeling she was only there out of guilt. Trying to make me feel better for her havin' alone time with you last night."

Pause. "Son of a bitch. She did the same damn thing after we left Muddy Gap. That afternoon in Gillette, she sought me out to reassure me and we ended up . . . Ah, hell. She shouldn't be reassuring us, Hank; we oughta be reassuring her."

"I know. I ain't bein' a dick when I say it'd be easier all around if we nixed the individual alone time with either of us from here on out—unless she requests it."

"Agreed."

Hank shot Kyle a look from beneath his hat brim. "That was quick."

Kyle shrugged. "Don't make much sense to argue when we all want the same thing."

"True. Don't know what we'll be able to do about reassuring her tonight, since we've got a long-ass drive to Miles City after we leave Red Lodge."

"We have to come up with something. Figure out how to make time, bein's we'll be spending the majority of our time on the road the next two weeks."

"She asked if she could drive tonight."

"I say we let her."

Hank allowed a grin. "Then we'll be rested up."

"I'm in. I'll follow your lead. Until it's time for you to follow mine." Kyle pushed back from the fence and slung his bull rope over his shoulder. "Gotta get my head in the game."

∞

When the time came for Hank to hit the dirt, he was ready. The quality of both the bulls and the riders was high. But sometimes during afternoon events, in the hot sun, the livestock were lazy. Neither broncs nor bulls bucked hard. Which wasn't bad for him—a lethargic bull usually wasn't problematic. But riders needed ornery, rough stock to score well.

A few bull riders cleared the eight-second mark. None of the judges' scores were impressive. Except for the one they gave Kyle. He'd ended up with a replacement bull that wasn't happy to be in the bucking chute. When the slavering beast burst out, he tried like hell to get Kyle off his back by any means necessary. And Kyle stayed on, spurring like crazy. When the buzzer sounded, and the bull ran off with no prompting from the bullfighters, Hank suspected he'd just seen the winning ride.

They stood side by side in the dirt as they waited for the score. Eighty-eight. Hank slapped him on the back. "Looks like we'll be sticking around to get that winner's check, huh?"

The next eight riders didn't come close to Kyle's score.

Hank didn't bother to shower or change out of his

bullfighting duds after the rodeo. They'd be cutting it close to get to Red Lodge.

Kyle picked up his winnings and they booked it back to the camper. Lainie had made sandwiches, a thoughtful gesture that wasn't lost on him or Kyle. It was her sweetness, a genuine desire to please them, not for any reason besides that she liked to do it, that made Hank take notice. That kind of care was rare—and all the more prized.

When Lainie marched over to the driver's side, he and Kyle exchanged a look—which she returned with irritation. "What?"

"No offense, sugar, but we need to get there fast, so this ain't the time for you to be learning how to drive a rig with a three-thousand-pound camper attached."

Wrong thing for Kyle to say. Venom sparked in Lainie's eyes. "You think I can't drive a truck? I drive a goddamn ambulance! I'm certainly capable—"

"Whoa. Let's all take a deep breath," Hank said. "We're not questioning your driving skills. But the truth is, me 'n' Kyle have driven that stretch of twisty highway many times to go skiing or to unload cattle. You haven't. If you wanna argue about it in the truck on the way to Red Lodge, fine. But we need to get goin' now."

Lainie had that stubborn set to her chin and Hank braced himself for a fight. But she climbed in the back of the cab and slammed the door. Hank tossed Kyle the keys. "Let 'er rip."

She didn't speak until they were out of town. "I'm driving to Miles City tonight."

"Fine. You coming to the performance?"

"Nope."

Kyle slanted her a look in the rearview mirror. "So you're goin' shopping for fancy shoes? Or souvenirs for your mama while me 'n' Hank are risking life and limb?"

Fuck. Way to be a smart-ass. Hank was about to cuff

Kyle in the back of the head and apologize for him when Lainie laughed.

"You are such a jerk, Kyle. Only shoes I'll buy are the pointy-toed variety to kick your butt with."

"Bring it, sugar."

"I heard your name announced over the loudspeaker as the winner. Congrats."

"Thanks."

"You're on a roll. The CRA seems to suit you better than the EBS. You've ridden what? Your last twelve bulls in a row?"

"Something like that. You must be my lucky charm."

She rolled her eyes and turned to look out the window.

Kyle asked Hank, "Did you talk to Abe after all that shit went down with Celia?"

"Yesterday, while you guys were at the carnival."

"What'd Abe say?"

"Truthfully? He wasn't surprised. Said he suspected something like that, but wanted her to come clean about it before accusing her."

"What's he gonna do about it?"

"What can he do? She's of legal age." Hank slouched in the seat. The discussion about Celia wasn't what'd bothered him about the call. It was the weariness in Abe's voice. Abe indicated that when Hank and Celia were both home they'd all sit down and talk specifics about the future of the Lawson ranch. Hank felt sick when he thought about their home place being sold. He'd fight Abe to keep it.

Yeah? Why? You want it but you don't want to run it.

The hell he didn't.

You're either a bullfighter or a rancher. Better to give your all to one thing rather than do a half-assed attempt at two.

Aware that he'd gone off into his own little world, Hank looked at Kyle, but he hadn't noticed Hank's distraction. Lainie had sacked out in the backseat. Hank pulled his hat down over his eyes and let the *tharump, tharump* of the tires lull him to sleep.

∞

They made it to Red Lodge with thirty minutes to kill. Because the grounds were small, most of the contestants without horses parked in the lot across the road. Kyle's buddy Breck had called and invited them to his impromptu cookout.

Everyone was blowing off steam, hyped up on the bonus of a multievent day. Winning, or the promise of it, plus reconnecting with friends made for a lively group. Beer and food flowed freely. Hank felt Lainie hanging back as they traversed the crowd, which freaked him out a little, because she'd never acted shy.

Maybe she's embarrassed at being with two guys.

Kyle took them to Breck's setup. Bratwurst were sizzling on a grill next to a pot of beans. Lawn chairs were arranged but no one was sitting. When Breck caught sight of Kyle, he beamed a smile.

"Glad you could make it and drag your friends along." He held out his hand to Hank. "Good to see you again, Hank."

"Likewise."

Breck's assessing gaze roved over Lainie, even when Breck had a brunette hanging off his arm. "I don't believe we've met. I'm Breck Christianson."

"Lainie. And we did meet briefly in Denver, although I doubt you remember."

"You'd be a hard one to forget."

Kyle snorted.

Lainie smiled. "You had a pretty serious case of whiplash after getting tossed off a bronc. Doc sent you for X-rays to check for a concussion. I drove you to the hospital."

"That was you?"

"Yep. I work for Lariat."

"So what're you doin' with these two yahoos?"

"Keeping them healthy. Learning what you guys go through during Cowboy Christmas."

"And your opinion so far?"

She flashed her teeth. "No comment."

As they mingled, Hank realized he missed the socializing during a multiday rodeo. Racing from event to event limited their interaction. What was Lainie gaining from this experience?

Lainie chatted with a barrel racer who knew Tanna. When opening-ceremonies time neared, he and Kyle headed to the rodeo grounds and Lainie escaped to the camper to rest before the trip to Miles City.

Maybe it was his mood from earlier carrying over, but Hank was sorry Lainie missed the Red Lodge rodeo. High scores in the saddle bronc. A new record in tie-down roping. A couple of real close calls in the bull riding section. Kyle finished second. Not where he wanted but still in the money.

Another rodeo ended. Another trip to the winners' tent. Another long walk to the camper. Lainie was there fiddling with the GPS, as well as studying maps spread out across the table. They dumped their duffel bags.

Kyle spoke first. "You sure you're okay to drive? 'Cause the truth is, me 'n' Hank are bushed."

"I'll be fine. You guys go ahead. I don't need you to hold my hand, and if that changes, I promise I'll wake one of you up."

"Good, let's go."

On the road again, he and Kyle had flipped for shotgun and Hank won.

Before Hank drifted off, he said, "By the way? Because me 'n' Kyle will be fully rested when we hit Miles City, we've got plans for you. Naked plans."

That'd keep her awake, if nothing else.

Chapter Seventeen

Ten miles outside of Miles City, Montana, Lainie jabbed Hank in the ribs. His head was right beside her hip on the bench seat and she could've lovingly stroked his hair, but since he'd snored the entire way she wasn't keen on being kind.

Even Kyle, who usually seized the chance to talk to her alone while Hank slept, had immediately started sawing logs like a damn chain saw. Two performances in one day took a toll on both men.

Maybe they won't be up for a private performance with you.

But getting it up had never been a problem for either of them.

"Lainie, darlin', are you muttering to yourself or talking to me?" Hank asked sleepily.

"Muttering to you. Where are we stopping in Miles City?"

"There's a parking lot across from the rodeo grounds. The contestants' area doesn't open until eight."

"That's in four hours."

"Plenty of time for what we've got in mind." Hank turned and slapped Kyle's thigh. "Rise and shine."

Kyle grunted.

Lainie ignored his *what we've got in mind* comment and focused on driving.

But Hank wouldn't let her ignore him. The man was hell-bent on distracting her. He used his rough-tipped forefinger to trace the bones on the back of her hand. "Why're you white-knuckling the steering wheel? Did the drive make you nervous?"

She shook her head even as her heart raced.

Hank stretched his arm across the back of the seat and stroked the side of Lainie's neck.

Kyle moved behind her in the backseat, twining her hair around his fingers. "What're you trying so hard not to think about, sugar?"

"Right now I'm only thinking about driving." *Liar, liar.*

"So, you're not thinking about my hands on your tits, while Hank fingers your clit?"

A wave of desire swamped her and she forced her gaze to stay on the white lines on the road.

"You're not thinking about how much you'd like us to both have our mouths on your nipples?" Hank's finger drifted from the base of her neck down her chest. His big hand squeezed her breast and his palm rubbed her nipple outside the lacy cup of her bra. "I think Lainie needs a little reminder, Kyle."

"I do believe you're right, Hank." Kyle mimicked Hank's position on her left side. Holding the weight of her breast in his hand. "I can't wait to get my mouth on you."

"Kyle—"

"Hush. I'd suck just long enough to make you squirm.

Then I'd use my teeth and give you that tiny bit of pain to drive you wild."

"Not me," Hank countered. "I'd suck softly. Swirling my tongue around the tip. Blowing on the wetness to see you shiver. Teasing you until I heard the whimper you make when you need to come."

Her sex softened and heated.

"I'd kiss down the smooth skin of your belly. Stop to flick my tongue across every indent between the bones of your rib cage."

"I'd move up. Focusing on this sweet section of skin." Hank's thumb swept lazily over the pulse point in her throat. "See how it jumps for the attention of my mouth?"

Lainie choked out, "You guys trying to get me to wreck the damn truck?"

Confident male chuckles.

"No. We're just refreshing your memory," Kyle murmured silkily.

"Not that you're thinking about getting nekkid with both of us or anything," Hank said in her other ear. "You're just driving, remember?'

Good Lord. Even their voices got her hot. These men knew exactly how to rev her up. Hands caressed her. Breath teased her. The sexual tension in the truck cab was so thick it prickled across her skin.

"Cat got your tongue?" Kyle asked.

"Maybe Lainie needs a reminder of all the things we can do with our tongues."

"Stop."

Hank whispered, "No. We want you so ready for us that the crotch of your jeans is soaked clear through. Mmm. I'm getting a whiff of that sweet cream, Kyle. How about you?"

Lainie clenched her thighs together. Ha! Like that

would hide her arousal. Heck, it only drew the muscles up tighter and made the ache sharper.

"Now that you mention it, Hank, I am detecting a hint of her hot juices." Kyle toyed with her hair; his coarse fingertips scraped her ear as if he were fingering her clit.

Hank said, "Exit here."

Miles City was dead at four a.m. The way to the rodeo grounds was clearly marked with signs—lucky for her, since her concentration was shit. Somehow she continued to hold on to the steering wheel, follow Hank's directions, and get the truck parked in the back of the lot.

She killed the ignition. The engine clicked and popped as it started to cool. No one moved. No one spoke.

Finally Hank climbed out his side. He rounded the front end and opened Lainie's door. "We seem to have lost our momentum, darlin'. Lemme see if I can get it back." Hank didn't just kiss her; he inhaled her. Turning her sideways on the seat, tugging her closer until she had to hold on to his shoulders or she'd pitch forward onto the concrete.

Not that falling on top of Hank was a hardship.

When his hands clamped onto her butt cheeks, urging her against his body, she circled her thighs around his hips. Hank never broke stride, never faltered a step as he carried her inside the camper.

Once Lainie was on her feet again, Kyle crowded her into the bedroom. Her calves hit the edge of the mattress and she had to grip his biceps to stop from toppling backward.

Not that squeezing Kyle's muscular arms was a hardship.

"Strip."

By the time she'd gotten naked, Kyle was already in the middle of the bed wearing a come-and-get-it grin, a bright green condom, and nothing else. When he crooked his finger at her, she pounced on him.

Hank chuckled behind them.

Kyle yanked the ponytail holder free and his hands were in her hair, using pressure on her scalp to keep their frantic mouths fused.

Bracing her hands by his head, she straddled the outside of his thighs and rubbed on him like a cat. Purring at the sensation of his chest hair tickling her nipples. Dipping low to feel his washboard abs tightening against the softer curve of her lower belly.

The bed jostled. Another pair of calloused hands drifted down her back, eliciting a full-body tremble. Fingers dipped into the dimples above her hips, then followed the crack of her ass, past her tailbone and anus, stopping at the wet mouth of her sex. Hank groaned. "Lord, woman, I do love how you heat up."

Kyle's hands left her hair as he ended the kiss. "Bring them nipples up here while Hank gets you ready for us."

"I'm ready now," she murmured, nipping at the cord straining in Kyle's neck. "Really ready."

Hands kneaded her ass, pulling her butt cheeks apart. A slick digit brushed her asshole as Kyle's hot mouth started working her nipple. She barely noticed when a finger breached the opening. But she definitely felt the second finger.

Hank's razor stubble scored her spine and he murmured, "Relax a little."

"Lift up onto your knees," Kyle said. He placed his hands on her hips, keeping his molten gaze between their bodies. "Take me in, sugar."

Lainie aligned his cock to her pussy, smiling at the visual, despite the *now*, *now*, *now*, screaming in her head for her to just slam down until he was buried deep.

"What's that smile for?"

"Talk about a Jolly Green Giant."

Hank's chuckle against her skin vibrated up the nape of her neck.

She looked at him over her shoulder. "What color condom are you sporting?"

He grinned. "Yellow. Feel free to comment about a yellow submarine bein' long, thick, hard, and filled with seamen."

Lainie couldn't help it; she giggled.

"Can we get to the fucking good part and save the jokes for later?" Kyle prompted.

Locking their gazes, Lainie dropped her hips and took him in completely. She lifted and lowered, squeezing her pussy muscles around his cock. Oh, yeah. That was so good.

Kyle groaned.

A hand landed in the middle of her back and pushed her forward. "My turn," Hank breathed in her ear. He circled the wet tip of his cock around her puckered entrance and was balls-deep in her anal passage in one quick thrust.

Pain. A burning that made her want to scream. The feeling of fullness—of being overfilled—caused a moment's panic. Lainie bore down on both cocks.

"Sweet fucking Christ," Hank gritted out behind her. "Do it again."

"It hurts." She arched her neck and closed her eyes.

"I'm sure." A tender caress floated up her back. "It'll get better, darlin'; it has before, right?"

"Uh-huh."

"That wasn't real convincing."

Because I'm not convinced.

Just breathe. In. Out. You wanted this.

Kyle's hands framed her face. "Lainie. Sugar, look at me."

Her lids flipped open and she stared into Kyle's eyes.

"You want to stop?"

Yes! "Um. I don't know."

"It's okay. Let us take care of you." He pressed his mouth to hers and started kissing her in his take-no-prisoners way. While Kyle brought her back to the level of passion they'd started at, Hank touched her. Trailing those wonderful rough-skinned hands up her wrists and arms. Across her shoulders and neck. Zigzagging her spine from top to bottom. Even the backs of her thighs and calves received his tender caresses.

Mesmerizing touches and hypnotic kisses relaxed her to the point that she began to move on Kyle. Slowly at first, until she realized rubbing against Kyle's pelvis abraded her clit. The faster she moved the more intense it felt.

"That's it. You're in control," Kyle whispered against her lips.

Hank just kept touching her, staying with her as she rode Kyle, but holding back. Reverting to the gentlemanly Hank.

But she didn't want to hold anyone back. She wanted to feel that burning edge of desire full force.

Even if it hurts?

Maybe especially if it hurt.

Lainie lifted her mouth from Kyle's. "Hank."

That was all she needed to say.

He pulled out until his cock head rested against her sphincter and closed around the crown. Then he plunged his shaft back in to the root.

She slid forward at the same time Hank withdrew. When she pushed down onto Kyle's cock, Hank thrust into her back channel. That sharp scrape against the sensitive tissues, feeling both cocks wedged so tightly inside her, separated only by a thin membrane . . . was erotic as hell.

A half snarl sounded and Hank's hips pistoned faster. Lainie attempted to match his pace, but she couldn't. So they began a countermovement—Hank's cock in, Kyle's out—and an entirely different, more intense sensation zipped through her blood and pulsed between her thighs.

Close. So close.

"That's it, baby. Take us with you," Kyle said. He jacked his pelvis up and his body stiffened beneath hers as he came.

Hank followed a second later with a hoarse shout. She swore she felt the heat of his ejaculate through the latex as his cock jerked against her tight bowels.

She shifted her pubic bone, searching for the perfect friction on her clit, and it was right there. Like a sudden storm, her orgasm burst free, tightening her pussy, compressing her anal muscles around the male flesh invading her body. Her clit spasmed and her vision dimmed as pleasure washed over her in an eruption of heat and light.

Eventually, Lainie realized hands stroked her. Words were murmured to her. She also realized she still had both of them inside her. She attempted to speak but her mouth was beyond dry and only a tiny squeak sounded.

Hank pulled out first. After Kyle slipped from her body, he helped her to her knees. She fell face-first on the bed, spent.

"Sugar? You all right?"

Lainie rolled over to see that both men had ditched the condoms. Hank wore a pair of plaid boxer shorts; Kyle wore just his skin.

Both wore identical grins. Cocky grins.

"Smug bastards," she muttered.

"Now, is that any way to speak to the studs who just rocked your world? At the same time?" Kyle asked.

"Hell, we even rocked the camper," Hank said.

They high-fived each other.

"This is a first for me, but you guys act like you've never double-teamed a woman before."

They both froze.

Her gaze flicked between their telling faces. "You haven't?"

Hank looked at Kyle and he shrugged. "Nope. It's a first for us too."

"It is? Why didn't you tell me?"

"When we came up with the idea to share you, we weren't exactly sure how that was gonna work. And when you agreed to travel with us, we wanted you to trust us. Admitting we were a quart low on threesome expertise wasn't the way to win your trust, so we figured we'd wing it."

"You honestly thought I'd be upset that you haven't done this before?" She laughed, but inside, she was strangely touched. "That couldn't be further from the truth. Thank you, guys."

"Our pleasure." Kyle crawled next to her.

"Ditto for me." Hank flopped on her other side. "Let's try to get some sleep. Dawn's creeping up."

Covers were distributed. Bodies were situated. Lainie tossed and turned because she could not get comfortable.

Kyle sighed. "This ain't working for me. Too damn many people in this bed. I'll sleep in the bunk." And he was gone.

Hank attempted to drag Lainie into his arms, but she wiggled away. "No offense, but I am not a friendly sleeper."

A long pause ensued. Then, "Would it be different if I'd left instead of Kyle?"

"No. The night I slept in your bed at the ranch, did we wake twined around each other? No. Not the first night we were together in the camper either. Last night, when I was with Kyle? Same thing. Ask him. I stayed on my side of the bed. I'm just not cuddly. I like my own space." She smooched his nose. "Stop worrying that I've been cuddling with Kyle and not you. Go to sleep."

∞

She woke up completely out of it. No idea what day it was. No idea where she was. She ventured out of the bedroom and found Hank sitting at the dinette.

He smiled. "We drank all the coffee but I can make another pot if you like."

"What time is it?"

"Noon. Kyle's already checked in."

"Noon! Why'd you let me sleep that long?"

"No reason for you to get up. Plus you drove last night." Hank sipped from a bottle of water. "Hope I didn't overstep my bounds, but while you were sleeping I checked out the medical facilities for you."

Hank's thoughtfulness gave her a warm feeling. "What'd you find out?"

"Staffed by volunteers. Two EMTs from the local ambulance service and two doctors on call."

"They just told you this?"

A sheepish look entered his eyes. "Nah. Told them I might've pulled a muscle in my neck. I chatted them up while they checked me out."

She was immediately behind him. "Let me see."

"Lainie—"

"Why didn't you say anything to me about this before?"

"Because I don't expect you to be my nursemaid."

Count to ten and don't yell at him. "Hank. That's what I do, who I am, and part of why you and I ended up together. Part of why you like me and why you hate me."

He chuckled.

"Look, I won't think you're weak or stupid—besides the fact that you like to tangle with bulls—if you let me check your injuries." She ran the back of her knuckles across the rugged planes of his face. "Besides making me feel useful, I like to do it, okay?"

"Okay." Hank removed his shirt and draped it across the back of the chair. He swiveled his head side to side, showing her the limited range of motion in his neck. "Don't know when it happened. Might've been a combination of bullfighting and sleeping in the truck cab. It's sore as hell."

She traced the inflamed area with the tips of her fingers. "Have you iced it this morning?"

"Nope."

"Taken ibuprofen or . . . something else?" She'd watched cowboys wander into sports med looking for a doctor to write them a prescription for "cowboy candy." Lots of guys were addicted to painkillers due to constant pain from their bone-jarring profession.

"Nothin'."

"Will you let me rub it to see if I can work the kinks out?"

"Yes, please."

Lainie smiled. Now she was on solid ground again after feeling like she'd been adrift.

Hank stretched out over the table and made groans and soft grunts while she worked him over. It amused her that his noises were similar to when they were having sex.

"God, woman, you have magic hands."

"Thank you. Want me to spread some liniment on the area?"

"No. I'm good. You goin' to the rodeo today?"

"I planned to. Thought I'd wander around the vendors' stands to see if I can find souvenirs for my sister and brother."

He pushed up from lying across the table and blinked at her. "You never talk about them. Why is that?"

"Mostly because I don't know them. My mom and Marcus tried to have a baby for ten years before she got pregnant with David and Nerise. By then I was seventeen. Three months later I was out of the house and living in Oklahoma. Taking care of Grandma and going to school kept me busy. Two babies kept Mom and Marcus busy."

"Do you get along with your stepfather?"

She shrugged. "I guess. He's a nice guy. He worships my mom and he's very involved with the twins." She dug her fingertips into his trapezius. "Marcus never tried to take the place of my father. Sometimes I wonder if that was my fault."

He groaned when she attacked a knotted muscle. "Why do you say that?"

"Because to some extent my mom is right. I've always had this hero-worship complex about my dad." Her hands stilled. "Can I tell you something I've never told anyone?"

"Sure."

"The reason I won't talk about my father isn't because it's so incredibly painful, but because I don't remember him."

Hank turned and looked at her. "Nothin' at all?"

"Oh, a few little things, like him taking me out for ice cream. Or dragging me to the rodeo grounds so I could watch him practice riding the mechanical bull. One Christmas he helped us decorate the tree. But besides that? He wasn't around. It was just me and my mom. He was always on the road. I do remember he'd come home and drop his stinky equipment bag on the floor. Then he and my mother would disappear into their bedroom because he was 'tired.' I remember thinking my mom took a lot of naps whenever Dad came home."

He chuckled.

"But as far as Jason Capshaw teaching me to ride a bike or coming to my Thanksgiving play, or sitting by my bedside when I had the chicken pox? That was all my mom. And she handled all those things even before he died. I wasn't as important to him as bull riding. I guess maybe I've always had that girlish hope that if he had lived, he would've wanted to become part of my life. Stupid, huh?"

Hank sat up and brought her onto his lap. He didn't say a word; he just held her. Brushing his lips on the top of her head and running his hands up and down her back. Silently soothing her.

Comforted beyond measure, Lainie sighed. "So what I know of my dad as a bull rider I learned from TV, books, and magazines. The rest of it I learned from my grandma. His boyhood, his teen years, the start of his rodeo career. But I know nothing of him as a man. As husband. Or as a father."

"Your mother didn't fill in the blanks for you?"

"I didn't ask." Guilt swamped her. "I suppose you think that makes me a horrible brat, huh?"

"Never." Hank kissed her temple. "I think it's a horrible situation, Lainie. I lost my parents too, but I had my growing-up years to get to know them. To learn from them. To see all the circumstances and events that made them into the people they were. Things you're curious about that you never had the chance to understand about your father. That is pretty horrible. So I am a little surprised you've chosen to work in the world of rodeo as a career."

She felt tears surface and quickly swallowed them down. "Will you continue on the circuit when you have kids? Leave them with their mommy on the ranch as you drive off to fight bulls?"

His body went rigid. "I haven't thought that far ahead.

And bein's I ain't got a wife yet, it's a moot point." A couple of seconds passed and he playfully slapped her ass. "Unless you wanna marry me and we can hash out the details right now so we're on the same page before we walk down the aisle together."

Lainie smiled, appreciating his attempt to lighten the conversation. "I'll take it under consideration." She hopped off his lap. She fiddled with the coffeepot, unnerved by how easy it'd been, spilling her deepest, darkest secret to him. What did it mean that she trusted him with something she'd never told another living soul?

"Oh, before I forget, I grabbed these from the grocery store across the way this mornin'." Hank set a pile of paperback word searches and word puzzles on the counter.

Holy crap. She did not know what to say.

When it took her a bit to answer, he shuffled his feet. "Look, it's okay if you ain't interested. You mentioned you used to do them with your grandma—"

Lainie turned and hugged him, pressing her mouth to his, not allowing him to explain away his sweet, thoughtful gesture. Allowing herself a moment to get her emotions under control.

"Thank you. I love them."

"You're welcome."

That was when Lainie knew everything was about to change.

Chapter Eighteen

The next week on the road was a grueling test of endurance. After Miles City, they stopped in Glendive, Montana. Then Sidney, Montana. After that, Williston, North Dakota. Then back into Montana, hitting the Wolf Point, Brockton, Glasgow, and Sand Springs rodeos.

Lainie started to believe it should be called Cowboy Hell instead of Cowboy Christmas.

Several rodeos held an afternoon performance as the first go-round; the final go-round was the evening performance. If Kyle placed in the top ten, he had to return for the second performance for a chance at winning the event. Every night after the bull riding ended, they were back in the truck, on the road, racing off to the next event on the list.

So far it'd paid off. Kyle finished in the money at every stop except Miles City. Ironically, that'd also been the last time they'd indulged in the no-holds-barred type of threesome. Heck, some nights they weren't having sex at all. Hank and Kyle were too damn tired. Or she was bleary-eyed and exhausted from taking over the driving duties.

Part of her wondered if Kyle was superstitious. He hadn't covered a single bull after indulging in the double-rider special. Since that night, they'd gone back to the fuck-and-suck variety of threesomes, and Kyle's winning streak was back on track.

Lainie wasn't bothered by the decrease in steamy sexual interludes between the three of them, as much as it bothered her that Kyle spent his limited free time with other CRA competitors—not with her and Hank. She was happy he'd forged connections; after all, Kyle had jumped into a new circuit midyear, and being the new guy sucked. She also understood Kyle's desire to get the hell out of the camper.

Hank suffered from cabin fever and road weariness too. To combat it, he'd secured an entire day and one night at an actual cabin in the woods outside of Great Falls, Montana. Lainie had looked forward to it for days.

Rather than show gratitude about the small break in the taxing schedule, Kyle had turned surly. He hadn't gone on the road to sit in a damn cabin. His only goal was to ride bulls, win money, and hit as many rodeos as possible. It hadn't helped matters that Hank had reminded Kyle that he owned the rig they were driving. He made the final decision on their destination. Far as Hank was concerned, they were taking one day off. Period. If Kyle didn't like it, he was free to make alternative arrangements.

So Kyle did just that. He'd hang out with them during the day, but in the evening he'd be competing at a tiny rodeo an hour away. An event that didn't have official points or a decent purse, but one that allowed Kyle to stick with his goal to ride at least one bull every day.

Everyone was happy with the compromise.

So it made no sense that Lainie was cranky. She was in a beautiful secluded cabin, with all the amenities—a real shower, a puffy feather bed, a well-stocked kitchen.

Lainie didn't like being cranky, especially when she couldn't pinpoint the source of it.

"Why the sour face, sugar?" Kyle drawled.

Thwack, thwack, thwack. She slid the red peppers off the cutting board and reached for a cucumber.

"Lainie?"

Thwack echoed again as the knife sliced through the thick green skin.

"What's wrong?"

She looked up at him. "Oh, are you talking to me?"

"Who else would I be talking to?"

"The man in the moon," she muttered.

Kyle frowned. "Did you say you're in a bad mood?"

"Did you say you had stuff to do elsewhere?" she retorted sweetly.

"Jesus. What's bugging you today?"

I don't have a freakin' clue. "Nothing."

"Then why are you whacking the shit out of that cucumber?"

Lainie glanced down. Damn. She'd pulverized it. "It's supposed to be finely chopped. Can't you go annoy Hank for a while and let me cook?"

His eyebrow lifted. "Annoying you, am I?"

"Yep. Now scram."

His eyes took on a hint of challenge. "I ain't much liking your tone."

"Too bad. I put up with your surliness all day yesterday and the day before, so you can suck it up."

Silence. Not particularly pleasant silence.

"Oh, I think you'll be the one sucking it up. Put down the damn knife."

"I'm busy."

"I don't care. I said now."

"Fine." She let the knife clatter on the cutting board. "What do you want?"

"Same thing you do." Kyle ambled around the center island. Grabbing her wrist, he towed her right out the front door, down the steps to the grassy area between the barn and the house.

Hank exited the barn and jogged over to them. He gave them a puzzled look. "What's goin' on?"

"I think Miz Lainie is missing us. But instead of coming right out and asking us to fuck her, she's stomping around."

"You know, I do believe you're right, Kyle. She has been a mite sassy today."

"Think if we filled that mouth of hers with cock she'd still be sassy?"

"Only one way to find out."

Lainie rolled her eyes. "Funny, guys."

"Do you see us laughing? Strip down."

"I'll pass on a little slap and tickle. In the past couple of days, with you guys being so tired, I've taken care of my own needs, thank you very much."

"Don't need us, do you?" Hank shot back.

"Nope." She flashed her teeth. "I just need more double-A batteries."

Silence.

"That buzzing noise I heard when you were in the bathroom was you getting yourself off?" Kyle said. "Damn. I thought you were brushing your teeth."

Lainie laughed, tossed her head, and started to walk off.

"Stop right there."

She didn't.

"Lainie," Hank said sharply, "that wasn't a request."

She slowly turned around. Both her men gazed at her

invitingly, hotly even, but their mouths and postures were set with determination. A tiny shiver of desire surfaced, that she could elicit those types of looks. "You're serious."

"Completely."

She gestured to the great outdoors. "I'm supposed to get nekkid out here?"

"Yep."

"You guys plan on standing around in your birthday suits too?"

Hank and Kyle exchanged a look. "Not your concern. Your concern is getting them clothes off. Now."

"Ha! Convince me that stripping down for you guys would be a better way to spend my time than chin-deep in a bathtub."

Now she'd done it, questioning their sexual prowess. Hank and Kyle would be hell-bent on proving their mastery of her body. How easily they could wring a screaming orgasm or twenty out of her.

Lainie couldn't freakin' wait.

"Darlin', that was the wrong thing to say. You'll take whatever we decide to dish out. Now strip," Kyle said.

His adamant tone sent her scrambling to get undressed—even when part of her wanted to protest his bossy behavior.

T-shirt gone, bra tossed to the ground, she kicked her flip-flops aside and shimmied her jeans and underwear off. She stood in the front yard naked as the day she was born.

Lust and something darker . . . like male power, settled on Hank's and Kyle's faces. Her gaze fell to the bulging crotches of their jeans.

"Fair warning: Since you pushed us, we're gonna push you back."

"Our demands will be rough on you."

Not *might* be rough, *will* be rough. Another shiver worked through her. She wasn't afraid. Just curious. What would these sexually adventurous men, who hadn't exactly gone easy on her, do to kick the kink up a notch or ten?

"Touch yourself," Kyle commanded gruffly. "Put those fingers in your pretty snatch and get yourself off for us."

Shoving aside the fact that she'd never masturbated in front of another person, let alone two men, Lainie closed her eyes. She placed her right index finger and middle finger on her mound, rubbing the slit. Gradually she scissored her fingers closed, trapping her pussy lips and her clit together, adding a few light strokes to coax that nubbin from its hiding place.

Crazy how fast she heated up, how wet and pliant her pussy had become. Feeling Hank's and Kyle's burning gazes, she pushed her middle finger down the seam of her sex and thrust it inside her cunt. Moaning, she added another finger and fucked herself, trying to get deeper with every plunge.

Neither Hank nor Kyle said a word, but she could hear their stuttered breathing. She could almost feel their pulses pounding in time with hers.

Masturbating was never as good as real sex, but it was always a faster path to orgasm. Lainie knew this wasn't about her getting off as much as about their forcing her to pleasure herself for their pleasure. Still, it'd take just a few concentrated strokes on her clitoris and she'd come. Using her middle finger, she rubbed quickly on her clit until the pulses gathered and expanded into one rhythmic explosion. She threw her head back and gasped.

Her eyes fluttered open when the sound of footsteps came closer.

Kyle and Hank were unhooking their belts. Unzipping their jeans. Tugging denim and boxer briefs down their flanks.

Blowing them both at once? That would be something new.

Hank said, "We watched you. Now you're gonna watch us."

Oh, wow. Not what she'd expected.

"On your knees." Kyle pointed to her jeans. "Use them for a cushion."

"Hands at your sides," Hank instructed after she'd dropped into position.

Her eyes moved back and forth between her men. Holy buckets, that was hot as sin, watching them jack off. Hank's rhythm stayed steady. Kyle's started out fast, then slowed. The rougher yanking and twisting on their cocks fascinated her. Lainie hadn't exactly been tentative, but she'd never been that aggressive.

Hands moved faster. The *slap*, *slap*, *slap*, of rough fists on male flesh, coupled with the harsh breathing, brought a fresh wave of lust over her, especially when Hank grunted and stepped closer.

In her peripheral vision, she saw Kyle move behind her. He swore and the sounds of him beating off increased. She peeked over her shoulder when he groaned and bit out, "Yes. Fuck. Yes." Warm liquid landed on her butt cheeks as Kyle ejaculated on her ass. Her cunt spasmed and she clenched her thighs together.

"Fuck, yeah," Hank rasped. Lainie turned to look at him as the first explosion hit her breasts. Hank's fist pumped as he aimed the spurts at her nipples. After the last splatter, he curled one hand around the back of her neck. "Lick me clean, darlin'," and brushed his wet-tipped cock head across her lips until she opened her mouth.

Hank pushed his cock inside halfway. His shaft had softened a little but not much. She swirled her tongue around the rim, suckling softly, humming her appreciation of his familiar salty tang.

He pressed his thumb against her jawbone. "Open wider. Take it all." He growled when she let him slide across her tongue until the crown touched her throat. "You are so fuckin' sexy, Lainie, with my come dripping off your tits as you're deep-throating my dick."

His raunchy descriptions tightened her nipples, her skin, her pussy. She swallowed a couple of times against the saliva building in her mouth and Hank pulled out. "Keep your hands by your sides."

Kyle stepped into view. "Use that sassy mouth on me too, sugar," and slipped his cock past her lips. He cupped his hands over her ears, tilting the angle of her head, fucking in and out as he pleased. "I like seeing my seed running down the crack of your ass. Makes me hard. Makes me realize I ain't nearly done with you." He shoved deep and stayed there. "How about you, Hank?"

"Oh, not by half. Keep her occupied. I'll get the supplies we'll need."

Lainie wanted to ask, *What supplies?* But she couldn't speak with Kyle's cock buried in her mouth. His shaft was rock hard, as if he hadn't just come. All over her ass.

He kept a lazy tempo, murmuring, "Get me wet," and "Use your teeth," and "Suck harder."

Surrendering her will to Kyle made her wetter and hotter than she'd ever imagined. She focused on pleasing him, getting him to that intangible point where he lost control. Where she held all the power as she brought him over the edge.

Two, three, four thrusts and he stopped halfway so the tip rested in the center of her tongue. "Swallow. Yeah. Suck like that."

His taste flooded her mouth and she swallowed the slick mixture until she'd milked him dry with hungry, rhythmic sucks.

A moment later Kyle tilted her chin to look into her

eyes. He swept her hair from her temples with the tenderest touch. "You are beautiful." Then he helped her to her feet.

Her body was a sticky mess, fingers, chest, chin, ass, between her legs. But Lainie forgot everything when Hank ambled into view carrying a sawhorse. And a saddle. And, sweet Jesus, was that a . . . *rope* draped over his shoulder?

Hank flashed his bad cowboy grin and her stomach cartwheeled.

"Kyle, grab some rubbers and lube from the camper." His gaze wandered over the dried come on her chest and he smiled cockily.

He dumped the saddle on the ground as he set the sawhorse down. "Am I makin' you nervous?"

"Not you so much as your unusual . . . supplies."

That damnably alluring grin appeared again. "Ah, hell, darlin'. It ain't nothin'. We're just gonna have ourselves a private rodeo."

"Let me guess. Instead of bulls and broncs, you're gonna be ridin' me."

"Such a smart cookie you are. Got it on the first try." Hank crooked his finger at her.

Lainie automatically walked to him.

He rested his backside on the sawhorse and tugged her between his legs. His dark, hungry gaze might've scared her if she weren't one hundred percent certain Hank would never hurt her. Not by accident, certainly not on purpose, and not ever in a moment of passion.

"Turn around and close your eyes."

She obeyed and faced the pasture, letting her lids flutter closed.

Hank's wonderfully calloused hands slowly floated over her limbs, from the cup of her shoulder down her biceps, past the bend in her elbow to her wrists. God. She loved the way his hands felt on her skin. He'd memorized every hot spot. Sweet spot. Ticklish spot. Running those rough-skinned palms and fingertips across her quivering flesh blanked everything except her anticipation of his next thorough touch.

Then those same strong fingers braceleted her wrists and he pulled them behind her back. "Hold still. Keep your hands like that."

Something abrasive brushed her knuckles.

He coiled the rope from the base of her clasped hands, past her wrists, stopping midway up her forearms.

Lainie shot him a sardonic look. "How long have you imagined tying me up?"

"Or tying you down?" Hank tossed back. He spun her forward. "About since I figured out you'd let me."

Ooh. Snap. "Is this one of those scenarios where I regret giving you guys free rein?"

"No." He framed her face in his hands. "Hell, no. But you have to trust us."

"I do. Or else I wouldn't be outside in the middle of the damn day, trussed up like a turkey, stark nekkid, covered in body fluid."

Hank grinned, sweeping his thumbs over her lips before letting his hands fall away. "Sounds kinkier yet when you put it that way, darlin'."

The camper door slammed. Hank squinted at Kyle. "You ready?"

"Yep. I see you've got our girl all geared up."

"Maybe I'm not raring to go for a scenario that involves lube and a saddle," she said.

"Too bad." Hank stood and Lainie recognized that the conversation was over. He crowded her until she started to move back. He kept his gaze locked on her eyes as he lowered his face until she couldn't see anything but him.

The simple press of his mouth to hers brought that uncontainable passion to the surface again. Her skin sizzled from the sun. From anticipation.

He tormented her mouth with barely-there brushes of his lips. Hard. Soft. Flirty. Clinging. Fleeting. Without the use of her hands, Lainie couldn't grab him. He merely chuckled against her lips at her disgruntled growl.

Kyle said, "My turn," and turned her around. He clamped his hard-skinned hands around her biceps, hauling her to her toes for the type of consuming kiss she craved. He whispered, "I love the taste of my come on your tongue."

Before the pure deliciousness of Kyle's desire kicked hers up another notch, Kyle returned her to Hank.

Passing her back and forth, Hank and Kyle tried to outdo each other with their possessive kisses. Gentle caresses morphed into insistent touches. The pinch of her nipple. Wandering fingers and avid mouths were fogging her brain.

On the next pass, she braced her feet and held her ground. "Enough." She glanced from Hank's face to Kyle's, a bit uneasy at the silent communication passing between them.

Hank quirked a brow at Kyle. "First go. Header or heeler?"

"Header. Definitely." Kyle's wide, almost feral grin twisted her gut into knots.

"Come on, let's mount her up. The saddle's already on the sawhorse."

Before she asked what the devil they'd conspired, the men lowered her across the saddle. Her belly rested on the curved seat. Her chest hung over the edge. Her feet almost didn't touch the ground, forcing her on her tiptoes.

Definitely kinky. Especially since neither had undressed, merely unhooked their belts and dropped their jeans only far enough down their thighs that their cocks sprang out.

"Comfy?" Kyle asked sweetly.

"No. Did you guys see this girl-spread-over-a-saddle scenario in Western porn?"

"No," Hank said behind her. "A few years back I saw a couple of bull riders demonstrating this with a buckle bunny. Except she was blindfolded. Oh, and they used a riding crop. Man, that chick loved getting her ass smacked."

"No ass smacking," Lainie warned. Though, if she was entirely truthful, she wondered if a spank or ten on her bottom would . . . enhance an orgasm.

Kyle's cock, sporting a bright purple condom, was right in her face. "You're not as opposed to the idea of a few controlled love smacks as you're claiming, sugar." He reached down to pluck her nipples. He tweaked the right one with more force than she expected. Lainie reared up; her mouth opened at the sharp sting. Kyle used the opportunity to slide in until his balls slapped her chin. "That's it. Stay still a minute, and mind those teeth."

Then Hank's hands were caressing her ass as he adjusted the angle of her pelvis. Without warning he impaled her with one snap of his hips.

God. They'd kill her with pleasure. It felt so damn good. All of it. She moaned around Kyle's cock.

He hissed, "Do that again."

She did.

His hands fisted in her hair, forcing her head up so their eyes met. "I prefer ridin' your face bareback, watching you swallow all of me."

For the first time, Lainie wondered why he wore a condom when they'd never used one during oral sex.

Hank's fingers dug into her butt cheeks and he made a soft growling noise.

Kyle withdrew until the rim of his cock head rested on her bottom lip. Hank mimicked Kyle's position, his dick resting at the mouth of her sex.

They slammed in simultaneously. Over and over.

Sweat coated her skin. A hazy veil shimmered behind her closed lids. Then all action stopped when Hank said, "Switch."

Kyle held her jaw as his cock slipped free.

Hank withdrew from her pussy.

Lainie struggled to move, but when she was wedged in the saddle, arms tied, legs spread, it was pretty much a moot point.

They switched places. Hank stood in front of her, his orange-latex-clad dick bobbing happily. He pinched her chin down and worked his shaft into her mouth.

"That's it, baby," Hank crooned. "Show me how much you like having my dick in your mouth. Can you taste yourself?"

She moaned and nodded.

While slamming in and out of her cunt, Kyle snaked a hand between her legs and toyed with her clit. Pinching slightly, which sent a jolt up to her nipples.

Belly, ass, mouth, cunt, legs tightened. The climax teetered so close. They teased her to the point that she couldn't stop whimpering. Her hips bumped up, but Kyle held her down, pushing his palm into the middle of her back. She arched her neck, but Hank put pressure on the top of her head, keeping her mouth at the angle that allowed him to drive his dick into her throat.

Lainie was utterly at their mercy.

And she loved it.

"Switch," Kyle said.

Her body was momentarily void of thrusting man parts. She slumped forward, letting her neck muscles loosen. Taking advantage of inhaling slow, full breaths when a cock wasn't stuffed in her mouth. She yelped when her hips were hiked up and her feet left the ground.

"Put your feet on my boots and give your legs a break."

"But that's the only break we're giving you." Kyle's groin appeared in front of her face. She smelled her own arousal. Saw the proof of it clinging to Kyle's purple-covered cock.

"How many times are you going to switch?"

"As many as it takes to keep you from coming," Hank said. "Because, baby, when we do get you off, it'll fucking blow your mind."

Kyle braced his hands on either side of the saddle and rose up on the tips of his boots. "Turn your head, sugar, and suck my balls."

While Lainie rolled the tight globes over her tongue, using gentle tugs of her mouth to elicit Kyle's groans, he brushed his fingers over her face with a gentleness bordering on reverence.

Hank wrapped his left arm around her waist to hold her in place, but it also gave him total access to her clit. Which he teased mercilessly.

"That's enough," Kyle said. His shallow thrusts matched Hank's controlled flexing of his pelvis as he thrust only halfway into her channel. When Hank began rimming the seam of her ass with a slippery thumb, in tandem with the steady stroking of her clitoris, that lovely, fluttery, ethereal feeling hummed in her blood. She braced herself for a world-class orgasm.

They both quit moving entirely.

She made a wild sound of aggravation that was completely foreign to her.

Kyle said, "She's close."

"Switch."

"I can't take any more," she whimpered. Feet shuffled.

Sweat gathered on her belly, gluing her skin to the saddle.

Hank forced her chin up to meet his gaze. The raw look of possession in his eyes sent goose bumps skittering across her skin, even though the hot sun beat down on her. "I know, baby; brace yourself." Then he rolled the condom off.

Kyle spread her ass cheeks and coated her hole with lube. One finger, then two twisted inside the tight entrance.

She arched up and gritted her teeth against the sharp, and yet not unwelcome, tinge of pain as he stretched her.

Hank stroked her clenched jaw. "Sure glad my dick wasn't in there when your teeth snapped shut."

Lainie snarled at him, which made both Hank and Kyle laugh. Mean little masculine chuckles. Torturous bastards.

You love it.

More lube. Then the tip of Kyle's cock circled her hole. She clenched when he started to feed his cock in.

"Lainie. Sugar, relax." Kyle stopped and put his hand in the middle of her back between her bound arms. "Lemme feel you breathe in."

But her breath stalled in her lungs.

"Put the vibrator in her pussy to distract her, Kyle."

Vibrator? What the fuck? "Were you snooping through my stuff?" she demanded.

"Yep. I was looking for toothpaste."

Hank choked back a laugh.

"Great idea. It'll almost be like we're havin' a four-way. Me, you, her, and her battery-operated boyfriend."

"You call him Bob?" Hank asked with a snicker.

"Nah, I'll bet his name is Dick," Kyle said.

More laughter.

Then Kyle inserted the buzzing shaft into her channel and she groaned.

"That's a girl. You like that. You'll like this too when I'm balls-deep in your ass. Now push out when you breathe out. That's it. Let me in. You're hot as sin, sugar; let us make you feel good."

She curled her hands into fists as the plump head of Kyle's cock teased the tight ring of muscle. The blood-rich nerve endings pulsed. Protested. Relaxed. Throbbed in sweet agony.

He seated himself fully in her ass with one push.

God. That did hurt, but in a way that made her eager for the next stroke. She lifted her head and said, panting, "No more switching."

Kyle chuckled.

Hank murmured, "No more switching, I promise." He ran the back of his knuckles across her swollen lips. "Wrap your pretty mouth around me."

She suckled the broad crown. A hint of the taste of latex remained, but underneath was the familiar taste of Hank. He filled her. Ignited her need.

"More. Take all of me." He held her head in his hands and fucked in and out of her mouth, in a different rhythm from Kyle. Harsher. More determined. More possessive.

Kyle countered every stroke in her ass with a flick of her clit. A deep thrust in, a tissue-rasping withdrawal. With the continual buzzing of the vibrator, Lainie felt her orgasm gathering. She'd started to drift away, anticipating that moment when everything synchronized into a glorious explosion.

"Shit. I'm there," Kyle said. "Tighten around me baby, that's it."

Groaning, Kyle flexed his hips. Even with the vibrator buzzing against her vaginal walls, Lainie felt every plunging twitch of his cock as he roared out his climax.

Hank retained a tight grip on her head and switched from deep-throated thrusts to shallower dips where her tongue constantly sought the spot below the head. He swore, pressing the tip in the middle of her tongue, forcing her to swallow convulsively as her mouth filled with his seed.

As she hung suspended with her front and rear still impaled, the buzzing of the vibrator increased. A finger rapidly flicked her clit. Rough fingertips plucked her nipples hard enough to bring the sting of tears.

"Have we overwhelmed you, darlin'? You need a little more to get you there?" Hank asked, letting his cock slip free.

She nodded.

"Close your eyes."

Lainie heard Hank step sideways and mutter to Kyle. Then something cracked across both her butt cheeks.

She gasped.

Another blow landed in a different spot and she yelped again. But with the next blow, something happened. All that energy and expectation loosened, so the next lash sent her careening into a continual stream of pleasure the likes of which she'd never experienced. Tingling, stinging sensations coalesced into a breath-stealing, mind-bending orgasm that veered off the charts. She screamed and thrashed, wanting the delicious torture to stop as much as she never wanted it to end. She floated. Soared. Crashed. Burned.

Lainie went limp. She'd probably end up with a sunburn on her lily-white ass, but she was too blissed out to care.

Chapter Nineteen

"Holy shit. We fucked her until she passed out."

"I don't know whether to be proud or appalled," Kyle admitted as he untied Lainie's arms, rubbing the red rope marks.

"Got her shoulders?" Hank asked.

"Yep." Kyle placed his arm across the front of her thighs and lifted her, rolling her until she was cradled against his body.

"Here. I'll take her," Hank said, reaching for her.

"I've got her," Kyle snapped.

"Guys. Don't fight. Especially not after that stupendous orgasm. And sorry to burst your egos, but you did *not* fuck me until I passed out."

Kyle kissed her forehead and glared at Hank. "How about if I pop you in the bath while Hank cleans up out here."

"Sure." She snuggled into Kyle's chest with a sigh. "Just don't let me fall asleep in the tub and drown."

"No worries." Kyle headed up the cabin steps, feeling the heat of Hank's stare on the back of his neck.

Inside the cabin, he held Lainie on his lap as the tub filled. She wasn't sleeping, but she didn't attempt to talk either. When he shut the spigots off, she stood and stepped over the edge of the old-fashioned claw-foot tub. She sank beneath the surface of the water with a long, deep sigh.

Kyle couldn't help but twine one of her corkscrew curls around his finger. "Need anything else?"

"I'd ask for a beer but that'll definitely put me to sleep." She trailed her fingers across the surface of the water. "What time is it?"

"A little after four."

Her eyes widened. "No wonder you wore me out. You guys fucked me for over an hour."

"Complaints?"

"Not hardly."

"Good."

"I imagine you're leaving for the rodeo pretty quick."

"Yeah." He released her hair. "You change your mind about coming along?"

Lainie shook her head. "If Hank wants to go, tell him I'll be fine here by myself."

"I think that's why Hank ain't goin'. Because you will be here by yourself."

"He thinks he'll sneak in alone time with me?" She snorted. "Trust me. I won't be in the mood at all tonight."

"Sex is not all we want from you, Lainie. Hank and I both want more. Surely you realize that by now."

With an irritated expression, Lainie slipped her arm from the lip of the tub and hunkered deeper into the water.

Kyle wouldn't allow her snit. Mostly because he'd been in one of his own for the last few days. "Talk to me."

"Neither of you expects more than a fling and that's fine. That's what we *all* signed on for. So when you guys say shit like that—which you both do—I don't know if you're trying to convince me or yourselves."

"That's kinda harsh, don't you think?"

"Be honest, okay? If I said, 'Kyle, let's move in together,' you wouldn't yell, 'Yippee!' No. You'd balk. Backtrack. Suggest we take it slow. One, because where would we live? Colorado Springs? Rawlins? Cheyenne? Two, when would we see each other? I switch circuits, remember? I won't always be assigned to the CRA."

"Can you ask to be signed strictly to the CRA?"

"No. I'm part-time. Heck, I'd prefer no travel and stable nine-to-five hours."

That floored him. "You would?"

Lainie jabbed her finger at him. "Yes. And that right there is why it wouldn't work between you and me long-term, Kyle. You're just now getting your career back on track. You'll be chasing eight for the next couple years, or at least until you get the demons out of your soul. Settling down isn't on your itinerary. Maybe if you were forced out of the rodeo life, but I'll bet you weren't exactly pleasant when you were recovering from the blown-out knee that sidelined you for an entire year, were you?"

Admitting he'd been a total jackass would put him in an even worse light. He hedged, "Probably not."

"Same thing with Hank. He's killing time on the road with you, with the CRA, with me, waiting for that EBS tryout next week."

Kyle's jaw dropped. "He told you about that?"

"No. Celia let it slip when we were at the ranch. She assumed that as Hank's girlfriend I'd know his future plans."

"But you haven't said nothin' to Hank about knowing?"

"I haven't said anything because it won't change shit."

Drip, *drip*, *drip*, echoed as the condensation from the mirror hit the pedestal.

"You wanna explain that?"

"Hank will be pulled in a bunch of directions. I'd never add to that burden. No matter how much I . . ." She closed her eyes and gestured distractedly. "*This* is why I never date rodeo cowboys."

Lainie's assessment was dead on. Kyle wasn't ready to settle down, not even close to it. Not now that he was back riding bulls, winning money, and finding his footing after a year of struggle.

You wouldn't consider settling down with a woman like Lainie, who is everything you ever wanted?

As the answer *no* shimmered on the surface of his subconscious, it was weighted with both relief and sadness. The hardest part was the realization that it didn't matter—Lainie wasn't his and never would be. She wasn't in love with him. She was in love with Hank.

The truth sliced his gut with the pain of a slow, rusty knife.

Kyle swept his hand down the wet slickness of her arm and threaded their fingers together, knowing it'd be the last time he'd touch her like a lover.

Lainie looked up at him, confusion puckering her brow. "What?"

"I'll let you finish your bath in peace." He stood and leaned over to press a kiss on her damp forehead. "See you in the morning."

He made tracks for the camper to get his gear and was surprised to find Hank sitting in the swivel chair, his boots up on the table, drinking a beer.

First thing out of Hank's mouth: "Is Lainie okay?"

Hank always thought of Lainie first. Always. "Tired. Still soaking in the tub."

"So you and she . . ."

"Just talked." Kyle dug through his equipment bag, checking the contents. Tape, gauze, rosin, a tube of liniment. Spurs, bull rope, a package of Tums. Extra tape, extra rosin, extra gauze, an extra jar of arnica gel. Spare spurs, spare socks, spare shirt, spare belt. Yep. He was good to go.

"What did you guys talk about?" Hank asked.

"Mostly about you. She knows about your tryout with the EBS. Celia mentioned it to her, because it was something you'd tell your girlfriend."

Confusion replaced his stunned look. "Why didn't Lainie say nothin' to me if she knew?"

"She figured if you'd wanted her to know you'd tell her."

"So why are you telling me now?"

"Because I'm taking off. It'll be the two of you alone tonight. Thought you might want to talk." Kyle zipped up the duffel and faced his longtime friend. "If you wanna fuck her tonight, fine, go ahead. Just understand, it ain't jealousy when I say your time might be better spent talking to her. There's a little more than a week left before we part ways. It'd be good if you two hashed out your issues before then." *Now that I know where I stand.*

Hank drained his beer. "You're right. It's just that when it comes to her . . ."

"I know." Right then Kyle knew Hank loved Lainie. He loved her in a way Kyle never would.

"Remember to come back and get us in the morning."

"That'd be a real hardship for you, Hank. Stuck up here alone in a romantic cabin in the woods with Lainie for a few days."

He grinned. "You're right. On second thought . . ."

Kyle punched him in the arm. Hard.

"Hey! And here I was gonna warn you to be careful tonight."

"Especially since you won't be there to be my hero and save me from the big, bad, nasty bulls?"

"Kiss my ass, Gilchrist."

"Not in this lifetime," he shot back. Tossing insults was easier than Kyle being pissy that Hank Lawson was a lucky bastard. He just hoped Hank was smart enough not to blow the best thing that had ever happened to him.

∞

Hank returned to the cabin. He followed the sweet floral scent of Lainie's shampoo and lotion to the bedroom. She was sprawled facedown on the middle of the big bed. From the doorway he couldn't tell whether she'd fallen asleep. He turned away, only to hear, "Hank?"

"I'm here. Didn't want to disturb you if you were conked out."

"I wish. I've got this sharp pain in my lower back and I just can't get comfortable."

"The hot bath didn't help?"

"No."

Hank stopped at the edge of the bed. "I could rub it, if you want."

Lainie lifted her head and gave him a droll stare. "Really?"

He raised his hands in mock surrender. "No strings. Thought I'd return the favor for all the times you worked out my kinks."

"Do you have all the kinks out of your system?"

What a loaded question. He deflected. "Up to you, Lainie, whether you want my help or not."

"I'll take it. Thank you."

He started to strip.

"What are you doing?"

"These jeans are dirty and constricting."

"Fine. But promise me no funny business."

"I promise. But I'm a little disappointed. I'll just kick my clown shoes and rainbow wig under the bed."

She laughed. "Smart-ass."

Lord. Did he love the sound of her laughter. He'd gotten so used to it in the last couple weeks, he didn't know how he'd live without it.

Isn't that the point of this night? You finally telling Lainie how you feel about her?

Once he'd stripped down to his boxer briefs, he tossed the pillows to the floor. "Scoot up so I ain't falling off the bed."

As Lainie moved up, the towel came loose and she tossed it aside. Hot damn. She was naked.

"I feel you eyeballin' my ass, Hank Lawson, and I'm reminding you that I'm a little sore all around."

He swept his hand up her back and was mighty pleased when she shivered from his touch. "I know. But a man can't help but admire the beauty of your body when it's spread out in front of him like a feast for the senses."

"Sweet-talkin' cowboy," she muttered, and turned her face away.

Hank grinned. He straddled her thighs and sat on his haunches, careful not to put his weight on her. But he couldn't stop his greedy hands from following the delectable curve of her ass up to the equally delectable dimples above that fine, fine ass. His thumbs pressed into the skin at the base of her spine and worked outward. "Tell me where it hurts, darlin'."

"Up a little. There. Now move out away from—Jesus. Right there. Exactly there." Her body went rigid.

"Relax. If you tense up it'll hurt worse, remember? That's what you always say to me."

Neither said anything, beyond Lainie's soft grunts of pleasure or sharply inhaled breaths when he worked her a little too hard.

Since she didn't protest, Hank massaged more than just her lower back. He did her shoulders, her arms, her hands, her spine. He massaged her butt cheeks, but he was careful not to dip between the tempting cleft of her ass or between her thighs.

Just when Hank thought Lainie was relaxed enough to sleep, she murmured, "Kyle told you, didn't he?"

"That Celia spilled the beans about my upcoming tryout with the EBS? Yeah."

"Are you mad?"

His hands stopped kneading. "Why would I be mad? I thought *you'd* be mad."

"Why would I be mad? I thought *you'd* be mad," she teased. "It's a great opportunity for you. When it comes to career stuff, I understand why you'd want to keep it under wraps until it's a done deal. I would've done the same thing."

Hank frowned. "Really?"

"Absolutely."

"Part of the reason I didn't tell you is because we'll still see each other regardless if I'm on the EBS or the CRA circuit."

Silence.

When her lack of response lasted longer than he figured it should have, he prompted, "Lainie?"

"Sorry. You've definitely worked the kinks out to the point that I'm almost comatose. I think I'll crash for a little bit. If you'd shut the door on your way out, that'd be great."

Feeling dismissed, he rolled off the bed and left the room.

Two hours later, Lainie sauntered into the kitchen

looking like a million bucks in a green-and-white-checked sundress. She smiled. "Something smells good."

"Just burgers. You hungry?"

"Starved. But you didn't have to go to all this trouble for me, Hank."

"No trouble. To be honest, I like taking care of you for a change."

Lainie looked away.

Bull's-eye. Maybe the stubborn woman would get it through her head that he'd like to take care of her all the time. "You want to eat in here or outside?"

"Outside."

∞

After dinner they moved to the porch swing. The night was clear enough to see the explosion of stars above the tree line. A slightly cooler breeze reminded them that they were in the mountains. She shivered and Hank grabbed a fleece blanket from the living room couch.

Then he hauled her onto his lap and tucked it around her.

"This is a beautiful place. Why doesn't your friend live here full-time?"

"He's usually on the road. When he has time to get away, he wants to go where no one can find him."

"And yet you've been here before," she pointed out.

"Me, Devin, Kyle, and the rest of the guys have been buddies most of our lives. Devin's brought us up here to go huntin', but we're sworn to secrecy." Hank whispered, "And you are now too."

"Why the cloak-and-dagger business? Is he a secret agent or something?"

"Or something. Ever heard of Devin McClain?"

"The country singer? Yes. My God. I love his music." She grasped his meaning. "Whoa. This is his place?"

"Yep."

"No wonder it's so secluded, with every possible amenity. Ooh, just think, I'll be sleeping in Devin McClain's bed tonight."

Hank growled. "Not something I wanna imagine, woman."

Lainie's laughter rang out and she lightly elbowed him in the gut. "Sucker."

For the longest time they rocked together on the swing. Hank could easily imagine spending every night of his life like this, Lainie on his lap, by his side, and in his bed. At times he suspected she might feel the same. But after seeing the dejected look on Kyle's face as they'd been in the camper earlier, Hank had sworn he wouldn't address his feelings or their future until the three weeks were up.

When Lainie pressed a warm, sweet kiss to the side of his neck, he had the foolish urge to shout out his love for her, damn the consequences.

She yawned. Again. "You guys wore me out today. How long is the drive tomorrow?"

"Four hours. Kyle will come back and get us pretty early, so maybe we oughta get to bed."

"Mmm. Where are you bunking? Since I'll be in Devin's bed."

Hank gave her a light head butt. "Come on."

In the amber glow of the bedside lamp, Hank watched Lainie slip on a skintight white tank top and butt-hugging silver-and-blue boy shorts, which fueled his Dallas Cowboy cheerleader fantasy.

Her eyes narrowed as she climbed into bed beside him. "What's got you wearing that lewd smirk?"

"Nothin'. But if you say, 'Rah! Rah!' even one time, I ain't gonna be responsible for my actions." He clicked off the light and lay flat on his back, staring at the ceiling.

Lainie wiggled to get comfy, like she always did. But

instead of moving away, like she always did, she scooted next to him. Right next to him. Heck, she practically crawled on top of him. "Cold?"

"No. I just feel like snuggling with you tonight. Is that okay?"

I love it. I love you. "Yep." He tucked the top of her head under his chin and pulled her closer yet, hoping his actions spoke louder than the words stuck in his throat.

Chapter Twenty

The roar of the crowd was infectious.

Lainie watched two little girls, who were awestruck at the lineup of rodeo queens and dazzled by the rhinestone belts, tiaras, chaps sporting metallic fringe, and big satin sashes.

Hank had scored her a good seat above the bucking chutes. She found herself peering at the contestant area, hoping for a glimpse of him. Without a pair of binoculars it was impossible to discern one cowboy from another. Hank was probably in the back with the livestock, checking out the bull situation anyway.

Why aren't you searching for Kyle?

Question of the day. The year. Maybe of her life.

Everything changed two days ago when she and Hank were alone at the cabin. She realized Hank wanted more than a fling. He probably always had.

It touched her in the last week that he'd gone out of his way to do fun, sweet things for her every day. Little romantic gestures like making her coffee. Helping her with word puzzles. Finding a magazine to interest her. Hand-feeding her Skittles and M&M's when she was behind the wheel. Or just holding her hand. Even when he slept.

But those silly tokens hadn't been the tipping point. That'd happened last night, when she'd caught Hank's eye as they were driving to another rodeo. The glow from the dashboard seemed dim compared to the light in Hank's face when he'd looked at her. As if he was exactly where he wanted to be, in the cab of a pickup truck, in the middle of nowhere, with her.

The time at the cabin had also changed the dynamic with Kyle. When Kyle wasn't driving, he was sleeping in the camper. He'd distanced himself—not that he was acting like a jerk, but he'd become quiet, claiming his winning streak meant he needed more time to mentally prepare himself for an event, not less.

Lainie had gotten used to Hank. Used to being with him all the time. They meshed in so many ways, it scared her.

It scares you because you were a little bit in love with Hank when this started. Even when you said you weren't going to choose, you already had.

Did Kyle sense that? Was that the real reason for his retreat?

Maybe, but Lainie couldn't shake the feeling that for Kyle, this sharing thing had merely been convenient, but for Hank, it'd always been so much more.

She just didn't know how to address it.

The sun clung on the edge of the horizon. Once that fat orange ball faded from view, the stifling heat would abate. Folks fanned themselves with programs. Kids sprayed one another with water-bottle spray fans. Babies cried. Children ran pell-mell up and down the wooden bleachers. Food and beer vendors constantly shouted their wares. Welcome to small-town rodeo America.

The first bareback rider started the night out with a bang—a score of eighty-two. Most riders hung on for the full eight seconds, but none surpassed the high mark set from the start.

Saddle bronc scores were usually higher than bareback scores, which seemed weird, given that bareback riders didn't have the saddle to help them keep a seat on the animal.

Interspersed between the bulldogging and the calf roping was a rodeo clown act. Hank always bristled when people confused bullfighting with what passed for entertainment.

During the act, Lainie wandered to the fence separating the contestants from the general public. Rodeo promoters stationed a guard at the contestant entrance. But a pair of double Ds popping out of a low-cut shirt pretty much guaranteed entrance anywhere.

Pangs of loneliness settled low in her belly. She was surrounded by families joined together with their love of rodeo, from great-grandparents down to the tiniest baby. Rooting for hometown contestants. Gossiping. Betting on scores and times. Beer drinking and some even dancing on bleacher seats. Lainie was a part of it, yet not completely. Working for Lariat often left her with the same sense of disconnection. Disconnected from her life and from her job.

Dammit. She wasn't a brooder by nature. Drifting in that direction wouldn't change a damn thing in her life tonight.

For the next hour, she watched the team roping—heelers had a damn hard go of it—and the specialty act consisting of trick riders and more unfunny clown antics. What struck her as odd was that the venue didn't dictate the caliber of the entertainer. She'd attended big events where the clown's entire repertoire consisted of fat-mother-in-law jokes and seen smaller venues that hired a better than average performer.

Barrel racing reminded her of Tanna, and Lainie realized she hadn't spoken to her in a week. Time on the road was a blur.

"Who's ready to see some bull riding?"

The crowd went wild.

The announcer detailed bull riding rules while the barrels were picked up. Guys ran out with rakes and shovels to even out the dirt. Lainie's stomach did a little flip when Hank's name reverberated through the loudspeakers.

As usual, Lainie's heart leaped the second that chute opened. As soon as the rider untied his riding hand and landed on the ground, Hank was focusing the bull's attention on him.

Twenty bull riders were on the docket. Some guys took extra time getting ready in the chutes, which caused the announcer to fill the air with mindless drivel. A restless energy rippled through the crowd. As much as no one wanted to see a bull rider hurt, the projectile ejections, the close brush with hooves made for a great show.

Who didn't love a great show? Thousands of people had witnessed her father's death. For some, it'd been an event to brag about. Some ghoulish people even bragged to her that they'd been in Cheyenne that fateful day. She never quite knew how to respond, so most of the time she mumbled something lame like, "Good for you," and escaped as soon as possible.

Kyle rode twelfth, drawing Moneymaker, the rankest bull in the go-round. Moneymaker had a reputation for staying calm in the chute. But the second that gate opened, the slavering beast roared to life with a vengeance. Unpredictable on his best day, Moneymaker had been ridden only four times in thirty-four outs, and each one of those rides garnered scores in the nineties.

Lainie gleaned some of the information about the bull from the program guide, some from the conversations around her, and some from the announcer.

"Next up, Kyle Gilchrist. This cowboy hails from Rawlins, Wyoming. Kyle's been on a winning streak lately, and let's hope his luck holds tonight. He's taking a shot at Moneymaker, a CRA American Finals Rodeo veteran."

Please be safe. Lainie leaned over the railing, hoping to see the action taking place in the chute.

Kyle rosined his rope. Fiddled with it several times. He slipped in his mouth guard. Canted his hips. Free arm waving above his head, he nodded to the gatekeeper.

The millisecond that bull tasted freedom, he let 'er rip. Fifteen hundred pounds straight up in the air. Twisting a hard left as he swung his hips right. Then right again.

Kyle slid sideways. If the crowd's gasps were any indication, everyone thought he'd fly off. He didn't, which was a testament to his skill and his tenacity.

Another high jump. Another hard landing for man and beast. This time Kyle wasn't prepared for the jolt and he pitched forward. He overcompensated and the next few actions played out in slow motion. Kyle was ejected ass over teakettle, but his hand was still tangled in his wrap. More gasps sounded from the crowd as they recognized he was in the position known as "the well."

That was when Moneymaker started his notorious tornado spin. Kyle frantically tried to get himself free. The bull spun so fast the bullfighters couldn't get close enough.

Lainie's terror grew when she saw Hank dart in midspin and slap the bull on the ass, hard, with both hands. Moneymaker stopped abruptly, sending Kyle swinging as he smacked into Moneymaker's side. During the momentary lull, Hank stepped in and yanked on Kyle's bull rope, freeing his hand.

Kyle dropped to his knees, cradling his arm, gasping for breath. He lost his balance and face-planted, oblivious to the animal gunning for him.

Hank threw himself below the bull's head, right at the gigantic chest, blocking the bull from landing on Kyle's spine. Yelling at Kyle, Hank rolled to his feet to run interference, as it appeared the bull would make another run at both men.

Kyle stumbled upright, scrambling for the barrier fence, falling once, getting back up to scale the metal rails.

Before the bull gave chase, he whipped his massive head around and caught Hank right square in the chest with a horn. Hank flew back and hit the ground face-first like a sack of potatoes. As if that weren't bad enough, Moneymaker's hoof grazed the back of Hank's head before the other bullfighter lured the bull away.

The pickup men immediately swung ropes, cornering the bull, dragging the livid beast to the livestock gate.

Hank wasn't moving. The other bullfighters gathered around and Kyle raced back, dropping to his knees in the dirt beside Hank.

Lainie couldn't breathe.

The medics rushed in, first snapping a neck brace on and then slowly rolling Hank flat. A stretcher appeared, vitals were checked. Next they'd lift him onto the stretcher.

Dammit. She couldn't see. The stupid medics were blocking Hank from the crowd's view. From her view.

Fear glued her to the spot.

What if he's dead? What if the bull pierced his lung and damaged his internal organs and he's bleeding to death? Just like my dad?

This was an absolute nightmare.

"Miss? Are you all right?"

She managed to turn her head to look at the woman whose eyes brimmed with concern. Lainie shook her head.

"Are you sick? You're pale as a ghost."

"I . . . can't . . ." She worked up enough spit to swallow and forced the words from her throat. "The bullfighter is my boyfriend."

"Oh, sweet Lord, child, no wonder you're in shock. Let's get you down there."

Lainie nodded numbly.

"You have to let go of the railing, dearie." She squeezed Lainie's hands with her own.

Somehow, Lainie's fingers uncurled from the rail and she turned away from the medics still working on Hank. Part of her didn't want to look away. Part of her didn't know if she could continue to watch.

"That's it." The woman wrapped her hand around Lainie's waist. "One step at a time. Ready?"

Again Lainie nodded.

The woman led her up the stairs to the main ramp. "I suspect your young man will perk right up once he knows you're at his side."

If he's conscious. If he's not already a lifeless blob with the light completely gone from his eyes.

Clapping echoed, jarring Lainie out of her morbid thoughts. Clapping meant they'd taken Hank out of the arena.

That doesn't mean he's all right.

When they reached the contestants' entrance, the guard blocked them. "Sorry, ladies. No admittance."

"This young woman is the girlfriend of the bullfighter who was just injured."

The guard gave them an accusing stare. As he debated, she heard Kyle shout her name from behind the gate. The man stepped aside.

Lainie noticed Kyle cradling his riding arm, and the bruise on the side of his face. The wailing of sirens in the background snapped her back to reality: Hank was injured badly enough to justify an ambulance ride to the hospital.

Kyle was out of breath. "I was just coming to find you."

"Is he . . ." Lainie couldn't force out the rest of the sentence.

"He's still unconscious. That's all I know."

She would've crumpled to the ground if not for the Good Samaritan keeping her upright.

"Let's get to the hospital." He grimaced. "I don't know if I can drive."

"Neither of you should drive. I'll drive you both," the woman insisted.

Lainie inhaled a deep breath. She stepped away from the woman and offered her a shaky smile. "I don't even know your name."

"Marion Basham."

"Thank you, Marion, for all your help. If it wouldn't be too much trouble, a ride to the hospital would be appreciated."

"No trouble at all. My car is close and I'll get you there in a jiffy."

Marion didn't chatter beyond asking the basics. Lainie was grateful for the buffer between her and Kyle. It would've been hell on her nerves to rehash the accident—as she knew Kyle was apt to do.

At the emergency entrance, Lainie thanked Marion profusely, which Marion waved off with the typical ranch woman's response, "I was glad to help."

The place wasn't bustling like most big-city hospitals.

Lainie wasn't sure whether that was a good sign or a bad sign. The nurse behind the desk took one look at Kyle cradling his arm and inquired, "Broken bone?"

"No. We ain't here about this. Has Hank Lawson, the bullfighter injured at the rodeo arena, been checked in yet? He came by ambulance."

Her eyes turned sharp and businesslike. "Who are you?"

"We're his family."

"He's waiting for the doctor. If you want to have a seat, I'll let his nurse know you're here."

"Is he all right?" Lainie blurted, even when she knew they wouldn't tell her a damn thing.

"I'm sorry, I can't give you that information. Like I said, the waiting room is right over there."

"Thanks." Lainie gave her name and Kyle's name and stood by the desk, trying to see down the hallway.

"Come on," Kyle said, tugging her away with his left hand.

After they sat, she faced him and pointed at his arm. "Did the medics check that out?"

"They weren't concerned about me at all." At Lainie's stark expression, he squeezed her hand. "I meant—"

"I know what you meant. You should get that looked at."

"So do it. Ain't like you're doin' nothin' else right now."

"You are such a pain in the ass sometimes." But Kyle knew how to keep her mind occupied. "Where's it hurt?"

"The better question is, Where don't it hurt?" he quipped. "If I woulda measured it before the ride and now after, I'd bet money I gained a good two inches of length."

She gently moved his thumb back and forth. "Excessive pain here?"

"Nope. Mostly above where the wrist brace ended."

"Issues with the shoulder socket? Feel like the muscles are torn? Did anything pop?"

"Not that I recall. I was trying to keep fluid so the bull didn't rip my arm clean off."

"You're lucky he didn't." She poked a couple more spots and was satisfied when he didn't react with pain. "My advice is—"

"Rest, ligament cream, and ibuprofen every four hours," they finished in unison.

Lainie muttered, "A smart-ass as well as a pain in the ass."

"This ain't my first rodeo, sugar. I've heard that advice a time or twenty."

Silence floated between them as the minutes ticked by.

"Hank saved my life."

"I know."

"I was so tired from trying to break free that falling in the dirt and letting that motherfucker stomp me didn't seem like such a bad idea. Now Hank is in there, God knows how bad—"

"Lainie Capshaw. Please come to the front desk."

Her heart pounded. Fear lodged in her throat. Dread lodged in her gut, making the trip to the front desk excruciatingly long. At the kiosk she choked out, "I'm Lainie Capshaw," to the young female nurse who'd paged her.

"Please come with me," she said brusquely.

"What's going on?"

The nurse, who was three inches shorter than Lainie's five foot four, stopped abruptly. "Mr. Lawson is refusing any treatment until he speaks to you."

"Hank's awake?"

"Awake and unreasonable. Maybe you can talk some sense into the man, since he demands to see you." Her ponytail bobbed as Lainie trailed behind her down the corridor. She motioned for Lainie to wait.

A privacy sheet separated the exam areas. The nurse snapped, "Mr. Lawson. Lie down. Right now. If I see you sitting up again, I'll restrain you."

"Try it," Hank snarled.

Lainie ripped the privacy sheet back so fast the metal hangers sounded like a zipper.

Oh, God. There he was. Pissed off. Wearing a flimsy hospital gown, the front open to reveal his chest. A sheet twisted around his lower half. His bare feet dangled off the side of the hospital bed, giving him a childlike vulnerability. Her gaze landed on his chest. The bruised sternum stood out in stark misery.

She slapped her hand over her mouth to keep from crying out. She felt Hank's eyes on her, but she couldn't tear her focus away from his injury.

"Lainie. Baby. Look at me."

Her tears fell unchecked.

"Look at me. Only in my eyes."

Somehow she lifted her gaze to his face.

"That's it. Just look in my eyes. Let me prove to you I'm okay."

"I thought—"

"I know what you thought, and I've been goin' crazy trying to convince them to let you in here to see me. Come here."

Lainie wanted to move, but her feet failed her.

Hank's eyes darkened with fear. "Please. I think they're gonna drug me up, but I've gotta make sure you're okay before they do." He held out his hand to her. "Come here."

She shuffled four steps and reached for his fingers. More tears spilled down her cheeks. She let her gaze drop to his chest again and whispered, "Costochondritis."

"You know how I love it when you use medical sweet talkin' on me, darlin'."

Although she barely grazed his skin with her fingertips, she felt the heat and the swelling. "Does it hurt?"

"Some."

Any admission of pain from Hank meant it was probably excruciating. "Why wouldn't you let them give you a painkiller?"

"Because you needed to see me awake and alert. Able to talk to you. Able to reassure you I was fine, not passed out cold, lying on some goddamn gurney. I'd never do that to you, Lainie. Never, ever. Not if I can help it."

Oh, sweet baby Jesus. The man was in a hospital bed and his first concern had been for her, not for himself. *For her*. He'd worried that after what she'd seen in the arena, she'd draw parallels between his accident and her father's.

Hadn't you?

"Talk to me," he said softly.

As much as she wanted to burst out with her deepest feelings of love for him, she'd do it at a different time and place. A time when he'd know for sure that she'd spilled her guts out of love, not out of fear.

Her shaking fingertips traced the flattened line of his mouth. He was gritting his teeth so hard his lips had all but disappeared. "Now that you've calmed my fears, will you please let them give you relief from this goddamn ugly rodeo tattoo?"

"Yeah." His face was pinched with agony when he tried to swing his legs back up on the bed by himself. "Fuck."

"Let me help you or I'll call your devoted nurse back."

"You've got a big mean streak for such a small thing." He grunted. But he allowed her to help him.

As soon as he was situated, Lainie pushed the damp hair back from his hot forehead. He practically purred. She touched him, reassuring them both.

Lainie didn't budge when the curtain was jerked back. She shot a glance at the woman wearing a white coat, not scrubs. She clutched a clipboard and scanned it before addressing them.

"I'm Dr. Tortor, T-o-r-t-o-r, not Dr. Torture, as some patients have been known to call me." No smile. "So, you fight bulls for a living? Seems this one fought back."

"It happens."

"How do you feel?"

"Lousy."

"No surprise." She examined him thoroughly, then said, "A horn to the chest resulting in a bruised sternum. The medical term is costochondritis."

Hank gaped at Lainie.

"The CT scan came back with no brain swelling. Although, after being knocked unconscious for seven minutes, you've suffered a concussion. I'd like to keep you overnight for observation."

"No. Way." Hank focused distressed eyes on Lainie. "Why can't you take care of me? You're a licensed nurse and an EMT."

Dr. Tortor faced her. "Is that true?"

"I'm a sports med tech."

"You see injuries like this frequently?"

"Yes, but I defer course of treatment to those with more medical training."

"That'd be me, and a stay overnight is what this doctor orders."

Hank groaned.

"We'll get the pain meds started and move you into a regular room."

"Thanks, Doctor," Lainie said.

"And no bullfighting for a minimum of one week. I know you won't stay out of the ring for my recommendation of one month."

The doctor pressed the call button for the nurse. They conferred outside the curtain. Rather than eavesdrop, Lainie mapped the planes and hollows of Hank's face with her fingertips. She bent to kiss his mouth softly, then nuzzled his ear. Thank God. He was here, whole and wholly hers.

"Lainie? Stay with me until the drugs take effect. Please."

Hank's low, scratchy voice pulled at her, as did his hidden pride and the need he so rarely shared. She smooched his lips again. "Like I could leave you alone with Dr. Hottie, who, incidentally, was checking out all your nekkid body parts hanging out of this ass-baring gown."

A small smile. "All my nekkid body parts belong to you, baby."

"Don't you forget it."

After Hank received the meds, he conked out. She rode the elevator with him to his room, chatting with the orderly as he maneuvered the gurney. She'd never worked in a hospital, except for dropping patients off in the ER, and sometimes she wondered if she was missing out on an aspect of her medical training.

It wasn't until her cell phone buzzed with a text message from Kyle that she realized she'd forgotten him completely. Shame heated her face.

She stepped into the hallway to call him, but he didn't answer his phone. Not that she blamed him.

Chapter Twenty-one

Breck was sprawled in a lawn chair outside his horse trailer when Kyle ambled up. "Hey, Kyle. You look like you could use a beer." Breck gestured to the blue cooler. "Help yourself, and pull up a chair."

"Thanks." Kyle opened an icy can of Bud Light and sat on the picnic table bench seat. He sighed. "I needed that."

"I imagine so. What's up with Hank? He okay?"

"Concussion. Bruised sternum. They're keeping him overnight."

"He's damn lucky." Breck leaned over and toasted Kyle. "Then again, so are you."

"Don't I know it. Crazy man saved my life."

Breck shrugged. "I ain't bein' a dick when I say it's his job and what he signed on for."

Kyle chose not to respond concerning what he saw as the differences between what most bullfighters did and what Hank had done.

"What's the diagnosis on your ridin' arm?"

"Sore as fuckin' hell."

"So you're ridin' tomorrow night?"

"Yep. Wouldn't you?"

"Yep."

Kyle sipped his beer and glanced at the mostly dark campsite. "Quiet night for a two-day event."

"Most people are grabbing shut-eye while they can. We'll all be back on the road tomorrow night."

"Where you headed?"

"Council Oaks, Idaho. Then Red City. There's a good eight, nine days of action in Idaho and Oregon." Breck pushed his hat up on his forehead a little higher. "What about you?"

"We were gonna swing down through Jackson Hole. Pick up a few events in the western side of Wyoming and then Utah before we hit Colorado." Kyle fiddled with the metal tab on his beer can. "Now I ain't sure what'll happen, bein's Hank has to return to Muddy Gap to recover."

"No bullfightin' at all?"

"Guess not." Hank had no stake in finishing out Cowboy Christmas. The real payday for him would be getting selected to work in the EBS.

"Still don't answer my question. What're *you* gonna do?"

"Since it's Hank's rig and camper, I reckon I'll go back to Wyoming. Figure out what to do from there."

"Or if you wanna keep up the winning momentum, you can hit the road with me," Breck offered.

Whoa. That'd come out of left field, as so many things had today. Not just getting hung up on the bull, or Hank's going above and beyond to save his sorry ass. But seeing Lainie's reaction to Hank's injury. Mostly seeing Lainie's reaction to Hank. And how Hank reacted to her. Like she was everything.

When an hour passed and he hadn't heard from Lainie after she'd gone to the exam rooms, Kyle had sweet-talked the nurse into letting him sneak back there.

Damned ironic, after all the threesomes they'd been in, that he'd felt like a fucking peeping Tom, watching them together from a crack in the curtains.

Kyle had left the hospital immediately afterward. At loose ends, he'd sat alone in the camper, contemplating his options before wandering over here.

"No big deal if you'd rather pass," Breck said, breaking Kyle's melancholy.

"It's not that. What about Lee?"

Breck sighed. "He's already gone home. He ain't won money in the last fifteen stops, so he's hanging it up for this year. Feels guilty bein' away from his wife and baby girl."

"I would too. I ain't gonna spend my life on the road, but after spending last year sitting out, I missed it. Guess that means I'm not done with it neither."

"Good to hear. So's that a yes?"

"Yep."

The pinched look vanished from Breck's face. Smiling, he flipped open the cooler lid and fished out two cold beers. "Next case is on you, partner."

Hank snarled when fingers prodded his head, waking him up for the millionth time. He bit out, "Jesus, I'm fine," and squeezed his eyes shut against the intrusive light burning his eyeballs.

The nurse chuckled. "Open your eyes so I can check them and I'll go away."

Muttering, he complied.

"You're due for more medication if you want it."

His entire body throbbed. As he started to deny his need for it, Lainie spoke.

"Just give it to him. He's been restless the last hour. And he won't ask for it."

Hank looked at Lainie, sitting in a chair beside his

bed, her fingers threaded through his. The poor woman was exhausted. Dark circles beneath her eyes were the only color on her pale face. But she still looked beautiful to him.

She smiled wanly. "See? If I order it, you still get to be the macho tough guy."

The nurse snorted. "Cowboy, she's definitely got your number."

"Goes with the territory," Lainie said. She and the nurse chatted in medical jargon that made no sense to him. But Hank was just content to listen to Lainie's soft voice. Content that she was here by his side.

After the nurse left, Lainie stood. "I need to stretch my legs and use the bathroom. I'll be right back."

"Lainie, darlin'. That chair can't be comfortable to sleep in. You don't have to stay here all night."

She crossed her arms over her chest. "Then why did you ask me to stay tonight if you didn't want me here?"

He froze. "What? I asked you?"

"You don't remember?"

Hank shook his head.

Her eyes searched his. "What do you remember?"

"You bein' with me in the ER. Coming up here. Then the nurses waking me all the damn time."

"But nothing else you said?"

"Ah. No."

Lainie smirked an I've-got-a-secret smile.

"What? Did I say something . . . ?" A niggling sense of unease arose. Shit, had he been spouting poetry or something? A man under the influence of narcotics couldn't be held responsible for what he'd said, could he?

Fuck. Had he blurted out that he loved her? Body and soul? Straight down to the bone?

That'd be embarrassing.

Wouldn't it?

No. It'd be a relief. If she didn't feel the same he could blame it on the drugs.

She leaned across the bed. "So, you're not going to fuck me until I can't walk when you're feeling up to it? Because I was kinda looking forward to it."

He attempted to keep it light. "Since I feel like dog shit, it might be a while." After he said that, Hank held his breath, fearing she'd toss off something flip, like that Kyle could keep her motor running while Hank recovered.

Lainie let her lips cross his in a sweet, lingering glide. "Lucky for you I'm a patient woman, Hank Lawson."

His eyes felt heavy, his body went limp, and then the lights went out.

∞

The next morning, after Hank's discharge, they waited in front of the hospital for Kyle to pick them up. Hank crawled in the rear of the quad cab and stretched out across the bench seat. Fuck. It didn't matter if he lay down or sat up; his body hurt like a motherfucker.

"Hank, buddy, I'd ask how you're doin', but it's obvious you ain't back up to full speed yet."

"How's your arm?" Lainie asked Kyle.

"Fine. I iced it down last night. Put liniment on it this morning. Took some pills. I'll wrap it tonight before I ride."

"So you *are* riding tonight?"

"Of course. Different purse. More points." Kyle stretched his arm across the back of the seat so Lainie could examine it. Then he looked at Hank. "I figured you'd take off for the ranch. So I'm joining up with Breck. He lost his traveling partner. Won't be hitting the same rodeos we'd planned on, but going toward Oregon and Idaho."

Hank almost protested—but his greedy side reminded him that with Kyle gone, he'd be with Lainie. At home. For a week.

That alone was almost worth getting injured for.

He shifted slightly and stabbing pain shot through his midsection.

The rest of the drive to the rodeo grounds was quiet. Hank was starting to relax and lose consciousness as the throbbing in his chest abated and the pain pill kicked in. Doors opened and closed.

"Take care, Hank. You're a lucky bastard."

"I know."

"I'll keep in touch."

The last thing he heard was Lainie saying, "I'll help you pack."

∞

Outside the door to the camper, Kyle said, "Thanks for the offer, but I'm already packed up."

"Maybe I just want to talk to you in private."

Lainie glanced at the duffel bag and Kyle's equipment bag. She jammed her hands in her pockets. "You're ditching us for Breck, huh?"

"His traveling partner left yesterday, so it's actually great timing."

"Breck seems like a good guy."

"He is."

Her stomach roiled when she saw the wariness on Kyle's face. "I won't ask you not to go."

"I know. Which is why I'm goin'," he said softly.

She'd been a fool to believe no one would get hurt in this situation. "I'll be rooting for you."

"I appreciate it. I hope my luck holds."

"It will. You're a great bull rider."

A ghost of a smile appeared and vanished. "Don't give me those sad puppy-dog eyes, Lainie. We knew it'd end. It just happened sooner than we expected."

Lainie had no response.

"Hank will heal faster at home in Muddy Gap. Especially with you taking care of him. He's a great guy, but I don't need to tell you that."

"Kyle, I didn't mean—"

He held up his hand, halting her excuse. "I know. You didn't want to choose. But you have. I accept that. I'll admit to feeling a bit glum, as I'd hoped it'd be me. But to be honest, Hank is the best guy I know. You're the best woman I know, so in my mind, you and Hank are the best match."

She swallowed, determined not to cry.

"Don't worry. I won't be an ass to you or Hank, or blab to anyone about how we spent Cowboy Christmas. It'll stay our secret, because, sugar, I don't have a single regret."

"Me either."

"When I see you at CRA events, I won't make it awkward—"

"You won't see me at CRA events," she blurted. "Or at EBS events. Or at any events."

His eyes clouded with confusion, then sharpened with suspicion. "What are you talking about?"

Her shoulders slumped against the camper. "I'm switching to an administrative position with Lariat. Full-time. I can quit my part-time EMT job. No more weekends on the road. To be honest, it isn't as glamorous as I imagined."

Kyle frowned and she backpedaled.

"Don't get me wrong. I love the people part of my job. But all I see is the airport or the inside of my car, another hotel room, and the medical room."

"And you just realized this?"

"Maybe. This constant traveling opened my eyes. Showed me what my dad went through in his quest to be the number one bull rider in the world. Made me appreciate my mother's point of view." She inhaled and let out a sigh. "She's off base on a lot of things, but she was right about this. I'm getting the short end of the stick working half-time for Lariat. It'd be easier to be on the road full-time or not at all. I'm choosing not at all.

"It's another reason why this worked for us. We're at a crossroads in our lives. You, switching to the CRA. Hank, trying to decide if he wants to do the bullfighting gig full-time. Me, realizing I don't want my life to be work and sleep."

"Does Hank know about your job change?"

She shook her head. "I'd planned to tell you both at the same time. But since you're moving on, I figured you deserved to know the truth."

Kyle scratched his goatee. "I'm surprised, but not completely. I'd wondered about your change of heart from a big 'no' to throwing yourself into our threesome idea. Was the thought that you wouldn't have to face either of us afterward why you agreed at the last minute?"

"Yes."

Silence.

Lainie tried to remember why she thought this scenario would be an easy, fun fling.

"Hey." Kyle touched her cheek. "No regrets, remember? It's all good, Lainie. I'll be fine. I promise."

She looked at him. No anger or sadness lingered on his face. Just acceptance. "You are a great man, Kyle Gilchrist. Someday you'll find a woman who appreciates everything about you."

"I already did. But the problem is, she's in love with my best friend." He pressed his lips to her forehead. "Take care of yourself, Mel. I'll see you around."

He walked away and didn't look back.

∞

Lainie set the GPS. Eight hours' travel time. At least she was making the drive during the day, so she could enjoy a little of the scenery.

At first Hank flat-out refused to sleep in the camper. She'd dealt with enough belligerent cowboys that she wasn't cowed by his behavior.

When Hank realized Lainie wasn't bluffing about dragging his ass back to the hospital if he didn't fall in line, he shuffled into the camper. Making sure his cell phone was within reach, as well as a bottle of water and a barf bucket, she tucked him in with a kiss. Then she hit the road.

At the halfway point she topped off the tank, checked on her patient—still out—and took a bathroom break. After being in the constant company of Hank and Kyle, she found her own company didn't thrill her. She was lonely. How Tanna did this by herself week in, week out boggled her mind.

Dusk teased the sky when she started up the long driveway to the Lawson ranch. Abe had the cab door open almost before she'd parked. "Thanks for driving him home. How's he doin'?"

"Still asleep. Which is the best thing for him, although he'll tell you he's just fine."

"How are you?"

She hadn't expected that. "I'm okay. But watching him take that horn to the chest and the hoof to the back of the head about did me in."

"I can imagine."

"Is Celia around?"

Abe shook his head. "She'll be back the day after tomorrow."

"Who's been helping you with the stuff that needs doing around here?"

"Me, myself, and I. We're a good team." Abe grinned.

Lainie grinned back at him, because he reminded her so much of Hank. "I'd like to tag along tomorrow morning and help out, if that's all right."

"That ain't necessary; you've already done enough."

"Hank will be crashed all day, and I'm not the greatest at figuring out what to do with free time. So be warned: If you don't take me along to see the daily grind of a Wyoming cattle rancher, I'll find something else to occupy myself. Like rearranging your closets and cupboards. Fun stuff like that."

Abe measured her. "Hank don't get away with nothin' with you, does he?"

"Nope."

"He's always needed a good woman to keep him in line." He jerked his chin toward the camper. "How's about we get the patient inside?"

Hank walked inside mostly on his own. He took a pain pill, took a leak, crawled into his own bed, and was out for the night.

∞

The next day, between times of obsessively checking on Hank, Lainie hung out with Abe. Oddly enough, she never felt restless. She certainly never felt bored. She was completely relaxed. More content than she'd been in a long time.

So the cell phone call from Doc Dusty should've come as no surprise. Lariat had added three last-minute venues with the second tier of the EBS circuit: a two-day event in Santa Rosa, New Mexico, a one-night event in River Bend, Texas, and a two-day event in Salt Lake City. Since he'd sent everyone on vacation, Dusty was desperate for her to fill in as a Lariat representative.

It was damn difficult for Lainie not to feel resentment—even when she could've said no. But that was why Doc had called her; he knew she wouldn't turn him down.

So much for the remaining week of her vacation time. First thing in the morning Abe would take her to Rawlins. She'd rent a car and drive to Denver. From there she'd fly to Santa Rosa, stay three nights, rent another car for the six-hour drive to River Bend, stay one night, and fly out the next afternoon to Salt Lake City for two nights. Then she'd fly to Colorado Springs, giving her one day before starting her new position with Lariat.

Why wasn't she looking forward to any of it?

Because it means leaving Hank.

After a late-afternoon cattle check with Abe, Lainie peeped in Hank's bedroom, expecting he'd still be asleep.

But he was showered, dressed in ragged sweats, and unpacking his equipment bag.

"What are you doing up? Get back in bed."

"Nope." He piled his dirty clothes into a laundry basket. "Two days of sleep cured me."

"But—"

"Lainie. I'm fine." He finally looked at her.

She had to admit he did look better. Color in his cheeks. Clear-eyed. Belligerent posture.

"See? So tell me what you've been doin'."

"I drove yesterday. Hung out with Abe today. Watched over you. That's about it."

"Bored out of your skull, were you?" he said dryly.

"Not even close. I did ranch stuff, which was fun. But I did miss you. Although you do argue less when you're unconscious."

"Ha, ha."

"You hungry?"

"Starved."

"Sit. I'll bring you a tray." She started for the door.

"Like hell." Hank grabbed her hand and tugged her against his body. "Next time I'm in that bed you'll be in it with me. And we won't be sleeping."

"I wouldn't want you to strain yourself."

Hank gave her the naughty grin that turned her insides into pudding. "If I ain't straining myself to please you between the sheets, then I'm doin' something wrong."

When she didn't smile, he tipped her chin up. "Darlin', I'm okay. I promise."

"I'm glad."

"Then what's wrong?"

Lainie sighed and pressed the side of her face into his chest. "I hate to tell you, but Doc called me a couple hours ago. I have to leave tomorrow. A bunch of last-minute EBS events." She braced herself for his demand that she stay as he played the sympathy card about his injury. But Hank didn't.

He kissed the top of her head. "Well, we'd better make the most of tonight, hadn't we?"

∞

Abe vanished after supper.

Lainie supervised Hank while he stretched the kinks out, making sure he didn't push himself too soon. He appreciated her concern and he took it easy with the exercises. But as soon as she was gone he'd have to figure out a way to work through the pain. His audition in Tulsa was in five short days. No way was he missing it.

Later they sat side by side, swinging in the old porch swing. As much as he loved just being with her, he needed to touch her. To reconnect with her in the most elemental way so she truly understood he was all right physically. Emotionally the thought of her leaving was almost more painful than getting kicked around by a bull. But neither of them was ready to deal with that tonight.

"Lainie."

"Mmm?"

"I want you."

She brushed her moist lips across his ear. "Then take me."

Hank twined his fingers through hers and led her to his bedroom. "Get nekkid, woman."

She stripped and then bounced on the middle of the bed, causing her tits to jiggle nicely. "Hank, you're not convincing me you're recovered."

"Why's that?"

"You're a little slow getting them britches off."

"Darlin', you ain't seen slow yet. Not by half."

Lainie groaned.

"Kick those covers aside so I've got room to work." Hank lowered himself beside her. Looking into those shining eyes, he saw something more than lust. It knocked him for a loop, same as it had the first time he'd seen it: the night they'd been alone together at the cabin.

She whispered, "Why are you staring at me?"

Because I love you. I think you love me. And why can't we just be adults about this and admit the truth?

"Hank?"

"Because I'm trying to decide where I wanna start kissing you first."

"I can make a suggestion," she said huskily.

"Mmm. I'll bet you can." With barely-there kisses, he teased the plump, wet softness of her mouth until her breath hitched. Until she latched onto his neck to bring his mouth down on hers.

After letting her think she had control, he eased back to gaze into her eyes again. "Is that really where you want me to spend my time kissing you?"

Lainie scratched the beard bristle on his jawline. "No. I want to feel this rough beard between my thighs. On my nipples. My belly. My neck."

He growled. "Arms above your head."

She arched sexily, a long curve from her wrists to the wanton cant of her hips.

Hank placed his mouth on the hollow of her throat

and licked straight down the valley of her cleavage, not stopping to suckle the hard tips of her nipples or the rounded underside of her breasts. His tongue followed the shallow indent of her smooth belly. He circled the tip of his tongue around her navel and across the quivering skin of her lower belly, stringing kisses along the line of tight curls.

"I love that."

His answer was a long, slow, flat-tongued lick from the entrance to her pussy up the slit. He didn't intend to drag out her climax forever, but he wouldn't be denied the time to enjoy her thoroughly.

He nibbled into the soft recesses of her intimate flesh. Lapping at the pink folds, swallowing her sweet cream. Holding her hips down with a warning squeeze when her pelvis shot up.

"Hank, please."

He moved his mouth away a fraction of an inch and blew a stream of cool air across her hot tissues.

Her whole body trembled.

That was when Hank zeroed in on her clit, letting his tongue lightly flick the nub. As soon as her breathing changed he suctioned his mouth to it and sucked hard.

"Just like that—yes!" That sweet, hot flesh contracted and spasmed against his tongue and pulsed against his lips.

The friction of his cock head against the sheets was almost more than he could bear. He released her clit, rubbing his razor-stubbled face against her inner thighs. He loved this secret part of her. The pale white skin looked even more exotic against the tanned skin of his hands.

Hank meandered up her luscious body. He tended to her breasts, admiring the perfect weight of them in his hands, the slight upturn to the nipples, and how tightly the tips budded in anticipation of his mouth.

Lainie arched. Then she blinked and bestowed that secret womanly smile that made him nervous.

"What?"

"You are one damn handsome man." She traced his lip with the pad of her thumb. "And you sure know what to do with this mouth."

"Who's the sweet talker now?" He rested his forehead to hers. "Spread your legs, baby, and let me love on you."

"Anytime, anyplace."

He lowered his body to hers, hissing in a breath when her tits crushed into his chest. Pleasure rocketed through him when her soft belly brushed his. His eager cock aligned to her core of its own accord. He watched her eyes glaze with pleasure as he eased into her heat and welcoming wetness.

"That's always so good," she whispered against his throat. "Every time."

Truer words had never been spoken. "You don't mind that we're face-to-face?"

Lainie lightly slapped her hands on his cheeks. "I love being face-to-face with you. Especially now that I know missionary isn't the only position that you excel in."

"You had doubts?"

"Maybe at one time. Not now." She smooched his lips with each word. "You. Rock. My. World. Hank. Lawson."

"Lainie. I—I—"

She put her fingers over his mouth. "Don't. Just be with me like this."

Rough kisses fed soft. Deep, rhythmic thrusts became shallow rocks of his hips. Hank moved with her, on her, in her, gave her all of himself and received everything from her in return.

She was wholly his. She in turn owned him completely.

It was beautiful. And scary. And amazing.

There was no race to orgasm. Just the constant ebb and flow of skin sliding on skin. Heartbeat matched to heartbeat. Lips clinging to lips. Breath mingling with breath. His senses were awash in the feeling of connectedness. Of rightness. Of their making love to each other, bodies, hearts, souls, and eyes wide open.

She whispered his name and unraveled.

Hank found release right along with her.

In the afterglow they lazed in his big bed, Lainie resting on her stomach, head pillowed on her arms. Hank dragged his fingertips up and down her spine. Or he played connect the dots with her freckles and moles. "You really have to go?"

"Yes. I wish I didn't."

"Is that your way of saying you don't mind hanging out at the ranch? Even though I slept through the days you were here?"

She smiled. "Fishing for compliments about your spread, Hank—for shame. You know I like it here."

"I'm glad." He placed a kiss at the base of her neck. "You sure you want Abe to take you to Rawlins tomorrow?"

"It'll be easier."

Lainie didn't explain whether she meant easier on him because of his injury, or easier for them to say goodbye here, rather than in public. Either way, this wasn't a permanent separation. They'd see each other soon on the circuit.

Hank wouldn't push her for any kind of promises until after he knew where his career was headed. "Well, it ain't gonna be easier on me, darlin', 'cause I'm gonna miss you like crazy."

"Same goes."

Chapter Twenty-two

The trip had been a nightmare from the start. Delayed flights, long lines at the rental-car places. Brutally hot weather. Crappy motels. Snarly contestants. Jerky coworkers.

Lainie was ready to throw in the towel.

Tanna was making a special trip to see her tonight because River Bend, Texas, was a mere five hours from her family ranch. It was the only bright spot in Lainie's long day.

Since the sports medicine room was at the opposite end of the arena, Lainie had to schlep everything from the van through twisting corridors. Lariat was shorthanded. She'd anticipated a busier than normal shift. However, she hadn't expected Bobby, the other staffer—a local hire—to sit on his fat ass and direct her in an irritating king-to-peasant manner.

Bobby took great pains to point out that he'd earned a master's degree in sports physiology. He snarked that he'd limit her medical help to handing him adhesive bandages, emptying the medical waste receptacle, and fetching coffee.

It'd gone downhill from there.

The fill-in doctor was a pretentious prick. Between the two men, Lainie felt about an inch high. She kept her mouth shut and did what she was told.

The event was second tier—meaning none of the top sixty EBS riders were competing. It surprised her to see two guys from the big tour hanging out in the cramped medical room with their buddy. A lot of bull riders were unbelievably cocky, which was another reason she'd chosen not to date them.

You dated Kyle.

Kyle was different. He'd never pulled macho cowboy bullshit with her. She'd expected him to look down his nose at the CRA bull riders, as the rivalry between the CRA and EBS was legendary. But he'd fit right into the CRA circuit. She wondered how Kyle was doing. Lainie hadn't spoken to Hank since she'd left Wyoming five long days ago.

"Excuse me. If you're done starin' at Jake's ass, he could use some medical help."

Guffaws broke out.

Lainie's gaze whipped to Ace Newharth. Even though he was dead wrong about the direction of her unfocused gaze, trying to stop her blush was pointless. "What do you need?"

"What're you offerin' me, sweetness?" Ace said with a lewd wink.

A punch in the mouth. "Do you require medical assistance?"

"Yes. I've got this pain in my groin. You wanna get down on your knees and have a closer look at it?"

More braying laughter.

Lainie bit back her response—*I don't have a cure for*

small cocks—and said, "If you don't have a real injury, leave so we can assist those that do."

A male chorus of *ooohs* rang out.

Ace's mouth flattened. "You ain't pretty enough to get away with talkin' to me like that."

Direct hit.

Lainie turned her back on him. But he grabbed her arm and jerked her close enough to gift her with garlic breath. "Let me go."

"Ask me nice. Real nice."

What the hell were her male colleagues doing while this asshole was manhandling her?

Out of the corner of her eye she saw Bobby and Dr. Horrible engaged in conversation. They weren't paying attention to their own patients, let alone her. Swallowing her anger, she softened her tone. "Please. Let go of my arm, Mr. Newharth."

"You know my name."

"Everyone knows your name." *Everyone thinks you're an asshole* went unsaid.

He released her. Smiled nastily. "Lucky for you. Now see to my buddy; he thinks he sprained his riding thumb."

"I'm afraid I'm not qualified to help him with that." She pointed. "That doctor is."

All three bull riders harrumphed and ambled away. But Lainie felt Ace's eyes on her the entire time. It creeped her out. Not only was he married, but he proudly proclaimed himself a Christian cowboy. His crude behavior really rankled her.

Tanna had texted her that she'd pick her up out front at the main entrance to the arena. Three-quarters of the way through the event, Lainie started hauling stuff to the sponsor's van—with no help from Bobby or the bad doctor. Dusty always lent a hand. Did he do that at all events? Or just the ones she worked? Because she was a woman? Or because she was Jason Capshaw's daughter?

Didn't matter. She wouldn't say boo to Dusty about his nonhelpful workers. Wouldn't be her concern much longer anyway. She'd be working nine to five in the office, and hauling boxes would be someone else's responsibility.

She stopped to watch the last rider, hoping the guy didn't get injured, as she'd already packed up the medical supplies. He rode eight seconds without incident.

The door to the medical room was closed on her return but the Lariat Sports Medicine team sign remained up. Neither Bobby nor Dr. Horrible was in the room, but they'd left their marks: empty Styrofoam coffee cups, soda cans, food wrappers, blank pages of paper.

Dammit. She was not a maid. Grumbling to herself, she set the room to rights. She'd almost finished when she heard the shuffle of boots behind her. She whirled around and found herself face-to-face with Ace Newharth.

The hair on the back of her neck stood up. Her heart rate spiked. What was he doing here?

Stay calm. There could be a perfectly valid explanation for why he's shown up.

She couldn't muster a smile, but she managed to keep her tone even. "Mr. Newharth. The medical room is all packed up."

"And you're all alone." The sound of the door clicking shut was as loud as a gunshot.

"What do you want?"

"A little taste of your feisty side."

"I'm not interested. It'd be best if you left. Right now. Before Bobby and the doctor get back."

"They're gone. It's just you. And me."

"Get out."

Ace laughed and advanced on her. "I ain't goin' nowhere. Neither are you. 'Cause you gotta get past me to get out that door. And there's a reason my nickname is 'Tank,' so go ahead and try. I don't mind getting rough."

Lainie screamed. Twice. As loud as she could.

He was on her in an instant, shoving her into the cement wall. One hand clamped over her mouth; the other circled her throat. His lower body trapped hers. "Do that again and I'll wrap my hands around your neck until you pass out. Then I will fuck you while you're unconscious any fuckin' way I want to if I hear another sound come out of your stupid mouth. Understand?"

She nodded.

He rubbed his fingers over her lips. The garlic scent of his breath in her face made her gag. "Bet you can suck real good."

A sick feeling ran through her. How long before things started to go fuzzy from lack of oxygen to her brain?

"Shoulda been nicer to me." His hand pushed into her larynx hard enough to bring tears to her eyes. His lower body pinned hers to the wall.

Stay alert! Kick him in the balls. Do something. Don't just stand there! Fight back.

"Do you rape your wife too?"

Ace dug his fingers into her throat, lifted her head, and smacked it hard enough into the cement that her vision dimmed.

Don't pass out. Don't pass out.

"Shut up." His other hand circled her biceps, pinching the tender skin on the underside of her arm until she whimpered. "You brought this on yourself."

The door opened and Tanna's voice drifted in. "Lainie? You in here?"

Ace abruptly released her and stepped back.

Only by sheer will did Lainie stay upright.

"What the fuck is going on here?" Tanna demanded, closing the distance between the door and where Lainie stood.

Ace sidestepped Tanna and booked it from the room.

Lainie closed her eyes. Tears seeped out as she slowly slid down the wall to the floor.

"Oh, my God, Lainie. Are you all right?" Tanna dropped to her knees beside her.

She couldn't speak around the sobs gathered in her throat that hadn't yet burst free.

"Was that . . . Did he try . . . ?" Tanna clasped Lainie's hand between hers. "Did that son of a bitch attack you?"

She nodded slightly.

"Fuck. Fuck that and fuck him. I'm goin' after that bastard right fuckin' now." Tanna scrambled to her feet.

Somehow Lainie found the strength to grip her hand. "Don't go."

"I need to catch him before he gets away."

"I know him."

"All the more reason to grab him until the cops get here."

"No cops," she rasped.

Tanna's eyes turned sharp. "Did you hit your head? 'Cause, girl, you ain't making a lick of sense. What do you mean, no cops?"

"Please. Can we just go? I just want to get out of here. I don't think I can stand to be in this room another minute." Lainie started to cry.

"It's okay. Shh, sugar. We'll go. Lemme help you up."

Once Lainie was on her feet, she felt more in control. She shouldered her duffel bag and followed Tanna through the winding and dark corridors. Her body returned to panic mode immediately. The urge to run. To constantly look behind her. Every noise made her jump.

"Almost there. You doin' okay?"

No. "I think so." She was glad she hadn't run into anyone she knew. Or anyone she didn't know. She wanted to curl into a ball and cry until she forgot this ever happened.

Inside Tanna's truck, Lainie leaned forward, hugging her knees against the shakes she was trying to control. They seemed to be driving a long way, so Lainie lifted her head. "Where are we going?"

"I booked a hotel for tonight. But it's a ways out, since everything else in town was full."

In the hotel room, Lainie threw her purse on the bed and escaped to the bathroom. She cranked the water to hot. When the tiny space was filled with so much steam she couldn't see her hand in front of her face, she climbed in the shower. Water beat on her head and streamed down her body. She stayed enclosed in the heat until she'd calmed down. After slipping on her pajamas, she exited the humid space.

Tanna paced, a bottle of Jack Daniel's dangling from her fingertips. She stopped. Stared. Swigged. And passed the bottle to Lainie.

"No, thanks."

"Drink up. It'll help. Trust me."

Lainie knocked back a slug. Before the first shudder set in, she gulped another mouthful. "That always tastes like shit."

"I know. But gentleman Jack is one guy who's exactly as he appears: cheap, potent, trouble if you don't keep a lid on him, and mean as a snake the morning after." Tanna pointed to the bed against the wall. "Sit. Talk. I was fixin' to bust down that damn door if you hadn't come out."

"How long was I in there?"

"Forty-nine minutes. Start talkin'."

Lainie sighed and dropped on the mattress. "Everything is getting more surreal the more I think about it."

"I'm sure. It's called shock."

Another slug of Jack Daniel's and Lainie poured it all out. She finished with, "If you hadn't come in, he would've raped me." There. She'd said the word.

"You're being way too calm about this, Lainie."

"No. I'm not making light of this, but it could've been much worse than him shoving and grabbing me."

"That doesn't mean you shouldn't file charges. Jesus. He attacked you. At the very least it's attempted sexual assault."

Lainie signaled for her to pass the bottle over. She drank deeply. Once. Twice. "Maybe. I need some time to think. I don't want to talk about it anymore."

Tanna's brittle smile relayed her frustration. "God knows I want to get shit-faced, and it didn't even happen to me."

She lay flat on the bed and stared at the ceiling.

"So what's up with you and your guys?"

Another fucked-up situation Lainie didn't want to discuss, but Tanna could be a real bulldog. "The truth? I've fallen in love with Hank Lawson. Completely. Totally. I want to wake up with him every morning and have his babies—that kind of love."

"Really? Hank?"

"Why is that such a surprise?"

"If you'd asked me early on, I would've guessed Kyle was the front-runner in the 'win Lainie's heart' contest."

Lainie turned her head and looked at Tanna lying on the other bed. "Why?"

"Now, don't get pissed off, but Kyle had the advantage because he's a bull rider. Like your father was."

Lainie scowled. "That has no bearing on it."

"Plus, Kyle had bedroom tricks up his sleeve that Hank didn't."

"At first, but trust me when I say Hank more than made up for lost time and opportunities."

Tanna bounced up and snatched the bottle from Lainie. "You cannot toss that out there and then pull that silent crap. Spill."

"You know when you have those defining moments in your life? And everything that seemed so murky suddenly becomes crystal clear? I had one of those."

"When Hank was injured?"

"Ironically, no. Before that."

"Does Hank know how you feel about him?"

"I think so."

Tanna studied her curiously. "While you were in the bathroom did you call Hank?"

"No."

"Why not?"

"Because I'm fine. I don't want him to worry. His big tryout with the EBS was this weekend in Tulsa, and there's nothing he can do about it from there."

"Maybe you ought to allow Hank the chance to comfort you like you comforted him when *he* was hurting."

That statement jarred her.

"Think about it. You'd be pissed if it were the other way around and he kept something like this from you."

True. Quiet seconds ticked into minutes. The booze took effect, filling Lainie's body with a mellow heat. She blinked sleepily. Resting her eyes for a bit was a good idea.

An annoying buzz started by her head. Then it finally stopped. Tanna shook her shoulder. "Lainie? Wake up. Hank wants to talk to you."

She peeled her eyelids open. "Hank is here?"

"No. He's on your cell."

Lainie squinted at her. "Why were you answering my phone?"

"Because it buzzed like four times, so I figured whoever was calling needed to talk to you."

"Did you tell him?"

Tanna gave her that what-the-fuck-do-you-think look.

"Give me the goddamned thing." Lainie held the phone away from her ear in anticipation of Hank yelling at her. "Hey."

"Baby, are you okay?"

"I've been better. How'd your night go?"

"Don't you pull this subject-changing bullshit on me. Jesus Christ. I cannot believe you were attacked. Why didn't you call me right away? Do you have any idea how hard it is for me to stay fucking calm?"

"Which is why I didn't call you. I knew you'd be upset."

"Upset?" he barked. "I'm beyond upset. When I get my hands on that cocksucker I'm gonna break him in two. Then feed him to the hogs."

"I'm fine."

"I'm not. I won't be fine until I lay eyes on you, Lainie, so fair warning—I'm on my way to River Bend right now."

Butterflies took wing in her stomach, not from the whiskey. "Hank—"

"Not another fucking word. I'll be there in roughly seven and a half hours. We'll talk about how we're gonna handle it then."

"I can't believe you're coming here."

"Lainie. Darlin'. Did you honestly think I'd stay away?" His tone was as soft and sweet and loving as she'd ever heard from him. "Baby. That ain't the kind of man I am."

She teared up. "I know."

"Good. Rest up. I'll be there before you know it."

The tight feeling in her chest that booze couldn't loosen gave a little. She hung up.

Tanna sat beside her. "Don't be mad at me."

"I'm not. God. How could I ever be mad at you? Especially after you—" Her voice caught on a sob.

"Maybe the whiskey wasn't such a good idea if my tough-as-nails buddy Lainie is starting that 'I love you, man' crap," Tanna said.

Lainie laughed and sobbed simultaneously. Then exhaustion and Jack Daniel's overtook her.

∞

Hank's blood absolutely boiled. For the first time in his life, he truly understood what *savage* meant. The thoughts he entertained on the drive turned more bloody and violent with every mile. When he managed some semblance of control, he called Kyle.

It took Kyle a while to calm down from his burst of rage. Hank waited and watched as the mile markers passed by.

"So what's your take on this?" Hank asked Kyle. "You've competed with him. Do you know him?"

"Bottom line is, Ace Newharth is extremely cocky, with a holier-than-thou attitude and a huge following from hard-core fans who want religion with their bull riding. He's also the favored son of several prominent sponsors, as well as in tight with the president of the EBS."

"Which means what, Kyle? He can't be touched? He's immune to the law?"

"Yes. No. Fuck. I don't know what good it'll do to file charges against him, because they'll never stick. It fucking sucks."

Hank counted to ten. "Our only option is to sit around with our thumbs up our asses while that fucking lowlife can get away with attempted rape?"

"Hank. Listen to me. I hate this as much as you do. But it'll be Lainie's word against his."

"Tanna was there. She stopped it."

"For which I owe that girl a lifetime of thanks. But I've watched Ace spin things, charm his way in and out of good and bad situations. He'll claim it was a misunderstanding. And without pissing you off and bein' crude, if Lainie's clothes weren't ripped and she didn't have the typical signs of an assault, they'll question even what *Tanna* saw. Ace is slick as shit. He's probably already conned a couple of guys into backing him up with a legitimate reason why he'd shown up in sports med."

"So we just give up?"

No answer.

"Kyle?"

Kyle's voice dropped and Hank strained to hear him. "When a woman makes an accusation of attempted sexual assault, the woman's character is always brought into question, not the man's. Especially not someone like Ace Newharth. Although we've been discreet, it might come out that Lainie's been traveling with both of us. That's bound to add more fuel to the fire."

Fuck. Hank hadn't thought of that.

"Sure, we can say she's your girlfriend, but it'll still cast a shadow on her character, not his. Is it fair? Fuck, no. That's the way it is. I don't see that there's anything we can do for her besides just bein' there for her."

"It don't seem like enough."

"It ain't." He paused. "Look, the only other suggestion I have is to call Dusty. He knows Lainie wouldn't cry wolf, and Dusty might put pressure on the powers that be in the EBS to bring sanctions against Ace."

"You know, that's a damn smart idea. I'll suggest it to Lainie once she and I hash this out."

"You're on your way to River Bend now?" Kyle asked.

"Yeah. She claims she's fine. I just need to see her. To make sure she's okay with my own eyes."

"That's the best thing for her, havin' you there. Lainie needs you. Let me know how she's doin'."

"For sure."

"Good enough. Be safe on that blacktop tonight, my friend."

"I will. You too."

∞

The drive had been a blur after that.

Hours later Hank knocked on the door of room 212. Just as he was thinking Tanna and Lainie were probably both asleep, the safety chain clanked against the metal door before it opened.

Tanna held her finger to her lips and rolled a suitcase out behind her, keeping the door slightly ajar.

"How is she?"

"Sleeping. I encouraged her to drink a little Jack Daniel's for medicinal reasons and let's just say she had more than one. She's stayed asleep since right after you talked to her."

"What else?"

Her eyes searched his. Tired eyes. "Don't take this the wrong way, but don't grill her first thing when she wakes up. I've already done that. If we were playing good cop/ bad cop, you need to be the good cop."

"I can handle that. Has she changed her mind about filing charges?"

She shook her head. "The son of a bitch needs to pay. We haven't lost the window of opportunity, but it did close some when she didn't take immediate action."

Hank relayed Kyle's suggestion about contacting Dusty, and Tanna nodded.

"Makes sense. It might have an effect, but I ain't holding my breath that it's gonna change anything."

He frowned. "Why'd you push her to go to the cops if you didn't believe they'd take action?"

"You misunderstand. I believe the cops would take action. They'd see it as attempted assault, whereas the Lariat and the EBS guys will agree with Lainie's 'don't rock the boat' attitude and sweep it under the rug."

"Bullshit."

"Look, you've been in the world of rodeo for a long time, Hank. So have I. But being a woman in this world is completely different. I've lived and dealt with and cried and fought against the discrimination and chauvinism that abound in this sport. Everything from hiring all-male stock contractors, to the all-male event promoters, to the all-male prize awardment committees, to the all-male sports medicine team."

"Lainie ain't male. I know. I checked."

Tanna rolled her eyes. "Lainie is the *only* female working for Lariat down in the trenches on the circuits."

"So?"

"So there are some people—men, specifically, men in positions of power, specifically—who don't think she should be in what's basically a men's locker room."

"That's asinine."

"The attitude is what it is. Be a tough row for her to hoe if she sticks around after making the accusation. We both know what the bastard did, but there are a lot of folks who won't believe her. Who'll believe she's only saying it to get attention. Yeah, the whole situation sucks balls."

They stared at each other in miserable silence for a beat or two.

"I fucking hate this."

"Me too."

His gaze landed on her suitcase. "You taking off right now?"

"You guys don't need me around."

"You've already done more than enough." Hank cleared his throat. "I don't know if I can ever thank you. If you hadn't shown up there when you did, this could be a much worse situation to deal with. She could be . . ."

Tanna squeezed his forearm. "I love her too, Hank. Your racing here to be with her is more than payment enough. Tell her to call me later. The room is paid for through tonight."

Hank hugged her. "Thank you, Tanna. Safe travels."

His heart was pounding something fierce when he entered the room. He imagined the worst. But Lainie looked the same as ever. Except for the small thumb-shaped bruise on the side of her throat.

Still, she looked absolutely beautiful to him.

He didn't touch her, though he longed to smooth her wild curls. He longed to wrap her tightly in his arms and never let her go. He longed to pepper her sweet face with kisses. Feel her breath drifting across his chest.

Instead he pulled out the desk chair and watched her sleep.

Chapter Twenty-three

Hank had about half dozed off when he heard the covers rustling. His eyes flew open and he caught her staring at him.

"Hank?"

He stood. "Lainie. Are you—"

She jumped out of bed and launched herself into his arms before he'd taken a single step.

"Oh, God. You're really here."

Everything that felt wild in him settled. Surrounded by her scent, her body pressed against his, he held her, finally believing she was safe.

She spoke first. "Where's Tanna?"

"She hit the road. You're supposed to call her later."

Lainie placed sweet, tender, nuzzling kisses up his throat that made him sigh in pure contentment. When she reached his mouth, she kissed the corners of his smile, teasing his lips into parting, sweeping her tongue inside for a full-blown kiss.

Her potent taste sparked the desire that always simmered between them. But Hank was content to let her lead. To let her show him how much she could handle.

She touched him thoroughly. Running her hands through his hair. Over his face. Across his shoulders. Down his chest. "I missed you."

"I missed you too, darlin'."

"Will you crawl under the covers with me? I'm tired and I can't seem to get warm."

"That I can do."

He stripped to his boxers and spooned her. Tucking the covers around her so only her face was exposed, he rested his chin on the top of her head and closed his eyes.

Hank actually relaxed enough to drift off. But when Lainie stirred and he knew she was awake, he said, "I need to know what happened last night."

Her body stiffened immediately. "Didn't Tanna relay all the sordid details?"

"Some. But I want to hear it from you."

Lainie was facing away from him. At first her voice was low enough that he barely heard it. By the time she finished, her tone was clear and strong, which he took as a good sign.

"I'm sorry. I'm pissed as hell. My anger won't help this situation, but I have an idea about something that will help."

She rolled back toward him. "What?"

"When this attack happened you were at the event as an employee of Lariat. It's their job to provide a safe environment. When your coworkers took off, they left you alone in a dangerous situation. So in my mind, Lariat needs to be aware of what happened. Specifically, Dusty needs to be told. Dusty also needs to contact Bryson Westfield, from the EBS, so he's aware of what happened at an EBS-sanctioned event."

Lainie's defeat morphed into defiance. He continued, "I can deal with this if it's too hard for you. And FYI, that wasn't a suggestion. Either you call him, or I will."

"Don't bully me, Hank."

He curled his hand around her neck, bringing her close, so she'd make no mistake about his intent. "Don't confuse bullying with my ensuring that this matter is handled swiftly and properly. Do you have any idea what the thought of you being hurt does to me?"

He foiled her attempt to look away.

"It's all I can do not to track that worthless fucker down and shoot him for the animal he is. Ace was stopped before he succeeded in his attempt to rape you. We could be dealing with a lot different—a lot worse situation."

"We?"

"You can't honestly believe I'd walk away and leave you to handle this alone?"

"Hank—"

"Don't brush me aside. Not now. Not ever. You know how I feel about you, Lainie, even when you won't let me say the actual words. But it doesn't change them. Or negate them."

Lainie didn't answer, but Hank hadn't expected her to.

"This isn't something I can stand back and do nothin' about. I'm here for you. No matter what happens. But one of us is gonna make that call. You choose."

Neither spoke. Neither moved. Finally Lainie closed her eyes and said, "All right. I'll do it."

Thank God.

Hank brushed his lips over her forehead. "I'll be right here with you, if you want."

"I'd like that." Lainie wriggled out of his arms. "In fact, I'll call Dusty now. He's harder to get hold of as the day progresses, and I don't want to put this off any longer than I have to."

∞

After Lainie hung up, she knew she'd done the right thing. Dusty was suitably appalled by the defection of the other medical personnel as well as Ace's behavior. But when it seemed Dusty might balk at contacting Bryson Westfield about the incident, Lainie put the screws to him. She'd wait four hours for Bryson's response and plan for disciplinary action against Ace, or she'd head to the police department and file formal charges against Ace Newharth before she left town for the next EBS event.

Dusty's reaction left her unsettled. She understood the EBS was half Lariat's source of income, but wasn't it hypocritical for an organization devoted to healing to turn a blind eye when one of its own workers was the injured party?

Hank dragged her to the vending machine to load up on snacks. Back at the room, he tucked her against his big body so they touched from head to toe. He held her, constantly soothing her with his loving caresses while they waited for her cell phone to ring.

"Whatcha thinking about?" Hank murmured.

"I don't want to get on a plane and fly to Salt Lake City."

"I don't want you to either." He stroked the bend in her elbow. "Given what happened to you, I expected Dusty would insist that someone besides you could finish this fill-in gig."

"He offered; I declined," she lied, knowing Hank would be even more infuriated if he knew the truth: Dusty hadn't mentioned finding her a replacement. There wasn't anyone else in the company who could drop everything and fly off at a moment's notice. Not because she was indispensable, but because she was cheap, she had no other life, and she wouldn't say no.

"Please reconsider," he said gently. "I'll drive you to Colorado Springs myself."

Lainie turned and looked at him. "Aren't you supposed to be in Kansas City?"

"Yes. But the CRA would understand."

"What about the EBS?"

Hank hesitated. "I don't know if I can—"

Her cell phone rang. She disentangled from Hank's arms and glanced at the caller ID. Not a number she recognized. "Hello?"

"Is this Melanie Capshaw?"

"Yes. Who's this?"

"This is Bryson Westfield of the EBS."

Her heart thumped and she scrambled to the edge of the bed.

"I just got off the phone with your boss, Doc Bowman. He indicated you'd had an unfortunate incident with an EBS rider last night."

"Yes, sir."

"Can you explain what happened?"

Lainie resented having to prove that she'd been attacked. She'd done nothing wrong except show up for work. After she finished, Bryson Westfield put her on hold.

Five minutes later he clicked back on the line. "Thanks for holding. You said Ace Newharth was responsible? He wasn't listed on last night's docket of riders."

"I've treated Ace in a medical capacity, so I know who he is. The other Lariat employees can verify that he was in the room with his friend Jake Nelson last night during the event."

More muffled sounds.

"I assure you, Miss Capshaw, I don't condone Ace's behavior."

"But are you going to condemn it?" she demanded.

"I'll ask that you refrain both from filing charges with the local police department or from contacting your legal counsel until we've thoroughly investigated this matter. Naturally I'll keep you informed of how the investigation proceeds."

Her mouth nearly hit the floor. "That's it? Ace attacks me and he won't be reprimanded at all?"

"I didn't say that," he cautioned.

"You implied it. At the very least I would expect Ace would be suspended from EBS events pending a full investigation."

Silence.

Hank hopped up and paced in the small walkway between the beds, practically growling his displeasure.

"I'll oversee Mr. Newharth's disciplinary action personally."

"Thank you." But she didn't feel relief; she wasn't sure he wasn't feeding her full of shit.

"In the meantime, I'll expect the usual discretionary measures. No media alerts."

"I'm not looking for publicity, Mr. Westfield. I prefer this to be handled as discreetly, expediently, and fairly as possible."

"Consider it done. Someone from my office will be in touch with you soon, Miss Capshaw." And he hung up.

Hank crouched in front of her. "What happened?"

"They're checking into it."

"What's to check into? Ace attacked you. End of investigation."

Lainie rubbed the ache between her eyes. "Can we just forget about this whole shitty mess and snuggle up until it's time for me to leave?"

Emotionally drained, she rolled over and faced the wall. If she could just make it through the next two days, she'd be home free. The clerical job started Monday.

"Talk to me. What aren't you telling me?"

"My position with Lariat is changing. Which is why it's ironic that this happened at one of the last events I have on the road."

"Last events? Are you . . . quitting?"

"No. I'll be working in the Lariat offices full-time, not traveling the circuits."

"How long have you known?" When she didn't jump right in with a response, Hank said, "Since Lamar. Dusty offered you the job and told you to go on vacation for three weeks before you started." Pause. "When were you going to tell me?"

"I'd planned to tell you. Things were going so great between us that I didn't want it to end on a bad note."

End hung in the air like a dirty cloud.

The mattress moved beneath them as Hank draped his arm over her side and pulled her flush to his body. His warm breath teased her ear. "Well, darlin', we don't have much time left today. I sure as hell don't want to spend it fighting with you."

That was when her tears surfaced. This man was so unbelievably sweet. Thoughtful. Fierce. Loving. "I don't want to spend it fighting either."

"Good." He placed hot, wet, openmouthed kisses down her neck. "When does your flight leave?"

"Four."

"Mmm. That leaves us plenty of time."

Her body tingled from the eroticism of his mouth on her skin. "For what?"

"For me to prove to you that this shouldn't end. Ever."

And prove it he did. In the bed. In the shower. In the chair.

Hank systematically left his mark on her body, her

heart, and her soul. Their parting at the airport was bittersweet. When he whispered that he wanted more than three lousy weeks with her, she asked him to give her a little time to get her head together.

Lainie felt more confused than ever. She kissed him and forced herself to turn away.

Chapter Twenty-four

Lainie figured the summons from Dusty on her day off meant he wanted the lowdown on what happened in River Bend—without interruptions. She rapped on his office door.

Doc motioned her to a metal stool, the one piece of furniture not mounded with papers.

His clinical gaze swept over Lainie. "How are you?"

"Fine." When he looked as if he didn't believe her, she said, "Seriously. I'm fine now. But I won't lie: Having Ace Newharth corner me scared the piss out of me."

"I imagine so. Have you called your mother to let her know what happened?"

"I intend to. I took a three-week sabbatical from her too."

"So Sharlene and her husband don't know what's going on?"

Since when did Doc care about her stepfather's involvement in her life? She shook her head.

"Good enough."

He tapped his fingers on the desk blotter.

The first bit of niggling doubt surfaced.

"You wondering why I called you in today?"

"I thought it was about the River Bend incident."

"No. There are a few things we need to discuss."

"Pay rates for my new job?" she joked.

Doc sagged back in his office chair and pinched the bridge of his nose. "Look, let me just say this straightaway."

Not good. Seriously not good.

"I offered you something I had no right to."

"Is this is about the office position?"

"Yes. I'm afraid the job's already been filled."

Her hopes sank to the tips of her boots. "By who?"

"A woman with previous experience in office management. She started last week. I'm sorry. It was out of my hands."

Bullshit. "When was this decided?"

Dusty didn't answer.

She forced herself to remain calm. Forced herself to swallow the ugly reality. "You never intended to hire me for the full-time office position, did you? You used it as a carrot to force me to take vacation time, knowing that when I returned you could pull this 'the position was filled' crap on me."

He didn't deny it.

"After you talked to me in Lamar, I came back to Colorado Springs and quit my EMT job, thinking I wouldn't need it." She laughed bitterly. "How wrongheaded that decision was."

Dusty wouldn't meet her gaze—an indication that this situation was worse than she'd initially believed. "Are you firing me outright?"

"No. When we spoke in Lamar I told you the organization was being restructured, remember?"

"The entire organization? Or just this office?"

"Mostly this office."

Liar. Dusty could do whatever he wanted, hire whoever he wanted. Something else was at play here.

"The good thing is, I can keep you on in your current capacity, part-time, as a med tech, but only on the CRA circuit."

Lainie was stunned into speechlessness.

"We feel it's best for our employees to stick with one rodeo organization, rather than switching back and forth between them like you've done."

Her disbelief expanded. "You're penalizing *me* because of Ace attacking me on the EBS circuit?"

"Not a penalty," he chided. "We're making a business decision. To be honest, sending you to the EBS wearing the 'Mel' name tag was a joke gone awry. I'm rectifying that mistake by assigning you solely to the CRA."

The EBS was blaming her for getting attacked. She'd bet money Ace wouldn't even get a slap on the wrist. "So I'm being reassigned because of my gender?"

"No. But Bryson did contact the Lariat corporate office questioning your medical qualifications."

"And?" she demanded.

"His phone call brought up an oversight. So corporate revised the med tech standards for employees working in the Lariat Sports Medicine division, specifically relating to our professional relationship with the EBS. New criteria, effective immediately."

"Which is?"

"A four-year degree in a health-related field. So, see, you don't qualify with your CNA, LPN degree, and EMT certificate."

Shame, hot and thick, expanded in her throat. She couldn't speak. She'd been so proud of her accomplishments. So confident in her ability. Certain Lariat Sports

Medicine had hired her as a qualified medical professional on her own merits. When the truth was, Dusty had hired her out of pity, or worse, solely out of an obligation he felt to her dead father.

Had her mother been right all along? Dusty used her, overworked her, knowing she'd be thrilled with any menial job in the rodeo world because it was a connection to her father? Knowing she wouldn't complain about the shit wages?

She'd never felt so betrayed. So heartsick. Her future was as much in shambles as the past she couldn't get away from.

"Do you have any other questions?" Doc asked.

She shook her head.

"Look. I can get you on the docket Thursday for—"

"No." Blindly, she stood. "I quit. Have corporate send my last check to the address you have on file. I should be there for a few more weeks until the lease on my apartment is up."

"Don't be ridiculous. So what if you can't work in the EBS? The CRA doesn't have the same rigid medical requirements. The CRA is happy to have you, Lainie. I'm happy to have you here."

"Because of what I do? Or who I am?" She whirled on him. "I believed you hired me on my own merits. I moved here and worked another job so I could keep this one. For what? The hours suck. The pay sucks. The travel sucks. Everything sucks. Why didn't I see that before now?"

"Lainie, you're confused and hurt. I don't blame you. But don't make a rash decision and throw everything away until you've thought it through."

"You're damn right I'm confused and hurt. I have to take a good hard look at my life and I can't do it while I'm looking at you."

Surprise registered on his face. "What?"

"I see broken promises and outright lies on your face, Doc. I deserve better. I always have. So, no, I don't need time to think it through. Maybe I'm thinking clearly for the first time." She stumbled out of his office.

"Lainie. Wait."

She didn't.

Lainie climbed in her truck, her mind racing as she sped away. She'd never been unemployed. She could get her EMT job back. She could apply at a nursing home. She could return to the health club as a massage therapist. She could start over. But she didn't want to do it in Colorado Springs.

Why had she been in a holding pattern for the last two years? Putting off making any decisions about her life and her future?

Because she was stuck in the past? Mourning her grandmother? Living her life in the shadow of a man she hardly remembered? Had she been deluding herself? Choosing to work in the rodeo world her father loved in some misguided attempt to feel close to him?

Enough. Get a grip on the here and now.

Problem was, Lainie had no freakin' clue where to start.

Her grandmother's voice drifted into her head. *Sometimes getting on the right path takes a step back to see where you've been.*

Once Lainie returned to her apartment, she paced until she mustered the guts to just pick up the damn phone and call her mother.

Sharlene answered. "I'll admit I'm surprised you're calling me, Melanie." Pause. "Although I am really glad to hear from you."

Lainie looked at the receiver as if it were playing tricks on her. "You are?"

"Yes. I've been really worried about you. And I hate

it when we fight, even though it's all we've seemed to do in the last few years. Are you okay?"

No. Stupid tears started again.

"Lainie?"

She swallowed hard at the soft, concerned way her mother said her name. "No, Mom, I'm not okay. You were right about Dusty. About the whole situation. God. I feel like such an idiot."

"Oh, sugar bear, what happened?"

Sugar bear. She hadn't called her that in years. And for the first time in years, Lainie found herself spilling her guts to her mother. About her job. About seeing the real rodeo world. About the hardships of life on the road. About her relationship with Hank. About her confusion over it all.

When she finished, Sharlene was quiet. Too quiet. Like the kind of stillness one felt in an animal about to attack and rip its prey to shreds. Lainie braced herself when her mother expelled a drawn-out sigh.

"Thank you for telling me. I'm horrified and sick to my stomach about what you went through. But I'll be honest. If it were me? I'd sue the living shit out of both the EBS and Lariat."

Lainie froze. No wonder Dusty had asked about her stepfather. He feared a lawsuit.

"But it's not about me. And I've overstepped my boundaries with you too many times already. So my next question is, What can I do?"

Not the response she'd expected.

Maybe because you're putting lousy expectations on your mother that she never deserved. Good or bad.

"I don't think there's anything you can do. I just needed to let you know. To thank you, I guess, for giving me an insight I didn't have. Or I didn't believe, is probably a more accurate statement."

Her mother laughed. "We always seem to be at cross-purposes, don't we? I never intended to hurt you, sweetheart, and it seems I always do. I know our relationship has never been easy."

That was putting it mildly.

"There's a lot I haven't told you, or you've misunderstood. I kept hoping you'd come to me with questions, but you just closed down. Resented me. I know this will sound harsh, but I resented you for that resentment. I hated that you made assumptions."

"Assumptions about . . . you?"

"Yes, about me. But also about your father. About what happened after he died."

Lainie's stomach lurched in the brutal silence.

"Twenty years have passed and it's still so damn hard."

Lainie actually felt her mother's anguish over the phone lines. "I'm in a place where I can listen with an open mind. And a closed mouth," she added.

Her mother let loose a half laugh, half sob. "I forget how funny you are. I miss that. You're so like your father sometimes it makes me crazy. So determined to make your own way. So helpful to others at the expense of your own happiness." She sniffed. "Do you know you even have his cowlick?"

Lainie closed her eyes. "You mentioned that a time or two when I was a kid."

"I loved Jason. He was . . . everything in the world to me. He *was* my world. Without going into too much detail, we fought hard, we loved hard. We were happy. Even when he wasn't around as much as I wanted, especially after you were born, we made the most of our time together.

"When Jason died . . . I wanted to die right along with him. Everybody mourned him. He became more famous in death than he'd been in life. Which pissed me off. I'd lost my everything, you'd lost a father, and all anyone could talk about was the lasting legacy he'd left on the bull riding community. Your grandma Elsa, God rest her soul, loved talking to the press about her only son. She was no stranger to tragedy, but I was. I'd never lost anyone important in my life. And I was so damn young. All I wanted was to hole up and mourn. In my own way. Not in public.

"But Elsa saw my grief as a weakness. She'd lived through heartbreak several times and figured I was being a drama queen by letting sadness consume me. She took over your care and I let her. I remember about a year after Jason died I finally woke up from my fog of misery."

"I don't remember any of that."

"I know you don't. I'm actually glad. Anyway, I'd met with Marcus a couple of times about a wrongful-death lawsuit. But mostly I was interested in setting up a foundation in Jason's name, where any use of his likeness and his image would be under my control." An edge entered her voice. "Elsa accused me of profiting from Jason's death. But she didn't understand that if I didn't have legal protection in place, other people would profit. It wasn't about the money. It was about retaining some goddamn dignity. I didn't want to see the man I'd loved become a commodity. I wanted to ensure that his face wouldn't end up on a commemorative fucking spoon or something."

Lainie's heart squeezed painfully at the raw anguish in her mother's voice and the rare burst of profanity. How had she not known any of this? Had she really assumed her father's death had no impact on her mother at all? How could she have been so clueless? So selfish? So self-involved?

Because you were a kid, and kids are notoriously selfish. But you've never given yourself a chance to have a decent adult relationship with her.

"Is that when we moved out of Oklahoma?"

Silence.

"Mom?"

"Yes. I needed a fresh start. Away from rodeo, away from the memories. By that time I'd fallen in love with Marcus. We both knew I'd never overcome the stigma of being Jason Capshaw's widow if we lived in Oklahoma. And I didn't want you to grow up a curiosity."

Sharlene had succeeded there. No one in California had heard of bull rider Jason Capshaw or his tragic end. Since she'd been involved with rodeo, and with the questions she constantly fielded about her father, she had a better appreciation for her mother's choice.

"You were unhappy. We'd left Elsa on bad terms because she'd threatened to sue for custody of you."

"She did?"

"I hated that it'd come down to that. She cooled down—it took her over a year—and I agreed to let you spend summers with her. As long as she kept you away from the world of rodeo."

"And I ended up there anyway," Lainie murmured.

"When Dusty told me he'd hired you, but only part-time, I knew he'd taken advantage of your curiosity, your grief over your grandmother's death, and your restlessness. I worried you'd schedule your life around those twenty hours a week in some attempt to relate to your father's life on the road."

"Maybe. Probably. I was flattered that he thought I was qualified. I feel like such a fool that Dusty had counted on that reaction from me."

"He's shrewd. He saw how much you were like Jason. I hoped after Elsa died you'd come home and we could talk about some of this stuff. When you went to work for Lariat immediately, I'll admit I went off the deep end. I called Dusty and he was so fucking smug. . . . I called him every name in the book and hated how he was using you. I thought that if I encouraged you to go back to school . . . but you mistook my encouragement as an indictment of your abilities. I never intended that." Her mother made an exasperated sigh. "Lainie, sugar bear, I seem to go about this all wrong with you all the time. I'd like to figure out a way to make it right for both of us."

Lainie said, "Me too," and for the first time, she meant it.

"As much as I'd like to see you, I won't guilt you into coming to California. I know this won't happen overnight, but can we stay in touch? Take it a step at a time?"

"I'd like that."

"Are you going to talk to Hank now that you're unemployed and unencumbered?"

"Yes. But there's something I have to do first."

The intent hung between them.

"Maybe someday I'll get up the guts to go too," her mother said softly. "Call me if you need me."

∞

Even after the enlightening yet surreal conversation with her mother, Lainie was restless. Staring at the bare white walls of her apartment the next two days while Hank was in Omaha wasn't an option. As she packed a bag, her cell phone rang. Lainie attempted to put a smile in her voice. "Hey, Tanna, how's it going in Lubbock?"

"I finished top of the leaderboard in the first go."

"That's awesome."

"Yeah, but it's a two-day event and there's no one cool to hang with since you're not here. By the way, I finally ditched that asshole Steve. I can't believe I wasted four months of my life on him."

"Glad you finally saw the light, and you'll get back to the wild Tanna I know and love."

"We'll see. Anyway, enough about me. Are you excited to start the new job?"

"No. I'm . . . done with Lariat."

"What?"

Lainie began to explain calmly, but with all that'd happened in the last week, she lost it. She babbled about her mother, her future, her past, all her realizations in the past three weeks. When she took a breath, she realized Tanna hadn't uttered a peep. "Sorry." She sniffled. "It just hit me all at once."

"Where are you?" Tanna demanded.

"Getting ready to leave my apartment."

"Stay put. If I leave right now, I can be there in eight hours."

"No." Lainie teared up again. "God, Tanna, I appreciate that you'd drop everything for me, but you're in first place. This is a big rodeo with a big purse and you have to stay there and win it."

"Fine. You don't have a job. Drive down here. We'll get shit-faced and act like total idiots. Then you can come home with me to the ranch for as long as you need to."

She pressed her neck into the back of the couch. "I may take you up on that later. But there's something I need to do first."

"Girl, are you finally goin' to Hank and letting him know how you feel?" She allowed a thoughtful pause. "Please tell me you called him about what happened with Lariat today."

"Hank's got enough to worry about. His first event with the EBS is this weekend."

"Lainie, you know I love ya, but sometimes I wanna strangle you. Hank's a big boy. He deserves to know."

"I'll tell him. I promise. Soon. Just not tonight. Tonight

I have to do something I've been putting off for a long time."

"What? Where are you going?"

"Cheyenne." Her cell phone beeped, signaling low battery. "Look. I have a ways to drive and my phone is almost dead. I'll call you tomorrow, okay?"

"Okay," Tanna said grudgingly. "Drive safe."

"I will."

Lainie turned the phone off. She threw her bag in the back of her truck and lit out. As soon as she pulled back onto I-25 north, she knew that this time there'd be no detours. No excuses. No more running from the past. She'd face those demons head-on.

∞

Hank paced. Unproductive, but it eased some of his rage. He'd promised Lainie he'd stick to their agreement of giving her time to think. He'd been doing pretty well, except for the ten times a day he picked up his phone to call her, only to remember at the last second that he shouldn't.

The fact that Lainie hadn't relayed this disturbing turn of events, that he'd had to hear it from Tanna again, chapped his ass. Big-time.

Maybe she didn't tell you because she knew how you'd react: huffing and throwing your weight around like an out-of-control bull.

Worked for him.

He passed the T-shirt stand and the section over-loaded with EBS everything. Belt buckles, neckerchiefs, posters, program guides, DVDs, CDs, even wispy lace thongs were displayed.

The EBS was big business.

The little slip of a secretary was no match for Hank. He bulled his way into Bryson Westfield's traveling of-fice in the back of an EBS-logoed semi trailer.

Miz Bony Secretary cut in front of Hank and glared before directing her comments to her boss. "Sir, I'm sorry. He just blew right past me—"

"It's all right. This man is damn near unstoppable, which is why he's a fine bullfighter." He gestured with his pen. "Just make sure it doesn't happen again."

"Yes, sir." Her beaklike nose nearly brushed the floor, her head hung so low on her retreat.

Not that Bryson Westfield noticed. He shooed away the men wielding papers and didn't speak until the door clicked shut behind them.

"Mr. Lawson. This is your first official EBS event, but it ain't your first rodeo. Do I really need to detail what constitutes rude behavior?"

"No."

"Good. Storming in here and bullying my secretary is unacceptable. You'd better have a damn good reason why you saw fit to make yourself my priority today."

Inhale. Exhale. Stay fucking calm. Deep breath in. Long, slow breath out. "For the record, I apologize. It wasn't my intention—"

"The road to hell and all that springs to mind, Hank, so get to the point. I'm a busy man."

There's still time to slink away. To back down. Do your job, collect a paycheck, and smile like an idiot.

"Well?" Bryson demanded.

Buck up. But no half measures, no compromises in this situation. Black and white. Right and wrong.

Hank threw back his shoulders and drew himself up to his full height. He stalked closer to the balding fat boy. "I'm here about Ace Newharth."

"What about him?"

"I saw his name on the roster for this weekend. He's still on the tour?"

Those flat black reptilian eyes turned appraising.

"Yes, he is. He's a top-twenty-five-ranked bull rider and he deserves to be there. Why?"

"After what he did to Lainie Capshaw last week? You're not reprimanding him?"

"What I choose to do or not to do with my bull riders is none of your concern. I handled it in the best way I saw fit."

"Meaning you're ignoring it," Hank spat.

Bryson shrugged. "It's her word against his. I've known Ace a long time. He's a devout Christian man, with a loving family supporting him and a large fan base. I know nothing of this Lainie woman beyond that she expects the Capshaw name will grant her special privileges."

He stared at Bryson, wondering when the man had gotten kicked in the head by a bull. Attempted sexual assault was a special privilege?

"This is typical reactive behavior for a female in a male-dominated sport. They get their little feelings hurt, or they send off mixed signals, or their advances are rebuffed and the next thing you know, they're crying foul." He pointed a fat finger at Hank. "This is also why I told Doc not to send me female medical technicians. Did he listen to me? No. I've never once had to deal with sexual harassment shit like this when the staff and the riders were all men."

Hank slapped his hands on the desk with enough force that his palms stung. "You ignorant son of a bitch. This is not about Lainie getting her feelings hurt. This is about that bastard putting the hurt on her. Ace left fucking bruises on her neck. Bruises. If Tanna Barker hadn't come in . . ." Jesus. A red haze of fury consumed him when he considered what might've happened.

"I don't know who you think you are, but you can't speak to me like that—"

"We're not talkin' sexual harassment, Bryson. We're talkin' attempted sexual assault. Big fucking difference."

"Says you. Might I remind you that Miz Capshaw didn't file charges against Mr. Newharth?"

"She didn't file at your request! She didn't want the bad publicity any more than the EBS did. You promised her you'd handle it discreetly. Nothin's been done. Except Lainie's been penalized. She's been pulled from the EBS circuit permanently."

"Oh, really? I didn't know."

"The fuck you didn't. I'll bet this is your doin'. Ace hasn't been penalized at all. This isn't fair and you goddamn well know it."

"Fairness is relative, and as far as I can tell the matter is over."

"It's far from fucking over," Hank snarled. "You either drop him from this event—"

"Or you'll what?" Bryson supplied sarcastically. "Hover over me and snarl idle threats?"

"No, I'll let the bull he's on stomp him into the dirt like the piece of shit he is. In fact, I'll encourage it. I sure as hell won't rush in and risk my life to save his."

Bryson's face turned beet red, but the fat folds in his jowls remained milky white lines. "Get out of my office. You're done here. For good. I'll be pulling *your* name off the roster, not Ace's."

"Do it. And fair warning: You have no idea the shit storm that's gonna rain down on you and the EBS when the media gets wind of this. The almighty EBS. The premier organization dedicated to the art of riding bulls turns its back on the only daughter of the most beloved bull rider of all time."

Another piggy-eyed glare.

"Because of Jason Capshaw's death, bull riders now wear safety equipment. Lainie Capshaw has centered her career around helping injured cowboys. In memory of her fallen father. Yet this organization failed to protect her—not from the bulls, but from the bull riders themselves. The very men she was hired to help."

"Miz Capshaw didn't want the media attention before—"

"It's different now. She gave you her faith the EBS would do the right thing . . . and you gave her the finger. Her only recourse is to try this in the court of public opinion, and in the legal system." He angled forward across the desk, invading his personal space. Bryson, the dickless wonder, flinched, causing Hank to grin. "We both know she can still file charges against Ace. She can file charges against you and your organization for everything from conspiracy to discrimination to endangerment."

"Get. The. Fuck. Out." Bryson seethed. "Your bullfighting days are over."

"With the EBS? Good riddance. I'm damn happy to stay in the CRA, where honor and family and respect mean something."

"The beloved CRA, where a man is considered a real John Wayne for standing up for his little woman?"

"No, in the CRA a man doesn't have to stand up for his woman, because the organization is already standing behind her. This assault never would've happened within the CRA."

"Well, this ain't the CRA."

"Of that, there's no doubt in my mind. Pretty soon it'll be crystal clear in everyone else's mind too."

"Threats don't work on me."

"Yeah? Let's test that theory, shall we?"

Hank spun on his boot heel and stormed out.

Halfway to his truck, he dialed directory assistance. "Connect me with United Airlines."

Chapter Twenty-five

Cheyenne looked far bigger than what the population sign indicated. The orange glow of the sodium lights along the four-lane interstate turned the black sky an abnormal shade of purple.

Lainie forced herself to uncurl her fingers from the steering wheel. Her knuckles were white. Her palms were scored with red marks from the death grip she'd maintained on the hard plastic since she'd hit the Wyoming state line.

The lights of the Warren Air Force Base blinked across the prairie. A dark, jagged outline of mountains loomed in the distance. Several sizes of missiles were grouped together along the side of the road. The welcome to the "equality state" seemed appropriate.

She rounded a sloping corner on the interstate and there it was, Frontier Park. Carnival rides towered above the chain-link fence surrounding the park. Then everything disappeared behind rows and rows of trees.

No going back now.

She exited and followed the signs. Traffic was light this time of night. It didn't take long to reach the big wooden sign hanging above the rodeo grounds, welcoming visitors to "The Daddy of 'Em All," the Cheyenne Frontier Days rodeo.

Her stomach was twisted in knots. Her mouth was as dry as the dust kicking up beneath her tires. Her heart whomped against her chest. A cold sweat—she'd never believed that phrase until just now—coated her skin. Her body trembled so hard her legs bounced of their own accord.

One step at a time.

As Lainie parked alongside the visitors' building, she prayed they'd locked up for the night. Maybe if she stayed in the pickup, a cranky security guard would swing by and shoo her away. At least she could honestly say she tried.

Get out of the damn truck.

Why had she decided to make the pilgrimage to this place after all these years? Her father wasn't here. His soul or spirit or whatever had moved on long ago. What remained of Jason Capshaw was the tragic legend, the reverence regarding his flawless bull riding style, and a memorial statue at the place where he died.

And you. You're what's left of him. You're part of him.

Lainie pictured her grandmother Elsa's sweet face and the fierce pride when she spoke of her son. Her sadness at losing him at such a young age. Her joy that she'd at least had Lainie as a reminder. Grandma had traveled all the way from Oklahoma for the unveiling of the statue the Cheyenne Frontier Days Booster Club had presented on the fifth anniversary of Jason Capshaw's death.

Sharlene hadn't attended the ceremony; nor had she allowed Lainie to attend. *People move on*, Sharlene had pointed out. Sharlene had said that a lot. Now Lainie knew why. Now she understood.

Lightning zigzagged across the sky. As soon as Lainie opened her door, a blast of dry air hit her, stealing her breath. She glanced at the sky again. No clouds.

Rain, dammit. Then I'd have an excuse to hide.

Gritting her teeth, she shoved her keys in her back pocket. She skirted the front end of the truck and followed the line of the fence until it ended. The gate was wide open. Lainie looked up.

There it was. Less than forty feet away.

A metal handrail circled the statue. The bronze was centered on a gigantic piece of sandstone, prominent in the spotlight. Even from this distance she could tell the detail was amazing on both the bull and the man.

Lainie cut sideways so she'd get a full-on view of the face. His face. Her father's face. A face she hadn't seen in such detail since she was five years old. The artist had perfectly captured the look of determination her father wore when seated on the back of a bull. The twist to his lips. The squinty-eyed stare. The slight flare to his nostrils. The hard set to his jaw.

She blinked the moisture from her eyes as she drank in every facet. The tilt of his summer-weight cowboy hat, centered high on his forehead. The precise angle of his free arm thrown up in the air, parallel to his upper torso. The gloved fist wrapped in frayed bull rope. The forward pitch of his lean body, knees tucked tight, spurs digging in.

Other elements jumped out. The flowing look of the fringe on the chaps, as man and beast caught air. The deep creases and faded spots in his jeans. The worn-down runnels on the spurs. The scuff marks on the toes of the boots.

She gasped. How could she have forgotten those old boots?

A childhood memory surfaced of her father returning home from an event. She'd helped him air out his equipment bag, filled with a mixture of scents: wet leather, dust, and a hint of manure. The pungent trace of liniment. The cool tang of metal. The oily scent of rope. The bitter, powdery aroma of rosin. The rich smell of chewing tobacco. The dirty sweat-sock odor of his boots.

His beloved ragged, stained cowboy boots. Her mother complained about his unnatural attachment to those boots and threatened to throw them out. It'd been the only time Lainie had seen her laid-back, good-natured father mad enough to spit nails.

She'd asked him why he didn't just buy a new pair. He'd told her those boots had absorbed a lot of great memories and brought him good luck. It seemed a waste for a man to throw good luck and memories away.

Jason Capshaw had been buried in those boots. A fact that she now realized would've pleased him.

Her focus returned to the figure astride the bucking bull. The artist had denoted the wrinkles of his shirt, as well as the gleam and size of the championship belt buckle centered between lean hips. Her gaze lingered on his face before moving up. She'd definitely inherited her dad's hair. Wild curls peeped out from the sides and back of his cowboy hat. Springy strands so perfectly detailed, she was half tempted to climb up and see if the ringlets smelled like the Prell shampoo he'd favored. But the shampoo never quite masked the leather scent left in his hair from his ever-present cowboy hat.

Lainie checked out the backside of the figure. The contestant number was pinned below his shoulders. Number one. He'd entered the bull riding competition that fateful day as the number one bull rider in the world.

Her gaze fell to the memorial plaque. It read:

In memory of Jason Arthur Capshaw—
son, husband, father, friend—a bull rider to the very end.
We miss you. We'll never forget you.

Lainie didn't bother to hold back the tears. She cried silently. Her grief was almost worse now than in her childhood, as she faced everything she'd lost.

"Lainie."

She wheeled around.

Hank stood in the shadows.

He held open his arms. She ran straight into them. Her sobs escalated. Hank merely held her tighter. He kissed her crown and murmured, "It's okay, baby. I've got you."

Twenty years of grief poured out of her. Through it all, Hank stayed strong and steady. Holding her. Soothing her. Being there for her in a way no other man ever had. Once the storm of emotions subsided, she looked up at him.

The tenderness in his eyes as he gently wiped away her tears almost sent her into another sobbing fit.

Lainie managed to hold it in. Her throat was raw from crying. Her voice was an unrecognizable rasp. "How did you know?"

"Tanna called me. She was worried sick about you."

She couldn't be mad at her friend for knowing exactly what she needed. "Did she tell you all of it?"

"Yes. I won't chew you out for not calling me. *This time.*" He twined a curl around his index finger before pushing it behind her ear. "When Tanna told me you were coming to Cheyenne . . . I couldn't get out of Omaha fast enough. I didn't want you to deal with this alone, Lainie. Kyle's mom picked me up at the airport and dropped me off."

"How long have you been here?"

"Just an hour." His thumb wicked the tears from her cheeks. "I was prepared to stay all night if I had to."

"What if I'd chickened out?" She swallowed hard. "I had a devil of a time getting out of my truck."

"I know. I watched you struggling. It about killed me, but I let you be until you needed me."

Take a chance. Tell him.

"I've come to realize I need you all the time, Hank, not just once in a while." Before he spoke, she blurted, "Cheyenne was just a pit stop on my way to Muddy Gap."

"Why?"

"Because I quit my job. But as I was driving here, I began to worry."

"Worry about what?"

"I didn't want you to think I was coming to you because I had nowhere else to go. You're not a last resort, Hank. You're my first choice."

"Lainie. Darlin', I love you. Love you like crazy. I tried to tell you before but you didn't want to hear it."

"I wanted to hear it. God, I wanted to hear it more than anything. I didn't tell you how I felt when you were in the hospital because I didn't want you to think I'd said it out of pity. After the attack I worried that *you* tried to say it to me out of pity. That's why I asked for time to think. Not for me, for you. I wanted you to make sure *I* was who you wanted."

Hank lifted a brow. "Good Lord, woman, you're a bossy little thing. How is it that *you* get to decide how *I* feel about you?"

She blinked at him. "What?"

"Don't you know I've been half in love with you since I saw you helping an elderly lady find her way back to the stands? I fell the rest of the way in love with you after you started traveling with us and I got to know you."

"I thought you'd say you fell the rest of the way after we slept together."

He flashed her that sinful smile again. "Oh, I definitely fell in lust with you. But lust fades. What I feel for you won't. I believe that with all my heart, Lainie."

"I do too. When I realized I loved you, it scared me. For the first time I understood why my mother walked away from the rodeo life after my dad died. For all her faults, she loved my father. After she lost him, she needed to start over."

A beat of silence passed between them.

His eyes searched hers intently. "Did you pick me over Kyle because you couldn't see yourself with a bull rider? Or because you didn't want to repeat the path your mother had taken?"

"No. I chose you because I love you, Hank. Bullfighter, garbage man, it doesn't matter. I want to be with you." She smiled. "If you're willing to take on an unemployed med tech."

"I'll take you on anytime, anyplace, baby." He touched her cheek. He couldn't seem to not touch her, just another sweetness about him she loved. "So you quit, huh?"

"Yeah. My mom advised me to sue everyone in sight, but her husband is a lawyer, so I'm considering the source." She smirked. "Besides, I want to be done with it. Really and truly move on this time. Getting caught up in legal battles isn't the way to do it."

"I agree. I made some threats to Bryson that in hindsight I ain't proud of. After all the garbage that's happened with the EBS . . . I'm taking this as a sign to go back to full-time ranching. To be honest, I'm looking forward to moving on too."

"Not even part-time bullfighting with the CRA?"

"Nope. It's time to let Celia chase her dream, now that I've found mine and she's standing right in front of me."

"But you like being on the road as a blacktop cowboy, Hank."

He swept a damp curl from her cheek. "Now I have a more compelling reason to stay corralled at home."

She blushed and stared at him, her heart racing, her hope soaring.

"Is there anything for you in Colorado Springs?" he asked softly. "Any reason you have to—or want to—live there?"

"No."

Relief crossed his face. Then he pushed back and dropped to one knee.

"Hank! What are you doing?"

"Since I can't ask your daddy for your hand in marriage, I figure it'd be fitting if I asked you to marry me here, in front of his likeness." Hank snatched both her hands and squeezed them in his. "Lainie Capshaw, will you marry me? Make a home with me? Let me spend my life loving you? For all those reasons and about a hundred others I can't remember because I'm so damn nervous."

Lainie thought she was through crying. Not so. Tears spilled down her cheeks. "Yes, Hank. I'll marry you."

He jumped to his feet and let out a whoop of delight that was very un-Hank-like. But it made her smile.

"Hot damn. We have lots to talk about."

"I know. Like what I'll do for a job."

"There's plenty of work on the ranch, if you're interested. Abe told me how much you helped him out after my injury. If you want to stay active in the medical field, I'm sure the hospital or any of the clinics in Rawlins have openings. But if you need some time to think about what you really want to do, that's fine too."

"Really?"

"Really. Lainie, I don't care, just as long as we're together." Hank pushed a curl from her damp cheek. "Let's talk about this on the way home."

Home and Hank. Two words that fit together perfectly. Lainie looked at the statue of her father one last time. Then she faced Hank, faced her future, and finally left her past behind.

"Come on, cowboy. Take me home."

Can't get enough of the sexy
Blacktop Cowboys® series?
Read on for an excerpt from Lorelei James's

Turn and Burn

Available now from Signet Eclipse.

"Sweet darlin', what did you say you did for a living?"

Sweet darlin'. Did this dude really think she'd buy into his fake cowboy shtick because he'd shown up at a Western bar wearing alligator boots and a Stetson? *Please.* She was a Texas girl, born and bred. And if there was one thing Tanna Barker knew, it was cowboys—*real* cowboys.

She smiled coyly. "I didn't say. But a shot of Patrón would loosen my tongue a whole lot."

Mr. Alligator Boots flagged down the bartender.

Sucker.

Tanna would've almost felt bad for this guy, except he'd approached her. Buying her a shot was the least he could do after he'd laid on the bullshit so thick, she felt it seeping into her boots.

After knocking back the tequila, she confessed, "I don't normally share my occupation because it tends to be viewed as . . . a bit raunchy. But I'll make an exception for you, puddin' pop."

She saw his gears spinning as he pondered her raunchy occupation. Paid escort? Hooker? Exotic dancer? His eyes roamed over her skintight Miss Me jeans, her pink rhinestone b.b.simon belt and her shimmery ruffled blouse cut low enough to garner interest in her abundant cleavage.

Then Mr. Alligator Boots frowned at the bandage on her forehead. "What happened to you?"

"Hazard of my job." She confided, "I'm a professional roller derby girl. I'm the pivot for the Lonestar Ladies. I hit the cement in the ring last night after some bitch hooked me and I ended up with a skate to the head. It bled like a mother, I guess. I didn't notice, 'cause I play to win. Only took ten stitches this time. Last month I ripped the shit outta my calf and ended up with twenty-five stitches."

Silence.

"I can show you the scar. Bet a tough cowboy like you is into scars, ain't ya?" she taunted.

Mr. Alligator Boots backed away and waved at someone across the room. "Would you look at the time? I gotta go. I see my friends are here."

Tanna held in her laughter until he disappeared.

Within five minutes another friendly guy sidled up. Younger than Mr. Alligator Boots. But he still wore the *Hey, baby, I'm all that and a real cowboy* look of a smarmy douche bag. She smiled and waited for him to strike up a conversation.

Hello, free shot number two.

Talk about shooting fish in a barrel. Over the next two hours, and after multiple complimentary shots of tequila, her injury had been the result of a bow hunting accident, from getting clipped by her gear after jumping from an airplane, from a drunken brawl with her fellow missionaries, from hitting the roll bar during the demolition derby finals, and her personal favorite—the whip she'd used on her lover recoiled and sliced her in the face. Truly a classic. As the queen of tall tales, she couldn't wait to share these fun little fibs with her buddy Celia Lawson Gilchrist.

Hopefully pregnancy hadn't affected Celia's sense of humor.

Tanna ordered a Corona, lamenting the lack of Lone Star beer this far north. Still, she was grateful for her friends who'd offered her a place to live in Wyoming while she got her head on straight. Her life had been in turmoil these past two years, more than she'd let on. She just wanted a place to hole up, lick her wounds and figure out what the hell to do with herself.

Rather than imposing on Celia and Kyle Gilchrist or Lainie and Hank Lawson, even for one night, Tanna had checked into a dive motel in Rawlins within stumbling distance of Cactus Jack's Bar. This wouldn't be her last night of freedom, but it'd be her last chance to be anonymously wild for a while.

Right. Tell yourself that. You can't go more than two weeks without getting into trouble.

Another guy, this one with too many tats and too few teeth, slunk up next to her. "What's a looker like you doin' drinking alone?"

"Celebrating that I just got out of jail last week."

His bleary eyes lit up. "What a coincidence. I just got outta jail too. What were you in for?"

A real jailbird was hitting on her? Awesome. That'd teach her to lie. "Arson. I allegedly"—she made quotes in the air when she said "allegedly"—"set fire to my ex's trailer and blew up his truck with a couple of incendiary rounds. The man has no sense of humor, and if I ever see that lyin' bastard again . . ." Tanna squinted at him suspiciously. "Hey. Come to think of it, you look an awful lot like him. An awful lot." She sneered and poked him in the chest. "LeRoy, I swear to God, if you think you can pull some kind of lame disguise with me—"

"I ain't LeRoy, and, lady, you're plumb crazy." He backed away. Ran away was more like it.

She couldn't help but snicker before she upended her beer.

"Word of advice, sugar twang? Bein's the town of Rawlins hosts the Wyoming state penitentiary, there's a higher-than-average population of ex-cons around. And they're not all so easily conned as him."

Tanna glanced up at the man.

Oh, hello, sweet darlin'.

How hadn't she noticed this giant? At least six feet five, he easily cast her five feet three inches in shadow. And holy *frijoles* was this guy hot. Like, really hot. After being approached by wannabe cowboys all night, she had no doubt this guy was the real deal. So she shamelessly took in his banging body, from his summer-weight cowboy hat to the tips of his dusty boots—and every inch in between.

His age looked to be midthirties. In this part of the country, his reddish gold complexion had to be from Native American ancestry. Her avid gaze took in his angular features. A high forehead not marred by a single wrinkle. A slash of dark eyebrows arched over eyes the color of warm topaz. His cheekbones were prominent in a wide-set face. A thin blade of nose. The corners of his lips turned up in an indulgent smile. And check out that ridiculously strong-looking, chiseled jawline. His thick neck tapered into shoulders so wide, it appeared he wore football pads, until she realized this hunky man couldn't hide bulky equipment under his skintight T-shirt.

"You done looking your fill? Or did you want me to turn around, so you can ogle my ass too?"

"Better to know up front that I'm staring at your package, and not considering the size of your wallet, don'tcha think?" Tanna retorted with saccharine sweetness.

He laughed. A deep, sexy rumble that caused a little flip in her belly. "So will you let me buy you a beer if I pull out my wallet?"

"If you're sure you wanna spend money on an ex-con."

"You're not an ex-con by any stretch of your imagination." He waved down the bartender. "But I *am* interested to hear which lie I'll rate." He shot her a grin. "I'm hoping you'll claim to be a secret agent."

Tanna leaned across the bar. "Got a Bond girl fantasy you wanna tell me about, ace?"

"I'm more a fan of Lara Croft or Sydney Bristow. Chicks who kick ass turn my crank."

"Hot women who know how to kill and how to dress to kill *are* the ultimate asset."

"Oh, those women ain't got nothin' on you in the asset department." His gaze dipped to the deep V of her cleavage.

It didn't bother her that he was blatantly checking out her rack. When he finally dragged his gaze to hers again, the unbridled lust in his eyes sent a wave of liquid heat through her.

"You are trouble," she murmured, unable to look away from him. Something about this man pulled her in and revved her up.

"No more trouble than you are, spy girl." He held out a twenty for the bartender without breaking eye contact. "You wanna grab us a booth and we'll talk about what kinda trouble we can get into together?"

She nodded. Just as she stepped back, a man jockeying for her spot at the bar jostled her, sending her off balance. Her tall, dark and handsome stranger kept her from falling by using a firm arm to pull her forward. Her breasts met the hard wall of his chest and all the air left her lungs in a rush. Good God was he solid.

He sucked in a sharp breath at the sudden intimate contact.

The side of her face smashed against his pectorals. She remained like that, inhaling his scent until he tugged on her hair to get her attention. She glanced up into his eyes, feeling a blast of pure sexual heat.

"Might be dangerous to keep looking at me like that," he said softly.

"Because you're afraid I wanna do more than look at you?"

"No." His rough-edged fingertip traced a line down her neck, from the dent in her chin to the start of her cleavage. "But maybe I want more than you're willing to give."

Tanna stared at him. Normally such blatant sexual talk so soon after meeting had her stepping back. But something about this man kept her right where she was—completely entranced by him.

"Say the word, sugar twang, and I'll walk away."

"And if I don't want you to walk away?" she countered boldly.

"Then our night just got a whole lot more interesting."

"Sounds good to me." Opening her mouth over the hard curve of his pectorals, she blew a stream of hot air through the shirt, then lightly bit down. "I'm game for whatever you've got in mind."

"Grab your beer." He led them to the only unoccupied booth, by the front door.

She slid into the bench seat opposite him and raised her bottle for a toast.

"What're we toasting to?"

"Ex-cons and little white lies." She smirked. "And a guy with a big . . . bullshit meter."

"I'll drink to that." He grinned.

Sweet Lord. There was damn dangerous wattage in those pearly whites of his.

He rested his massive shoulders against the back of the booth. "So, what's your name besides Hot Trouble?"

Tanna shook her head. "How about if we keep it simple and don't exchange names?"

He didn't even blink. "Because you'd probably give me a fake one anyway."

"Yep. I see this ain't your first go-round in this type of rodeo either, cowboy."

"I'm good with no names—I like 'sugar twang' better anyway—but there are a couple of basic questions I've gotta ask first."

"Shoot."

The twinkle vanished from his eyes. "You're not married and out on the town looking for one night with a stranger to cure your marital boredom?"

"No, sir. I don't cheat. So no boyfriend either." She pointed with her beer bottle. "Back atcha."

"No significant other in my life. Or in my bed on a regular basis."

"That clears that up. Next question."

His eyes flicked to the bandage on her forehead. "What happened there?"

"Nothin'. It's a prop to garner sympathy, start conversations and con men into buying me drinks."

That seemed to amuse him rather than annoy him. "What brings you to Rawlins, Wyoming?"

"Just passing through on my way to start a new job." Not exactly a lie. "What about you?"

"I'm on the road a lot too." He let his bottle dangle a

couple of inches above the table and swung it like a pendulum. "You're not really on the run from an ex?"

Tanna snickered. "Nope. I'm just killing time in a honky-tonk before I move on."

"So you're not looking for Mr. Right?"

"More like looking for Mr. Right *Now*."

His handsome face remained skeptical.

"Let's cut to the chase. I like sex. There isn't a substitute for the way naked flesh feels sliding together in the heat of passion. There isn't a substitute for a long, wet kiss. There isn't a substitute for a heart-pounding, blood-pulsing orgasm. There isn't a substitute for sex. Period. I'm not supposed to admit I get antsy and snappish if I go too long without it. I'm not supposed to admit that satisfying the craving for intimate physical contact is all I want. I don't want messy emotional entanglements. Just. Hot. Sex."

He leaned forward and took her hand, staring deeply into her eyes. "I think I love you."

She laughed.

"In all seriousness, it's refreshing that you're so up front about what you want."

"Or what I don't want." Tanna swallowed a mouthful of beer. "So, you interested in taking me for a tumble?"

"Oh yeah." His smile turned decidedly predatory. "But I'm not gonna shake your hand like this is a business arrangement." He lifted their joined hands and kissed the inside of her forearm, from her wrist to the crook of her elbow. "I'm gonna seduce you."

"Right here, right now?"

"Just giving you a sneak peek at my playbook." His thumb lazily swept an arc from her knuckles to her wrist. "But I won't attempt an all-out blitz. I'd rather make the plays drive by drive. Trust me. I'll still get us to the goal line."

Tanna squirmed in her seat. "I've never been turned on by a football analogy before."

He chuckled. "I'm happy you caught the right sport reference."

"Bite your tongue. I'm a Texan. Football is not a sport—it's a religion."

"My mistake. That said, I'm gonna jump ahead in the offensive playbook and score us a room at the motel across the street. Be right back."

He slid from the booth, leaving her staring after him feeling . . . what? Guilty? Like she should offer to pay for half? Or tell him she'd already booked a room? Or was she feeling like a skanky ho for picking up yet another guy in a bar?

Nah. It'd been a while since she'd hooked up. And what was wrong with acting on her baser impulses anyway? Nothing. Men did it all the freakin' time. Her body, her choice. All pleasure, no emotional pain. Just what she needed.

Tanna ordered another round of Coronas and let her head fall back. Her mind filled with thoughts of roving hands and hot mouths. Of cool cotton sheets beneath her. She imagined the taste of his mouth. His skin. She thought about his hair teasing her as he kissed down the center of her body. By the time she'd finished fleshing out all the sexual scenarios she'd like to put into play, the bench seat creaked. She angled her head and opened her eyes to see her hot stranger sliding next to her.

His big hand curled around the side of her face and he swept his thumb over her cheekbone. "I was afraid you'd be gone."

"Why? I meant what I said."

"I believe you. But me heading off to secure a room before I even kissed you is a little rude on my part."

Tanna's heart galloped when he leaned closer, letting

their lips almost touch as he gazed into her eyes with such heat and tenderness. She managed to eke out, "Maybe you oughta prove that you're not a bad kisser before this goes any further."

"Be my pleasure." His breath continued to flow over her lips, but he didn't kiss her.

"Is there a problem?"

"No. You're just so dang pretty," he murmured, and pressed his mouth to hers.

A soft, quick brush of moist flesh as his lips teased hers. Then another. And another. When Tanna parted her lips, his tongue slipped inside her mouth.

The kiss started out a slow, sweet exploration. Heat built gradually as their lips moved and tongues dueled. She gave herself over to him and this amazing first kiss.

By the time he eased back, Tanna knew her face was flushed. Her heart raced. A warm throb of need had settled between her legs.

"Damn, woman," he finally said.

"I'm feeling a little buzzed after that too." Good Lord. He'd kissed her with such intensity, she was out of breath.

"I take it I passed the kissing test?"

She nodded. "With flying colors."

"Good. Because I want another taste of you."

Heat spread between her thighs. "And then what?"

"Then I'll probably throw you over my shoulder and run across the parking lot." His mouth meandered down her throat. He stopped to trace his tongue along her collarbone before he planted kisses straight down to her cleavage.

Somehow he'd maneuvered her into the corner of the booth. His big body blocked her from the view of other bar patrons, which allowed him to leave openmouthed kisses on every exposed inch of her breasts.

Tanna's head fell back, letting his greedy kisses on her

skin consume her. When she realized her hands were gripping the booth and not his rock-hard flesh, she reached out and placed her palms on his pectorals.

"I like your hands on me," he murmured against the upper swell of her breast.

She curled her fingers into his torso, allowing her nails to scrape down his belly to the waistband of his jeans. Then she put her mouth on the salty skin beneath his ear. "Imagine me doin' that down your back." She nipped on his earlobe. "At least two times."

He groaned and then his mouth was back, overwhelming hers with passion. Not sloppy, wet, *I wanna fuck you* kisses. But hot, hungry kisses that drove her to another level of need. This wouldn't be a one-off fuck. The first time might be fast. But the second time wouldn't be. Nor would the third time. The fourth go-round would be spectacular.

Looked to be a long, sweaty night.

And she couldn't freakin' wait.

She slapped her hands on his cheeks to pull his mouth off hers. When she stared into his face and saw that devilish gleam, she smirked back.

"What?"

"Didn't you say something about throwing me over your shoulder and getting us outta here?"

"Let's go."

New in Trade Paperback From

Lorelei James

TURN AND BURN

A Blacktop Cowboys Novel

Tanna Barker is a world champion barrel racer. But now, a rodeo injury has left the restless spitfire holed up in Muddy Gap, unsure what her next move should be.

Veterinarian August Fletcher has always put his job first. He's never found a woman who could handle his on-the-road lifestyle. But when sassy, sexy Tanna blows into town, he finally finds the woman of his fantasies. How can Fletch prove that he's in it for the long haul... and that their sizzling relationship is better than winning any rodeo medal?

"[James's] sexy cowboys are to die for!"
—*New York Times* bestselling author Maya Banks

Available wherever books are sold or at
penguin.com

facebook.com/LoveAlwaysBooks

S0495